# A
# REAL
# SOMEBODY

# A
# REAL
# SOMEBODY

*a novel*

# DERYN COLLIER

LAKE UNION
PUBLISHING

Text copyright © 2023 by Deryn Collier
All rights reserved.

Published by Lake Union Publishing, Seattle

www.apub.com

Amazon, the Amazon logo, and Lake Union Publishing are trademarks of Amazon.com, Inc., or its affiliates.

ISBN-13: 9781662512643 (paperback)
ISBN-13: 9781662512636 (digital)

Cover design by Mumtaz Mustafa
Cover image: © Martin Bergsma / Alamy

Printed in the United States of America

*For my great-aunt, June Grant (1925–2014):*

*You asked me to finish your story and then
gave me everything I needed to complete the task.
For that, I say thank you.*

*I gave myself over to your story, and in the process,
the line between truth and fiction became forever
blurred.
For that, I say please forgive me.*

*Your devoted grand-niece,
Deryn June Collier*

# Part 1

"I was young in the days when girls were brought up in old-fashioned families, convinced they were helplessly dependent on two Male Persons: a Supreme One in the Sky and a Prince Charming who would come along if you were good and if you had a well-filled hope chest."

—June Grant on CBC's *The Sunday Edition*, 1998 (approximately)

There's a framed photograph on the sideboard of the Abbott Street apartment that explains everything about our family.

In it, Father stands at the beach in Old Orchard Beach, Maine, the endless Atlantic stretched out behind him. He's wearing a bathing suit, the black shorts rising over his waist and up his shoulders into a sleeveless tank, exposing his arms and the sides of his very white chest. His white canvas beach hat shadows his eyes, but you can see that he's smiling right at the camera, his face relaxed and open.

In front of him stand two young girls in matching swim dresses, Missie on the left, Daisy on the right. Missie looks like she was interrupted in the midst of building a sandcastle. Her bathing cap has slipped down and almost covers her eyes, her arms mid-movement, as though, like any five-year-old at the beach, she can't wait to get back to something else.

But not Daisy. Daisy poses like she's been waiting for the photographer to show up all morning. Arms straight and long, wrists together, swim cap angled up, she is the very picture of a pretty daughter on a fun holiday. But there's knowing too, in her eyes and smile, like she's aware of the performance of it. Convincing her audience is more fun than playing at the beach. At eight years old, Daisy already knows about persuasion.

There's no sign of me, of course. This photo was taken before I was born, which is when all of our family's happy memories were made. Soon after, *there was no more money for trips to Old Orchard Beach, or anywhere else for that matter.*

*The sideboard itself is a relic of better days. In the old house on Côte Saint Antoine, it used to stand in the spacious dining room under the leaded-glass windows. Now it blocks half the entrance to the sitting room; we have to squeeze past it to reach the sofa. Its surface is crammed with photos of us three girls, though there are many more of Daisy and Missie than there are of me. School photos from the convent school we all attended, and photos of each of our debutante balls, and there are wedding photos too: of Mother and Father, of Daisy and Geoff, of Missie and Robert.*

*Next to these is six square inches of mahogany that Mother keeps polished and ready. "For your wedding photo, June," she always tells me. "One day soon."*

# Chapter One

During the war, we waited. Waited for news from the London bombings. From Pearl Harbor and Kursk and Normandy. We wrote letters and waited for replies. Waited for our grocer, Mr. Lublin, to have sugar and coffee again. We waited and prayed, but mostly we lived quietly, kept rations, curled our hair in victory rolls to keep the boys' spirits up. Those of us who needed to, or wanted to, went to work. The war ended almost two years ago, and now we wait to get married.

Waiting makes me sick. It's always been this way.

I keep telling myself it's a regular day, that there's no reason for the dread that started when I woke up this morning, but nothing has helped. Not even the dry toast or the cold air on my walk to the streetcar. Not the extra milk in my coffee or the sweet bun I wasted a nickel on during my break.

Today I am waiting to see whether a certain young man will ask me on a date. Will he? Or won't he? I can't decide which option is worse.

I focus on the seven-layer carbon-and-paper sandwich I've rolled into the typewriter, ready for the updated agreement between McAulay Advertising, where I work, and Eaton's department store, where I wish I could spend my earnings. Miss Pomeroy was quite pointed with me when she said she wants this finished before lunch—no mistakes—though as far as I can tell none of the other girls are getting anything at all done today.

I start with the McAulay Advertising address: Sun Life Building, 1155 Metcalfe Street, 11th Floor, Montreal, Quebec. Then the full Eaton's address, which seems silly, since it is right around the corner. I could walk there in under five minutes myself, and the boy from the mail room runs there in three.

The young man who might ask me out is named Mr. Jack Ritchie and he is from Toronto, so in my mind his name has become "Mr. Jack Ritchie from Toronto." He's studying law at McGill and he's Catholic, and both his mother and mine are pleased at the possible match. To them, the only question is whether I will be pleasing to him. No one asks whether *he* will be pleasing to *me*, but this is always the case when my mother and sisters arrange dates for me.

I look around at the other girls in the office, each one prettier and more tidily put together than me, with dresses and skirts in the new styles. I am sure Mr. Jack Ritchie from Toronto would pick any one of them before me. My brown tweed skirt has been passed down through so many female relatives it might well be from before the First World War. My white blouse has been pressed so many times the fabric shines at the collar and cuffs.

"June?" Abbie appears in front of my desk, cheerfully irresistible as ever. She's holding out a coffee can that she's decorated with yellow and green ribbons. "Will you contribute to the gift for Rita's bridal shower?"

"Why are you whispering?" I look around. Miss Pomeroy has stepped out. Marie-Céleste has stopped all pretense of typing and is filing her nails. Helen disappeared to the ladies' room ages ago and hasn't been back, and Rita, the bride-to-be, is serving coffee in one of the conference rooms. After the bridal shower tomorrow she will disappear, off to the land of the happily married, as promised by the very advertisements that are created here at McAulay's.

"I'm whispering because it's a secret." Abbie's blonde curls bounce and she crooks her head. I look back to my fingers, perched over the keys. I will not let her distract me this time, I tell myself, though Abbie has been distracting me ever since we met on our first day of secretarial school, and every day of the almost three years since my brother-in-law got us both jobs at McAulay's.

Between getting cards signed, arranging for lunches and bridal gift collections, and her special talent for repairing Dictaphones, Abbie gets very little typing done. For her, it's all a lark. Something to fill the time until she gets married. My own reason for working here is no joke. Without my salary, my family would be in dire straits indeed.

"So, will you?" She shakes the can, rattling the coins at the bottom. "Come on, June. If everyone puts in fifty cents or a dollar, we can collect enough to get her two pairs of nylon stockings and the usual casserole dish."

I shake my head. "No, thank you. I'll do what I normally do."

"Oh, June, not the poem again?" Abbie crouches down in front of my desk, as though I am a child she needs to convince. "Won't you at least try to get along? Even just a little?"

I keep my fingers poised above the keys. "I wish Rita a marriage where new stockings are the only thing she has to worry about, but perhaps a day will come when my poem will bring her comfort," I say.

I want to tell Abbie that a poem written for the newlyweds is the greatest gift I can imagine giving or receiving. After all, my mother was gowned in white duchess satin and carried a bouquet of white roses as she walked down the aisle of Saint Patrick's Basilica on her wedding day, but it is the poems she cuts out of the newspapers that give her comfort now. She memorizes stanzas and recites them aloud to Father as she feeds him his dinner.

Abbie sighs. "I'm going to put in two quarters for you," she says, standing up. "So at least you can sign the card."

"Abbie, don't." She's wearing her green wool vest over a wide-pleated green skirt with yellow appliqué details at the pocket hems, and I realize she's decorated the can to match her outfit. The two quarters clink as she drops them in.

"Too late." Her eyes are the same green as her skirt and the ribbons on the collection tin. It's impossible to stay mad at her for long.

I feel a wave of affection wash over me. She's gone to so much trouble for Rita, who hardly any of us really know, but that's Abbie's way. All of a sudden I want to tell her everything. About my unsettled stomach. About waiting. About how, this evening, at the Shrove Tuesday pancake dinner at the church—the last bit of fun we will be allowed before Lent starts tomorrow—Jack Ritchie from Toronto might ask me on a date. How, though I'm already twenty-two, there may still be hope for me, which will make my mother so happy. But also, how I dread each new suitor, each embarrassing date, and the charade of it all. It's all ready to spill out of me when I hear Miss Pomeroy's heavy step in the corridor.

"She wants this contract by lunch," I say.

Abbie has the collection tin out of sight and Marie-Céleste tucks her legs under her desk before Miss Pomeroy sees a thing. The room fills again with the steady tap of keys.

———— ❧ ————

At three o'clock, Miss Pomeroy sends me to the supply room, which takes me past the copywriters' offices. Their windows stretch right to the ceiling so the rooms are filled with light, even through the ever-present swirl of smoke. To me, those offices are where magic is born. Imagine coming to work and writing all day.

Mr. Sands's office is the one right next to the steno pool. He likes to keep his door open so he can watch us steno girls go by and comment on our best features. (Rita's small waist and swinging hips, Marie-Céleste's legs, Helen's glossy hair. He calls Abbie the full package, whatever that means.) Mr. Sands thinks every girl, no matter how tall or awkward, has at least one redeeming quality, though he has yet to proclaim my best feature, saying he needs to think about it more.

I try not to stir up so much as a breeze as I pass by his half-closed door.

The supply room is golden in the afternoon light. Sometimes I come in here on my lunch break and pretend it's my office—the office of an important lady poet. I sit on the windowsill and let the beauty of the city enthrall me until the feeling spreads through me, out my fingers, and onto the pages of my little notebook. The ever-changing rectangle of color that is Dominion Square, the golden brownstone of the grand Windsor Hotel, Dorchester Boulevard leading west to building after building, fine stone- and wood-framed windows—I imagine the people in those buildings looking back at me. I write verses about them, those invisible people and their grand lives. Sometimes I forget to eat my lunch altogether and I'm famished all afternoon.

There's no time for all that today. I hold the door open for Abbie, who wheels in the metal rolling cart full of wax cylinders, which we are to shave clean for tomorrow's dictation. Two Dictaphone shavers wait side by side on a plain table, and we set to work. Soon their whirring fills the room, like the static of a record left on a phonograph after the waltz is over.

"I got a nice collection for Rita. All of the writers and most of the art department." She juts her chin toward the wall opposite. "There's a new artist who started this week. Have you met him yet?" I can tell by the sparkle in her eyes that she knows something.

I shake my head and feel the blush coming, as it always does when I hear of new artists and writers being hired. My chest gets tight and fear fills me to the brim so I can barely speak. I clench my hands and look down, waiting for it to pass. Of course, Abbie knows what's happening right away.

"Oh, June, don't worry. It's been so long, no one remembers."

She knows that nothing has been the same since last year, when my brother-in-law, Geoff Collier, McAulay's star copywriter, left to start his own agency, taking an illustrator and six important clients with him.

They offer a fresh approach for new times, Geoff says. I have worried about my position here since the day Collier and Moore opened its doors—worried that I will be seen as a traitor by association.

"I only got this job in the first place because he recommended me," I say. He recommended both of us, really, though the job matters much more to me than it does to Abbie.

She shakes her head. "But you're still in the job because you don't make mistakes. You've been here for almost three years! Think how lost Miss Pomeroy would be without you. The rest of us are going to—"

She holds her hand up to cover her mouth and stop the words. She looks at me wide-eyed, but I know what she's going to say. The rest of the girls will get married. Miss Pomeroy needs to keep me around, because the chances of me—plain, poorly dressed, too-tall, awkward June—getting married are slim. Even Abbie knows that. She's not being cruel, just speaking the truth, and it's a relief to me to hear her say it, even when she changes the subject right away.

"The new artist—Lewin is his name—that's his office right there." She points to the wall in front of us. She raises an eyebrow. The walls are notoriously thin, and some of the girls have devised a system for listening in on conversations.

"Abbie, we shouldn't," I say.

"I know," she says. Then she grins, her curls bobbing. "But we will anyway. When we hear him come back. Mr. McAulay says he's a rising talent and we're lucky to have him. And even Mr. Sands admits that he's said to be one of the best."

The machine before me clunks to a finish. I extract the clean cylinder and slide it into its cardboard sleeve and then into one of the empty slots in the box on the lower tray. I take a used one from the front of the box and start the whole process over again.

Once the whirring has started up, I screw up my courage and blurt out: "Mother has arranged for a man to ask me on a date. At the pancake dinner tonight."

Abbie turns to me, her eyes bright. "How wonderful!" Then, when she sees my expression, her face crumples. "It's not wonderful? I'm sorry, June. Is he horrible?"

"I don't know. I don't know anything about him. Well, except that his name is Jack Ritchie and he's from Toronto."

Abbie shakes her head as though she's supposed to have heard of him, but of course she hasn't. The pool of English men in Toronto is much larger than in Montreal, after all. "Anything else?"

"He's at McGill. In law."

"A catch then."

"So says his mother, who has been on the telephone with my mother for a week arranging all this. No doubt she wants to find a good Catholic girl for him, before he finds a Protestant one for himself."

We both fall silent, and the air fills with the sound of static and the glow of the afternoon light. I'm thinking of all the specifications set out for a proper match for me—an English-speaking, Catholic man from a respectable family and working in a good profession. He should be tall, too. Taller than me. That's all that's supposed to matter.

Abbie must be thinking along similar lines, because she says: "Fathers bet on horses. But mothers bet on their daughters."

I can barely hear her over the whirring machine. The feeling of dread sinks deeper into my stomach.

"But what if I don't like him?" I ask. Or worse, so much worse I don't dare say it out loud: What if he likes me and wants to marry me? What will I do then?

Abbie plunks a fresh cylinder into the machine, her finger over the lever. "They say that in time, you'll grow to love him."

I turn to her. "Even you?" Abbie has been unofficially engaged since she was sixteen. Her fiancé is a diplomat and has been transferred all over the world for the past five years of their engagement.

She nods. "Even me." Then she holds up a finger at the sound of a door closing next door. "There they are."

Abbie grabs the whiskey tumbler, hidden behind a box of envelopes expressly for this purpose. She holds it up to the wall, narrows her eyes as she listens, her pink lips pursed.

"It's Mr. McAulay and the new fellow—Mr. Lewin." She's quiet again, listening. "They're talking about Eaton's. Lewin is going to take over the Eaton's account." Her eyes widen.

"What is it?" I whisper.

She flaps her hand for me to be quiet. All I can hear is the soft rumble of male voices, the words indistinct. After a minute, the rumble fades. The wall shakes as a door closes. Abbie pushes herself away and returns the glass to its hiding place.

"What is it?"

Abbie presses the lever on her Dictaphone shaver so that the sound covers our voices. "Mr. McAulay said that Eaton's wants a fresh look for the summer catalog. He's worried they think we're stodgy and that they want a new firm."

"Eaton's?" Surely they can't go to Collier and Moore too? That would be a disaster. Eaton's has been McAulay Advertising's major client for the three years that Abbie and I have worked here, and for twenty or more years before that.

Abbie nods. "Mr. McAulay said it's up to Lewin to come up with a fresh campaign so they won't even think of leaving us."

We stare at each other.

"Let's hope this Lewin fellow is good," I say.

After that, we work in silence until the box is full of cleaned cylinders.

"Should I take these around?" Abbie asks, which is kind of her. We both know I'm much too clumsy to handle the rolling carts, which are awkward even for the most coordinated girls. Miss Pomeroy never sends me to serve coffee for that exact reason.

"Yes," I say. "I'll see you back in steno."

I hold the door for her, then return to the table to straighten the Dictaphone shavers. In the process, my hand brushes against the box of envelopes and I reach behind them for the whiskey glass with its delicate band of silver around the base. I hold it up to see if the light of the sunset will catch it, but the sun has already dropped below the horizon at the end of Dorchester Boulevard. The storage room is back to a dull gray light that even the electric ceiling lights can't pierce.

I press the glass up to the wall. I have never done this myself before, preferring to leave it to the other girls to tell me what they hear. I set my ear against it and listen. There's nothing at first. No voices. No clack of typewriter keys, though of course this Mr. Lewin is an artist, not a writer. No pencil against paper. No sound at all.

And then I hear it. Softly. A sound I recognize at once. The sound Father makes when he falls asleep in his wheelchair.

Mr. Lewin, the great hope for saving the Eaton's account for McAulay, is snoring.

# Chapter Two

"This is the dress that Missie wore that summer she turned sixteen and got fat, remember?" Daisy folds into a crouch in her narrow skirt and silk stockings, tugging at the hem of the dress she has me trying.

"I'm not fat, Daisy," I say.

"Of course not, June." This is from Mother, at the ironing board. "You're big-boned. You take after your father's side of the family."

I know that Daisy spent the whole afternoon rehemming Missie's old dress so it would be passably long enough on me. I know I should feel more grateful, but instead I feel the sour knot that has been in my stomach all day tighten further. It's a gray linen tea dress with lace at the dropped waist, which our Aunt Lucie had made in her flapper days. Well, on Missie and Aunt Lucie it was a dropped waist; on me the waist is at my actual waist.

And if there is a date? What will I wear then? And a second date? How many different dresses will I need for this endeavor?

Daisy looks up at me, a cigarette clenched between her scarlet-painted lips. "'Big-boned' is just another way of saying 'fat.'" Smoke spews from both sides of her lips as she speaks.

I blink the smoke out of my eyes and wish for Missie. There's a seven-year gap between Daisy and me that is simply impossible to overcome. Missie, our middle sister, always smoothed things over. But Missie is gone now.

Gone, as in married. She lives in Philadelphia, just a short train ride and a world away, with her husband of two years. They are expecting a baby in April and between the fuss of getting married, moving away, settling into her role as a housewife, and now preparing for the baby, Missie has moved on from our family. Well, aside from the occasional letter and a phone call on the last Tuesday of each month.

In the mirror I watch as Daisy screws her lips to one side and then drops them back down into her regular expression. A sort of bemused blankness is what I'd call the look, her face a mask of powder and lipstick. The black liner makes her look severe, like you don't want to waste her time, and she's spent a lot of time on me today.

I should appreciate her more. She is trying, after all. We all are. No one expected us to end up like this—in a squashed-up town house, resorting to dressing me, the youngest, in a dress two generations old, in the hopes of giving me some kind of chance at marriage and a normal life. What if I told them all not to bother? But I can't do that. Mother has so much hope that things will work out for me, too.

"Thank you, Daisy," I say. Our eyes fix in the mirror—both bright blue like Father's. I drop my eyes down, feeling the familiar grip in my belly, sourness in my throat at the impossible position I am in.

She shakes her head and mutters under her breath, so Mother can't hear her. "What will become of Mother and Father if you marry?" Then she steps away, as though she hadn't said anything at all.

"Are the boys ready?" Mother asks.

"I'll go see to them," Daisy says. "And don't stay there forever. I need to meet Geoff downtown."

Mother frowns but only says: "Thank you for staying with Father so we can go."

Daisy shakes her head with impatience. "It's fine. Just have dinner and come back. No lingering over coffee."

I would never dream of speaking to Mother this way, but Daisy has no qualms. And Mother is so relieved that Daisy is safely married off, she just wants to keep the peace. We all remember what a handful Daisy used to be.

I take one last look at myself in the mirror. It's like I can see the imprint, over the top of my reflection, of the women who wore this dress before me. I'm a little bit of Missie and of Aunt Lucie. There's only a small part of me left at all, and I wonder if Mr. Jack Ritchie from Toronto will like me this way.

— ⊙∕∖⊙ —

Mother and I line up with Daisy's boys in the basement hall of Ascension of Our Lord church. The air is thick with the smell of pancakes, hot syrup, and burnt butter, prepared by the members of the Men's Club.

Stephen, at three, practically still a baby, whimpers as Christopher, his older brother and far too serious for a boy of seven, holds him back by the shoulders. They both look out into the expansive room, the tables set with white cloth and centerpieces of evergreens and berries, left over from Christmas and starting to show their age. Steve wriggles, trying to free himself. They want to run, as boys should.

"Stay still, Stephen," I whisper.

"That must be him," Mother says. There is only one man behind the counter young enough to be my would-be suitor. He's wearing a hand-knit cardigan that is rolled up at the sleeves. As we approach, he turns his back to the counter, standing over the grill, spatula in hand.

"Ah, Mrs. Grant, nice to see you." A man of Mother's age addresses us. Mother nods at him and takes the plates he offers her. "And June, the last daughter left," he says with a wink.

I smile automatically. I can't remember his name; there are dozens of men like him in the congregation. A businessman like Father, but more favored by fortune. Not struck down by stroke, and having navigated the Depression years unscathed. A man whose wife has time to serve on church committees. If this man has daughters, they are all married by now.

"Thank you." I don't know what else to say, but he doesn't seem to require an answer. Jack Ritchie is monitoring the pancakes, still with his back to us. He hasn't noticed me at all. The kindly church man hands me my plate, and one for Steve, and already he's smiling at the women behind us. We shuffle off to find a seat.

I look down at my pancakes with the awareness that I'm being watched, though when I look around, Jack Ritchie is too busy serving pancakes to pay any attention to me. Will I be suitable for him? As much as a date with him is sure to be a disaster like all the others, the idea that he won't like the look of me, and won't ask me at all, is somehow worse.

I try to remember the basics from deportment class—sit with your spine erect—but right there I'm caught, because will he really want to go on a date with someone so tall? By the time I settle into my pancakes—the last morsels of joy before Lent—they are cold and the syrup is congealed.

———— ৩৶৶৶৽ ————

After dinner, Mother and I struggle to get Stephen's coat on over his arms, which he holds out, stiff as Christ on the cross. Christopher is watching from the sidelines, and when I look up, wild-eyed, to ask for his help, I see Jack Ritchie standing behind him. They are both watching me with the same serious expression on their faces, as though they aren't sure what to make of me.

"Go talk to him," Mother hisses in my ear.

"Miss June Grant?"

I step closer to him, wondering whether to him I've become Miss June Grant from Montreal. This makes me smile and hold back a laugh, and then blush terribly. "Y-yes."

"I'm Jack Ritchie, from Toronto."

He doesn't hold out his hand to shake. I nod, but can't think of anything to say. I wait.

"Would you like to go for dinner with me?"

"How kind," I say, because that's what Daisy would say, at least to his face. I'm sure once she was away from him she'd quip about his flat, plain features, his badly fitting sweater. "I'd love to," I add, to make up for my ungracious thoughts.

"Thursday at five o'clock?"

I look down at my coat, which is a hand-me-down from Father and much too big for me in the shoulders. "I need to go home from work and check on Father, and then change." Do I need to explain these things? Surely not. "Is six okay?"

Christopher stands between us, his serious face swinging back and forth as he follows the volley of our words.

"The early dinner special ends at six. I'm a student. I thought you knew that?"

Mother steps forward, propelling Stephen, his coat finally on, in front of her. She gestures for Christopher and he comes to her. He leans against her beaver-fur coat and she smooths out his hair. Then she smooths over the mess I'm in the midst of creating.

"I think you can be ready by five thirty, June."

Jack Ritchie is satisfied with this and does not look to me for agreement. "Five thirty, then? I'll come to your house. Your mother already gave my mother the address."

We all watch him go. I'm sweating now in my coat.

"He must have been nervous," Mother says.

"I suppose."

"Come, let's get these boys home and to bed. Maybe you can still write a poem tonight."

"Yes, maybe," I say, but I think every poem inside me has shriveled up under Jack Ritchie's assessing gaze.

———— ❧❧❧ ————

We walk back from church in full dark, the boys running as far ahead as Mother will let them, skidding and sliding along the slick ice on the sidewalk. Once home, Mother and the boys head inside. I pause to look up at the clear, dark sky and feel into the space in my mind and throat where poems sometimes press their way out, but it's empty. My moment of peace is interrupted by a sudden flurry of activity. The door opens and Mother is there with her two spaniels, George and Elizabeth, on their leashes.

"I'll take them, Mother," I say, stepping up onto the stoop to take the leashes from her hands. But Daisy is there too and gets tangled up as she tries to step over them.

I hear the squeak of car brakes on the street behind me and turn. There's a taxi idling there, its roof light casting a red glow across the snowbanks at the side of the road.

"Damn dogs," Daisy says and she holds onto the doorframe and untangles herself.

"Daisy!" Mother cries. "Don't swear."

I hold the dogs close. Daisy looks back at me, buttoning her coat over her blouse, which is tucked in tight to her tidy pencil skirt. I watch her shake off her impatience and stand still, waiting, like a queen, as the taxi driver steps out and navigates the icy walk to take her arm. She practically glides to the waiting back seat, as though ice-crusted snow-banks and frozen slush do not exist for her.

Mother has closed the door against the cold. I skid and stumble my way, pulled by the dogs, down the sidewalk to the strip of snow-covered scrub along the fence line where the street ends at the railway tracks.

I hear the taxi brakes squeak again at Saint Catherine Street and Daisy is gone, but she stays in my mind as the dogs do their business. Daisy, and Geoff. Daisy has never worn a hand-me-down in her life. No one would think to ask that of her. And now, married, with children of her own, she has a husband to buy her all the clothes she likes.

I know I should be grateful to both of them. Daisy hemmed my dress today, even if she wasn't gracious about it. And Geoff—there is so much we can't do in the world without an able-bodied man to help us. We count on Geoff for our heat and lights, since women can't have utility accounts themselves. Without his help, we'd freeze in the dark every winter.

I do wonder, though, whether Daisy and Geoff might help Mother and Father a little more? So that it's not just my salary that keeps us going? So that I might have a new dress now and then, or even a new hat? So that perhaps I could get married, if I wanted to. (Do I want to? Who will look after Mother and Father if I do?)

I feel a thickness at my throat when I think of Daisy, as though I need to swallow down something sour. Then the acid swirl of envy in my stomach. Envy. At my own sister. Envy is a terrible sin.

And then the rush of hot shame with the knowledge that this feeling is constant. I am always envious of Daisy.

# Chapter Three

Monsignor McDonagh makes his way along the line of the penitent, each waiting for absolution, which today, Ash Wednesday, comes in the form of a cross of black ash on our foreheads.

It's hard to concentrate on my prayers. As always, I'm wearing an old dress of Daisy's that rides up almost to my knees when I kneel. I arrange Father's coat around my calves so as not to shock the monsignor, or anyone else, and focus on my sacrifice for Lent—to stop being jealous of Daisy.

It's almost my turn and I close my eyes and whisper a fervent prayer:

"Heavenly Father, let me be satisfied with my lot in life. Tall and with big feet and outdated clothes that never fit properly but looked lovely on my sisters. Help me to appreciate the gifts you've given me, and let me overcome my envy of my sister Daisy. I can take dictation and type fast without errors, and I can write poems. I have a job and can pay the rent and electricity bill all on my own. And I have a date tomorrow. Maybe there is hope for me after all, I mean, if you want me to get married, Heavenly Father."

I end with a request for intercession—that I remember not to touch my face so I don't end up with ash smudged all over as I have every other Ash Wednesday of my life.

The monsignor has reached me now. "Bless you, my child."

He smells of hot paraffin and shortbread cookies. His touch on my forehead as he draws the cross in ash is so soft that I do feel, for just a moment, that it is the finger of God, washing me clean.

———— ⌇⌇ ————

I wrote a love poem as a gift for Rita and her husband-to-be. I typed it up on special paper of Mother's; she has a small stack left over from when each member of the family had their own monogrammed stationery. It would be stingy to point out that my gift took three sheets of paper and my writing time for two whole evenings, which, altogether, is worth much more than the dollar each that the other girls contributed to Rita's gift.

Miss Pomeroy contributed too, and offered a ribbon to tie the package of nylon stockings. Marie-Céleste finagled an illustration from someone in the art department—of Rita and her beau changing a tire on their way to their honeymoon—and made it into a card that everyone signed but me. It would not be right to pretend that I had contributed to the stockings when I hadn't, aside from the two quarters Abbie snuck into the can on my behalf.

"I hardly know what the newlyweds will do with a poem," Marie-Céleste says, perched at the edge of her desk. "Do you, Helen?"

Helen, sitting wan before her typewriter, doesn't respond. Marie-Céleste turns to Abbie, hoping for a better reaction.

"Our Miss Grant is unique, isn't she?" Abbie says, as she puts her hand out to take the poem from me. "Mind the ash," she says under her breath.

I look down to see black whorls of my fingerprints on the thick cream paper.

"Don't worry," Abbie says, taking the sheets from me. "It'll brush off. But you'd best go wash your hands."

In the hall I keep my head down, my fingers curled inward and tucked against my thighs so I don't mess anything else up.

"Ah, Miss Grant. Where are you rushing off to?"

Mr. Sands lounges in the doorframe of his office, smoking and idle. I slow my steps and raise my eyes to look at him.

I've always thought there's something childish about Mr. Sands. He's a few years older than me, but has the air of a schoolyard bully who suddenly finds himself a grown man with a job and isn't sure how it happened. Maybe it's the flop of blond hair that he's always pushing out of his eyes. Or the fact that his suit is too big, with fabric pooling around his ankles and sleeves that hang down over his wrists. I look up to his face, and he tosses his head back and laughs so hard he chokes on his own cigarette smoke.

He holds up his hand, as though I were a dog and he's telling me to stay. It would be rude of me to go on with my errand, but it's intolerable to stand there, watching his breath catch again and a drop of spittle escape one side of his wide, soft lips. Frustration burbles up in me and I press my fingernails into the meat of my palm to contain it. With one final cough, Mr. Sands pulls himself together.

He eyes me for a moment and takes another drag on his cigarette before he finally speaks. "How does someone with a Scottish name like Grant end up a Catholic? You should go to the mail room, all the Irish boys there have the same dirt on their faces."

I look away from him, down the empty hall and then down at my shoes. My cheeks burn. Despite trying to hold them back, my words come out, strong, my voice clear. "I'm not Irish," I say.

I look up at him. He holds his hands up as though to push back an assault. "All right, I'll bite. What are you then?"

I blink my eyes closed and sigh, knowing that there is no use in answering, but I answer him anyway. "My mother is French. Well, half-French."

This elicits another round of laughter. "A Scottish papist? I've never heard of one of those before." Sands's cigarette is burned down now, and he holds the burning stump of it vertically. "You really should check in with the mail room. You'll feel right at home there."

He holds a finger up, telling me to wait, but when he steps inside to put out his cigarette, I rush down the hall.

The ladies' room feels like an afterthought, as though the great architectural minds of twenty years ago never expected women to work in offices. In fact, the stall used to be a janitor's closet, and the room itself is fashioned from an old office.

I climb up onto the wide windowsill and pull the sash up a foot, though there is a drift of snow on the stone ledge outside. Below me, the city stretches downhill, gray limestone office buildings against the gray sky leading down to the darker gray river; the green copper of church spires the only color. But as I'm watching, the clouds break open a fissure just large enough for the sun to pierce through and bathe the old part of the city in warm yellow light for just a moment. Then the clouds shift again and it's all back to gray.

I should get back. I slide down from the windowsill, and when I inspect the damage to the ash on my forehead, I can see why Mr. Sands laughed at me. My cross has turned into a blob. I pause, hand over my forehead, tempted to wipe the whole thing off. But what would Mother say when I got home? Never mind Mother. What about the fate of my soul?

With a damp finger I tidy the edges back into shape, then wash my hands clean again and resolve not to touch my face for the rest of the day.

I do not know Rita well. She was only in steno for a short time before she became a secretary. The other girls have stayed connected with her through after-work drinks and movies and double dates on weekends. I have hardly seen her since she started at her new desk, where she's been secretary—to Mr. McAulay himself—all this time.

Today she is radiant, her light-brown hair pinned expertly, curling in all the right places, shiny. Her eyes have a slight sheen, as though the world surprises and delights her.

"So thoughtful of you, Miss Grant," Rita simpers when she unties the ribbon that Abbie must have secured around my rolled-up poem. She holds the sheet of paper loosely between her fingers as though it has a bad smell. Marie-Céleste takes it from her, and Rita squeals when Abbie hands her the package of nylon stockings.

As Miss Pomeroy presents the grandest gift—the casserole dish, neatly boxed and wrapped and ribboned—I keep my smile pinned in place. I glue my knees and ankles together and tuck them at an angle. I fold my hands prettily in my lap so as not to touch my face, and I wait for it to be over.

The one game, a roll-your-own-cigarette race, comes to a sudden halt when Mr. McAulay stops in the doorway.

Miss Pomeroy rushes to greet him, and they step out into the hall. Rita holds the casserole on her lap like she's won a prize. Helen starts to collect our punch cups, Marie-Céleste tucks the hand-rolled cigarettes away in her purse. Abbie flattens my poem with care, and the other girls start to roll up the streamers. They have all fallen into their roles so naturally, without consulting or instructing one another, and I wonder, How do they know what to do? I should help too, and I stand, looking about for something to do, just as Miss Pomeroy calls me into the hall.

"Miss Grant, Mr. McAulay needs a contract typed this afternoon. I've told him you'll be able to find calm after the excitement of the party."

Mr. McAulay leans against the doorframe. I can barely meet his gaze, though we are at eye level. A quick look and I see that his white hair and long face are just as handsome close-up as they are from a distance. His blue eyes take me in with a fatherly smile.

"You don't mind leaving the party, Miss Grant?"

"No, Sir," I say.

"You can go work at Rita's desk," Miss Pomeroy says. My eyes fly up to her face, and she's quick to squelch any hope. "Just for this afternoon."

"Thank you, Miss Pomeroy." I look back to Abbie and she winks at me.

"Come on then," Mr. McAulay says, leading me toward the executive offices that circle the main reception desk. "This way."

——— ⸙ ———

I skip off the streetcar when it reaches my stop. Not even the half-frozen puddle of slush at the curb, which threatens to suck my boots right off my feet, can strip me of my good mood. I have discovered something: working as Mr. McAulay's secretary is far preferable to working in steno.

I did my very best. I was cheerful and efficient and I made not one mistake. I answered the phone and told callers that Mr. McAulay was out, because that's what he told me to say (even though I knew he was right there in his office). I did not smear the cross on my forehead, and no one commented on it. I didn't trip over my own feet, and no one asked me to deliver a coffee cart.

I'm later than usual and there's little traffic as I cross Saint Catherine Street. There's a spring in my step despite the cold and the drizzle that threatens to turn to freezing rain. There's a buzz working at Mr. McAulay's desk that is nothing like working in steno. And a few times, when the writers and illustrators left their copy and draft ads for approval, I had a chance to look at them as I brought them in to Mr. McAulay, and I realized something: each ad is a tiny, convincing poem. Copywriters get to write poetry all day long.

I hope Mr. McAulay will ask for me again tomorrow.

Mr. Lublin is outside his corner grocery, smoking his evening pipe. "You make an old man smile this evening, Miss Grant."

When Mr. Lublin was growing up in Poland, he never expected to end up owning a corner grocery at the forgotten edge of Westmount. We've all had to adjust to such changes because of the war. These are the quiet confidences Mr. Lublin and I share most evenings as he hands over the wrapped ground beef, the half loaf of bread, and the piece of cheese that Mother has called ahead for.

"You are hardly an old man, Mr. Lublin," I say with a smile, though honestly, I have no idea how old he is. Older than Father? There's no way to know.

"Your mother's order is ready. François will get it for you." He opens the door for me with a flourish.

François, who helps in the shop and rides the shop bicycle around for deliveries, is behind the cheese counter. His father used to be our gardener, back when we lived at the Côte Saint Antoine house. He came every Tuesday and once a month on Saturdays. Sometimes, on the Saturdays, François would come with him to help. It was Mother who helped François get his first job here, at Lublin's, after we moved to Abbott Street and let all the staff go, and he still treats her, and all of our family, with the same deference he did then.

"Here's your order, Miss," he says to me. "Mr. Lublin said to put in an orange. Says your father has a cold. I wrapped it up real careful." He hands me a small box, the cardboard slightly damp under my fingers.

I look down to see the quarter pound of wrapped ground beef, tied with string, a square package in brown paper that must be cheese, a can of condensed milk. A pack of Chesterfields that lets me know Daisy must be visiting. I douse a flash of anger as soon as it flares. Surely she could have come to the store for Mother?

"That was kind of him. Thank you, François." I reach for the box and end up tugging it when François doesn't let go. I look down to see his long fingers, tinged with pink on the inside tips and wrinkled brown on the outside, holding the box back.

I look up into his eyes again. They bore into mine as though he's trying to tell me something important. Something more than about the cheese. "I wrapped the orange real careful, Miss Grant," he repeats, emphasizing the words *real* and *careful.*

I nod back, as though I understand. "I'll be sure to point that out to Mother." This seems to satisfy him, and he lets me take the box.

Finally, I'm on Abbott Street, our street. It's full dark, and I almost miss the car parked right in front of our house. A taxi with its roof light out. The driver leans against the hood, tall and shrouded in a black coat. I can't make out his features under his hat, even when he lifts his cigarette to his mouth. I can't see his eyes but I can feel his gaze following me all the way to our door.

"Finally. What took you so long?" Daisy steps out onto the stoop, cinching her dark-brown wool coat tight. She reaches into the box, pulls out the pack of Chesterfields, and skips across to the waiting taxi without another word.

As the taxi pulls away, its red light flashes briefly and I read the words in cursive, painted along the side of the car: *Red Lantern Taxi.* The light goes off and the taxi turns the corner. In Daisy's wake, the street smells of wet cigarettes, juniper berries, and CHANEL N°5, along with the usual reek of coal oil.

I pause in the kitchen doorway. What a picture they make. The spaniels, George and Elizabeth, scuffle at Mother's feet with each step she takes, always hopeful for her attention. Mother, her hair secured in her usual old-fashioned bun, is holding a cigarette between lipsticked lips. She's dressed in her fur coat over her housedress, her legs in thick tights, her feet in mohair slippers knit for her by her former maid.

Until we moved to Abbott Street, Mother had never set foot in the kitchen. We had a maid, and a cook, and a girl for the laundry at the house on Côte Saint Antoine. We shared a seamstress and François's father, the gardener, with four other families.

Christopher, serious as ever, is at the table, my typewriter in front of him, index finger circling midair as he searches for the next key.

"He's brilliant, see? A writer just like you were, June."

The hope that I carried home from my day sinks and sputters out. I'm still a writer, I want to shout, but it would not do to cause trouble for Mother. None of this is her fault. I slide the box onto the counter and begin to unpack it. "Mr. Lublin sent an orange for Father. How's he feeling?"

"He's always so kind, Mr. Lublin. Go see Father for yourself. He's still up."

"I will. In a minute."

"There's a bowl of lentil soup for you there."

I take the wrapped orange out of the box and set it on the table. All is quiet except for Christopher's unrhythmic jabs at the typewriter and the shuffling of the dogs' paws on the linoleum.

Though dinner was a simple soup and sliced bread, Mother has set the table with silverware and linen napkins. It's while taking this in, and sulking—How am I to write poetry if the boys are using my typewriter?—that I notice Stephen staring at me from his spot on the floor. His eyes are blue and as clear as Father's.

His gaze is frank and so open, so trusting that I want to turn away from it. I want to wipe the fleck of lentil off his cheek with a soft cloth and sing him to sleep at bedtime. But his gaze also makes me want to weep and yell and smash the typewriter keys with the words that have been stuck inside me all day with nowhere to go.

Instead, I pick up the orange.

A quiet has come over the kitchen. Stephen is still staring at me, and Christopher has paused his typing while Mother leans over his page to admire his words.

The orange is wrapped in a scrap of waxed pink butcher paper, crinkled around the fruit and pressed into the indent made by the bud end.

"Oh!" Stephen whispers as I expose the bright-orange fruit. He gets up from the floor and comes to stand next to me. I flash a smile at him, hold the orange up, a magician, waiting for applause.

"Lovely of Mr. Lublin," Mother says again.

"Will Father want it tonight?"

"Oh, that's too much for Father to eat all on his own. What do you think, boys? Shall we all share it for breakfast in the morning?"

"Yes!" Stephen calls.

Christopher is more solemn, but his eyes follow the orange as I hand it to Mother.

"The boys are staying again tonight? Where's Daisy gone?"

"Daisy and Geoff have a client dinner."

It does seem that Geoff needs her help an awful lot with entertaining clients for his new agency. I press the wrapper flat on the table and smooth it out, feeling the softened wax along the creases with my fingers. It's only then that I see the writing in black wax pencil. *1919 Saint Jacques.*

I mouth the address but don't speak it aloud. I fold the paper and put it in the pocket of my dress before Mother sees it. *I wrapped the orange real careful, Miss Grant.*

A secret message from the deliveryman at the grocer's? Mother would be shocked if she knew, and Mr. Lublin would not be happy. We may have fallen on hard times, it's true, but Mother and François are from two different worlds still. The message must be important, but what can it mean?

My chair screeches along the floor as I stand, and Mother looks up sharply. "I'll go say good night to Father. Then I'd like to use my typewriter," I say. I press my hand to Christopher's shoulder, hoping my uncharitable thoughts don't show through. "If you don't mind, little man."

─── ⚬∾⚬ ───

When I go into his study off the kitchen, the room is dark. Father is in his wheelchair. In the early days, Mother and I would move him every night, from chair to the little cot in the corner. It took both of us, but that was when Father could help a bit by holding some of his weight and sliding one foot along to propel us all forward.

I'm not sure if he's not capable of helping anymore, or if he's simply given up, but he's too heavy for us to manage on our own. These days we only move him to his bed on Sundays, when Geoff and Daisy are here for lunch and we can all help. Mother says he's content to stay in his chair the rest of the week, and I think that is probably true: before his stroke Father was always in favor of the solution that was less trouble for his beloved wife.

He's not neglected, though. Mother has changed him into clean pajamas and tucked a wool blanket around him with a hot-water bottle at his feet. The chair is leaned back and the legs raised, so Father is practically in a lying position. He's snoring softly, breathing through his mouth because of his cold. He sleeps so much now. Poor Father.

Father does not stir when I kiss him on the forehead. I know that he would not want me to fret over him. Not when I could be writing. Before his stroke, Father always wanted to hear my poems and stories when he got home from his own long days at work, even once the hard times started. Especially then. Father knew a poem could soothe both the poet and its audience, and he'd listen, sherry in hand, eyes closed, head tipped back against the generous velvet-covered armchairs of the Côte Saint Antoine house. My poems felt complete only once Father had heard them.

Mother would object—"Should you really encourage her?"—and he'd reply there was no harm in it. Once, I overheard him say, "She's really talented, you know. She's got something."

Some days the memory of that overheard remark is the only thing that keeps me writing at all. Especially on days like today. Even in his wheelchair, even with his cold, I know that Father would want me to go upstairs and write the poem that has been growing in my head all afternoon—about a golden ray of sunlight piercing the heavy winter sky like an arrow, pointing to a life I'd never thought of before, filling me with impossible hope.

# Chapter Four

In the morning, my mind skitters between worry and dread. Worry over the note in wax pencil on the orange wrapper, which I have tucked into my skirt pocket, and dread about tonight's date with Jack Ritchie. I'm laying my hat on the shelf when I hear Miss Pomeroy's voice in the hallway. "I simply don't have anyone to spare, Mr. McAulay. We will have a new batch next week, and you can choose from one of those."

"What about the one you sent yesterday? Can't I have her back?"

I freeze, holding my coat up to the hook. Should I rush to my desk? Pretend that I haven't heard?

"She's not what you're looking for."

"Why not? She seemed capable enough." He is so close now I can hear the petulance in his tone. He's not used to being told he can't have something. He steps into the steno office.

"Look, here she is now. Do you have any objection to coming back to work at my desk again today, Miss?"

I look from Mr. McAulay's long, sad face to Miss Pomeroy's sharp one.

"Would you like to go, Miss Grant?" Miss Pomeroy asks me. I can see what she wants my answer to be by her punched-up eyebrows and pinched-in lips.

I think of my daydreams on the streetcar home yesterday. The excitement of seeing the writers coming and going with their tiny gems of poems. The ray of yellow sun illuminating an idea I can't bring myself to say out loud. And yet, the hope is there.

If it were just me, I know what my answer would be. I want to write advertisements, too. I know I can do it. But I must think about Mother and Father and go to the desk where I will still have work next month, next year, and the year after that.

"I would like to go where I'm most needed," I say.

"Well, that settles it then," McAulay says. He heads out the door and I turn to follow, but Miss Pomeroy stops me.

"She'll be along in just a moment, Mr. McAulay," she calls after him.

Once we are alone she inspects me, her eyes slits.

"Freshen your lipstick," she says. "I don't suppose we can do anything about your hair. And tuck your feet under you when you sit down."

I know she'd rather send one of the prettier girls. One of the girls with dainty feet and hair that doesn't frizz.

"I won't disappoint you," I say.

"That's not what I'm worried about," she says, handing me a steno pad and a fresh sleeve of pencils, sharp as spears. I want to ask what she is worried about instead. But Mr. McAulay has paused in the hall, and I certainly must not keep him waiting.

———— ✽ ————

Abbie appears at my new desk at the start of the morning break, carrying my coat and hat. "Come smoke with me."

Miss Pomeroy has taught us that it is indiscreet to talk in elevators, so aside from saying hello to Constant, the elevator attendant, we head down the red-velvet-lined carriage in silence. As soon as the doors open, Abbie catches my arm in hers and steers me outside and across the street into Dominion Square. The air is crisp and clear and oh so cold.

I let Abbie guide me along the diagonal pathways, the recently shoveled snow loosely piled along the edges, snowflakes bright as prisms.

"Here, sit." Abbie chooses a bench overlooking the Boer War monument, the statue of Scottish poet Robbie Burns behind us. Across from us, the granite of the Sun Life Building gleams white as though preening in the sun. I look up, counting the floors, until I find the window to the supply room, and the long hallway of offices for the artists and copywriters. I imagine them looking down at us as we look up at them.

"June, are you all right?"

"What? Oh, yes," I say.

Abbie lights a cigarette, sucks deep into her lungs, and then exhales the smoke into the cold air. She knows me well enough to not even offer me a cigarette.

"Mother says I should not sit in a public square like I've got nowhere to go," I say.

"My mother tells me I must educate myself about art and history, so I can be a dazzling hostess for the diplomats that will come to dinner once I'm married. By sitting here, you are helping make me a better wife one day."

I lean back on the bench and try to push away the heavy apprehension I've felt all morning. I can ruin a whole day with worry, and I know it does not make sense. All around us the city is alive, secretaries and businessmen alike, lured outside by the sun and now hunched into their coats against the frigid air.

Abbie sits up, her expression turning serious. "But tell me. What's it like at Mr. McAulay's desk?"

I sigh, pulling the sleeves of Father's old coat down over my hands to keep them from freezing. "It feels like a dream. Miss Pomeroy only has time to check on me every hour, and as long as I'm typing something or on the phone, no one bothers me at all."

"And Mr. McAulay?"

I shrug. "So far he's been mostly out. A few letters. A few messages. Passing on files from the writers and artists. Some notes about the new Eaton's campaign."

"It won't be long before he finds out you're a better writer than the whole lot of them."

I bat this comment away, along with some of her smoke. "Oh, Abbie. You know that's not even possible. There are no lady advertising writers."

She flings an arm out along the back of the iron bench. "I know no such thing. What about that poetry contest you won?"

"That was nothing."

"That's not true. You beat out all those men."

I wave this comment away, and we fall into the comfortable silence of old friends. Abbie smokes, I stare at the monument, until she asks: "What is it then, June? What's bothering you?"

That's the other side of being with a good friend. I can't hide from Abbie. I can't bring myself to mention Jack Ritchie—what is there to say, after all? Instead, I slip my hand into my coat pocket and pull out the slip of waxed butcher paper.

Abbie takes it from me. "1919 Saint Jacques? What is this?"

"The clerk at the grocery wrapped an orange for Father in this paper. He made a point of telling me to give it to Mother."

Abbie holds the paper away as though to see better. "Did you give it to her?"

I snatch it back from her then. "No, of course not."

She laughs. "Can you imagine it? Mrs. James Grant, formerly Miss Blanche Routh, daughter of the great F. A. Routh . . ."

"Stop! Stop!" I smooth the paper over my knee and say, quietly, "I know how far we've fallen. There's no need to tease."

Abbie's eyes widen with dismay. "Oh, dear June. You know that's not what I mean." She takes my hands in her gloved ones and rubs my fingers to warm them. "Plenty of great families are living in reduced circumstances through no fault of their own. No. What I meant was that, that . . ." She falters, then takes a breath and tries again. "Your mother will always be

Blanche Routh. A grand lady from a grand family. Under no circumstances should she be receiving a note from a grocery clerk. Don't you see?"

"Of course I see. But I don't know what it means, or what to do about it." I steel myself taut against the tears. Abbie's just trying to help, I know that.

She takes the paper back from me and crumples it. "Well then, you'll just have to find out, won't you?" She stands and tosses the balled-up paper into the trash bin.

I jump up after her. "What are you doing?"

She raises her eyebrows with a smile and skips out of reach. "Memorize the message, and then dispose of it," she says with a laugh, then, just as quickly, her smile fades. "Something Edward told me once."

"Oh, really? Sounds like something a spy would say. Abbie?" I ask quietly. Her expression is so focused, so far away, I don't want to disturb her. I've seen her like this before, in what I think of as her secret moods. Gone are the bright smiles, the cocked head, the bouncing ringlets. Abbie's father has a line of steamships; he managed well enough through the Depression and war years. Her engagement is more of a business alliance than a love match, though she says she likes Edward just fine. Next week, when Abbie turns twenty-one, she'll come into her own money. There's little doubt she'll be married before her next birthday.

"Abbie?" I ask again, louder this time.

She shakes herself and steps back toward me, taking my arm in hers once more. "Come. Let's get back before Miss Pomeroy loses all patience with me."

———— ⚬⁓⁓⚬ ————

Before lunch, Mr. McAulay steps out of his office, buttoning up his wool coat.

"Everything all right, Miss Grant?"

I press the lever to pause the Dictaphone and look up at him, sliding the headset away so I can hear him. "Fine, Mr. McAulay, thank you."

He tucks his hat over his white hair. "I'll be out for the rest of the day."

"Do you need anything else this afternoon?" This morning he dictated three letters, speaking so loudly into the Dictaphone that I could have typed them up from here. I'm already finishing the last one.

"Just those letters. Leave them on my desk with any messages."

He heads down the hall, nodding to each smiling secretary who has paused in her work to wish him a good afternoon as he passes by. I watch his lanky figure, his slow walk, as he accepts the fealty of his staff, until he steps around the corner into the main reception hall and out of sight.

I turn back to the letter at hand—a bid to the Montreal Association of Advertisers to be nominated as their chairman. I slide the headset back in place and press the lever, and once again, Mr. McAulay's voice fills my ears.

It does not take long to finish. I slide the letter from the carriage and set it atop the others. Then I sit perfectly still, fingers in formation above the keys for a minute, waiting.

The afternoon stretches before me with nothing to fill my time except my own imagination, which at the moment is fixated on what a disaster the date with Jack Ritchie will be. Will I make it to the table without tripping on my own feet? Will I get through the dinner without spilling something on myself (or worse, on him)?

To distract myself, I think instead of the note on the orange wrapper. *1919 Saint Jacques.* What is at this address that François wants me, or Mother, to know about? It must be important, or else why would he be so forward? What was it that Abbie said? *You'll just have to find out, won't you?*

I wait a full twenty minutes before heading into Mr. McAulay's office with the letters, my heart beating louder than a ticking clock. The walls of his office are covered in a collection of hieroglyphics prints. I noticed them earlier, but now, with Mr. McAulay out, I linger over each one. I could marvel at them for hours.

I step behind his enormous desk to inspect the prints along the wall more closely. These are symbols only, circles and lines and squiggles. I imagine they form a poem, one that is indecipherable to modern man. A poem forever lost. I tear my eyes away. I must focus on the task I've come here to do.

Below the gilt-framed prints are bookshelves lined with magazines and catalogs. The Eaton's catalogs, dating back to 1922, alone take up one full shelf. Then there are the magazines and newspapers—*Chatelaine*, *Canadian Home Journal*, and bound volumes of the *Montreal Gazette*. I know without even looking that these contain the work of McAulay Advertising over the years.

I find a half row of textbooks, including three copies of *Scientific Advertising*, and next to these I find what I am looking for: Lovell's Directory. The red leather-bound book is as fat as a medical encyclopedia. I haul the volume out and place it on Mr. McAulay's desk. I bypass the section that lists Montreal residents by name and flip to the section that lists every street address in the city, along with the resident and their occupation, or the name of the business at that address.

The streets named after saints take up a good chunk of the directory. I manage to find the Saint Jacques pages without tearing the tissue-thin paper. Running my finger down each number, I finally find what I am looking for: *1919 Saint Jacques.*

It seems the building contains several businesses, most of them related to the railroad. On the second floor there's a railway agent named Fairleigh, a railway supply company, and something called Superior Models, which I assume supplies model railways like the ones Daisy's boys collect. There's a jazz club called Le Salon du Jazz. And the office of Red Lantern Taxi.

I settle back on my heels and think of Daisy slipping into the taxi the night before. The flash of red light illuminating the words *Red*

*Lantern Taxi* and the phone number painted along the side of the car. But surely that's a coincidence? A taxi is a taxi, isn't it?

I look through the names of the businesses again. What do any of these places have to do with Mother, or any of us? Why did François write down this address for us? Is it possible that I misunderstood the whole thing? *I wrapped the orange real careful, Miss Grant.*

I write the list of businesses on a sheet of notepaper with the words "From the Desk of J. N. McAulay" printed across the top and rip it from the pad.

I fold the sheet and slip it into my skirt pocket. I close the directory and slide it back in place. Then I straighten Mr. McAulay's desk, leaving the three letters, ready for his signature.

I look around the office once more. Everything in its place. Just before stepping back out, I turn and reach down again, pausing with my finger on the spine of one of the copies of *Scientific Advertising*. Surely Mr. McAulay won't mind if I borrow it for a few days?

# Chapter Five

Mr. Ritchie is waiting at the door in a brown trench coat, a tweed hat at an angle that seems to perk up his bland face. He holds out my coat for me, and I slide my arms in. I smile to thank him, but he doesn't notice. He's watching Daisy.

She is at the hall mirror, mouth open, painting her lips deep red. Each motion is graceful, slow, as though she is aware of her audience. (Of course she is.) She runs two fingers along her hairline and pauses to admire her own reflection.

Mr. Ritchie sighs, freeing us all from our momentary trance.

"Have fun, you two," Daisy says. She waggles her fingers at us, and then crouches down to receive the hugs and kisses her boys are waiting to give her.

Out on Abbott Street there is a taxi waiting, the light on its roof shining red. "You called a taxi?" I ask Mr. Ritchie.

"No, I thought we could walk." He does not take my arm. "You can walk, can't you? It's only a few blocks."

"No, I just thought—" I break off. "Never mind." We're not even on the sidewalk yet and already I've said the wrong thing. How am I supposed to get through a whole evening of this?

We reach the corner of Saint Catherine before the taxi passes us, the writing along its side easy to read in the fading daylight, as though mocking me: *Red Lantern Taxi.*

Daisy sits in the back seat, staring straight ahead like a celebrity actress being driven through the streets of Hollywood.

———— ⤷⤶ ————

"You don't look like your sister," Jack Ritchie says once we're seated, before ducking his head behind the leather-bound menu.

I swallow down the curdle of jealousy as I think of Daisy applying her lipstick. Of Mr. Ritchie's frozen stare.

"She takes after our mother," I say. "I take after our father."

"I see." From his tone it sounds like he thinks I had a choice and made the wrong one. I want to tell him about Missie, who is a perfect blend between Mother and Father, between Daisy and me, but he is intent on the menu.

"How about we both order the special? It comes with a soft drink, appetizers, and dessert."

I can't help scrunching up my nose.

"Something wrong with liver?"

"I thought the chicken looked good."

"But it's just an entrée. Twenty-five cents more, no salad, no dessert."

I've disappointed him twice already and we haven't even ordered yet. I put the menu down. "I'll have the soup of the day. And coffee." It's what Daisy would order.

"I'm on a student budget and the special is really the best value," he says, laying his menu down over the top of mine.

Without the menus between us there's nowhere to look but at each other. He's got a cowlick that curls like a little boy's. He blinks slowly, like he's trying to bring something into focus. "If you want to order the chicken and nothing else, that's okay. It's only a little more."

I smile in relief. "I don't really like liver."

He blinks again. "Liver is my favorite. I eat it twice a week." Thank goodness the waitress comes then. She takes the order from Jack Ritchie without greeting or comment.

I haven't been to Murray's since before the war, but it hasn't changed at all. Brown leather banquettes, filled, at this time of day, with diners looking for economy above all else. People older even than my parents. The dark paneled walls are decorated with pastoral scenes, soothing and unchallenging to the eye. The daylight coming through the rectangular windows seems like an intrusion.

"You're working? Supporting your family?" His question draws my attention back.

"That's right. Father had a stroke, you see. And Mother's only got a small income."

The waitress is back with his tomato juice, which he swallows in one go. I place my hands on my lap, trying not to fidget, watching one shiny, wet globule run down the outside of his glass, leaving a tiny circle of red on the wooden table. Jack Ritchie does not notice, and neither does the waitress, who is back already with his salad.

I watch him eat this too, sectioning the coleslaw into small portions. What would it be like to sit across from him and watch him do that to the food I'd cooked for him? Night after night. What would it be like to cook liver for this man, twice a week, week after week, year after year, for the rest of my life?

Would I ever write a poem again?

"Mother said you are a law student? How do you like it so far?"

It's such a relief when he starts talking that I hardly pay any attention to his words. Professors and cases and something called moot court, all between furtive bites of coleslaw, his lips ringed with a coating of mayonnaise dressing.

He keeps talking, even when the waitress's arm comes between us to deliver our main courses. His knife squeaks against the plate as he cuts the whole liver into bite-size pieces. He pauses in his monologue only to segregate the mashed potatoes and boiled carrots from the gravy.

My chicken is too dry to absorb the gravy it's drowning in, and I wish I had a soft drink or a coffee to help wash it down. I wish I was at home, having the usual cheese and crackers and can of soup for dinner, with Father as our silent sentinel. I smile between bites and try to sustain a look of captivated interest—eyebrows raised, eyes bright, slight upturn to the corners of my lips, even while chewing. He's telling me about his professors now.

"Are you going to eat your carrots?"

I shake my head. "I don't like carrots," I say.

"Really? May I?" He doesn't wait for me to answer, just reaches over and starts eating off my plate in that same squirrel-like way. I tuck my utensils together and lay them at an angle as he finishes my carrots. Then I tuck my hands together and lay them in my lap while I watch him eat a bowl of red Jell-O with a swirl of whipped cream on top.

He blinks at me, then takes a final swig of his coffee and signals for the bill. I offer to leave the tip and he accepts, and then goes to the door. I dither over my change purse, deciding on the amount, and finally settle on a dime. I get my own coat from the rack, as Jack Ritchie is already outside.

It's dark now and the air has warmed. The stores along Sherbrooke Street are lit up, their brick facades look inviting in the softly falling snow.

"I love walking in the snow," I say.

He gestures to the "Pickwick Apartments" sign above the entrance next door. "I'm right here. I suppose we should find you a taxi."

"Oh no! Not at all," I say. "I'm fine to walk from here. I really do walk everywhere."

He doesn't protest and makes no move toward me, though it seems he is waiting for something.

I step away, about to turn, then think better of it and step back. "Thank you for dinner," I say, holding out my hand. He shakes it, brushes the snow off his own shoulders, and heads toward his apartment.

I take my time, walking along Sherbrooke Street, past row houses that, over time, have been converted from homes into shops. I pass a pharmacy, a dry cleaner, and the branch of the Bank of Montreal where I will come tomorrow after work to deposit my pay. I pass the Bradner Fur Company, which used to buy coats from Father's fur manufacturing company. Before his stroke. Before the Depression. *Before.*

Back then, Father was a force. He started with little. Made his name trading furs, and gradually worked his way up to manager, and then proprietor, of one of the most respected fur coat manufacturers in Montreal. His furs were sold here, but also in Paris and New York. That is, until the crash, when suddenly it was no time to be in a luxury goods business.

All of the shops I pass—the upholsterer's shop, the oriental rug gallery, the pastry shop—were places Mother used to frequent. Now we buy all our food at Lublin's, but before the Depression, the proprietors at Young's Fruit and Vegetable Market, the National Food Shop, and the Golden Flower Shop all knew Mother, and her maid, Christine, by name.

There's a chance one of them might still remember me, if I were to walk in. They might call out to me, "Aah, Miss Grant, there you are," as though our family had been away at the seaside for a few weeks, not struck down by poverty years ago. Mr. Greenbaum might insist on sending home some of the Oka cheese he'd just gotten in, for Mother to try. Mrs. Griffin at Golden Flower Shop would prepare a bouquet of freesias and daisies, without even asking, and insist on sending it home for Mrs. Grant. Such kindness is hard to resist, and would no doubt please Mother. But when the accounts came in the mail at the end of the month, what would we do then?

At Westmount Park, I watch the snowflakes lingering in the angles of light from the streetlamps, and I feel a poem bloom at the edges of my mind. I glance from the soft snow underfoot to the warmly lit bay windows of the row houses across the street, to the velvet dark of the sky above. These graystones here have verandas and enough room for a garage or small driveway.

If I were to marry Mr. Ritchie, I could expect the deep stone walls of one of these homes to protect me, and our inevitable children, from the outside world. But then, what of Mother and Father? Mr. Ritchie clearly expects a wife who will cook liver for him twice a week, not one who will go out to work to support her own family.

*What will become of Mother and Father if you marry?* Daisy's words come back to me now, and I know that she is right. Even a kind and generous son-in-law, like Geoff, can only do so much. We may need Geoff's name on the electrical account, but it's my salary that pays the bill.

At home, the house is quiet. The boys are asleep on the sofa. Mother has finished her evening smoke and has settled into her room with the dogs. It is later than I thought.

I go down the hall as quietly as possible. I take a padded cushion from one of the kitchen chairs and lay it on the floor in Father's study, next to his chair. He is completely still, but awake, his eyes glistening in the dark room.

I sit on the floor next to him, fold my legs to one side, and tuck my skirt around my knees. I take Father's arm and put it over my shoulder, leaning my head against the sheets of his bed chair. I sit quietly for a moment, wishing things were different. Wishing Father was still in charge of the handsome building on Notre Dame Street, with the fur coat boutique on the main floor, two floors of manufacturing above, and the top floor where wide office windows overlooked the spire of Notre Dame Basilica. If he were well, we could meet downtown for lunch sometimes. Except if he were well, he would balk at the idea of me working at all.

When my hand touches his, he makes a guttural sound, which I take for a contented greeting. He doesn't say anything more, but soon I feel his fingers relax and hear his raspy breath slow. I stay there long after he has fallen asleep, feeling his rumbling snores vibrate through me.

# Chapter Six

Mother slides my coffee over to me and I take it, grateful for this quiet morning time together. She lays yesterday's *Gazette* flat on the table and looks across at me.

"How was Mr. Ritchie?"

I grimace into my coffee cup as I take my first sip.

"That bad?"

"A disaster." I feel the warmth of shame spread across my chest and up my cheeks. I don't want to be unkind, but I need to tell her something so that she won't make me go on another date with him. "He'll be a catch for someone, I'm sure."

"But not you?"

"I think he wants someone more . . ." The coffee is having its desired effect, and I pause to take another sip while deciding on the right words. "Someone who will give him their undivided attention."

Mother raises an eyebrow and cocks her head at me. "Come now, June. You know that every marriage involves some compromise."

"You're planning our wedding already? We had dinner once." I put my coffee cup down and pick up my toast, which Mother has spread with a little marmalade for me. I take a bite, considering what to tell her. "He likes to have liver twice a week," I say flatly.

"Oh, dear. That will never work." Mother says that I was, for the most part, an easy child. So long as I had my books and writing things,

I never gave anyone trouble. I would do as I was told and eat what I was given. But when I decided not to go along with something, there was no changing my mind.

"Did you tell him?"

I smile and shake my head, remembering. I was about five years old when our maid, Christine, made liver for our family dinner. I refused to touch it. Mother had her put the plate away, then serve it to me every breakfast and dinner for five days but, hungry as I was, I would not budge. (Missie snuck me toast and cheese and other treats, but still, I was hungry.) After I confessed my obstinacy at Mass on Sunday, Mother relented and let me have roast for lunch with everyone else. I haven't touched liver since.

"I doubt he'll ask for another date, in any case."

She nods and pulls a letter out of her pocket. "When his mother calls, I'll suggest that you are perhaps incompatible. Now, let me read you Missie's letter. There's hope yet."

She reads as I finish my toast and the rest of my coffee. Mother has a lovely voice, with a barely detectable French accent that makes her seem elegant and mysterious. While she is tired and hoarse a lot of the time these days, she sounds bright and young as she reads in Missie's voice. I close my eyes and let the images come to me: *"I've chosen yellow and green for the baby's nursery, never mind that Daisy will say they don't match . . . I could not find any dresses that I liked but then a neighbor showed me a brilliant way to add panels to practically any A-line pattern and I've made three dresses so far . . . The doctor says the baby will come in April, so it won't be too much longer now . . . Oh, and tell June . . .'"*

I sit up at this last part; Mother cocks her head in a teasing way that is a dead ringer for Missie.

*"'Robert has a man coming to Montreal for the General Motors conference soon. Single and handsome and on his way to success. I've told him all about her, and he says he will ask her to dinner while he is there! Mr. Hearn is his name. I told him to call her at McAulay's.'"*

"That's all really; the rest is a message for Daisy about shoes and swollen feet. You know Missie: Why write three letters when she can write one?" Mother says this but I know she's pleased. Pleased that Missie has made such a good match and is doing so well. "Isn't that exciting? About Mr. Hearn?"

I take the last bite of my toast and chew it slowly. Now I understand why Mother didn't insist I try again with Mr. Jack Ritchie from Toronto. Because there's a Mr. Hearn from Philadelphia.

I take a deep breath and ask, "Mother, what will happen to you and Father if I marry?"

"You're not to worry about that, June," she says, and then whispers a prayer under her breath.

At the door, I shrug on my coat and tuck the book of Emily Dickinson poems that is due back at the library into my pocket. Mother joins me at the door, and the dogs rouse themselves to follow. She's smiling, happy, I think, at the thought of another date for me. Hope is the thing with feathers, indeed. She hands me a sandwich wrapped in wax paper for my lunch.

"Today is my day for the bank and the library," I say. "I'll be a little late."

"You'll get out the money for the electricity bill? Geoff says he'll pay it for us tomorrow."

A familiar frustration washes over me. Why can't a woman have her own electrical account, if she's got a job and earns the money to pay the bills all on her own? We have this conversation every time the bill is due, and I know what Mother will say. She'll say, that's just the way it is. She'll say we should be grateful to have Geoff, who's willing to look after these things for us. What would we do without him?

There's no point bringing any of that up now; it will make me late for work, and I must not be late for what will most likely be my last day at Mr. McAulay's desk. "I'll get the money for the electricity bill," I promise.

"Good, and—" She starts to say something, then breaks off.

"And what, Mother?"

"Well, it would be nice if you could keep something for yourself this month. It's just . . ." She hesitates again.

"What is it?" We've learned to be direct about bills, Mother and I. We have no choice. It's not like her to evade.

She sighs. "It's just, I'm not sure this tank of heating oil will last until spring. It's been so cold. But never mind. We'll try, all right? Keep something for yourself."

"I will, Mother." I press Father's old hat down on my head. As I open the door, she reaches up and adjusts the angle of the brim.

"Maybe you can get a new hat," she says. "Or something for your hope chest." I have this urge to wrap my arms around her and tell her a new hat does not matter to me one bit, and neither does my hope chest, which is an old trunk of Grannie's that is all but empty. But Mother was raised in the Victorian age. She does not approve of hugs, and she takes great stock in hope chests. Instead, I step outside and wave from the stoop.

---

I barely have enough time to hang my hat and coat when Mr. McAulay asks me to take notes at a meeting. I follow him to a conference room, where he gestures to a chair in the corner. I perch on the hard edge of it, so that I have enough room to cement my feet and calves together and tuck them underneath. I open my steno pad, ready.

The room is smoky as the billiard room at a men's club, or at least how I imagine such rooms to be. Sands and three others stand around a table at the center of the room, their attention focused on a scattering of folders in front of them. I recognize a young man from accounts and a fellow from the media department, but I don't know their names. All the young men at McAulay's are new since the war, even Mr. Sands. There's also a tall man I've never seen before.

"I like this one," Sands says.

"You always go for the blondes. Too obvious," says one of the others.

"I like that knowing look in her eye." The third fellow—really, they are interchangeable—jostles the one next to him as he says this.

"That knowing look might not fly with the client." This more measured, almost clinical comment comes from the tall man.

"Ah, come on, Lewin, lighten up. Sands likes 'em with a knowing look."

"If she gets picked for the Eaton's insert, her face will be all over the city. Imagine how grateful she'll be, Sands!"

There's a general guffaw at this idea. I look up from my steno pad for a moment to take in Mr. Lewin, the artist brought on board to revive the Eaton's campaign, the man I heard snoring through the supply room wall.

I notice his height first, tall and thin with dark hair that is a little wild at the top. He's older than me by ten years, I would guess. His tie is an afterthought, his eyes dark and intelligent as he looks up to welcome Mr. McAulay.

McAulay walks into the space they've made for him and slaps a folder down. "Gentlemen," he says, "I don't need to remind you how important the Eaton's account is to this firm. We've got to get this right." He pauses, looks to each of them, and I feel the tenor of the room settle to meet the tone he's set.

"We'll pick our catalog models from this group, which has been reviewed and approved by Eaton's," he says, his hand still on the folder. Sands stands up straighter, mouth open as though to object.

Mr. McAulay silences him with a tilt of his head. "We need three options by the end of today. The girls we pick will model in the Eaton's spring preview fashion show next week, and we'll choose our cover girl from there. After that we prepare our Montreal-exclusive campaign, as you'll remember from yesterday's presentation, before the new clothes hit the racks in April."

"Yes, Sir," the young man from media says.

Mr. McAulay waits for the men to sit before opening the folder, then he sits down himself. He hands the first photo to Lewin, to his right. "Numbers only. No names. This is Girl Number One, Miss Grant."

I write "Girl Number One" in shorthand on my pad, and they begin, all business. Analyzing everything about her shape, her eye color, her bosom on its own and then in proportion to her waist and hips. No more joking about knowing looks. They could be talking about cars or carpets or shaving cream.

I have just written "Girl Number Four" when Sands snorts, breaking the spell.

"Too old. She looks like she's married and has kids already."

"She is lovely, though." This from Lewin. "Tiny waist. How most women hope to look after a few children." There's a tinge of wistfulness in his voice that has me look up from my notes, but from where I'm seated I can't see either his face or the girl's photo.

"I agree, Lewin. I have to say she's my top pick." This from Mr. McAulay, and from where I'm sitting, it seems like there's a boyish twinkle in his eye, like he's about to cause some trouble. But surely that can't be right. I simply don't know him well enough to read his expressions.

I look back to my notes, and then through the gap between suited shoulders, trying to get a glimpse of Girl Number Four.

The younger men jab each other with their elbows until the one from accounts comes forward as the spokesperson. "Her proportions are all wrong, Sir."

"What he's trying to say is she's flat as a board," Sands interrupts. "Besides, I like my girls a little fresher."

Mr. McAulay waves his hand in the air in front of him, dismissing these words. The jokes jigger to a halt, the three men eyeing one another like chastised schoolboys.

I wait, pencil poised.

"Since you fellows have forgotten, it seems like a good time to review the very first premise of advertising. What would that be, Mr. Lewin?"

Lewin coughs, stuck as he is between the boss he works for and the men he needs on his side to get his work done. Finally he says, "The visual needs to appeal to the customer. Not the adman."

"Exactly. And who is our customer, in this case?"

"Eaton's, Sir?" The accounts man again.

McAulay shakes his head as though disappointed. "Who do we need to convince to go to Eaton's for their summer dresses, not Simpson's down the street?"

No answer.

"Lewin? Will you enlighten these young men? They must not have read the research file, or perhaps they can't read at all."

Lewin pulls over a file folder and flips through until he finds the page he's looking for. "'In Toronto, Simpson's is seen as the choice for fashion-conscious female shoppers. Eaton's has a reputation for good quality and solid value.'"

"The place your mother buys her white cotton undies." Sands's joke is met by silence.

Lewin coughs, and then continues reading. "'In Montreal, things are quite a bit different. Largely because of the popularity of the L'Île-de-France restaurant, regular fashion shows, and lounge rooms where ladies can smoke and visit with friends while they shop, Eaton's has become very popular among affluent housewives who are looking to add interest to their outings, as they pass the time while their children are at school and their husbands are at work.'"

Mr. Lewin looks up, as though surprised that all the others are listening to him.

"Thank you, Mr. Lewin. And what is the average age of these girls with time on their hands?"

He runs a finger along the page. "Thirty-one to forty-three," he says. Then adds, "With an average of two school-age children."

Lewin's voice fades off and McAulay's comes in again, forceful as a priest admonishing against sin.

"Who is our customer? Sands? Who does our cover girl need to appeal to?"

"Housewives in Westmount and Outremont, Mr. McAulay." Sands sulks.

"Housewives who aspire to be as lovely as Girl Number Four, even after they are married and have had an average of two children." No one speaks. "In my view she's the best of the bunch. We'll try her at the fashion show on Monday and see how she does. Moving on. Girl Number Five now, Miss Grant."

They wrap up soon after, having chosen Girls Number One, Four, and Six to bring forward for consideration.

"Lunch?" Sands asks no one in particular, and all the men move to the door as one, Sands with one catalog of models under his arm and Mr. McAulay with a slim folder that reads "Superior Models."

I gasp and clap my hand over my mouth, then let my hand drop. I sit up straight, trying to appear calm, but I need not have worried. No one noticed my lapse in composure. The men leave without a word to me, almost as though they had forgotten I was there. I relax my legs out of their iron fold and I look over to the table, but the photos are all gone. I close my eyes and picture what I saw. The folder under Mr. McAulay's arm that read "Superior Models."

One of the businesses at 1919 Saint Jacques was called Superior Models. I'd assumed it sold model trains, since most of the other businesses in the building were related to the railway. That part of town was where trains got serviced, porters lived nearby with their families, and tankers and railcars were loaded and unloaded with goods and supplies for the factories along the Lachine Canal.

I stared down blindly at my notes. Superior Models. Surely there couldn't be two businesses with the same name? And to come across it twice—at the address that François gave me, and here at McAulay's. What could any of this have to do with Mother, or anyone in our family, for that matter, that François felt compelled to write that note?

The sound of squeaking wheels in the hallway draws me out of my reverie, and I jump to my feet. Helen is in the doorway with a rolling coffee tray. Her face is ashen.

"Helen, are you all right?"

She looks up at me but does not say anything. I help her with the ashtray, still smoking with cigarette ends, and the dirty coffee service. There's one file left on the table, labeled "Research."

"I'd better take this to Mr. McAulay right away," I say. "He might need it."

Helen looks up and nods. "I'll look after the rest."

I hurry down the hall. Most of the secretaries have gone for lunch already, and McAulay's office, when I get there, is dark. His coat and hat are gone.

# Chapter Seven

There's a lineup at the sinks in the ladies' room after lunch, all the steno girls reapplying their lipstick. I jostle in with the rest, just so I can wash my hands. When I get to the sink, Abbie is on one side of me and, on the other side, Marie-Céleste coats her lips in bright red. I drop my eyes down so as not to stare, looking instead to the gritty soap as I scrub my fingers clean under the cold water. I shake them dry—there's no hope of reaching the towel dispenser—and look up to find Marie-Céleste watching me, her right eyebrow arched in disdain.

"Poor Mr. McAulay," she says, turning away to admire her reflection.

Cheeks burning, I resist the urge to rush out. I need to say something, anything, or the teasing will never stop. I feel my throat tighten and I know that, if I dare speak, my voice will be raspy with tears. Abbie pushes in next to me and presses her foot lightly against mine. She hands me a pink lipstick.

"Whatever do you mean, 'Poor Mr. McAulay'?" Abbie's voice is light, innocent. She leans in so her face appears next to mine in the mirror, blotting her lips with a tissue from her handbag.

I brush the pink across my own lips, which are thin and straight, nowhere near the pillowy heart shape they are supposed to be.

"He loves nothing more than to be surrounded by pretty girls," Marie-Céleste says. As far as I can tell, she's done at the mirror now, but she ignores the girls behind her and takes her time. She smooths her dark hair, which frames her pale face and red lips in perfectly symmetrical double victory rolls. "He says it cheers him up, since his wife died." She drops her shoulders with a sigh, as though it can't be helped.

Abbie fluffs her blonde ringlets and puckers her lips at her own reflection. "I'm sure given the choice, Mr. McAulay would pick well-bred over simple prettiness any day." Her gaze locks with Marie-Céleste's in the mirror, and it's Abbie's turn to raise an eyebrow.

Marie-Céleste looks away first, moving aside to make room for Helen. Abbie nods, as though all is correct in the world, and hands me a tissue to blot my lipstick.

"Come do the cylinders with me this afternoon, if you can get away," she says.

"I will," I promise, following her out into the hall. My lips feel sticky and thick. I do my best not to chew the lipstick off before I get back to my desk. Poor Mr. McAulay, indeed.

———— ⬬⟿⟿ ————

As it turns out, I don't have time to think about whether or not I'm pretty enough to be Mr. McAulay's secretary. There are two men waiting when I arrive back at my desk.

I show them into Mr. McAulay's office, though he has not returned yet. The first man, the older of the two, introduces himself only as Bruno. His spine is rounded as he takes a seat on the long couch, his face red as though his tie is choking him. The second man is younger and does not introduce himself. He's not wearing a suit or tie, but rather black trousers and a white dress shirt with the top two buttons open. His dark hair is slick with pomade, and his dark eyes are what Daisy would call dreamy.

"Would you like coffee, gentlemen?"

The older one looks to the younger one, who shakes his head.

"No thanks, doll."

Relieved that I don't have to make a spectacle of myself with a coffee tray on my last day as a secretary, I duck my head out the door to see Mr. McAulay rushing down the hall.

"Are they here?"

I nod and hold out my hands for his hat and coat. "Yes, a man named Bruno and—"

"Yes, Bruno and J-P from Red Lantern Taxi."

It's like I'm frozen in place, his coat and hat in my hands. "Red Lantern Taxi?"

"Yes. A new account. They just got a license for a taxi stand at Westmount Station, and a few other places. Are you all right, Miss Grant?"

I swallow and nod, force myself to move again. "They don't want coffee," I say, hanging his coat on the coat-tree outside the door.

"Good. Is Sands here yet? Or Lewin?"

I shake my head.

"Can't be helped. Just come in and take notes, will you?"

Stenography only takes about 65 percent of my concentration, which leaves me plenty to notice everything else.

"I want Red Lantern to stand out from the others," says Bruno. "That's why we came to you, McAulay. I want those men, those prosperous professional men that live all the way up the hill like you do—The Boulevard, Summit Circle—to ask for us by name. Right, J-P?"

J-P sucks on his cigarette, leaning back in his chair. "You know what I think, Bruno."

"Yeah." Bruno turns to Mr. McAulay again. "J-P here thinks a taxi is a taxi and a station is a station. People at stations need taxis. No need to advertise."

"I understand both of your positions completely," Mr. McAulay says. He's in his element here. Smiling and relaxed, much too handsome for a man old enough to be my father. "I used to think like you, J-P, when I was on the money side of things. But then when I started working on the creative side of advertising, I saw the possibilities. The power of suggestion."

"Right. Suggestion. Exactly what I was saying, J-P. Like telling them Red Lantern is better," Bruno says.

Mr. McAulay nods slowly, taps a finger in the air as though Bruno were a star pupil. "We find something that makes Red Lantern stand out. And then make your customers want that thing."

I make a note of this, though normally side conversations are not recorded. The whole meeting feels like a side conversation, and I need to write something down. I try to imagine what could make one taxi better than another. Red Lantern Taxi, the only one with a red light on the roof. Like a siren, to get you home in a hurry. Like a visiting dignitary or a conquering hero.

I snap back to attention and stop myself before writing those words down. They've moved on now; discussing budget and media. Mr. McAulay promises to handle the file personally. Bruno accepts, eager to see campaign ideas. Mr. McAulay invites them to lunch next week, to meet the artist and writer who will work on their ads.

J-P stubs out his cigarette. He's not said another word, but he hasn't put a stop to things either. I know the girls in steno would call him handsome with those troublemaker eyes, but there's something off-balance about his features.

They are all standing now, shaking hands. Mr. McAulay escorts them to the elevators, and I'm left alone again with the filled ashtrays and Mr. McAulay's collection of hieroglyphs.

———— ❧❧ ————

"You can't let her push you around like that." Abbie stands in the supply room, arms crossed, her back to the view of a snow-covered Dominion Square.

I leave the cart of cylinders and join her. The snow is falling so hard I can barely see the facade of the Windsor Hotel across the square.

"It's going to be hard to get home tonight."

"Oh." Abbie turns and looks out with me. "Do you want us to drive you?" Abbie's family chauffeur drops her off each morning and picks her up at the end of the day. She would be happy to include me in their daily route, but it won't do for a girl like me to get used to being shuttled around by a chauffeur.

I shake my head. "I have some errands to do. But thank you."

"All right then, but listen. You have to speak up. To Marie-Céleste and the others. I won't always be here to do it for you."

There's something in the way she's standing, arms crossed, slightly away from me, that makes me look at her more closely. "Abbie, has something happened?"

She reaches into the pocket of her dress and pulls out a single cigarette. There's a strict rule against steno girls smoking in the office, despite the fact that the men, from the mail room to Mr. McAulay himself, smoke all they like. Abbie fishes in her pocket for a lighter and holds it up, sucking hard on the long cigarette. Only once she's exhaled the smoke, which smells like mint, does she speak again.

"Something happened. Something is happening."

"Oh, Abbie," I said. "But still, you can't smoke here. Miss Pomeroy—" My heart beats fast at the thought. Abbie will lose her job, and so will I. But the look on her face stops me cold.

"What difference does it make? Edward is coming for dinner tomorrow. A formal dinner, Mother has taken the trouble to tell me. She's bought me a new dress, and her hairdresser is coming at three o'clock."

"Do you suppose—"

"I suppose he's going to propose, properly this time, and they will set a date." She inhales deeply and looks over at me, and I can see the tears she is holding in with the smoke. She allows the smoke to billow out and looks out the window. I stare out too, at a lone pedestrian, pressing against the falling snow, crossing the square at a diagonal.

"But Abbie, aren't you pleased? You knew this was coming, and now it's finally here."

"That's just it." She leans her elbows on the windowsill, chin in one hand. "It's all laid out in front of me, a week before my twenty-first birthday. I thought maybe . . ." Her voice trails off, and I follow her gaze. The pedestrian has made it to the corner of Peel Street.

"What did you think, Abbie?" My voice seems loud against the hush from an afternoon lull. "What did you think?" I ask again, quieter this time.

"I thought I'd have some time. A few months maybe, with money in my own name, before going from my father's house to my husband's." I've never seen her green eyes so fierce. "But no. I can't be trusted even with that."

I slide the window open a few inches to try to clear some of the smoke. Abbie reaches out and stubs the cigarette on the stone windowsill, then turns to me. "Well, that settles it then," she says.

"What?"

She shakes off her mood as though it was a layer of snow. "I'm going to need a camera of my own."

"Really? Aren't they terribly expensive?"

She shrugs. "I'll tell Edward I want it for my birthday. He'll know where to find one for me. I'll insist on it. A project of my own. If I have to spend the next year looking at china patterns and tablecloths I will become a complete bore."

"You'll never be boring, Abbie. Think of all the showers you've planned here. It's always been fun for you, hasn't it?"

"But that's just an afternoon. Don't you have two older sisters? You know that girls talk about nothing else for their whole engagement. And Mother will want mine to be a full year long. So, you'll help me?"

"Of course. I'll do whatever I can. But what do you mean?"

She smiles, but she doesn't have time to answer as the door swings open. "You'll see," she whispers, just as Miss Pomeroy fills the doorway. She takes in the two of us, the open window, the untouched Dictaphone cylinders.

"Miss Grant, there you are," she says. "You must not leave Mr. McAulay's desk unattended."

I duck my head and step toward the door. I don't dare look back at Abbie as Miss Pomeroy leads me away.

"On Monday morning, you'll be back in steno where you belong."

"Yes, Miss Pomeroy," I say as I take my seat outside Mr. McAulay's office. Pretty enough or not, this is where I belong, at least until the end of the day.

I walk along Sherbrooke Street after depositing my paycheck at the bank. The shopwindows illuminate the freshly fallen snow, calling me inside. Should I buy Mother's cheese at National Food Shop instead of at Lublin's today? Perhaps a pastry from the patisserie for Mother and me to share?

I don't, of course. If Lublin's is good enough the day before payday, it is good enough on payday, but the daydream itself is pleasant enough to carry me to the library, where I return my Dickinson without choosing a new book.

I've brought *Scientific Advertising* home in my satchel and have decided it will be my reading for the week. There's no point to it really; I will never be a copywriter now. I'll be back in steno on Monday and never leave again, if Miss Pomeroy has anything to do with it. But what is the harm in learning more? No one will know.

It's still light enough to cut through the park. My boots sink in the snow of the unshoveled pathways. I pass the pond and the copse of trees where I like to sit on Friday evenings in summer and read my new library books. I wish I could sit here now under the rustle of green leaves and spend the evening writing poems in my notebook until the sun sets. Today I'd write a response to Emily Dickinson, to tell her what it's like here in Montreal at the end of winter, when the little bird makes no sound at all for days on end. Days when it is cold as the Arctic, yet there is no extra money for heating oil.

Mr. Lublin has Mother's order ready and accepts my payment for our month's worth of groceries with a smile but no comment. I don't see François, and it seems untoward somehow to ask where he is, so I take the small box of the usual groceries—cheese, ground beef for the dogs, and a can each of milk and soup—and head home.

Daisy is at the door, ready to go out. Little Steve tugs at her legs and she wrenches him off, redirecting him to me.

"Mother says you're to give me the money for the electricity bill."

I narrow my eyes. She's wearing her black wool suit again, this time with a bronze-colored silk blouse that makes her white skin glow like a gilded statue. Her eyes are lined and smoky. Her lips are as thin as mine but somehow, in painting them deep red, she's made them as inviting as Marie-Céleste's.

"I always give it to Geoff," I say.

Daisy hitches one hip and rolls her eyes. "Who do you think I'm going to give it to?" She holds out her hand as I open my pocketbook and count out the twelve dollars and the change. "Really, June. Don't you think Mother has enough to worry about without you being difficult?"

Stephen has been tugging at me this whole time and I want to shake him off, but instead I put my hand on his small head. I allow the warmth at the nape of his neck to seep into my palm and try to calm myself. Through the glass I can see the watery reflection of the red light at the top of the taxi outside.

"You're going out again tonight? Where?"

"I'm going to help Geoff entertain some clients. Not that it's any of your business."

"Yes, but where? Where are you going?"

She shrugs as she heads out. "Dinner. And then some jazz club, I expect."

I watch the Red Lantern taxi drive away along Abbott Street until it is out of sight and Mother asks me if I think money grows on trees and tells me to shut the door.

"I know perfectly well where money comes from," I mutter as I finally come inside and take off my boots and coat.

# Chapter Eight

Mother is in the kitchen, dressed for the day in a wool dress and tights with her beaver fur coat over the top. She's standing on a chair, stringing the system of clotheslines across the kitchen, getting ready for laundry day.

Mother hands me one end of the rope and I loop it over the hook close to the ceiling, which I can reach without a stool. I hand the length back and she hooks her end. We continue until the kitchen is strung like a tree with lights. I hold up a hand to help her step down. The spaniels are so eager to have her on the floor again, they whine at her feet as though she has been on a long trip.

"Come, my dears, let's get June her coffee." The spaniels follow her as she keeps up her chatter. "And yes, your breakfast too." It's like she's said magic words. George gives a little growl and Elizabeth yips and they wait at her feet, looking up at her in adoration while she hands me my coffee and then leads them to their bowls.

While they eat, she refills her own cup and joins me. Her face is pale, long lines drawing her features down, making her bright-red lipstick almost clown-like.

"How was your night?" I ask.

"I waited up for Daisy, and then Father had a coughing fit, so I stayed up with him."

"Oh, Mother, did you sleep at all?" I put my coffee cup down without taking a sip; my stomach churns with guilt. My sleep was interrupted when Daisy crawled into my bed at almost dawn, but at least I slept. "I should have stayed up and helped you."

"Nonsense, dear. I napped on the cot for a few hours," she says, then smiles. "I'll be fine."

I get up and put my toast on. I think about Mother waiting up for Daisy. How Daisy said she was going to meet Geoff, but now she's asleep in my bed, her boys on the sofa.

"Where's Geoff?" I ask Mother, taking my seat with my toast.

Mother just shakes her head and mutters a snippet of prayer under her breath.

"But Mother," I say. "If Daisy was out with Geoff last night, why did she come back here and sleep in my bed? Was she with Geoff at all last night?"

Mother shakes her head more firmly. Her lips are set in a grim line. "She's not like you, June. Or even like Missie. It's been hard for Daisy."

My mouth is so dry all of a sudden that I can barely swallow my bite of toast. "Hard for Daisy? What about you? What about Father?" What about me? I almost ask, but stop myself.

Mother reaches her hand across the table. I inch my fingers forward, thinking she's going to take my hand in hers. I'm anticipating the paper-smooth skin of her thin fingers, but instead, she takes my coffee cup and stands, bringing it to the counter to replace the few sips I've taken. Fresh-filled cups back on the table, she reaches down and strokes George's ears.

"Do you remember your debutante ball?" Mother asks.

It was two years ago, but I remember every embarrassment as though it were yesterday. My aunt offering to pay for my dress. Daisy loaning me a fur stole and Missie scrounging up a pair of elbow-length kid gloves from her own ball, which had been before the war. At the tea at the Ritz-Carlton that Grannie paid for, the flowers were left over from some other debutante's more lavish luncheon. Even my escort was borrowed—the boyfriend of one of Missie's friends, an RAF commander in uniform.

"I remember the worry, the upheaval, the scrimping. Keeping up appearances for Grannie and for all of Westmount." I clamp my mouth shut when I see the raised inner corners of her thin eyebrows, the pinch of her lips.

"It was only fair, June, that you should have a chance to come out like your sisters, despite everything."

"I'm sorry, Mother. I didn't mean to sound ungrateful." And it's true, if I hadn't gone—for all the good it's done me—I'd probably have thought it wasn't fair.

Mother sips her coffee and nods and I know she has accepted my apology. That's Mother's way. She doesn't hold grudges or let things fester. She accepts and moves on, though I know she'd rather not mention unpleasant topics at all.

"I asked you, because I can assure you that Daisy's memories of her ball are just as fresh and no doubt more painful. Do you even remember Daisy's ball? You were only a girl."

I was only ten years old.

"You sent me to Grannie's. When I came back, it was after the ball and Daisy was away. Gone to a friend's chalet in the Laurentians." That's all I can remember.

I look at Mother. Her features strain from the effort of holding them still against the emotion beneath. "Things were different after that," she says. "It's been hard on us all, but it's been hardest on Daisy. Please try to be more understanding, June."

She lifts her chin and stands. "I'd better take these dogs out. Seems like the boys are having a lie-in this morning."

George and Elizabeth follow her to the door, excited all over again at the prospect of the slightest activity. I eat my cold toast and take a sip of my coffee as Mother's admonition echoes in my head.

*More understanding. Of Daisy.* The vise of envy grips my stomach. I put the coffee down, giving up on it altogether. I grip my hands into fists and close my eyes tight, but still the selfish voice in my head will not stop asking, What about me?

———— ⚬~⚬ ————

I need to clear my head, so when Mother and the dogs come back, I head out for a walk of my own. As I pick up my satchel, my hand brushes against Daisy's much more stylish pocketbook, a soft caramel-colored leather. Its gold clasp must have only been partly closed, because that light brush of my hand is enough to pop it open. The little purse is stuffed so full that crumpled paper falls out.

No, not paper. Bills. Dollar bills, seven or eight of them, a cluster of two-dollar bills, and more. I reach out to touch a wrinkled five-dollar bill. The movement of my reflection in the mirror makes me jump, and I look up. The look of stern disapproval on my face scares even me. Is that really what I look like? I shift my gaze over to take in the sleeping boys, reflected behind me. They have not seen a thing.

I pick up Daisy's purse. Below the crumpled mass is a man's money clip, with bills neatly folded in half and sorted by denomination. I count close to one hundred dollars. I dig deeper. Below this I find three kinds of lipstick, a silver lighter that used to be Father's, and a half-empty pack of Chesterfields. There's a small satin pocket sewn into one side, and it's in there that I find the money I gave Daisy—five two-dollar bills, two one-dollar bills, a quarter, and a dime, along with the carefully folded stub from our electricity bill, stating that Geoff Collier owes $12.35 for his Abbott Street residence for the months of December 1946 to February 1947.

*Try to be more understanding, June.*

Fine, I think. I shut the clasp on Daisy's purse and put it back on the table before Mother can see. I pick up my own satchel and head out into the cold morning sunshine.

I set a quick pace along Saint Catherine, trying to push the thoughts of all that money in Daisy's purse from my mind. As long as she gives Geoff the money for the electricity bill, what concern is it of mine?

But where did all that money come from? I am not sure how things work between married couples, but I am quite certain that wives don't carry around pocketbooks full of crumpled-up bills.

I wish I could walk to Abbie's house and talk to her about it all and escape for a little while. Christine, who worked for Mother for most of her married life, works for Abbie's parents now. She still pampers me when I go there. Abbie has a lovely bedroom and a chauffeur who will take us downtown if we want to go. But I know that the whole house will be preparing for the formal dinner that night—Abbie's engagement dinner, if that's indeed what it is—and I'll only be in the way.

Instead, I turn my thoughts to the puzzle of the address: 1919 Saint Jacques.

I reach Greene Avenue and turn south, my steps hesitant. Brick houses line the street, and the sun shines equally on both sides of the railway bridge, and yet I know that across those tracks is another part of town altogether. Saint Henri, where everyone speaks French. Saint Charles, where the servants and the railway workers live. These are the neighborhoods where I imagine the poets must live. Across those tracks, just a short walk away, is 1919 Saint Jacques Street.

I stop short when I reach the railway bridge.

For a girl like me, Saint Henri and Saint Charles are more of a warning than a destination. A place you end up, not a place you walk toward. It's like there's an invisible barrier, anchoring me in the known, the English, the respectable streets of Westmount.

We have not fallen that far, not yet. Our little Abbott Street abode, rented to us out of kindness by an old business associate of Father's, might be a mere three doors up from these very tracks, but it's still Westmount.

It's me that's keeping my family from ending up on the other side of these tracks. My salary. My job. It's up to me. I think of the address written in pen on the slip of butcher paper, of the crumpled bills in Daisy's purse. I think of Mother's drawn expression as she tells me to be more understanding.

I resist the pull of the sunshine and mystery and turn around to head back home to help Mother with the laundry.

# Chapter Nine

I have noticed that married couples become a single unit that is greater than the sum of its parts. To ask questions, to doubt what they say, to pass judgment, would be to cast aspersions not on two distinct persons, but on that greater being—their marriage.

Geoff and Daisy are at their most omnipotent when they arrive on Sunday morning in time for Mass. Geoff stays with Father, and Daisy takes communion, and Mother, no longer anguished over Daisy's eternal damnation, is almost girlish.

"Let's eat now," she says. "I don't want the roast to get dry."

"Oh, Mother, your roasts are always delicious," Geoff chimes in. This is sheer flattery, as Mother's roasts are dry no matter what, but who dares question? "Come wash your hands, boys."

Geoff winks at me. He is so handsome I find it hard to look at him without blushing. Daisy is beyond pretty in that way that will awaken the jealous monster in me if I'm not careful.

If my date with Jack Ritchie had gone better, I wonder if we could have presented such a united front someday. But I think not. There was something missing in the mixing of us, some elemental spark. I could never overcome my hatred of liver to cook it for him twice a week, and as far as I can tell, catering to each other's preferences is a large part of what marriage is about, isn't it? At least on the wife's side.

And yet, Mother would be so pleased if I were to get married. Could I not pretend? I know I could not keep it up for long, not like Daisy does.

Is Daisy pretending now? Is Geoff?

"Come to the table, boys," Daisy says, shepherding them ahead of her down the hall.

To keep a formal dining room that we only use once a week, in such small house, seems a waste to me, but Mother insists on keeping her standards and Aunt Lucie's Chippendale table. The boys clamber underneath the carved mahogany legs and then squeeze themselves like little eels up from the floor and into position, their chairs side by side at the head of the table.

Next, Geoff sidles right to the back, into the seat closer to the boys. Daisy slides in next to him, under the portrait of Great-Grandfather Routh, who no doubt would be appalled to have his likeness hung over such a modest table.

I place a tray, laden with the gravy, peas, carrots, and sliced bread, on the table, then climb into my seat, opposite Geoff. Mother reaches over to hand the roast, a shrunken brown lump on a platter, to Geoff for carving.

Then, with great dignity, Mother maneuvers Father into place at the head of the table, then slides into her own seat next to me.

"Geoff, will you say grace?"

In this moment, even the boys are still. Geoff coughs, then begins. I drop my head down and close my eyes, hoping that the prayer will quiet the question on my mind: Did Geoff pay the electricity bill, which was due yesterday? (And if he pays it late again, will he cover the late fee?)

"Amen," Mother whispers, and I do as well.

"How are things at McAulay's, June?" Geoff asks. His voice is jovial, but I feel a wire of tension from Mother, next to me.

"It's fine. Same as always."

"Do they miss me at all, do you think?"

I brave a look at him to see if he's teasing or testing, but he's as earnest as Stephen over his peas. It's been almost a year since Geoff and Fletcher Moore left to start their own firm, Collier and Moore. If Geoff's name is spoken at McAulay's, it's in a whisper.

Mother passes the gravy boat to Daisy, who holds it for a moment without pouring any on her plate. She hands it to Geoff, who douses his beef in it before serving some to Stephen. Then he makes a big show of passing it to Christopher, who manages to put the gravy boat down in front of himself without spilling too much. I don't dare ask him to pass it on, and it's too far for me to reach.

"June worked at Mr. McAulay's desk this week, didn't you, dear?"

There's a screech of knife against plate as Geoff pauses in cutting Steve's meat for him. He looks at me, and I can see it's an effort to hold his Sunday dinner face in place. His skin turns red, his eyes bead out, and a cloud of unformed emotions darken his expression.

"You watch out for him, June. You hear me? That man is a leech who will suck you dry." Geoff's voice is low and dangerous. "I had to go out on my own to get out from under him."

I look to Daisy, expecting her to smooth things over, but she merely looks up from pushing her food about her plate, slicing it into smaller and smaller bites, without putting any of them into her mouth. She stares back at me and raises her eyebrows with a bright smile, as though the entertainment is just starting. She pulls a cigarette out of the pocket of her skirt and puts it in between her lips.

"June," she says. "Take my advice. If you're going to get sucked dry by a leech, make sure he's a rich one at least."

Daisy lights the cigarette as though she's lighting a spark and waiting for the bomb to go off.

"Dammit, Daisy," Geoff mutters, eyes bulging further. He tries to stand, but there's no way out. The boys stare at him, and Stephen, his mouth full of peas, opens his mouth to cry. Geoff sits down again and begins to console the boy.

"Daisy, no smoking at the table," Mother says, restoring decorum.

Daisy gestures to Father, silently pointing out the practicalities. There's simply nowhere she can go. She crosses her arms and sits back.

Everyone is silent as the unpleasantness settles like dust that no one meant to kick up.

"Well, you'll be back in steno tomorrow, won't you, June?" says Mother.

I nod, my mouth full of tough roast and peas.

"That's good, then," Geoff says.

I think of Miss Pomeroy's unrelenting criticism and Marie-Céleste's ironic glare. It seems everyone wants me to go back to steno and forget all that I learned about this week. But I'm not at all sure that is possible.

# Chapter Ten

I find Abbie at the center of a circle of girls in the steno office. She holds her left hand up to display her engagement ring—a diamond surrounded by emeralds.

I join the fray and Abbie winks at me, as though it's all a fun game. I try to see under her smile for a hint of the hard anger I glimpsed in the supply room on Friday, but it seems to have disappeared altogether. With Daisy I might feel envy, but with Abbie I feel nothing but sadness. But why should I feel sad when Abbie is getting the thing every girl wants? I swallow my doubts and smile back.

Miss Pomeroy coughs in the doorway. The girls scatter. Abbie drops her hands down over her typewriter keys, and I step over to my desk and settle into my own chair. Miss Pomeroy looks over at me and nods. Not approval. No, I wouldn't call it that. I would call it a look of affirmation; I am back in her sights, where I belong.

Miss Pomeroy circles the room like a headmistress as we get down to the typing she has assigned to us. I have a series of letters from the accounts department to various clients, all dictated in the rumbling voice of one of the account executives. I am so engrossed that I don't see Mr. Sands until he's standing right in front of me.

He picks up the letter opener on my desk—largely ornamental; I type letters for others to send, it's a rare thing for me to open one—then he touches the three sharp pencils that I have lined up at the front of my desk like little sentries. He shoves the pencils aside. Lifting the fabric of one pant leg at the knee, he settles one cheek of his behind on the edge of my desk. Blushing, I tear my gaze away from his rump and the scattered pencils to his face. He's taken over my desk and stopped me from working, but he's not even looking at me. He's winking at Marie-Céleste, who rolls her eyes and smiles, her pink painted fingers poised on the roller knob of her typewriter as if the page is going to take itself out.

"Miss Grant," he says at last.

His cultivated mustache does nothing to offset his weak chin. I don't care what the others say, I don't think Mr. Sands is handsome in the slightest.

"How can I help you, Mr. Sands?"

"There's a dress rehearsal for the Eaton's spring fashion show today. Mr. McAulay wants you there."

Marie-Céleste and Helen stare openly. Abbie smiles.

"What time?"

He shrugs. "Now." The too-long sleeve of his suit jacket reveals his fingers: thick as sausages and flecked with blond hair.

I remove the headset and mark the metal clip to show my place on the Dictaphone. I stand and adjust my skirt. I want to tidy my desk, but Mr. Sands is still half sitting on it. I weigh the merits of Miss Pomeroy scolding me for a messy desk against the girls teasing me for touching Mr. Sands's thigh; they are watching my every move now. I leave the pencils askew. I close the file folder with the letters I've already typed and carry it back to Miss Pomeroy.

She raises an eyebrow at Sands, then claps her hands for the girls, who resume typing as one.

"Mr. McAulay asked for her on Eaton's account."

"He asked for Miss Grant specifically?"

"Oh, yes. He was very clear."

"Very well, then, though I don't believe Miss Grant has anything more to offer than any of the other girls." She holds a hand out for the file. "I will reassign her work."

She eyes me as she takes the file and shakes her head. I'm much too tall. I eat my lipstick. And that hair of mine. She doesn't even need to say the words anymore, I can hear them in her eyes.

———— ❧❧ ————

A Red Lantern taxi is waiting outside. The driver holds the back door open for me and smiles as I get in. I notice how tall he is—taller than I am—and his ringless fingers as he holds the door for me. Tall and unmarried. He smiles, showing a black line of rot along his gumline.

"Haven't got all day, Grant." Sands presses against my arm, and I see he expects me to slide across the back seat to make room for him. Daisy would call him a beast. I don't say a word, but it's a trick to slide across without showing my legs above the knee or snagging my stockings.

The driver ducks his face in and looks past Mr. Sands. "You all right, Miss?" His English is deeply accented.

"Fine, thank you," I say, though I'm sure Mr. Sands would not have treated Marie-Céleste or any of the prettier girls this way. The driver limps around to the front, and Mr. Sands watches, his eyes slits.

"Would have been faster to walk," he says. "Damn DPs."

I cross my ankles and fold my hands in my lap. It is true that we could have walked most of the way by now, but the driver seems happy for the fare. Besides, it would be rude to get out now, and aside from Sands's curt manner, I'm quite enjoying being inside a taxi.

"It must be hard to be a displaced person," I say.

"Driving a taxi is pretty much the same everywhere," Sands says, missing the point completely. He changes the topic as the driver lowers himself into his seat. "Not like writing advertising. Now that's a hard job. Lots of people think they can do it, but it's no joke. Eaton's, please."

I settle back into the leather seat and imagine I'm in better company. A fashion show at Eaton's is plenty exciting, but Mr. Sands doesn't seem to think so. He mutters to himself and fidgets, which makes it hard to focus on my daydream. The Boer War Memorial flashes by, and I see a man sitting on the bench Abbie and I think of as our own. My attention is pulled away again as a car pulls out in front of us and our driver slams on the brakes.

"Look, I don't know where you are from—"

"Italia." The driver says it cheerfully. "Firenze."

"What?"

"You ask where I am from? I am from Firenze."

Another car cuts in, and we miss the light to turn onto Saint Catherine.

"There! There. Get in there. Just nose right in. That's right."

A chorus of honking sets up behind us. The driver grins at us in the mirror with his crooked, rotting teeth.

"Here, here. Just pull over here."

The driver lurches to a stop across from Eaton's. Sands hands him a taxi chit and steps out. I scramble along the seat again, then rush across traffic as Sands strides into the street. I keep pace with him, step for step, glad of my height for once.

Together we enter the grand lobby of Eaton's, and for a moment I am transported by the promise—fragrance and music and color and style in every direction. My head spins at the magic of it as I follow Sands down the main aisle to the elevators. He looks back at me and smirks, shaking his head.

"No girl can resist Eaton's," he says. "Not even a sensible one like you."

I want to tell him he's wrong, but I don't trust myself to be polite. Besides, is he wrong?

We find Mr. McAulay at the back of the ninth floor, in a high-ceilinged room that is divided by a raised runway. There's a stage at one end, decorated with flounced curtains and white columns that are painted to look like marble.

The room is set up with rows of chairs on both sides of the runway, as though ready for a full audience, but there are only a few people here. Three Eaton's matrons in lab coats, and Mr. Lewin, standing on the runway, talking to the photographer.

"Strike a pose, Lewin," Mr. Sands calls out.

Mr. McAulay shakes his head. "Come, Miss Grant, let's sit over here." I follow him to the opposite end of the runway. Sands pulls three chairs out of their alignment and clusters them right at its base. Mr. McAulay gestures to the middle one. "Sit. Sit. Did you bring a notebook?"

"Of course," I say, pulling my steno pad from my satchel.

"Good. We need descriptions for these outfits."

"Descriptions?"

"Yes, look." He points up to the stage where a model has stepped out. "We're short a writer today. Sands won't be able to keep up with all of it. We need you to take notes on everything, then type them up this afternoon."

Music starts playing. The lights dim. I look over to Mr. Lewin, who is now seated in a chair next to the photographer, a sketchbook open on his lap. The model steps down the four stairs from the stage and sashays along the runway toward us. She's dressed like a smart secretary, though in a pencil skirt so tight I doubt she'd ever be able to sit down.

"See her outfit? Describe it. Write down our impressions. What does this ensemble say to us? Where would you wear it? That kind of thing," McAulay whispers in my ear.

The model pauses in front of us and sways from one hip to the other, her gaze firmly set on something far beyond the back of the room.

I look up at the outfit and say, "My boss has an important client meeting today."

"Yes, like that, exactly." Mr. McAulay pulls out his own notebook and scrawls "client meeting" in a hand that is less tidy than my young nephew's. "Then later on, one of the copywriters can add his piece to our notes. 'You'll always be just right at the office in this number,' or some such thing. We tell a story about the outfit and the girl wearing it."

I nod as though I understand. I watch Mr. McAulay tuck his own notebook back into his suit jacket pocket.

The model is already on the move again. She steps over to the other side of the runway and, without looking down, stands right on top of a spot marked with masking tape. She poses there for a minute, her head turned at an angle as though she is listening for a faraway sound, while the photographer takes a photo and Lewin sketches. Once the flash has gone off, Lewin flips over the page in his sketchbook. A lab-coat-clad matron snaps her fingers, bringing the model back to life, and she floats back down the runway.

I start scribbling in my notebook as I watch the next girl parade onto the stage, pert and lovely in a pleated, flowered skirt that falls just above the ankle. I scrawl in shorthand, "Stand out at your husband's company summer garden party," and then capture a few details, the bright flowers, soft material, wide pleats, long hemline, as she approaches and pauses in front of me.

As a girl, I used to play with paper dolls. The dolls were old—hand-me-downs, of course—from when Daisy was a girl. By the time I got them, their edges were frayed and most of the paper tabs had fallen off. Even the tape used to repair them had dried and was coming unstuck. There was no way to play with those dolls without ruining them, so instead, I gave them names and wrote down stories about where they were going in their pretty dresses.

I draw on this experience now as the next model takes the stage. I give the girl the name Effie. Just that sets my imagination free. Effie may only be a secretary, but she'll make an impression at the office Dominion Day picnic in this flower-patterned, flowing rayon dress with its tucked waist and embroidered Peter Pan collar.

Thinking it will be easier if I name the ladies in alphabetical order, I call the next one Fran. Everyone says how stunning Fran looks in this sunshine-yellow frock. With its slimming cut, no one at the salon would guess she had a baby just last month. (And her husband can't take his eyes off her.)

I scribble furiously, getting into a steady rhythm. On either side of me, Mr. McAulay and Mr. Sands smile as the models parade before them, taking no notes at all. The models modulate their steps to the jazz music playing from a phonograph. I watch from the moment the girl steps from behind the black curtain. She takes three steps, and by the time she pauses next to one of the columns, I've named her. A half dozen more steps down the stairs to the runway and I've jotted the outfit details. By the time she's standing before me, hip jutted out, smiling down at us, I've created a story.

Just as the model I've named Janet retreats down the runway, Mr. McAulay lets out a little sigh of regret.

"There she is, Sands. Girl Number Four."

Mr. Sands whispers in my ear. "This is the girl he wants for the cover." Then to Mr. McAulay, in a voice loud enough the model might hear him, he says, "I still think she's too old."

"No, she's lovely. Eternally young. A real beauty. Look at those eyes." There's no mistaking that troublemaker look in Mr. McAulay's eyes this time when he sees her.

Mr. Sands settles back in his seat, and I snap my eyes up to the stage for my first look at the famous Girl Number Four.

"We'll see about that," Sands says, but his voice is distant in the buzz that suddenly fills my head. I jump out of my chair so fast that it screeches across the floor.

Girl Number Four is Daisy.

# Chapter Eleven

Mr. McAulay has to hold my chair to keep it from knocking onto the floor, and Daisy, terrible Daisy, looks down and sees me.

"Everything all right, Miss Grant?" Mr. McAulay asks.

Daisy's mask does not slip, precisely because she is that kind of girl. The kind of girl I wish I could be. The kind of girl I would trade places with if only I could, and I know that my quest to give up envy for Lent is doomed.

But none of this matters to Daisy, who smiles down at Mr. McAulay as though he were Father Christmas and she'd like to sit on his knee. In return, Mr. McAulay has forgotten about me completely. He gazes up at her, his eyes drained of thought and intelligence. She snaps around and struts to the marker in front of the photographer to strike her pose without looking at me again. I watch her ramrod-thin figure, her hips as small as a young girl's, swinging.

"She is a tidy package, I will give you that," Sands says as the flash-bulb sounds and, cued by the matron's nod, Daisy resumes her walk, impervious to it all.

I sit back down and turn to a new page on my steno pad, willing my hands to stop shaking, my heart to stop racing, the rush of wind in my ears to subside.

Before she married, before children, Daisy was a model. She'd practice, endless loops of the wide and long hallways of the old house. Daisy was married off before we moved to Abbott Street, where the cramped hallways would not have suited her one bit. She met Geoff at a show just like this. He was a young adman, working for McAulay on the Simpson's cruise collection of 1938. They were married in a big rush.

"Geoff wants me to stop modeling," she'd told us, flashing her diamond ring like a prize she'd won.

She said this while repacking her honeymoon trunk for the fifth time. "From now on, I wear all the lovely new outfits I want, because he buys them for me. He promised."

I turn to Mr. McAulay again, wondering about that look in his eye when he saw Daisy's photo. And again now. I miss the next girl completely, and I have to ad-lib, based on the back of her outfit. I admonish myself to pay attention, and I start taking notes again.

Words spill out on the page, outfit after outfit, girl after girl. *Lianne knows that even a day of running errands for her family is not a day to let herself go. These trousers, paired with a pretty, sweetheart-collared blouse, are just the right blend of practical and feminine.*

Daisy appears three more times, and each time I give her a new name. Sissy. Annabelle. Felicity.

I turn to the last page of my notebook, ready for the next model, but it turns out Daisy in her Felicity evening dress is the finale. Black silk with a deep V-neck, a belt with a rhinestone clasp, and a flowing pleated skirt that would never have been allowed during the war years. *When you want your husband to know you've only got eyes for him, and he can't wait to show you off!*

The spotlights go out and we are left with the regular gray light of a cloudy winter afternoon. The Eaton's matrons stand in their lab coats, clapping. A bevy of models appear and clap along, some already in street clothes, with coats and purses over their arms.

I hurry to the back of the room and out of Daisy's sight, taking shelter behind Mr. Lewin, who is packing up his sketches and saying goodbye to the photographer. I watch Daisy glide across the stage, in an outfit I would name Blanche, after our mother, more classic than anything on the stage today. Mr. McAulay hurries to the front and helps her step down. She holds his arm for balance and doesn't let go, even when she has both feet solidly on the floor. She smiles up at him, and he smiles down at her. There is no doubt they recognize each other.

Mr. Sands has turned himself into a veritable banister, helping girl after girl step down from the stage, even though all of them managed it multiple times on their own in the last hour. "Come to the Windsor tonight, girls, six o'clock, drinks on me."

"Well then, time for lunch," Mr. McAulay says, and stalks away behind Mr. Sands, who has the girls I've named Izzie and Minette on each arm.

When I look at my watch I see that it's well past my own lunch hour.

Everyone else is gone except for the Eaton's matrons. When the elevator finally disgorges me into the lobby, the bright lights and smell of perfume and the smiling shopgirls are too much all at once. I barely make it to the street before the tears start to fall.

———— ⚬⁓⁓⚬ ————

By the time I reach the Sun Life Building my face is a blotchy mess, but no matter how sternly I tell myself to, I can't stop crying. I can't go inside. I wish I could call up and have Abbie come meet me, but I can't spoil her day, which is full of happy news.

There's only one place left for me to go.

When I step into Saint James Cathedral, the smell of candles and mystery in the nave calms me immediately. My steps echo against stone and marble. The light pierces the stained-glass windows, transforming the dead gray afternoon light into pinpoints of golden color.

By now, my tears have turned to hiccups. What do I have to be sad about? But underneath the tears burns the frustration, the anger, I've been tamping down for weeks. Anger, at Daisy.

It's cold in the confessional. "Forgive me, Father, for I have sinned," I say as I kneel. The air is closed with trapped smells: damp wool, stale cigarettes, and overcooked brussels sprouts.

"Tell me, child."

At convent school, the nuns would have us prepare ourselves for confession. I have rushed in straight from Eaton's today and don't have my thoughts in order. I blurt out: "I'm worried. About my sister. I think she's sinning, and I don't know how to stop her."

"In what way is she sinning?"

"She's lying, Father. To her husband. To our mother." She must be doing that, at least. But what else?

"These are serious concerns, my child. Has she been to confession? Or to Mass?"

"She did go yesterday, Father."

"And did she take communion?"

"Yes, Father."

"Well then, it is between her and God." He sighs. "Sometimes, between sisters, there can be jealousy. Are you jealous of your sister?"

I feel the hot knife twist again. Envy, anger, frustration all at once. How is this *my* sin, when Daisy is up on that stage?

"My child? Envy is a sin all its own. One only you can do something about."

"Yes, Father."

"Let us pray, to ease your worries." He begins muttering a prayer for contrition in a monotone. I hug my thin coat to my shoulders and follow along, though impatience claws at me. Why should I have to pray for Daisy? I have enough to worry about. She should look after her own soul.

He sets me free with a final blessing and I rush out. I can't be late. I am sure Miss Pomeroy won't believe me if I tell her that I worked through my usual lunch hour and that I had to go to confession urgently. Most girls' sins can wait until after work.

———— ❧ ————

I tell Miss Pomeroy that Mr. McAulay asked me to type up my notes and to answer his phone, which is only sort of a lie. He asked me to type up "our" notes, but did not specify where I should type them. If he hadn't been bewitched by Daisy, I'm sure he would have.

But I don't know how he wants them. Would he want the names and stories that I invented? Or just the descriptions of the clothes?

"Are you working on the notes for today? Sands asked me to give you his notes from the show."

I look up, to take in Mr. Lewin. A flop of dark hair, kind brown eyes, and a soft smile. I look down to his fingers, tapping out a beat on a single page of scrawled notes, torn from a notebook.

I take it from him. "Thank you," I say.

He drops his fingers to my desk and they land on the first page of my own notes, which I had just pulled from the typewriter.

"You are Miss . . ." He takes up the page beneath his fingers.

"Miss Grant."

He's stopped listening. "Miss Grant, you say . . ." He runs a finger along the page. "I like this idea with the names. Fresh. Frankly, I'm surprised Sands came up with it." He cocks his head and looks at me, a question in his eyes. "Didn't I see you at the show?"

"Yes, I was there, Sir. Mr. Lewin. Isn't it?"

"Yes, that's right. I'm the illustrator on the Eaton's account. These notes"—he holds up my page—"will be my next two weeks of work. Do you normally work here, at Mr. McAulay's desk?"

I shake my head. "I'm normally in steno. I'm just here . . ." My voice fades off. I'm not sure when I'm here or even why. I want to ask him what's fresh about what I wrote, but before I can ask anything he holds out his hand.

"Well, it's a pleasure meeting you." His fingers are long and cool. "They lock me in the art office in the morning and I spend the whole day sketching hemlines. And if they lock you up in the steno office, well, it's no wonder we haven't met properly before. But a pleasure." He lets my hand fall and looks back to my notes. "Brilliant, really, this idea of naming the girls. I don't expect that from Sands on the whole."

*Brilliant.* My heart thrills at the word, but still, I don't claim the work as my own.

"I'm surprised really. It didn't look like Sands was paying attention." He winks again and I know that he knows. I smile up at him. His wedding band flashes back.

"Have a good afternoon, Miss Grant."

"Thank you, Mr. Lewin."

I don't watch as he walks back down the hall toward the art department. A tall man. Charming. Kind.

Married, I think, reminding myself of the gold band on his finger.

Still, everything inside me is fluttering.

For once the boys aren't here when I get home. The house is quiet and I have my typewriter all to myself. Daisy must be at her own house, pretending to be a good housewife. I want to storm over there and ask Geoff if he knows what his wife is up to. I want to ask what she was doing with Mr. McAulay.

I imagine Daisy on that runway, wearing a dress from next season, all eyes on her. The moment when I stood up and she saw me. I know I will pay a price.

She will make demands, pinch and press me until she has me firmly under her thumb. Like she used to do, in the old house, so I wouldn't tell Mother she was sneaking out her bedroom window at night. She'll make me promise. She won't be afraid to leave bruises.

In order to keep that promise, I'll have to lie, to Mother, and to Geoff. Think of all the Hail Marys I'll have to say, just to keep up with Daisy and all her sins.

I must remember to confess, for lying to Mr. Lewin, in letting him believe that the notes were Sands's. If I'm telling a lie to protect my own job and someone else's, is it really a sin?

Up until now, I've always kept track of those lies, so I can confess and repent, but over the course of a day, a woman has to tell so many. It seems the more I am out in the world, the more I lie. And the more I lie, the more time I need to spend on my knees, repenting for lies I've told so as not to offend anyone. If I continue at this pace, there will be no time to write poetry at all.

I could write a poem now, but I simply don't have the heart for it after today. My insides feel as raw and ragged as the ground beef that Mother feeds the spaniels, and I need to be the picture of calm before I go back to work tomorrow.

Father's cough is worse. I will go sit with Mother and keep her company. I will pretend that nothing is bothering me. I will agree that Daisy and Geoff are the perfect couple. I will pretend I never received a note from the grocery clerk with a mysterious address on it. I will smile when she asks me if I've heard from Mr. Hearn, the man Missie says is going to ask me on a date. And I will promise that when I do hear from him, I will be pleasant and open-minded and do my very best to get married. After all, I must not make a fuss.

# Chapter Twelve

I arrive ten minutes early and am already hard at work when the steno girls are still in the ladies' room, adjusting their hair and lipstick from their streetcar ride. I had a realization in the night—a much better way to organize my Eaton's fashion show notes—and I am determined to get them down on paper before I am summoned back to steno.

There's no sign of Mr. Lewin or Mr. McAulay this morning, and Miss Pomeroy is nowhere to be seen. I retrieve the typed notes that I left on Mr. McAulay's desk the night before and shove them into my desk drawer. Then I go back to my original shorthand notes in my steno pad and start again. Instead of a new girl for every outfit, I organize the outfits according to what one girl would wear in a day. I think of Daisy, who might wear a pair of trousers in the morning to drop Christopher off at school, then a simple dress to do the shopping, and then change into a nicer dress to go to a charity luncheon. In the evening she'd wear a cocktail dress for a client dinner or a party. Organized this way, there are only ten girls. The story of ten days, four outfits each.

I start typing again, taking care to build the story of each woman in each outfit as part of the story of her life.

"And just what do you think you are doing?"

I yelp and jump up at the sound of Miss Pomeroy's voice behind me.

"Miss Grant," she says. "You must maintain calm. It's unseemly."

I stand up fully and turn to face her, clasping my hands chastely. "I'm sorry, Miss Pomeroy. Mr. McAulay asked me to type up my notes from the fashion show. I didn't have a chance to finish yesterday." I grip my fingers tighter at the lie.

"Let me see," she says. She holds out a hand and looks off to my right, as though she can't bear the sight of me. I reach behind me for my steno notebook and hand it to her.

A wraith of doubt swirls up as she reads my shorthand. I press it down hard, push it under the rug with the mess that is already there, and feel a tightness at my throat at the effort of keeping it all down.

Miss Pomeroy turns the pad over and flips a page, and then another.

"Mr. McAulay dictated this to you? Or Mr. Sands maybe?"

I look down at my shoes, which look scuffed and enormous next to Miss Pomeroy's polished Oxfords. I should lie and say yes. I should tell her that I am simply transcribing Mr. Sands's notes, but I am sick of lying. I took those notes myself, and Mr. Lewin called them brilliant. And suddenly I am frozen. Lying is a sin, but then so is pride, and I am not sure which one is worse.

"Miss Grant?"

"Mr. McAulay asked me to type them," I say.

"Very well. You can stay here for today only. Tomorrow you will be back in steno."

I nod again and manage to whisper, "Yes, Miss Pomeroy."

She hands the notebook back to me. She steps away, and I feel relief wash over me, but then she steps back.

"Miss Grant," she says, and I steel myself again. "You are just a steno girl. Don't let Mr. McAulay make you think otherwise. At McAulay's, ladies are secretaries or stenographers. Nothing more."

"Yes, Miss Pomeroy. I won't forget," I say, but I know it is yet another lie. I would like nothing more than to write notes like this all day. I wait for her to be out of sight so I can get back to my task.

It takes a long time to type my notes in this way. Each story needs to be different, and I dig deep into my memory for all the things Daisy and Missie have told me they do as married women. I decide that Effie is engaged, not married yet, and she needs outfits for the types of activities she will do. Thinking of Abbie's recent experience, I start with a dress for a formal engagement dinner, but after that I am at a loss.

Mr. Sands finds me like this, my fingers over the keys, eyes staring out into space.

"Daydreaming, Grant?"

He doesn't sit on my desk this time, thankfully, but rather stands in front of it. I can't help but feel small with him standing over me like that.

"Are these my notes from yesterday?" He picks up the top sheet from the growing pile next to my typewriter and turns it over.

"Your notes?" I ask.

"Yes, didn't Lewin give them to you? I asked him to."

I pull up the single, crumpled sheet from the top drawer.

"These notes?"

"Yes. Are those included in here?"

I am at a loss for what to say. Half my mind is still choosing a china pattern with Effie, so I nod without thinking.

"Good. Good. Bring them to my office when you're done, will you? McAulay's finally giving me a chance to be the lead writer on Eaton's."

I feel my spine curving, like I'm shrinking under his gaze.

He nods slowly, as though the understanding is sinking in. "I see. Did you think you'd get a chance?"

I can't look at him. I must look as green as Helen, and I think I might be sick right there.

"Bring me my notes as soon as you finish typing them, Miss Grant," he calls after me.

Just before lunch, Mr. Lewin pulls a chair from a nearby desk and sits next to me. I pause in my typing but he makes a gesture as though for me to continue and so I finish the sentence.

"Effie has just left the hairdresser and is going home to dress for lunch," I tell him.

Mr. Lewin has taken up a few finished sheets and is running his finger along the side as he reads.

"I see." He looks up at me. "I can also see why Mr. Sands is in such a hurry to get his hands on these."

I am not sure what to say to this, but I'm saved from having to respond.

"Oh, there you are, June," says Abbie. "Hello, Mr. Lewin. Why so serious, you two?"

"Abbie," I say. "Is it time for lunch?"

Abbie lifts her hand and says, "I came to tell you that, sadly, now that I am engaged, my lunch hour is fully booked. Today, I am to have lunch with my future mother-in-law. And tomorrow, I am to shop for china. Mother has my days so full of wedding planning, I hardly have time to come to work."

Mr. Lewin stands and puts the chair back against the desk in front of mine.

"Congratulations, Miss Howard," he says. "On your engagement."

"Thank you, Mr. Lewin. You do know that June's a writer, don't you? A poet. Her talents are wasted in steno."

"Oh, Abbie," I say.

"Don't 'oh, Abbie' me. I'll shout it from the rooftops before I leave."

Mr. Lewin holds up the pages in his hand. "I was starting to get an inkling about that."

"Well, I hope you will put her to proper use. Now, before I rush off, did I mention that Friday is my last day?"

"You did," I say. "Will there be a shower?" I try to sound hopeful, as though a shower is the most exciting thing I can think of, but it's going to be sad here without Abbie.

Abbie explains to Mr. Lewin that she will have showers galore over the next year, and what she really wants is a night on the town. Starting with drinks and dinner at the Windsor.

"My father is treating us all, so of course everyone is invited."

"Generous of him," Mr. Lewin says.

"He's just relieved I won't be out in the world anymore, causing trouble. Isn't that right, June?"

I smile at her barely restrained energy. She's wearing a simple pink dress with a wide skirt and a frilled collar. Classic. The perfect dress for lunch with her future mother-in-law. "Somehow I doubt that even marriage will change your ways," I say.

"Of course you're right. That's the other thing to remember about Miss Grant. She's almost always right. Now, Mr. Lewin, promise me you will come to my party."

"How could I refuse such a generous invitation?" he says, touching his forehead as though tipping his hat. "Miss Grant, I'll hold Mr. Sands off for a few more hours. Will that give you enough time?"

"Thank you, yes," I say.

After he's gone, Abbie says, "And you are coming too, June."

"I'll have to check—"

She interrupts me. "It's all arranged. My mother called yours this morning, and you are to spend the night at my house afterward. So you'll come, won't you?"

"Of course I will," I say. "If it's all arranged." I slide my hand into my pocket and feel the list beneath my fingers. I pull it out.

"I have to go now, of course." She smooths the front of her dress. "Edward's mother is terrifying, I'll have you know. I can't be late."

I see a flash of the Abbie from the other day at lunch, just there, under the surface. Abbie won't be easily tamed. I know she is in a hurry, but I don't know when I'll see her again.

"Just quickly," I say. "Look," I say, smoothing the notepaper with the list I had written down.

"What is it?"

"Remember, you told me to find out what is at that address? 1919 Saint Jacques?"

"Oh, yes, from the delivery boy at the grocery store." She's looking down at the sheet, nodding.

"Yes. This is the list of businesses at that address."

She takes it up and looks more closely. "Well, Superior Models I've heard of. A lot of our models come from there."

"Yes, and Red Lantern Taxi is a new account." I don't mention Daisy. I don't know what to say or where to start, and I don't want Abbie to be late.

"What do you think it means?" Abbie looks up at me, a tiny furrow between her brows.

"I still don't know. But I wonder if we can—"

She interrupts me: "Look at this, Le Salon du Jazz." She smiles. "That's where we'll go. After dinner on Friday. Who knows if I'll ever be allowed to go to a jazz club once I'm married."

"Are you sure? What if it's . . ." I stop. I've never been to a jazz club. I can't imagine what it might be like.

As usual, Abbie knows what I'm thinking. "Everyone goes to jazz clubs, June. It's all the rage." She takes the list, folds it, and puts it into the satin-lined pocket of her wide-cut boiled-wool coat. "Leave it with me," she says. "Don't you worry about a thing."

With everyone gone, I head back to my Eaton's ladies, knowing perfectly well what Effie will do next—have lunch with her future mother-in-law, where she won't worry about a thing, because she knows she's wearing the perfect dress.

———— ✨ ————

I get home that evening to find Mother and Father in the living room. Mother is dressed as though for a night out, in her wool dress with sheer stockings and shoes, hair curled and face carefully made up, her fur coat over it all. Father is in clean pajamas with a fur car blanket over his lap. There is no sign of Daisy, which is both a relief and a worry.

"Keep your coat on, dear," Mother says, gesturing to me to come join them. "It's no warmer in here than outside."

Mother takes a seat on Father's old armchair. She's rolled Father's wheelchair into the room next to her. Between them is a small table, with the heavy black telephone, stretched to the very end of its cord, on its surface. It is the last Tuesday of the month. The night that Missie will call.

Mother goes to the sideboard and pours me a tiny glass of sherry. I take it and sit across from them on the sofa and wait. It is as though we are at the theater, waiting for the play to start.

"How is Father today?" I ask.

Mother looks at her watch and waves at me to shush. I sip my sherry and take in the scene. Father's mouth is open on one side, his eyes as clear and intelligent as ever. I smile at him, though he does not smile back, and I wonder if he sees me at all.

The room is warm with lamplight. The furniture is crowded and heavy, with its tapestry-upholstered armchairs and oriental-style velvet sofa. Mother has set lamps in every corner and hung landscapes and hunting paintings over every inch of wall space, and the overall effect, once you are seated and no longer worried about bumping your knees, is of a room where a man of substance might relax after a long day.

Even with my coat on, I am colder than I was on the streetcar. I reach for one of the folded blankets left after the boys' last stay. "Should we call about more heating oil?" I ask, but just then the phone rings.

"Hello? Missie? Hello?" Mother yells into the receiver. She crouches down next to Father, turning the receiver between them. "You'll have to speak up so Father can hear you."

I cannot make out her words, but I would recognize Missie's cadence anywhere. She's full of news, and Mother smiles and laughs and does not interrupt. Even Father's lips have relaxed into something of a smile. I turn my head slightly, hoping to hear what she is saying, and focus on the top of the sideboard. Mother has set up a tray with the decanter of sherry and set out enough glasses for a party of eight. The tray is surrounded by family photos in cheap wooden frames—we sold the silver ones when Father had his stroke, after we sold the car and before we sold Mother's engagement ring.

Mother is talking now, yelling into the phone. Telling Missie about Father's cold, and that Daisy has been helping Geoff with his new agency and that the boys are healthy and handsome and she does not mind looking after them one bit. I listen for Missie's reply, but keep looking at the photos.

Mother says, "June is here," and she stretches the receiver out to me. I stand in the middle of the room in a half crouch.

"Missie?" I ask.

"Of course, who else would it be? How are you, June?"

"Yes, I'm fine, work is fine."

"I heard about your date. Sounds like a bit of a fail."

I laugh. "Yes, but I've been working at Mr. McAulay's desk, as a secretary. I've been helping with some of the campaigns. Writing copy," I tell her. "It's like writing poems, only brighter, and faster." I know I am talking too fast, and probably not making any sense.

Missie interrupts. "Yes, but did Mother tell you about Mr. Hearn?"

"Who?" I ask.

"Mr. Hearn," she says. "He works with Robert. He's coming to Montreal for a conference, and he promised me he'd take you out."

"Oh, yes," I say, my voice faltering. "Yes, Mother mentioned it."

"Well, promise you'll sound more excited when he phones you. And don't bore him with stories of writing advertising poems. Let him talk a little."

"Of course, I will," I say. "But how are you, Missie?"

"I just told Mother all that. She can tell you. Listen, I have to go, these calls cost a fortune. My love to Daisy," she says, and hangs up.

I hand the receiver back to Mother and I realize I'm breathless with the shouting and the anticipation. Mother looks like she's had enough excitement for one night too.

"Should we go into the kitchen where it's warmer?" I ask. "I'll take Father."

Once we are settled in the kitchen, Mother sets my soup in front of me. I take in her tilted head and her perfectly applied lipstick. "Why are you writing copy, June?" She hands me a napkin and takes a seat across from me.

"Because Mr. McAulay asked me to." Pride swells in my chest.

"Mr. McAulay? He asked you? Are you sure?"

The pride is swept away by a hot surge of shame. Mother leans forward. Takes my hand. "Tell me what happened, June."

And so I tell her. Not about Daisy modeling, but about the Eaton's fashion show, about the ideas that came, unbidden, ideas that Mr. Lewin called "brilliant."

"That's hardly asking you to do it, is it, June?"

"But no one else was taking notes. He asked me to write notes and type them up. That's exactly what I did."

Mother takes my other hand now, her face serious. "This won't do. Not at all. June, can you even see what a risk this is? What does Miss Pomeroy think?"

I look down at Mother's thin fingers, the plainest gold wedding band in the place where a diamond engagement ring used to sit. "She doesn't like it."

"Of course she doesn't. June, you must go to her, tomorrow. Apologize. And go back to your contracts. Promise me?"

"Why? If I can earn more as a writer than as a stenographer, why should I?" I think of Daisy up on that stage, wearing those stylish dresses and shiny new shoes. Mr. McAulay's adoring stare. Being shuttled by taxi in the evening to God knows where. All that money crumpled up in her purse. I am sick with not only envy, but anger. Daisy can do anything she wants. Anything at all.

Mother shakes her head. "It's too risky for a girl, June. Remember before Geoff had his own agency? Ad writers, even the best ones, even the men, get fired for the slightest thing. Offending the wrong person, a dull campaign, the whim of clients. And then what? It's one thing for a man, but for you? A girl? Who's going to hire an overly ambitious stenographer?"

I feel my throat closing over my mouthful of soup. It all seems so silly now. The idea of naming the girls. Of telling the stories. Mother is right, of course. Did anyone ask me to do that? Take notes and type them up, is all Mr. McAulay said.

"We are all counting on you, June."

As if to emphasize her point, Father coughs, low and wet and deep in his chest. Mother stands to go to him. "Promise me, June."

Still, I don't answer. I can't look at her. Lying to a parent breaks two commandments. I bring my bowl of now-cold soup up to my lips and slurp the last of it without my spoon.

A moment later Mother is back, clearing the dishes. She stands at the sink, her hands on the bowls, and leans against the counter, head dropped down, eyes closed, as though the weight on her shoulders has at last become more than she can bear.

I stand, move to her, take her small shoulders in my giant hands. "I will, Mother. I promise."

Mother doesn't answer, her body a steel rod under my fingers. "Come, Mother. I'll do the dishes. I'll stay up and listen for Father. You go to sleep now. I'll look after everything."

Her shoulders shudder. "Thank you, dear June," she says at last.

She leaves the kitchen without another word, gliding on silent feet, spine so straight that if she'd had a dictionary balanced on her head it would not have fallen off. The dogs rouse themselves from their slumber by the warm stove and follow her, single file and silent; her loyal subjects.

# Chapter Thirteen

Miss Pomeroy meets me at the elevator in the morning, her eyebrows pinched.

"Miss Grant, you are to go to Mr. McAulay's desk for the rest of the week."

I follow her, like one of the nuns is leading me to Mother Superior's office. She's wearing her brown wool skirt and blazer set today, which the girls in steno have declared the least attractive against her pale and pocked skin. Miss Pomeroy has three identical suits; one navy, one charcoal gray, and this medium-brown one she is wearing. She also has five identical white blouses, one for each day of the week. I find her approach very practical, but the other girls laugh at her lack of fashion sense and say it's no wonder she's not married.

The Dictaphone has already been rolled up to my desk, and Miss Pomeroy points to a cardboard canister on the desk.

"Mr. McAulay has been called away this morning. He outlined ideas for a new campaign and needs you to transcribe them and get them to Mr. Lewin as soon as possible." Her forehead is deeply creased from raising her eyebrows so high. Disapproval wafts from her in waves.

"Of course, Miss Pomeroy. I'll get this done right away," I take off my hat and twirl it in my hands. "Is there anything else?"

She tilts her head as though she thinks I am tricking her. "You'll have to rise to the occasion for this, Miss Grant. Don't let it go to your head. You'll be back in steno next week."

"Where I belong," I say.

Miss Pomeroy tilts her head. "Don't be sharp with me. You're not the first he's picked from the litter, and you won't be the last."

I take a step back at the fierce expression on her face.

"The others? None of them are still here. Rise to the occasion, but no further." She steps toward me, her voice a low growl. "I am looking after you."

I drop my gaze to my shoes. "Yes, Miss Pomeroy."

She watches as I hang up my hat and coat; I have to step around her to sit at the desk. Only once I've placed the cylinder in the machine and adjusted the headset over my ears does she finally leave.

---

"Red Lantern Taxi." Mr. McAulay's voice is so loud I almost look behind me to see if he's come in. I start transcribing.

For the first minute Mr. McAulay's voice is strong and confident as he summarizes the new account. Then he stumbles and repeats a word, and I realize he is simply reading aloud the notes I took during the first Red Lantern Taxi meeting.

After that his voice becomes muffled. He mutters and there's the sound of slurping. I can make out the words *important man* and *rides a taxi*—which he repeats several times. There's the sound of a match and a pause as he inhales, so close to my ear that I expect to smell a freshly lit cigarette.

"But if a man is truly important, he'll have his own chauffeur, won't he? Taxi be damned." I pause. There's no sense typing that. Next there's a long string of words slurred together and then a long moment of static until Mr. McAulay's voice comes back loud and clear.

"Book lunch for four at the Mount Royal. Charge to Red Lantern. Tell Lewin to meet me there." The recording ends.

I listen again from the start.

In vain, I go into Mr. McAulay's office and search his desk for another canister, or perhaps some scribbled notes I can work from. The desk is perfectly clear, no bottle of scotch or glasses or filled ashtray on the desk, which the sounds on the recording would indicate. I wonder whether Miss Pomeroy has cleaned them up already.

I look at my watch. In two hours Mr. McAulay and Mr. Lewin will go to a client lunch with no ideas.

I go back to my own desk and sit down. I pick up the phone and call over to the Mount Royal. I book the lunch and fill out the requisition to accounting to have it charged to the Red Lantern account.

Then I sit with perfect posture, fingers in formation over the typewriter, and think.

Should I call a writer? Is that what I'm expected to do? I'd rather eat my own shoe than call Sands. Besides, everyone is busy on the Gillette campaign, and the Eaton's campaign is already short of writers. I imagine myself going door to door of the writers' offices, knocking, asking for help. "It's an emergency," I could tell them. But is it?

I remember Miss Pomeroy and her disdain—*You'll have to rise to the occasion. Don't let it go to your head*—and I understand now what she meant.

I think back to the Red Lantern meeting. The one man, Bruno, who was keen to advertise. The other man, J-P, who didn't think taxis needed to advertise at all. *Find something that makes Red Lantern stand out. And then make your customers want that thing.* That's what Mr. McAulay had said.

I remember Daisy's taxis over the last week. Daisy, who has been secretly modeling. Troubled Daisy. Eternal damnation was the least of her worries.

Was there some kind of connection? Did Daisy take Red Lantern taxis to her modeling agency, since both offices were in the same building? But why would she be going to her modeling agency at night?

All these thoughts flow through my head as I listen to Mr. McAulay ramble once more, my fingers ready to type. I think back to the Eaton's fashion show, Mr. McAulay and Sands in thrall of the pretty girls, of Daisy, while Mr. Lewin and I worked away diligently.

Should I ask Mr. Lewin for help? He would not make fun of me, but surely he has his hands full saving the Eaton's account? It would not be fair to burden him. Besides, he's an artist, not a writer.

I start typing. "Red Lantern Taxi Campaign," I write across the top, under the McAulay letterhead.

I write the date.

Then I start listing, in point form, my recollections from Friday's meeting, mixed with Mr. McAulay's slurred words about chauffeurs. "Your personal chauffeur."

It seemed like a failing, though—certainly it sounded to me that men like Mr. McAulay saw it as a failing—to not have a personal chauffeur. But what about another kind of man? What about Mr. Ritchie? He eschews taxis as a student, but once he is established as a lawyer in a firm with his name on the door, won't he see it as a badge of honor? I make a face. Likely not. I imagine Mr. Ritchie would be perfectly happy coming home by streetcar if it saved him a dime.

The only other man I know is Geoff. I put myself in his shoes. Arrive at the station and you still need to make the long, uphill trudge toward home. The prospect of a bus would be disheartening after such a long day. Both of those options might defeat a man, who, at this moment, wants to feel his most victorious. After all, he's conquered the world of business and now is going home to a warm meal, clean-haired children tucked up in bed, his wife in a pretty dress and with freshened lipstick, ready to mix his favorite drink. In my mind, Geoff grows into all men, every man, any man.

I start typing the man's dilemma on the page. And then my own words come back to me. The ones that had popped into my head during the meeting, but which I had not written down.

Red Lantern Taxi, the only one with a red light on the roof. Like a siren, to get you home in a hurry, like a visiting dignitary or a conquering hero.

I stop typing. I've filled the page.

I pull it out of the typewriter and lay it inside a clean folder. I type a label for the folder—"Red Lantern Taxi Campaign Ideas"—and affix it to the side. Then I lay it on the side of my desk, with an hour to spare for the lunch meeting.

With the notes ready to go, it seems there is nothing more to do at Mr. McAulay's desk. It is Wednesday now, and I have not seen him since the fashion show on Monday. I roll a clean sheet of letterhead into the typewriter and I slide on the headset. Then I open *Scientific Advertising* on my lap. The author says that being a fine writer is of no help to an advertiser, that having a unique literary style is in fact a disadvantage. An advertiser must write like a salesman, expressing himself briefly, clearly, and convincingly.

"Typing many letters this morning, Miss Grant?"

I slam the book closed and press it between my knees under the desk. "I'm sorry, Miss Pomeroy . . ." I slide the headset off and look up to see Mr. Lewin.

"Sorry, Mr. Lewin, I just . . ."

He waves a hand. "Let me see what you are reading."

I blush, look down, and pull the book out. "Ah," he says. "Mr. Hopkins does have an interesting perspective. And he makes a good point about headlines, don't you think?"

I cast a sideways glance through my peripheral vision.

"Don't worry, Miss Grant, your secret is safe with me. McAulay asked me to pick up his Red Lantern Taxi notes before the lunch."

He drums his fingers against his leg. He's always moving, fingers waggling, spine bending, long limbs angled into the space around him. "Ah," he says, as his fingers spider to the one file on my desk. He flips it open and reads. Nods, dips his head to one side, and finally laughs out loud. "Did McAulay write these?"

I stare straight forward. I can feel my saliva glands pinch as though I'm sucking on a sour candy. I would like a glass of water, but of course we girls cannot keep water at our desks, we might knock it over.

"John McAulay fancies himself a creative director, but really, the true creative genius behind the agency was his brother, Duncan. Did you know that?"

I shake my head. Mr. Lewin pulls up a chair and sits across the desk from me.

"Duncan was the dreamer of the family," he starts. "John was the practical brother—did what needed to be done. Studied business and accounting. Duncan studied poetry and art. He fell into advertising as the only application for his talents—much like it is for mine. Art feeds the soul, advertising pays the rent."

He leans back as though he's settling in to tell me a long story, his voice quiet, mesmerizing. Now that he's seated at my level, I can take in his face a little bit more. He's quietly handsome, not handsome all at once like Geoff.

"Duncan had the vision. John was the moneyman."

His voice is warm and his face kind. And he's married, I remind myself, looking down at his fingers, which have floated up in the air expressively as he continues his story.

"It was a tragedy when Duncan died. Just one of those things that happens, you know, a silly mistake that anyone could make. He got on the wrong train. He was headed to Toronto, but he got on the train to Ottawa. At some little town along the river, the first stop, he jumped off and ran across the tracks so he could get on the train to Toronto that was to arrive just a minute later.

"But then it just so happened, at that moment, the train he was so eager to catch was coming into the station. There was no time for the driver to stop."

I look up at him, my eyes wide, not worried about staring now. "He . . . ," I start.

"Yes. He died."

We sit in silence as I let the tragedy of it sink in.

"When did this happen?" I ask finally.

"Oh, thirty years ago, or more. They say that John McAulay has never been the same since. He was thrust into running the whole business, including the creative side. And he's proud. He won't simply hand it over."

Mr. Lewin taps the file folder in his hand to the edge of the desk. "And here you see the result. He keeps it all afloat by aligning himself with creative people, people who are willing to work in the background and not take the credit." He looks at me as he says this.

I take in a shaky breath and look away. I remember the stumbling sounds and the clink of glasses, Mr. McAulay's slurred voice on the Dictaphone. I think of Geoff's warning over Sunday lunch—*That man is a leech who will suck you dry.* And of Miss Pomeroy's words—*You're not the first he's picked from the litter*—and it all makes sense.

"But you just started here. How do you know all this?"

Mr. Lewin nods and smiles, a sad smile. "The advertising community in Montreal is very small," he says. "And we gossip more than your mother's hairdresser." He sighs as he shrugs his shoulders up, then down.

"I knew what I was getting into, Miss Grant," he says. "I want to paint. Landscapes, that is, not women's dresses. I don't need to be known for my advertising work. And there are certain advantages to that, but there are risks as well. You have to know what you're signing up for. And what you are willing to do."

He stands and puts the chair back in its place. "Now, I'd best get going to the luncheon, to present Mr. McAulay's campaign ideas," he says with a tilt of his eyebrows that makes me laugh.

I stop laughing as he walks away, and think about his words. Am I willing to write copy and let Mr. McAulay take all the credit? As I pack away the Dictaphone, I nod to myself. It doesn't seem too much to put up with, if it means I get to write.

———— ✦✦✦ ————

"Of all people, I didn't think it would be you I had to worry about."

Without turning to look at her, I can hear the threat in Daisy's voice. I stop typing my poem and turn to see her standing in my bedroom doorway. She's dressed to go out in a silky dress in one of the new fabrics, colorful and too light for the weather. The easy smile is nothing more than a mask; the glint in her eyes is there, if you know what to look for.

"Is that one of your dresses from the fashion show?" I ask. My words invite what's coming. I have been waiting for it, each minute since I saw her on that stage.

She takes in the room and dismisses it with one sweep of her eyes. It's true that I've given no thought to decor in my bedroom, other than to add these two boards across the dormer windowsill to make the tiny desk where I am sitting. For me, it's simply a place to sleep and change my clothes.

Daisy steps toward me, her red lips twisted into a smile. Before I know what's happening, she's at my chair, her fingers on my earlobe, twisting hard.

"Daisy! Let go!"

She lets go of my ear, then wrenches my arm back with one hand and yanks my hair with the other. "Promise first."

"Promise what?"

In response, Daisy pushes my face deep into the typewriter keys. "Say it."

"Say what?"

"You know what."

"I don't know, Daisy. All I know is I saw you in a fashion show."

She presses harder. My cheek against the keys, I take a breath and say the words she made me say as a child. "I promise I won't tell."

"Won't tell what?"

I try to push against her but she slams me harder into the typewriter. When she relaxes the pressure, I lift my head and yell, "I promise I won't tell Geoff you're going to be on the cover of the Eaton's catalog."

"Don't tell him I'm modeling at all."

"Fine," I say. "But I don't know how you expect to keep it a secret once your face is in every mailbox in the city."

"Is Auntie June choking, Mother?" I can hear Chris from my doorway.

"That's right, Chris. June was choking. Weren't you, June? I was helping her."

I press my hands into the boards to push myself up.

"What I came to tell you," Daisy says, back in the doorway, her hands on her son's shoulders, "is that Mother will need help with the boys tonight."

I rub my sore cheek and look at her face for confirmation. Her expression is relaxed once more, enigmatic and sultry with a strong hint of the angelic. No one would believe if I told them Daisy had caused the marks on my cheeks.

"Are you really asking for my help? After what you just did?"

"No, I'm not asking. I'm telling you that Mother needs your help. Isn't that what you are? The good one that helps Mother?"

I don't answer her.

"And Saturday night. I need your help then too. Don't I, Christopher?" She smooths his cowlick over his forehead. He nods, so solemn that I know he does not dare contradict her. "We're having a dinner party, and I need you to come look after the boys. You'll spend the night."

I want to argue with her, but it would be cruel to tell her to look after her own boys with Christopher there, watching us.

Daisy pulls out a compact and checks her reflection. There's a creak and squeak of brakes outside. "There's my taxi."

She kisses her son on the top of his head, and he looks up at her uncertainly. I don't blame him. There's a knife edge to her right now. She tugs at the waist of her dress and brushes away some invisible lint. She runs her fingers along the thin curve of her hips and, satisfied, nods. "Don't wait up," she says.

Left behind, Chris comes to me and takes my hand. "Did you touch her things?" he asks. "She doesn't like it when we touch her things."

I shake my head and take his other hand in mine. If only I knew why Daisy does what she does, perhaps I would tell him. Instead, I say, "Let's not mention anything to your grandmother. It will only upset her."

"I promise I won't tell, Auntie." Chris is seven. He already knows the rules.

# Chapter Fourteen

On Friday morning there's an audible buzz in the air of the steno department, in anticipation of Abbie's going-away dinner at the Windsor Hotel. It seems the entire office is planning to attend. The other girls have their best hats displayed on their desks like so many peacocks. The coatracks hang with party dresses cloaked in garment covers, waiting to be revealed.

The coffee I swallowed down this morning sits like hot lava in my stomach, and I don't think the sweet bun I bought from the cart in the lobby is going to sit well on top of that. I'm navigating a very narrow track and there is no room for error. Between Daisy, Mr. Sands, Mr. McAulay, and Miss Pomeroy, I've spent days waiting for something to happen—for the other shoe to drop.

Will Geoff find out that Daisy is modeling and blame me for not telling him? To him, modeling is an indulgence for single girls, not for wives of respectable men. Certainly not for his own wife. He's the provider, not her. It won't do to make him angry. What if he got fed up with looking after all of us, as well as his own family? Then where would we be? Cold and in the dark, that's where.

Then there's Miss Pomeroy. She won't be pleased if she finds out I'm writing copy, and Mother has made me promise to go back to steno. Of all the voices, shouldn't I listen to hers? And yet Mr. McAulay keeps giving me more copywriting work. Do I say no to him?

I settle in to my work and slide the earpiece over my head. When the voice starts up, it's someone from the accounts department summarizing McAulay Advertising's major clients and the firm's profitability since the end of the war. The names roll into my ears and out onto the page through my fingers: Eaton's, Gillette, CP Rail, Elizabeth Arden, J. Pascal Hardware. McAulay Advertising, according to the voice in my ear, is doing well indeed.

At lunch I head to steno to look for Abbie, only to find the door blocked by Marie-Céleste, Helen, and a new girl that I haven't met yet.

"Your savior's not here. Called in on her last day," Marie-Céleste tells me.

I retreat to the supply room with my sweet bun and my notebook. Someone has placed a desk in front of the window and I sit on top of it and look out into the gray blank of the day, trying to find the song of the city this view usually evokes in me. But Dominion Square looks empty and cold, the leafless trees stark black against the snow.

I can hear the after-lunch buzz in the hall even from my quiet nest here in the supply room. A buzz that will only get louder as the afternoon wears on; as the girls parade to the ladies' room to change their dresses and freshen their lipstick. As the excitement all around me notches up, I feel the dread sink deeper into my belly. I can't shake the feeling that after today, everything will be different. And not just because Abbie won't work here anymore.

--- ◦◦◦◦ ---

Mother told me this morning that Father used to love to come to the Windsor for dinner. That they'd come on their wedding anniversary each year, and sometimes he would bring important clients here. That when he'd travel north and west to buy furs, he'd dream of the civilization waiting for him back in the city—the warmth of home, his big office with its carved mahogany desk and view of the cobblestone streets leading down to the port, and a fine dinner of creme andalouse soup and roast ribs au jus at the Windsor.

Mother is sure I've eaten here plenty of times, but I do not remember any of them. I think she is mixing me up with Daisy and Missie. I want to savor every moment so I can tell Father about it. I wish I could save some of my soup to bring home for him, but of course that is not practical. Instead I eat slowly and watch the party bubble up around me.

Our party takes up two long tables, and all around me is a blur of laughter and movement as people change from seat to seat, to tell a story or share a joke or move to the center of the excitement. There's champagne and fancy cocktails and cigarettes handed out even as the food is being served, and I wonder if the waiters have ever seen a party like ours. I smile over my shoulder as the waiter places my plate of minced chicken and peppers à la king in front of me. His face is impassive and this calms me somehow, to know that we have not shocked him.

I enjoy every bite, including the Florida salad and pistachio ice cream, as Marie-Céleste takes to the dance floor with one of the account managers. Sands starts a game of balloon volley across the table with the boys from the mail room. Lewin raises a toast to Abbie, and Abbie flits around the tables, arranging her guests into tableaux and taking pictures of them with her new camera, an engagement gift from her fiancé, whose diplomatic work has already called him back to Europe.

And then, as I finish my second cup of coffee, it's all over. We roll out the door in a wave to the row of waiting Red Lantern taxis. I end up in a taxi with Helen on my lap and the boys from the mail room jostling in next to us. Mr. Lewin gets into the front seat.

"Hello again, Miss," the driver says, looking at me in the rearview mirror. It's the same driver as before, the man from Florence. Surprisingly handsome, until he smiles.

"1919 Saint Jacques," Mr. Lewin says, and the driver pulls up close to the red light, waiting to turn onto Dorchester.

Helen leans forward and asks to be dropped off on the way. "Saint Ambroise Street, I'll show you where." The light changes and the taxi sweeps along Dorchester and then, with a smooth right turn, drops down below the tracks. Just like that, we are in Point Saint Charles. Like there is no barrier at all.

The taxi creaks as we turn onto the cobblestones of Helen's street, so narrow we have to pull to the side to let another car pass. "A little farther," Helen says.

It's like the city has swallowed us. The row houses crouch closer as we reach the next corner.

"Here. You can drop me off here."

As we stop, a figure peels from the building and steps toward the taxi.

"Helen, are you sure?" I ask. I have to climb out of the car so she can get out.

The man, all dark clothes and stubble, dressed to go out in a wool coat and cap, steps toward me, crowding me to the edge of the sidewalk. "Hélène," he says, reaching out to her. "Donne-le."

"Non," she says. "Laisses-moi."

Mr. Lewin steps out of the taxi, stooped as a reed in the wind but taller than the man by a foot. "You heard her. Leave her be." The mail room boys spill out of the taxi onto the street, ready for a fight.

The man scowls and pulls his hand back, then turns and lumbers off in the direction of Notre Dame Street. Mr. Lewin and I walk Helen to the door, one on each side. I want to ask if that was her husband, but she lets herself in the unlocked bottom door into a dark, narrow staircase without saying anything.

"Do you want us to walk you up?" Mr. Lewin asks.

Helen shakes her head and closes the door without so much as a good night. By now the mail room boys have made a new plan and wander off in search of a tavern one of them knows. When we get back in the taxi, it's just Mr. Lewin, the driver with the rotting teeth, and me.

"Now we go to Saint Jacques," Mr. Lewin says.

"Le Salon du Jazz," says the driver as the taxi bounces along the cobblestones again.

The building I've wondered so much about is an old Victorian painted house. There's a line of Red Lantern taxis in front, and the club is on the first floor. Mr. Lewin scrawls his signature on a taxi chit and hands it to the driver. "On the McAulay account," he says.

Then Lewin turns to me. "You should have some of these," he says, giving me a handful of blank taxi chits. "Everyone on the Red Lantern account has them. Take a taxi everywhere you go. It's part of the job."

I take the squares of white paper from him as the driver steps out to open my door. When I get out, he hands me a business card, with the Red Lantern phone number and his name handwritten in pen. "Ask for me, Tomasso," he says. "Anytime."

———— ⚬⌇⚬ ————

Inside I can't see Abbie for the smoke and the crowd. There's a wooden staircase that curves upward, just inside the main door. I look up to see where it leads but can't make out anything in the dark. Mr. Lewin takes my elbow and jostles us through the smoke to what would have been the main living area of the old house.

A pair of fox eyes glint up at me from a lady's fur stole; a cigarette in a long ebony holder almost sets my coat ablaze as I brush past. We land at a small table where there are not enough chairs. Marie-Céleste is sitting on Sands's lap, his arms around her waist. Abbie makes space for me to share a chair with her. Lewin rustles up some more chairs, signals to the waiter, and gestures for me to sit down, which is a relief. The smell, the noise, the warmth, the music—all of it has me in a state of high alert.

"Isn't he enthralling?" Abbie whispers in my ear. "I want to take his picture."

I turn my attention to the stage at last. It's no more than a few feet higher than the floor, and with the low ceiling, the bass player has to dip his head down. There are five musicians, all men, all Black, playing to an all-white audience.

"This guy is good." Lewin wags his cigarette at the piano player. He's pointing to François from Epicerie Lublin.

I take a deep breath and let it out, trying to get rid of the tension that has taken hold of my whole body. François is here. Is this what he wanted? For me to come see him play? Surely he was not suggesting that Mother come here?

There's a pause in the cacophony and then François starts to play. Sands bites his front lip as he bobs his head. Lewin is tapping on the table along with the swing of the beat, like it's coming right through him. It's hard to fathom that the fingers flying with such precision over the keys are the same ones that wrap up Mother's cheese, and that wrote the note on the orange wrapper.

I have not really listened to jazz before. Is it music? It is nothing like the hymns at Mass. Or the cheerful songs we learned at school, or even the love songs on the radio. It feels like a bird has got trapped inside my rib cage and is fighting to get out.

I stand up. Abbie looks at me in surprise. "Powder room?" I mouth.

She gestures to the back of the room, a small door under the stairs, but doesn't offer to come with me.

The powder room, when I make it there through the smoke and the crowd, is made up of a rust-stained sink and toilet. I do my business as quickly as possible, and exit with wet hands—there is no soap, no towel.

Instead of braving the press of bodies to head back to the table, I decide to look around, to see if I can find what François wanted me to see. To my left is another room, closed off by a red velvet curtain. I duck my head behind to see a large kitchen, jumbled with open instrument cases and music stands. Jackets hang on the backs of chairs, and the kitchen table is strewn with sheet music, but there is no one in sight.

I enter, past the counters covered with dirty glasses and empty wine bottles. I pull out a chair, gritty with coal dust, and sit. I'll have to brush my skirt later, but it is such a relief to be away from the frenetic music that I don't mind.

I shut my eyes and immediately hear Daisy's voice. *What did you think, that you would actually enjoy a party?*

Her taunts inside my own head remind me that it's because of Daisy that we are all here. What is this place? Why did François need to tell Mother about it? I will wait here until the music is over to ask François himself when he comes back for his coat. I lean my head back against the window frame behind me and close my eyes, just for a moment.

———— ❧⁓❧ ————

"Shhhh! She's sleeping," a girl whispers.

I open my eyes, and in the moment it takes me to find my bearings, the girl disappears up a set of stairs at the back of the kitchen, a man in a business suit trailing in her wake.

I give them a moment and then follow them. The stair treads are narrow and angle sharply as they curve upward. I walk on my tiptoes and try not to clunk my feet. I duck my head as the steps climb to the second floor. I exit through an open door and find myself in the middle of a hallway, with doors on both sides. Walking close to the wall so I don't creak, I head toward the sounds—more giggling and then new sounds, bumps, whispers, a slamming door.

The only light is from a streetlamp outside, but it barely penetrates this far back. I can see a plaque hanging on the wall next to each door, a black rectangle with engraved lettering: *Fairleigh Railway Agent, Montreal Railway Supply*. After that it is too dark to read the signs.

The sounds are coming from farther down the hall. I know what those noises are. I have two married sisters, after all. Yet somehow, I wasn't expecting it to be like this. Snuffling and grunting like animals.

There's a steady rhythm too, even over the dissonant echoes of piano and saxophone from downstairs. I reach the closed door just as they reach a crescendo—cawing like the crow outside my window and snuffling like the pig we saw the day we went to visit the Villa Maria convent farm. Then suddenly, silence.

Does the girl need help? Should I knock? I'm just lifting my hand when the door opens. The girl stands there, applying lipstick without the benefit of a mirror.

"Oh, it's you."

"Who?" The man, buckling his belt, strides to the door. Lazy. Unhurried.

"The girl from the kitchen."

"We're all set here, honey. We don't need anything from the kitchen," he says. "And where do you think you're going?" He grabs the girl by the waist of her blue silk dress and pulls her back inside. "I've still got fifteen minutes left."

By the asymmetrical closing triangle of light as he slams the door, I read the sign on the wall outside. *Superior Model Management Inc.*

I make it halfway down the main, curved staircase before sinking down onto one of the steps. I hug my knees and drop my head down, taking deep breaths, the roaring in my ears drowning out the music from below.

# Part 2

"In our family we never discussed reality. Unpleasant things were politely ignored, like a faux pas at a dinner party. But something inside of me was howling: 'I never want an engagement ring, or a husband, or a family. Never.'"

—June Grant on CBC's *The Sunday Edition*,
October 2001

*I do remember Daisy's debutante ball.*

*I remember the elegant dining room in the Côte Saint Antoine house filled with white lace and tulle and satin and moiré silk, all laid out for Daisy by the dressmaker hired to make the dress of her dreams. I remember Daisy stretched across two dining chairs in her silk slip, pulling faces at each option the increasingly frantic dressmaker presented to her.*

*In the end she designed her own dress. Sketched it on a piece of Mother's stationery, drawing out each detail, the pleated cowl of silk across her collar bones, the paisley pattern in chiffon velvet on the sleeves, the skirt fitted to her knees and then falling into sharp, angled pleats that barely allowed her to walk.*

*I remember coming home from school and seeing her there, in the dress she designed. The image is clear in my mind to this day. Daisy in the grand dining room under the gilded framed portrait of one of Mother's stern ancestors. Her skin pale as soapstone against the ivory silk and velvet, she stood in an angle of sun coming in the leaded-glass windowpanes; a tiny, perfect angel.*

*She was breathtaking.*

*I remember something else, too. There is something there. Something threatening but undefined. A hush and rustling in the corridors. Daisy in tears. Father in his study, the door closed, yelling. A man rushing out.*

*I was only ten years old.*

*Now, my eyes land on a portrait of Daisy, taken before her debutante ball. A portrait in a plain wooden frame.*

*She's wearing a satin dress with a lace collar that slouches around her graceful neck and flounces at her hips. It looks nothing like the dress I remember her wearing in the Côte Saint Antoine house.*

*What happened to Daisy's dress?*

# Chapter Fifteen

When I open my eyes, everything is wrong. I'm in a sunny and bright bedroom, sunk deep into a soft mattress, and covered with a white eyelet comforter. The air smells of bacon and toast, and sun streams through the frilled curtains. When I put my feet on the ground, they sink into a cream-colored carpet that's softer than a cat's fur.

Abbie's house.

I remember now. Mr. Lewin took charge when they found me, seated on the curved staircase, so shocked and speechless that I wasn't even aware the music had stopped. They each took an arm, Abbie and Mr. Lewin, and led me out of the thinned crowd to a waiting taxi. Too late, I remembered I wanted to talk to François, but they steered me into the back seat and would not hear of it.

"Where to?" Lewin asked, and Abbie gave her address. I must have fallen asleep in the cab, and I have a pang thinking of who might have carried me up the stairs—the butler? Abbie's family does have one. I'm not sure what would be worse, the butler or her father.

I gasp out loud. No, worst of all would be Mr. Lewin.

"Ah, you're up. Here, I brought you a housecoat." Abbie is pretty as a picture in a lemon-yellow house frock, all frills and flounces just like the curtains.

I look down at my thin and mended slip and cover it with the pale-blue version of what she's wearing. Of course it is too short, and my frayed hem sways below.

I look at her and my eyes brim with tears.

"Now, don't worry about a thing. I called your mother and I told her we needed you today, to help with some wedding plans. It's a lie, of course, since we have a whole year, but we can have breakfast and giggle for a while. I'll curl your hair the way you like and you can try on my sweaters."

"But—"

"No buts. Go wash. I've left you a skirt that won't be too short, and a blouse, in the closet. Then come downstairs before Mother tells Christine to put the breakfast away."

Mr. Howard doesn't look up from his paper, but Mrs. Howard sits at the head of the dining table as we serve ourselves from the sideboard. A full English-style breakfast: bacon, piles of toast, fluffy eggs, and sliced fruit.

"I've made a pig of myself, I'm afraid," I say as I sit down.

Mrs. Howard only gives me a raised eyebrow in response and looks at my plate.

"That's all right, isn't it, Mother? Good that it won't go to waste."

"I assure you that nothing in this house goes to waste." Mrs. Howard is birdlike with faded hair and a permanent slight frown.

"How is your father?" she asks now. The Howards know my parents in the way that everyone English in Westmount knows one another. Through business circles, from the shops, from the neighborhood. Not from church, of course, since the Howards are Protestant, but in the forever calculation of who matters, being English and living in Westmount make up for our being Catholic. At least they used to.

"He has a cold," I say.

"You'll be needing to get back home then, won't you?"

I nibble a piece of bacon. It's crisp and dripping fat at the same time.

"Nonsense, Mother. June and I have things to do today. Don't you think June deserves a day off?"

"Well, I certainly think Blanche deserves a day off."

"If you're so concerned, why don't you send Christine down there for a few hours? It's not like this house needs to be polished all over again today."

"Watch your tone, young lady." This from Mr. Howard, with a rustle of newspaper. My mother's maid was the last staff member to go after Father's stroke. She ended up with the Howards soon after, though she's been known to come sit with Mother on her day off and has come on laundry day more than once.

I drop my head down so that all I can see is my plate. I want to devour it all, but restrain myself to a few dainty bites. As much as I'd like to tell Mrs. Howard that I will go home immediately to help Mother, a day off sounds like heaven. Especially since I need to babysit for Daisy tonight. I take a bite of the eggs and they remind me of my childhood—so rich they must have been scrambled with cream—and look around to see if I can catch sight of Christine. But all I see are the gleaming table and chairs with ample space around them. The bright sun pours through the window, illuminating the polished dark paneling of the dining room. The French doors to the living room are closed, their glass as clear as the crisp winter air. Christine is well out of view.

Abbie stares at her mother. Mrs. Howard stares back with a look that would have me running to the kitchen to wash the dishes, but Abbie does not look away.

"We'd like John to drive us downtown, Father, if that's all right."

Mrs. Howard's eyebrows arch dangerously, but Mr. Howard rustles the paper in what Abbie takes for consent. She runs to his side, kisses his cheek, and heads toward the stairs.

"Come on, June. Let's do your hair."

———— ❧ ————

Once we are in the car, Abbie adjusts her camera carrying case on her lap and hands the driver a slip of paper.

"Mr. Howard said you wanted to go to Eaton's, Miss."

"Oh, Eaton's. Is that the only place a young lady can go?"

"He won't be pleased if I take you to this address. Saint Jacques is below the tracks."

"He'll be even less pleased if you force two young ladies to walk there. Just take us to the Saint Cunigunde church. They can't object to that, surely?"

He doesn't say that it's a Catholic church, which her father definitely would object to. He simply aims the big black car down the steep curves of Forde Crescent like a slalom course.

"What are you up to?" I whisper to Abbie.

"It's not what I'm up to. It's what we're up to. Don't you think it's time we found out what's going on upstairs at 1919 Saint Jacques? Aren't you curious?"

———— ❧ ————

"Saint Cunigunde church is richly decorated in the neobaroque style," Abbie says as we enter the nave, surrounded by stained-glass windows that reach to the sky. As soon as the great doors to the church close behind us, she drops the playacting.

"Here, hold this," Abbie says.

She hands me the molded leather case and holds the camera to her waist to take a picture of the stained glass. It whirs and clicks and then she winds the camera again.

"There," she says. "Done." Then she pulls my arm. "Okay, let's go." It's as though she's responding to some signal that I can't hear. "We only have two hours until he comes back for us, and it's a bit of a walk."

"How far?"

"A few blocks this way," she says, taking my arm. We exit through the side door and down the steps.

The wind kicks up the coal dust from the nearby railway lines. There's the familiar rumble of a passing train, and I pause to look up the hill and see the train snaking along the tracks. The same train that will pass by our house before stopping at Westmount Station.

"We are on the other side of the world," I say. "Or at least our world."

"And we haven't been eaten by goblins yet!" She pulls my arm again and down Saint Jacques we go.

The sun has come out and it's as though winter has looked the other way. There's the sound of rushing water as the bases of the snowbanks melt into the gutters. A store owner, sweeping the stoop, stops to smile at us, and Abbie calls out to him in French. At this time of day, the street is alive with children and workers, not the groups of jazz clubbers we saw last night. Abbie ducks us into a dépanneur, its windows gritted with coal. Inside the offerings are sparse, nothing like Mr. Lublin's grocery with its wheels of cheese and big bags of flour. This one sells Coca-Cola and Molson beer in quart bottles and little else, though I admit I stop looking as soon as Abbie speaks to the man slouched behind the counter.

"Apartement à louer?" She pulls a scrap of the morning paper out of her coat pocket. Apartments for rent from the classifieds section.

"Pour vous deux?"

"Non, just moi."

"Just you? Abbie, what are you doing?"

"Shhh," she says. "Just wait."

The sullen young man is no match for Abbie's Swiss finishing school French and manners. He pulls a key from behind the counter. It's attached to a large metal soup spoon by a chain and he hands it to her.

"En haut," he says, pointing to the ceiling.

She takes it in both hands like a hatbox.

"Upstairs. Come on, June. Let's go see."

———— ⚬✺⚬ ————

There's only one step of a dusty stoop; the door leading to the upstairs apartment opens practically straight off the street. As Abbie pushes the door open, a pile of empty cardboard boxes threatens to topple. The stairs themselves are a de facto warehouse, with cases of beer and canned goods stacked on each step. We have to turn sideways to walk up. The smell is the same mousy cardboard smell from Mr. Lublin's shop—the smell of every dépanneur, I imagine—though here it is mixed, as is everything, with coal dust. Abbie fumbles with the key, trying the second door.

"It's stuck," she says.

I squirm with impatience and uncertainty, sure the slovenly young man from downstairs is going to come, or Abbie's chauffeur, or, for some reason, Monsignor McDonagh. I imagine his displeasure at finding a girl from his parish in this hovel.

"Here, let me try." After all, Abbie is used to having doors opened for her. I know that each one has its technique, and there's no entering until you've learned it.

"You have to lift the handle, then it will turn," I tell her, squeezing against the wall so she can go in first.

Abbie steps inside with a gasp. "The light!"

I join her at the center of the light-filled apartment. It's two rooms, open to each other with an archway between. In one corner there's a hot plate and in another there's a coal fireplace. The floors are wood, and the sun pours in through the two windows. Below, Saint Jacques Street teems with life. There's a tiny door that opens into a windowless space in the eaves—too big for a closet, too small for a bedroom.

"This will be the darkroom," Abbie says, stepping into the cave-like space. She comes out again, bringing the smell of pent-up air with her. "And this," she says, sweeping one arm around the rest of the open space, "will be my studio."

"Your studio?"

"Yes, my photography studio," she says, shaking her curls as though ridding herself of protests. "They can't expect me to just sit there for a year while Mother plans my whole wedding. I will simply tell Edward that if that is the case, he'll end up marrying a woman half-mad with boredom. He says my dazzling charm will be a great asset in London or The Hague or wherever it is we are to be posted. I am simply planning to preserve this asset until my wedding day."

"But what will your mother say?"

"Mother? She'll go along with whatever Father says. And Father has never been a problem."

"And Edward?"

She tilts her head at me. "Please, June. I'm not entering into this marriage blindly. Once I've spoken with him, Edward will not only agree, but he'll buy me all the supplies I need and have them delivered here. He'll even find an instructor and send him here to teach me how to develop my own photographs. Edward will not be a problem."

"Oh," I say. I wonder what it must be like to have Abbie's utter confidence. And to not spend a minute of the day worrying about money.

The fireplace looks meager for such a large room, and I imagine it will never be warm in here, not really. There's a rickety chair by one window, an ashtray full of burned-down cigarette ends on the sill. "It is warm—the light, that is," I concede.

"The light is perfect."

The view is not unlike the view from Abbie's bedroom window, though she's much higher up the mountain. A long stretch of rooftops, the occasional silver spire of a church steeple, silos, and brick factory buildings all coming to an abrupt end at the Lachine Canal.

She approaches the window and gestures to the view. "The people and the streets of Saint Henri and Saint Charles will be my subjects. And this view, of course."

"You're serious?"

Abbie looks at me and holds my gaze. The windows begin to rattle as a train passes. I would not hear her if she spoke, but I can see she is perfectly serious.

Once the rattle subsides, she asks: "Do you want to wait here, while I make the arrangements?"

A cloud has momentarily blocked the sun, and the room feels slovenly and full of shadows. If we needed to, could Mother and Father and I live in an apartment like this?

"I'll wait outside," I say.

———— ✌ ⁂ ⁂ ————

I wait in the street for what seems like forever until Abbie finally appears, tucking a folded paper into her purse. She takes my arm and leads me in the opposite direction of Saint Cunigunde church.

"Don't we have to get back?"

"Yes, but first let's go see what happens at 1919 Saint Jacques during the day."

As we walk the few blocks to the jazz club, Abbie fills me in on the studio she's just rented. She signed a lease for twelve months, paid in full in advance. "One year to be a photographer," she says. "I'll have charming stories to tell for the rest of my life. Why waste my year of freedom taking pictures of monuments and great buildings? There's so much life right here."

"You're sure your parents will allow this?"

She shrugs. "They can't really stop me."

We've reached 1919 Saint Jacques. A line of Red Lantern taxis waits out front, parked, lights out, no drivers in sight.

Abbie stops at the door of the jazz club. It's not yet two o'clock. The bar is shut up tight, and with it, the front entrance to the offices on the second floor.

"It is Saturday," I say.

"You're right. I'll come Monday. First thing. Well, first thing after I get Christine to clean my studio and arrange for supplies and furniture. Come, let's get back."

We walk back, sucking on candies from the bag Abbie bought at the dépanneur. "Smile, Junie," she says.

I try to smile. I do, but it's just pasted on. I can't help feeling this is going to end badly, this playacting on Saint Jacques Street. For her it's a game, ending up here.

For me, it's a very real possibility.

# Chapter Sixteen

Daisy answers the door in her dressing gown, hair in curlers, a crying and snotty Steve on her hip. She's got the long coil of the telephone hooked over her shoulder, a cigarette between her fingers.

"Oh, June, thank God you're here," she says as the receiver clatters to the floor and slides back toward the kitchen. Steve's shriek turns to panic when she tries to hand him to me. She unwinds his arms from around her neck and maneuvers him in my direction, so that his arms, grasping as they are, now cling to me. In her kitten-heeled slippers, sucking on her cigarette, Daisy clips down the hall toward the kitchen. Steve wails even louder.

"Come see what I built." Chris, dressed for bed though it is only late afternoon, waits at the bottom of the stairs. Daisy's entry hall is grand, with its gilt wall sconces and wallpaper printed with lemon trees and butterflies. Grander than the tiny Abbott Street home where she and the boys spend so much time.

Geoff stands halfway down the stairs in his shirtsleeves, a tie in each hand. "Which tie?" he asks, then sees me. "Oh, hello, June. Aren't you a sight for sore eyes." He steps aside to make space for our little parade. Chris, holding my hand, leads the way. Steve, hiccuping now, collapses against my shoulder and snuffles into my coat.

"Isn't that kind of June to come?" Geoff asks.

Daisy's eyes catch mine and slide away. "No, not either of those. I already picked a tie for you. It's hanging on the hook in the closet."

Then she's off to the kitchen. Geoff looks up at me and shrugs. My arm has fallen asleep, and I think Steve may be asleep too, and I feel the heaviness tugging down on my mood. Chris pulls my elbow again. "Come see, June. Come see what I built."

———— ✶ ————

Since his outburst earlier Steve has been quiet, resigned even. He doesn't make a fuss about getting under the covers, even though it's barely dark outside. He watches me wide-eyed with his thumb in his mouth as I tuck him in. I let him, though Daisy says it's a filthy habit. Let her put her own kids to bed if she wants him to stop.

"I'm not a baby," Chris tells me. "I'm going to go work until it's my bedtime."

I join him in Geoff's study. He's in a small task chair, pulled up to the folded-down desk of a secretary cabinet. I sit in the comfortable leather chair at Geoff's broad polished wood desk. Even this room is perfect as a *Good Housekeeping* spread, except for the desk itself, which is littered with papers and notes. The typewriter keys clack under Chris's fingers and I study the campaign that Geoff has been working on.

*Easy. Effortless. Attention-grabbing. A walk in the park. Straightforward. But also, mysterious, secretive, unknown.*

The words are scrawled across the blotter sheet. Geoff is working on a campaign for Derny, a makeup line.

The smell of stale smoke wafts from the heavy crystal ashtray at my elbow. I roll the words about in my head. I can sense what he's after—an uncomplicated beauty regime that still preserves all the mystery of being a woman—but none of these words are quite right. To start with, no one can use the word "easy" when talking about something to do with young ladies, or, even worse, married women.

Is Derny for young women? Or older women? Both?

I pick out a pencil from the cup on the desk, but it's not sharp. I pull out another one but it's not sharp, either. I open the top drawer to find a sharpener and sharpen all five pencils in the cup, then replace them, sharpened tips up.

I write new words in a blank space on the blotter: *Éclat, panache, style. Smooth, deft, skillful. Enigma, deceptive, unexplainable, riddle.* I'm so engrossed, I don't notice that Chris has stopped typing. I can hear music coming from downstairs.

"Aunt June, I'm going to get into bed now."

"Do you want me to tuck you in?"

He shakes his head. "I just do that because Grannie likes it. But I know that you don't."

It's a sad statement, but it's also true, and I don't correct him. Once he's gone, I sit back in Geoff's chair and let my mind wander, like I do when a poem teases at the edge of my thoughts.

A woman wants her beauty regime to be easy, but it needs to look complicated. She needs to preserve her mystery. She can't give away her secrets. An image of Marie-Céleste at the ladies' room sink flashes to mind. That's what he's trying to capture, whether he knows it or not.

Again, I wonder about the age range of women he's speaking to. Is it someone like Marie-Céleste? Or Mrs. Howard? Women have vastly different approaches to their makeup. I need to find the research file.

I reach for a pile of papers at the side of the desk, looking for more information about Derny Cosmetics, and exposing a list written in the top corner of the blotter in the process. It's in Geoff's handwriting, but neater, as if he's taken his time over this list. Elizabeth Arden, Eaton's, Gillette, J. Pascal Hardware, Canadian Pacific. Five names, which I know from my recent dictation for the accounts department are all top McAulay Advertising clients. Next to Elizabeth Arden, the name Derny is written in parentheses with an asterisk next to it. Eaton's has two asterisks next to it. I sit back as the excitement of the Derny headline seeps out of me.

There's a knock on the door and a cough. Geoff is there, an armful of coats in his hands. I jump up, scattering papers to the floor. "I got caught up . . . Sorry," I say. I gesture to the blotter. "I don't know what came over me. I like your Derny idea."

My blush deepens with each step he takes toward me, until he's standing next to me and I'm sure he can feel the heat coming from my body. My ears are itching and my neck might be covered in big red blotches.

His fingers trace the words I've written, and he nods slowly. "I see what you've done," he says, his nod turning into a shake of the head. "Interesting."

Propelled by embarrassment, I step away from him. It was almost better when he didn't notice me at all. I put my hand on the desk to steady myself. I swallow and manage to whisper, "Thank you."

He coughs. "Daisy's asking you to come help with the coats. You can put them in the guest room." He hands me the coats in his arms and leads the way out of his study.

———— ⚬⚬ ————

I sink into the soft carpet of the third step from the bottom, waiting for the doorbell to ring. From the living room, a man bellows hearty congratulations, which is how I learn that the party is a celebration of the first anniversary of the launch of Collier and Moore.

One year since the elevator doors at McAulay closed for the last time on Geoff Collier and Fletcher Moore. One full year of waiting for someone to make the connection that I am related to Geoff, the deserter. One full year of worrying I could be fired at any moment.

"And expanding already," I hear Geoff say. Daisy murmurs in the background, her tone charming though I can't make out the words.

The doorbell rings and I pad down the stairs to open it. Two couples, arriving at once. They hand me their coats until I can hardly see over the top of the pile. I lug the heavy coats upstairs and lay them with care on the bed where I am to sleep later. The doorbell rings again.

My face red from rushing, my breath heavy, I pull the door open to see Mr. Sands standing there with Marie-Céleste.

Marie-Céleste just steps right into the house, head swiveling, taking in the wallpaper, the sconces, the gilt-framed mirror. It's only when I say, "Welcome," that she notices me at all.

"Why, Miss Grant! What are you doing here?"

I manage a tight smile through the flurry of emotion. "May I take your coats?"

Marie-Céleste drops her head back and laughs and Mr. Sands says, "Grant. You're the coat-check girl now?" His eyes seek out mine as they both hand their coats to me.

The sound of laughter has drawn Geoff into the entry, all shaking hands and good cheer. "Sands, good of you to come. And hello there, I'm Geoff. Come on in, martinis are fresh." He nods the way and the two newcomers join the others, erasing me completely from their minds, or so I hope.

"All right there, June?" Geoff stands in the hall, watching me. "Those are the last of the guests."

"I'm fine," I say, holding up the coats. "I'll just bring these upstairs."

I scuttle up the stairs and lay the coats on top of the others, then lie on top of the pile, taking in the smell of mothballs and perfume. I wish I were one of the guests. Any of them, all of them. Anyone else but me.

Why is Mr. Sands at a party to celebrate Collier and Moore?

The sound of laughter erupts from the living room. It's unlikely the guests will come upstairs, but what if Sands comes to find me, or Marie-Céleste?

With a groan I go check on the sleeping boys. Then I go back to Geoff's study and sit behind the desk. I pick up a pencil and tap it on the blotter, under the list of McAulay clients, and think.

# Chapter Seventeen

The sound of yelling wakes me as the first light of dawn is creeping under the few inches of open blinds.

"Are you trying to make a fool out of me?" Geoff's voice.

"Don't you dare! No, don't you dare, after everything I did." Daisy, loud and shrill.

"Everything you did? You bought a cake. You hired a cook. You spent all day God knows where. You sleep at your mother's half the time. What do you do all day that you can't look after your own children? Can't have dinner on the table? Smoking and drinking and God knows what."

"Stop it! Stop it!"

I get out of bed and pull on my coat as a dressing gown over my slip. Halfway down the stairs I spot Daisy, crouched in a corner of the dining room, knees to her chest, hands over her ears, screeching like a caged animal.

The table is strewn with coffee cups, whiskey and wine glasses, overfilled ashtrays. The cake in question lays half-eaten at the center of the table, vanilla cream filling oozing from the edges, and I know this won't do. It won't do at all. Geoff likes things neat and proper.

"You want a maid and a cook, not a wife! You'd have me in that kitchen all day and all night!"

No one, except Missie, and sometimes Father, would dare speak back to Daisy. But Missie married and moved away, and Father—well, now there's no one that can talk Daisy down. Not when she gets like this.

"You want dull until you want sparkle. You can't have both! I can't be dull all day and then sparkle at night."

Geoff looks at me through the haze of a half-smoked cigarette. "June," he says. He raises his hands, palms open in supplication, then lets them fall. The cigarette spills ash on the carpet but he doesn't notice. Like a man who has tried everything and has given up at last.

I try to pretend I'm Missie. I make myself small, unthreatening. I crouch down and then, on all fours, crawl toward her. "Daisy, Daisy, Daisy," I croon. "Quiet now. Father says it's time to go to sleep."

She looks at me through raccoon eyes, her makeup a ruin. "Father?" Her breath in my face is gin-sharp.

I take her in my arms. "He's not upset. But he says it's time to go to bed now. Can you stand?"

She can't. I stand and she lifts up her arms. She's barely heavier than a pile of winter coats. Geoff steps forward but I shake my head. "I've got her."

Upstairs, I lay her on the master bed. She's passive as I undress her. I'm shocked at how thin she's become. She was always small and supple as a new branch, but now her ribs stick out and her belly is sunken. Her brassiere is stuffed with soft carded wool. I leave it in place so as not to embarrass her.

"Sit up," I say and slip a white flannel nightgown over her head. She hugs the soft fabric to her body and lies down, then curls up like one of her boys, staring at me as I adjust the cover over her.

"Go to sleep, Daisy. Father says so."

But she keeps her eyes open. Even when I turn out the lamp, I see her eyes glistening in the half dark of the room at dawn.

Geoff has not come upstairs. I go back to the guest room and take off my coat and get back into the warm, soft guest bed. It's my second night of luxury in a row, and I know I'd best not get used to it. I sink into the soft feathers, but any hope of sleep is gone.

I make an inventory of the questions in my head and run through them until they are in some kind of order.

Why did François write the address on the orange wrapper? Was that a message for Daisy? Or was it meant for me, or Mother?

And what about that address? What business could Daisy have there, other than the office of her modeling agency? I groan when I think of the sounds coming through the door, the girl in the blue dress. What did Geoff mean when he said Daisy gets up to "God knows what"? Surely not that.

Could Daisy have something to do with Red Lantern Taxi? And what about Sands and Marie-Céleste? What am I to do with the knowledge that they were guests at a party celebrating Collier and Moore? And the list of McAulay clients on Geoff's blotter?

And Geoff himself. Exasperated, and no wonder, with Daisy crying like a lost child on the floor. What if he just got fed up with it all? What if he got so fed up that he sent her back—damaged goods—to where she came from? To us.

There's no chance of sleep. I get up, wash, and dress in my own skirt and blouse from Friday. I slide my hand into the skirt pocket and finger the taxi chits that Lewin gave me, still nestled there. I head downstairs in my stockinged feet, tiptoeing past Geoff, who's sprawled on the sofa, mouth open, snoring softly. He does not stir when I spread a blanket over him.

In the kitchen I fill the sink with soapy water and start on the piles of dishes. When the boys wake I give them toast and milk and help Steve get dressed. There is no choice but to bring them to Mass with me. That's what Mother would want. It's one thing for Daisy to choose to risk her own soul for eternity, but she can hardly make that choice for her boys.

I use Daisy's phone to call Mother to tell her we are coming. Then I call Red Lantern Taxi and ask for a car to come and pick us up. Maybe with the day to themselves and a tidier house, Daisy and Geoff will sort things out when they wake up.

# Chapter Eighteen

"Good, there you are." Miss Pomeroy is waiting for me as I step off the elevator. The deep crease at the center of her face makes her look even more severe than usual. "That hat is a disgrace. You should take it off in the elevator."

I swipe Father's old hat off my head. She keeps talking before I can say so much as good morning.

"Mr. McAulay has asked for you again this morning. I told him one day only. You are to be back in steno tomorrow." She looks me up and down, shaking her head. "They want coffee. Three people."

I hang my coat on the hook outside Mr. McAulay's office and head to the coffee room, trying to order my thoughts as I prepare the coffee tray. Should I tell Mr. McAulay that Mr. Sands was at Geoff's party? This approach might cause problems for me, too. What was I doing there, after all?

I focus on balancing the heavy coffee tray evenly between my hands as I walk back to Mr. McAulay's office. By the time I am halfway down the hall, I have determined that it is best to say nothing at all, to Mr. McAulay, to Mr. Sands, or to anyone else.

"Miss Grant."

The voice is far away but I pay no mind, keeping my eyes straight ahead.

"Miss Grant. Do you need help?"

"Thank you, Miss Pomeroy, if you could open the door, please."

I can't look at her. I keep my gaze on the edge of the shag carpet, determined not to trip over it.

I pour the coffee with shaking hands. The cups clink in the saucers as I hand them, first to Mr. McAulay (milk and sugar) and Sands (sugar only). "How do you take your coffee, Mr. Lewin?" My voice is weak from strain as I ask.

"Black," he says, half rising to take the cup from me. He smiles and I remember how Friday night ended—with him carrying me into a taxi—but Mr. Lewin covers over any embarrassment. "What do you think of Mr. Sands's idea, Miss Grant?"

The other two men look up at me, McAulay curious, Sands smiling and smug.

"Which idea is that?"

"Sands gave the girls names," Mr. McAulay answers. "Not their own names, mind. The name of the lady they become, when they put on each look. And Lewin has captured it better than any photographer. Here." He hands a rough sketch of Simone, ready to serve Easter dinner for seventeen, just thirty minutes after church.

"Why . . . ," I say, my voice quiet. I look up at Mr. Lewin, who has abandoned his coffee cup in favor of a cigarette. "It's wonderful what you've done," I say to him.

He closes his eyes and blows out the smoke. "What we've done, together," he says. He looks at me as he says it, but gestures his arm, cigarette and all, to encompass the other two men. "Always a group effort, isn't it, Sands?"

Sands relaxes back, ankle on his knee, arms outstretched across the back of the sofa. "Sure thing, Lewin," he says. And then he winks at me, his confidence restored by my silence. *I won't tell if you won't,* that wink says. But what won't he tell? That the idea for the campaign was mine? That he was at Geoff and Daisy's party? That Geoff is my brother-in-law and Girl Number Four is my sister?

The phone rings. "I'll answer that at my desk, Sir."

They pay no attention, busy as they are laying my ideas across the expanse of Mr. McAulay's coffee table like so many playing cards.

———— ⟨∞⟩ ————

After lunch, Mr. McAulay calls me into his office. His tie is crooked and his sleeves are rolled up. His desk is covered with sketches and he has a sheaf of papers scrawled with notes in his hand. Mr. Lewin is still in the armchair, his sketches spread across the tabletop.

Mr. McAulay looks up at me and his eyes soften. "Close the door, Miss Grant. Come, take a seat. You were there at the Eaton's event, weren't you?"

"Yes, Sir," I say, standing across from him.

"Sit, sit. Mr. Lewin says you can help us, since Mr. Sands has been called away."

Lewin gestures to the chair across from him, and I sit down. "We are presenting this concept to Eaton's next Monday. We've got work to do, matching girls to their outfits."

"Yes," says McAulay. "And they want us on our toes."

I sit down and pull the top drawing toward me. I take in the easy lines of the sketch, the blush of color on the dress a suggestion only, but I recognize the model immediately. "This is Effie," I say to Lewin. And then, emboldened by his relieved smile, I ask, "Why does Eaton's want us on our toes, Mr. McAulay?"

"Anyone thinks they can make it in advertising these days. Upstarts," he says. He stands and heads to the window, his back to us. "Don't know the value of relationships."

"Yes, Sir," I say. I can't help but think he is talking about Collier and Moore. "Sissy," I whisper to Mr. Lewin, handing him a sketch of Daisy.

"But we know better, don't we, Lewin? Tradition matters. Experience matters."

Lewin dips his head to the side, as though measuring the statements against the facts. "Yes," he says. "Though we're hearing that style matters to the client now too. Current and fresh."

"Right. Exactly why we brought you on board." McAulay turns to face us. "But style can pair with tradition. You don't throw out your old friends, just because the suit styles have changed. Don't you agree, Miss Grant?"

"Absolutely," I say, looking down at the tweed of my skirt, which is older than my oldest friendships. Older than me, probably.

"You're a sensible girl. I like that," he says. Then he wanders to the door. "I've got an appointment. I'll leave you to it."

———— ❧~❧ ————

Mr. Lewin and I settle in to a steady pace of quiet work. We go through each girl, each outfit, each scenario.

He doesn't send me away, even once we are finished. Instead, he keeps me near him, like some essential element, which I suppose I am because Sands never does come back from lunch and Mr. McAulay's appointment takes the rest of the afternoon.

We review the scenarios again, one by one. The girls' names, their activities. Mr. Lewin asks questions, makes suggestions, while I take notes. My worries, about Mr. Sands, about Daisy and Geoff, about Collier and Moore, dissolve under the salve of work.

At the end of the day, we have the sketches organized and the scenarios ready to be retyped. "I can type these in the morning," I say, just as there's a knock at the door.

Miss Pomeroy ducks her head in. "Anything you need before I leave, Mr. Lewin?"

"No, I don't think so. Have a good night."

She pauses in the doorway, buttoning her coat. "Shall I expect you back in steno tomorrow, Miss Grant?" She makes a show of lifting her wrist and pointing at her watch as she asks.

I am about to nod when Mr. Lewin answers for me. "I'm afraid we'll need Miss Grant all week, Miss Pomeroy. I'll confirm with Mr. McAulay in the morning, but I'm sure he'll agree." She looks at me again but does not dare contradict him. Neither do I, even though I promised Mother I would go back to steno.

She buttons her coat and heads out and I'm alone again with Mr. Lewin.

He smiles. "Ready?" he asks.

"For what?" I'm ready to get my coat and go home, but that does not seem to be what he has in mind.

"We need to go through each one again, from the beginning." He looks at his watch. "I'd say let's give it two hours. Three at most."

"Three hours?" I won't get home in time to pick up Mother's groceries. No cheese for Mother. No ground beef for the dogs.

"Come, Miss Grant. Isn't this what you wanted? To become a copywriter?"

"I'm not sure I can." I slump down in my chair as I say the words, suddenly drained from the excitement of the afternoon.

Mr. Lewin sets the Eaton's folder aside and slaps down a fresh pad of blank paper. "Well, back to steno for you, then," he says with a laugh.

I look up at his kind face, and feel emptiness at his words. "Isn't that where I belong?"

He shakes his head, tipping it to one side. "I don't believe in fishing for compliments, Miss Grant, so I will only say this once. You've got talent. You deserve to be here, as much as any of the talented boys. More than Sands and a few others who get by on swagger alone. But you'll need to work harder than all of them. Evenings. Weekends. Long hours when it's needed, like tonight."

I nod, sit up straight again. Mr. Lewin's stomach grumbles. He scrunches his face, then laughs. "Of course, the advantage to staying late is they bring you dinner. Shall we call down for it now?"

I jump up and go to the phone, dialing the extension for the cafeteria.

"Ask for two desserts each," Lewin says, winking at me. "We've got to take our rewards where we can find them."

——— ❧❀❧ ———

I'm relieved that Mother has fallen asleep under her fur coat on the cot in Father's den. No need to explain why I'm so late; that I was working on a real campaign. That I didn't go back to steno like I promised.

In my own room, I pull on a pair of wool long underwear. I must call about the heating oil in the morning. Perhaps we can buy it on credit? But what good would that do? There won't be any extra money next month, either.

When the house is quiet like this, I can hear the neighbors' snores coming through the wall of my bedroom. Mother would never have tolerated living at such close quarters back when we were on Côte Saint Antoine, but I don't mind. It reminds me of how, when I was small, I used to wake in the middle of the night and check on everyone. That's how I found out that Daisy was climbing out her window. I'd go into Missie's room and wake her, and together we'd climb into Daisy's bed to wait for her to get back.

I'd half fall asleep to the sound of Missie's breathing, but only once Daisy returned, when, cradled by the rhythm of my sisters' breath on either side of me, would I fall into a deep sleep.

# Chapter Nineteen

I spend the morning at my desk outside Mr. McAulay's office, retyping the Eaton's copy exactly how Mr. Lewin and I discussed. Late in the morning, Mr. Sands, Mr. Lewin, and Mr. McAulay arrive all at once. Sands holds his hand out for my notes and then follows the others into Mr. McAulay's office. It seems I am not to be invited in today.

They are still in there well into the afternoon when the phone rings and I answer with my usual "Mr. McAulay's office."

"Is this June Grant?" The caller is a man.

"Yes," I say. I can't imagine who would be calling me. It's not Geoff.

"This is Ted Hearn, from Philadelphia. Missie gave me your number?"

"Oh, Mr. Hearn, yes. She mentioned you might call." I try to sound bright, like I'm excited to hear from him. I had forgotten completely about Mr. Hearn.

"I'm in town for business for a few days, and I wondered if you might like to have dinner with me?"

"That would be—" I start to say, then I hear the office door behind me open.

"Miss Grant, are you still there?" Mr. Hearn asks.

I look up to see Mr. Sands standing in front of me with the Eaton's copy I had typed this morning, covered in scribbled notes.

"Yes, I'm sorry. I'm here. That would be lovely," I say.

"I'm free Thursday night if that suits you?"

"Yes, Thursday is fine."

"Do you mind if we eat at my hotel? I'd offer to pick you up, but I'm sure I'd get lost."

We both laugh at that. Mr. Sands rolls his eyes and gestures with his hands that I should get on with it. "That's fine," I say. "Where would you like to meet?"

"In the lounge at the Mount Royal Hotel? Thursday at six?"

"I'll see you then," I say.

"I'm looking forward to it, Miss Grant. Your sister is a hoot. See you then."

I set down the receiver and Mr. Sands shakes his head. "Some advice, Grant. If they're serious, they'll pick you up at your house, not meet you there."

I manage to not respond, though I can tell the surge of heat to my throat and cheeks gives me away. Mr. Sands grins and looks around for someone to share the joke with, but there is no one to witness his mean-spiritedness this time. I hold my hand out for the notes. They are covered, front and back, in detailed scribbles in his handwriting. "So many changes," I say quietly.

"I need these back tomorrow morning, first thing."

"But it's the end of the day," I say.

Mr. Sands drops his head back again and laughs in that way that I find so unpleasant. "You do know how much McAulay hates Collier and Moore, don't you?" he asks. "Does he know that Collier is your brother-in-law? Or that the Eaton's girl is your sister?"

"What about you?" I ask. I want to ask him if McAulay knows that he's chummy with Geoff, but I can't bring myself to say the words.

"What about me? Well, I'm the writer on this account, and I say I need these notes by tomorrow morning, first thing. Any problem with that, Miss Grant?"

He walks off without waiting for me to answer. Mr. Lewin comes out of the office next.

"Everything okay, Miss Grant?"

I hold up the pages. "I can't stay late again today," I say. "I'm sorry."

Mr. Lewin takes the sheets and flips through them. "He's made a bloody mess, but really the changes are only minor. It's only a matter of typing them again. Go home, Miss Grant. Call it a day."

———— ❦ ————

I decide on a compromise between what Mr. Lewin suggested and what Mr. Sands demanded. I go home, and bring the notes with me to type on my own typewriter. I manage to leave in time to get to Lublin's five minutes before closing.

"There you are, Miss Grant. I was worried your mother would have to go without her cheese again."

"Yes, and the poor dogs without their ground beef," I say, smiling at Mr. Lublin. The cardboard box on the counter is larger than normal. Three cans of soup, a larger hunk of cheese, a full loaf of bread. Lying on top of the paper-wrapped ground beef is a pack of Chesterfields. I pull these out and lay them on the counter.

"Please send my regards to your mother. I hope your father is feeling better soon."

"I hope so too." I look down at the pack on the counter between us. "Mr. Lublin?"

"Yes, Miss Grant?"

"You know that Mother only smokes one or two cigarettes a day, and that they are Export A's?"

"Yes, I know that. These are for Daisy."

I try to stand like Daisy at her most imperial. "Mother is too kind to say anything, but with things as they are, she really can no longer buy Daisy's cigarettes."

Mr. Lublin looks down and nods at the pack on the counter. "It's difficult to say no to one of your children, even once they are grown." A cloud of sadness passes over his features as he says these words, and I wonder at Mr. Lublin's own story. He arrived sometime between the wars, from Poland, and he's all alone as far as I can tell. What would it be like to move so far from your family?

"It is. But Daisy can buy her own cigarettes." I think it would be a boon to move halfway across the world from Daisy at least, but the dark pools of Mr. Lublin's eyes tell me this is not something to make light of.

"I understand perfectly, Miss Grant." He sweeps the pack of cigarettes off the counter, dismissing the unspoken acknowledgment of loss along with it.

I take up the box at last. "One more thing, Mr. Lublin. Is François here? I have a question for him."

"A question for François? Why, no. He left early today, he's playing the jazz tonight." He pauses, as though waiting for me to explain what I want with François. "They say he's quite good, but I didn't think you'd be one for jazz clubs, Miss Grant."

He pauses again. I pick at an edge of the cardboard box.

"Would you like to leave a message for him?"

I shake my head. Mr. Lublin would no doubt read any note I might leave. "That's all right," I lie. "It's nothing important."

---

Daisy is waiting for me on the stoop. "About time. Give me my ciggies. My taxi is almost here." She holds out her palm.

The Daisy facing me now shows no trace of the whimpering, wasting-away version that I helped into her nightgown on Sunday at dawn. Her wool coat is cinched tight at the waist, her hair softly curled, her eyes smoky gray and mysterious. And yet I remain acutely aware of that moment of weakness—the folds of her ribs, that wool padding that must itch against the tender skin of her shrunken breasts. The exasperated look on her husband's face. I stand with my feet wide apart and straighten my spine just like I did with Mr. Lublin.

"It's not fair to ask Mother, or me, to pay for your cigarettes, when we don't even have enough to buy heating oil," I say. "You'll have to buy them yourself from now on."

As if in response to my words, the night sky becomes darker all of a sudden. Mr. Lublin has turned off his sign for the night.

Daisy takes a step down and walks toward me, her eyes narrowed with hate. She stops only when she's inches from my face. "Not you too," she snarls. "Everyone is turning against me. Being tight. Geoff, and Mother, and now you."

"Being tight?" I ask. "Is that what you think?"

"Yes. Mother crying poor all the time. Buying ground beef for the dogs, but won't help her own children. And you—you go out and work, but keep it all to yourself. And Geoff, telling me I can't buy clothes, as if I need his permission. Why is everyone so tight with money?" She punches her fist into her palm with these last words. She's so close I can smell her minty breath and feel tiny drops of her saliva landing on my cheeks.

"Do you think that's what this is? Mother pretending to be tight?" I think of Mother, washing the laundry by herself in the kitchen, wearing her fur coat as a dressing gown to keep warm.

I put down the cardboard box in front of me and pull the hat off my head and hold it out to her. "Do you think I want to wear this old hat?" I tug at the buttons of Father's old coat, heavy and dull on me, and hold it open. "Do you think I want to wear this old coat? This old tweed suit that belonged to God knows who before the first war? Is that what you think?"

The winter cold reaches the inch of exposed flesh where my blouse has crept out of my skirt. I pull the coat closed and hug my arms tight around me. I look down at Daisy in her new clothes, her shiny shoes, her lovely coat and hat. I think of her purse on the hall table, so full of bills that the clasp wouldn't close, and it's my turn to narrow my eyes at her. "You've got it all wrong if that's what you think."

"How dare you?" She screams the words, pummeling at my chest as the same broken, poisonous Daisy from last Sunday bubbles through an invisible crack in her smooth exterior. I stand firm. For once my big bones serve me. "How dare you," she whimpers. At the sound of a car turning onto our street from Saint Catherine, Daisy steps back. With a shake of her head she's composed once again. "This isn't finished."

I shrug. "I'm sure your taxi won't mind stopping for cigarettes. Maybe on the way to your modeling agency?"

The brakes squeal as the Red Lantern taxi comes to a stop in front of our house. I wonder if Daisy heard me. She freezes and turns back to face me. Through the anger she looks just mean, not pretty at all. "Don't you dare."

She arranges her face into a pretty-girl smile before she spins around. The driver has stepped out to open her door, and I wonder if it is the same one that comes every time. To me, he's nothing more than a shadow. Daisy slides inside the taxi without another word. The driver slams his own door and pulls right up onto the sidewalk to turn the car around and head back toward Saint Catherine.

— ❧ ❧ —

I'm at the kitchen table with the Eaton's drawings spread before me when Mother comes in.

"The boys are down. Well, Steve is down. Chris is thinking in the dark before he goes to sleep." She sighs and turns on the burner under the kettle. "An old man in a boy's body, that one. Would you like tea?"

"Yes, please." I slide a fresh sheet into the typewriter.

"Did Miss Pomeroy ask you to bring work home?" Mother fishes a tea bag from the bottom of the pot, gives it a shake, and sniffs it.

I shake my head but don't answer directly. "Mother, surely we can stop rationing tea? We never really had to, anyway," I say. And it's true.

Even with our ration cards, we could get most everything we needed. "I'll buy some more tea tomorrow."

Mother sighs. "But the bills are so high and we need heating oil."

"We have enough for tea. Besides, I've told Mr. Lublin no more Chesterfields. And Daisy too. It's just not fair, Mother."

Mother heats the teapot, places the sad old tea bag into it, and then fills it with just enough water for two cups. She assembles the tea tray and places it between us on the table, then sits down again.

I smile at her. "I wonder how long it will need to steep to have any flavor at all?"

Mother smiles back. "All night, I expect." Then she's serious again. "You're too hard on Daisy, June. You don't know what it's like, to have everything and then lose it."

"Because I never had anything, you mean."

"It's true. But it's easier for you this way, June. You are so much better off than Daisy."

Anger blooms in my chest all over again. Mother telling me I should not envy Daisy does not help my resolve at all. Already two weeks into Lent and I've made no progress at all on the envy front. The spaniels shuffle from their place next to the stove and resettle themselves under Mother's chair. Her face is lined and sad as she pours the tea.

I don't want to add to her sadness. I give her a grateful smile as I take my cup of weak tea. "I would like to buy new tea bags for all of us, rather than cigarettes for Daisy. Don't you think that's fair?"

Mother drops her head to one side, answering my question with one of her own. "What did Miss Pomeroy say?"

"What can she say? Mr. McAulay asked for me himself. But it's only for this week. Then I'll be back in steno for sure."

Mother's smile is as weak as the tea, and I know she's still worried. I pat her hand and she pulls it away. "Don't worry," I say. "I promise I won't work late on Thursday night, when I'm going on a date with Mr. Hearn."

# Chapter Twenty

I arrive at work the next day well before Mr. McAulay and Mr. Sands. There would have been plenty of time to finish typing my notes this morning; no reason to bring them home at all.

"Miss Grant."

I look up from my notes to see Miss Pomeroy, holding a message slip between two fingers.

"You know perfectly well that you're not to receive personal calls at work."

"Yes, Miss Pomeroy."

I wonder whether she will let me have the message, which I think must be from Mr. Hearn, canceling our date. I hold her gaze steadily for a moment and then look down, submissive as she expects me to be.

"Don't let it happen again."

"Yes, Miss Pomeroy."

The message, when she finally gives it to me, is from Abbie. *Come to my studio right after work today.*

After work, bold as anything, I hail a Red Lantern taxi from the stand outside the Sun Life Building. The driver, one I've never seen before, does not seem shocked when I give him the address of Abbie's studio.

He simply drives around Dominion Square, turns onto Dorchester, and slips along the side of the cathedral to come out on Saint Jacques. As we drive west into the sunset, the silver spires of a church are dark silhouettes against the golden sky. Was it just a week ago that I was afraid of crossing these tracks?

The driver accepts the chit without comment. I push open the door next to the dépanneur and make my way among the boxes, up the crowded steps to where the door to Abbie's studio stands open. The room is flooded with afternoon light.

"Why, Abbie! Look what you've done!" I stand at the center of the sun-washed room.

Abbie is draped across a red velvet divan under the double window. A coal fire in the grate warms the studio, which is clean to the corners. There's a table stacked with photography supplies along the wall next to the room in the eaves where Abbie has already set up her darkroom. I pause at a clothing rack in one corner and run my fingers over each hanger—kimonos and feather boas and men's suits and flapper dresses and silk blouses in cream and yellow and turquoise. Each outfit feels softer than the last under my fingers. The colors bright, patterns bold.

"I want to wear them all," I say.

"Of course you do, June." Abbie herself is draped in a kimono with a cherry blossom pattern. She sits up and jumps to her feet. "Come. Let's get dressed."

"What for?"

"We're going to that modeling agency. I checked. They're open until seven."

"I can't go to a modeling agency. What will they possibly do with me?"

Abbie pulls out a flapper-style dress from the rack and holds it over her torso. "You're right. We'll say you're my business manager. Hmmm." She turns back to the rack and pulls out a printed silk dress.

"You'll wear this, as a blouse, under your suit. And this." She hands me a wide-brimmed men's hat from the top of the rack.

I turn my back to change. When I turn around again, Abbie adjusts the collar of the blouse and the brim of the hat.

"Just right. My manager," she says. "Now, let me take your picture for my collection."

"Like this? What are you collecting?"

Abbie holds the camera to her waist and looks down at it to take my picture. "Well, if you ask my mother, I'm collecting pictures of stained-glass windows." She looks up at me and rocks her head from side to side as though measuring me up. "No, don't smile," she says, spinning a knob on the side of the camera. "There. Just like that." The camera clicks under her fingers, and she winds it again. "But since you are not my mother, I will tell you: I'm collecting people."

"People?"

"Yes. People in costume. Like you right now. The costume shows who you are." She says this dreamily, as though she's just thought of it for the first time. "There. Now, I'll get dressed and off we go."

———— ✺ ————

Abbie is a sensation on the street in a purple silk cocktail dress. Her hat is green and doesn't match, and she's pulled a black wool capelet over her shoulders. Her shoes are emerald blue, her handbag cream leather and ornamented with tiny pearl beads.

The children on the street know Abbie already and follow behind us as we walk the three blocks to the jazz club. "Miss Abbie," they call out, hoping for candies no doubt. They look at me as though I'm a storm cloud, which is how I usually feel walking next to Abbie, but today, in my man's hat and with the pretty-patterned collar of the blouse peeking out of my work blazer, I feel positively jaunty. I'm not nearly as stylish as Abbie, but I do have a pretend job to do as her business manager, and I'm dressed for the part.

We pass a line of Red Lantern cabs idling outside as we reach the front entrance to Le Salon du Jazz. I hold the door open and Abbie sweeps inside. The bartender stares out over the empty seats and nods a hello as we head for the curved staircase to the second floor. It's a blank nod, not a nod of recognition. He doesn't seem to remember us from Friday, and no wonder. This version of Abbie is like nothing I've ever seen.

She trips up the stairs like a countess on her way to a ball, pausing at the door of the modeling agency only long enough to wait for me to open it. I want to stop and formulate a plan, but Abbie smiles over her shoulder, her eyes bright. "Just follow my lead," she says, and steps inside.

We run straight into the woman from Friday night. Her blonde curls are hair-spray-ad perfect, her eyes crafty as they land on Abbie in her gown and cloak. "John-Paul," she calls back into the room. "New blood."

"Get out of here. Your taxi is outside." A voice I can only imagine belongs to John-Paul calls from inside the room. The girl's eyes look right past me. She does not remember me from Friday either.

When I enter the room, Abbie is already behind a privacy screen talking to John-Paul. Through the crack between the two corners of the screen I can see him. He's leaning back in his chair, and his dark eyes run up and down Abbie like she's a piano he's dying to play. I gasp. It's J-P, one of the executives from the Red Lantern Taxi meeting. The screen blocks a separate section of the room, and I realize that a wall has been removed and two offices are open to each other: Superior Models and Red Lantern Taxi.

"A bohemian. An artist. I don't have one of those," J-P says, as though Abbie were a new flavor for his box of chocolates. "Might be popular with some." His voice trails off.

"You're talking about modeling for photos, is that right?" Abbie's voice is chatty. She's not intimidated by talking to a strange man while pretending to be someone she's not. My knees shake as I silently compose the list of sins to confess at the first opportunity.

My eyes skim over the framed photographs of models on the wall until I find one of Daisy. It's in a grouping set apart from the others, which are obviously fashion photos. This small selection of photos, four total, is more artistic, and there's only one of Daisy. In it I can see her face and that long neck she likes to emphasize. She's got her head tilted to one side. There's a man's face in the frame, leaning down as though he's going to nuzzle her neck. The strange thing is that they are both looking at the camera. Daisy's gaze is clear-eyed and innocent, the lost-princess look that always used to get her out of trouble with Father before he got ill. And the man—he's older, and balding, and you can see only the edge of his shirt collar and enough of a tie to know that he's wearing one. He's looking up at the camera too, his eyes full of canny knowing. As I stare at the photo, taking in every detail, the conversation behind the screen floats back into my awareness.

"Modeling is a place to start, is all I'm saying. Look, I'll have my girl call you, shall I? Leave me your number. We can set up a photo session and talk about the possibilities. It's a little late for today. I will say, though, Miss Abbie . . ."

"Yes?"

"Well, you seem like a classy girl is all. It might be better for business if you dressed in the style of the day. Set your hair, got a new hat?"

"And look like everyone else? If you want girls that are as interchangeable as silverware, I'm not interested."

I hear the change in her voice and I know it's time to leave before she overplays her part. I step into the opening of the screen, my hat low over my face. What are the chances he'll recognize me?

"Time for your next meeting, Miss Abbie," I say, with a curt nod to John-Paul.

"My business manager," she says in explanation, pulling her cloak over her shoulders again.

Downstairs, the bar is just waking up, but we don't stop. Out on the street a driver steps out of his taxi, and the lazy assurance of his stance is instantly familiar. It's the same driver that comes to pick up Daisy.

I grab Abbie's arm and we walk back to her studio, the sidewalk lit by ineffectual circles of gas streetlamps and the rectangular reflection of the still-open shopwindows. The children are all inside and it's damp and cold now, though at least it's not snowing. The glow cast by the golden hour has faded, and the neighborhood feels every bit as threatening as a childhood fairy tale. We stop at the dépanneur long enough for Abbie to use the phone and then go upstairs and change. Back in her skirt and twin set, her hair combed smooth, she looks like any other Westmount girl.

We sit together on the divan, without turning on any lights, and watch the street below for her chauffeur to arrive to drive us back to our own side of the tracks. Abbie doesn't speak, and neither do I. My head is too full of my list for confession, and I'm afraid some of my sins will tumble out if I open my mouth.

# Chapter Twenty-One

"Miss Pomeroy wonders if you have time to help with the Dictaphones this afternoon, Miss Grant?"

"Helen! How nice to see you," I say, closing the file next to my typewriter. "Of course I will help."

I'm happy for any distraction. I have been pretending to work for much of the afternoon, and even the *Scientific Advertising* can only hold my attention for so long. Mr. Lewin is working on some new sketches for the Eaton's presentation next week. Mr. McAulay and Mr. Sands went for lunch hours ago to discuss the presentation, and I've had far too much time to fret about my date with Mr. Hearn tonight. I'm dressed in Aunt Lucie's tea dress again, the one I wore the night Mr. Ritchie asked me to dinner. It is too tight across my ribs and too light for a winter's day such as this one. I am convinced that Mr. Hearn will hate the dress and everything else about me, and it's a relief to have something else to do.

Helen seems even more wan and pale since the last time I saw her.

"How are you feeling, Helen?" I ask. I don't want to pry, but she's seemed unwell for so long now.

She starts to lift a hand to wave away my question, but then drops her hand down to her side as though even that small movement is too much for her. "Miss Pomeroy says it should be quiet since Mr.

McAulay will not be back this afternoon," she says, ignoring my question completely.

I stand. "Of course. Would you like me to collect the cartridges?"

"I'll get them," she says. "I'll meet you there in a few minutes."

In the supply room I don't let myself be drawn to the view for a daydream, as tempting as that is. Instead, I set up the Dictaphone shavers and then wait by the door so I can hold it open for Helen. When she appears, I help her steer the cart into the room. Her complexion is pale and her arms seem weak, as though pushing the cart over the threshold is too much effort.

Together we pull the cart inside and next to the counter. Helen releases it and leans against the counter as though she might collapse.

"Helen? Are you okay? Is there anything I can do to help?"

A shadow crosses her plain features. She is tidy as usual, but shrunken, as though weighted down. She shakes her head and stares out at me from the dark hollows of her eyes. She stands up again and reaches for a canister. She slides it into the shaver, and I follow suit and slide my own canister in. For several moments the whirring of the machines is the only sound. Once done, Helen hands me her clean canister and I give her another from the cart. In the quiet, she starts to speak, her voice haunted.

"You saw my husband's brother when the taxi drove me home."

I nod. "Yes, I did."

"He takes everything from my husband. Always has. His money, his belongings, his . . ." She stops and slides the canister into place, then finishes in a whisper. "Everything."

My eyes widen. I want to ask more, but Helen gathers a cloak of secrecy around her with a long intake of breath, and I don't know what to say that will reach her. I don't want to intrude on what she holds to herself so closely.

"Miss Pomeroy said not to dawdle and chat," Helen says. Her voice is quiet, but for a moment she's the efficient and practical Helen that I remember. She slides the metal tab into place and pushes her foot down on the lever. The whirring starts up again.

I reach for another canister and begin the process over again myself. We work in silence for the rest of the half hour that it takes to finish the job. Helen does not speak, even as I hold the door for her and she rolls the trolley back down the hall to deliver the clean cartridges back to the account executives' desks, ready for a new day tomorrow.

---

I head back to my desk, to read more *Scientific Advertising* and fret about my date, but Mr. Lewin is waiting for me, his face grim.

"Mr. McAulay wants us to do a run-through tonight. Then tomorrow we'll present it to him. That way he has time to make changes before he delivers it to Eaton's on Monday."

"You're going to start now?" I don't need to look at my watch to know it's almost time to leave. I can't help but wonder if everyone just took shorter lunches, there would not be this need to work in the evenings.

"Yes. Let's get it set up. Sands is on his way."

"Of course," I say, looking at my watch. I am meeting Mr. Hearn at six o'clock; surely that will be plenty of time?

"I've heard that this happens with McAulay, though this is the first time I've seen it," Mr. Lewin says, leading me to the largest boardroom. "He gets terrible jitters when he presents. He'll make us run through it all day tomorrow and maybe even over the weekend. He'll want a live audience too, before the presentation on Monday."

I've been part of the audience for Mr. McAulay's presentations before. It's considered a great treat among the steno girls. But I've never set up a presentation, or helped practice one, and I want to ask whether I will be expected to stay for all of this.

Mr. Lewin hands me a pile of sketches, which he's pasted onto boards. We work in silence, arranging the ladies around the room. A sketch of Daisy in a black evening gown is the cover image—we've called her Sissy. There are also Effie and Rosemarie and the others, a stack of four sketches on each easel.

Mr. Lewin and I sit down across the table from each other. He's got dark circles under his eyes. His voice soft, almost sad, as he starts to talk about each of our ten ladies for the Eaton's spring insert. I try not to look at my watch. Through the wall of windows, I see a secretary cover her typewriter and tidy the papers on her desk.

When Mr. Lewin has run through his part twice, he looks up at me.

"Should I try to find Mr. Sands?" I ask. "Or Mr. McAulay? Do you think they are together?"

Lewin shrugs. "I already called the shooting gallery and the bowling alley. And the cafeteria."

"I could try the barbershop?"

He shakes his head. "He closes at three. Besides, I think it's just Sands that's coming."

The secretary puts on her hat and adjusts it, takes out her lipstick and compact mirror. The clock in the conference room ticks closer to five. Outside, I can't even see the cupola of Saint James Cathedral across the street in the leaden sky. I pat my hair, smooth and polished for once since Mother helped me set it in pin curlers last night and I've somehow managed not to muss it today.

Lewin leans back in his chair, stretches out his legs, and loosens his tie. "McAulay is always unpredictable when he's the lead on a project. It's just better when he leaves things to us." Lewin taps his thumb on the arm of his chair, the rhythm mesmerizing. He shakes his head. "But then . . ."

His voice fades and I finish the sentence for him. "It's his firm?"

Lewin's head snaps up, as though he'd forgotten that I was there. He narrows his eyes at me. "You look different today, Miss Grant. Something special happening?"

It's my turn to sigh. "My sister set me up on a date. A friend of her husband's is in town for work and—"

The conference room phone rings, and I jump up. What am I doing telling Mr. Lewin about my date, anyway? This date I don't even want to go on. "Mr. McAulay's office," I answer automatically. "I mean, conference room. Can I help you?"

"Let me talk to Arthur. Is he there?" It's a woman's voice, rough and plaintive.

"Mr. Lewin? Yes, one moment, please."

Lewin is already on his feet, reaching for the receiver. I step away, but even from my place at the window, overlooking the heavy sky that has blanketed downtown in gray and rain that is turning to sleet, I can hear the wail coming from the other end of the line. I step out of the conference room to give him privacy.

"Miss Grant?" I look up to see Dot, in her coat and hat, leaving for the day with the other girls from steno. "Should we hold the elevator for you?"

The door to the conference room flies open and Lewin rushes past. "Finish up, will you, Miss Grant? He'll come eventually."

"Me? You want me to practice the presentation with McAulay and Sands?"

He shrugs on his coat and hat. "You know it as well as I do. You'll be fine. I've got to go."

Dot looks from me to Lewin, waiting for me to answer. "Hold the elevator for Mr. Lewin," I say.

He pats me on the shoulder. "You'll be great."

———— ❦ ————

I wait for an hour by myself before calling the Mount Royal Hotel to let Mr. Hearn know I will be late. The front desk tells me they have no guest registered under that name, and I don't know what to do. They patch me through to the lobby bar, where we were supposed to meet, but the man that answers the phone is curt and unhelpful.

What will Missie say, after she's gone to so much trouble? And Mother? Mother will not be pleased. And Daisy? At the thought of Daisy's scorn I let out a groan and drop back into my seat at the conference room table.

"Everything all right in here, Miss Grant?"

Mr. Sands leans in the doorway, hands in his trouser pockets, an unpleasant smirk on his face. He saunters into the conference room and closes the door behind him.

"What have we got here?" he asks, sidling up to sketches on their easels. He picks up the first of the ladies. "Ah, of course, Rosemarie. Good idea I had there, naming them, don't you think?"

I press my feet flat on the floor and cement my knees and ankles together at an angle. "Mr. Lewin has been called away. He asked me to wait, to run through the presentation with you and Mr. McAulay."

He flicks the page down, picks up another one. "Effie," he laughs. "Friday at the club. Did you write this?"

I nod. "Mr. Lewin and I worked on that together." I think back to earlier in the week. How simple it seemed, working quietly next to Mr. Lewin. Sands nowhere to be found.

"And of course the lovely Sissy on the cover." He picks up the cover board—a close-up sketch of a woman in a black evening gown that has a deep V in the back. She's looking over her shoulder and smiling. It's unmistakably Daisy. "Is that why you named her Sissy? Because she's your sister?"

I shake my head. "I—I didn't think of that."

"You didn't. I see." He circles around, lifts one pant leg up at the knee, and half sits on the conference room table, so close I can smell the soapy musk of his hair cream. He slams his hand down and leans toward me, his onion breath in my face. "But you did tell Mr. Lewin, right? When you were working so closely together, that this model is your sister?" He rubs his hands together, and I cringe at the sound of skin brushing against skin so close to me. "I thought there was something familiar about her. I met her at a dinner once, when I first started here. Back before Collier absconded."

"You knew all along?"

"I suspected. I didn't know for sure. Until I got myself invited to the party, that is."

Again I shake my head. I push my chair back and stand, taking several steps away from him. My voice still shaky, I ask: "Did you tell Mr. Lewin or Mr. McAulay about Daisy's connection to Collier and Moore? About going to their party? Did you tell Geoff about Daisy modeling?"

He's sitting fully on the table now, leaning back on his hands as though this is all fun for him. "A pointer for you, Miss Goody Two-Shoes: you only tell what you know when it works in your favor."

I go to the front of the room and start collecting the ladies into a neat stack. Lianne, Bridget, Grace. I've just picked up Deirdre when he slams his hand down again.

"Give them to me. I'll take things from here."

"But Mr. Lewin said—"

He drops his head back and laughs. "Oh, Mr. Lewin said, did he? What did he say? That you've got talent? You're a natural? I can only imagine."

He holds his hand out for the boards, and I, trained so well in doing what I'm told, hand them to him.

"I think we can all agree that you are a natural stenographer, Miss Grant." He straightens the papers on the desk and adds them to the boards that I handed over to him. "Miss Pomeroy says you are one of the very best, and I think we can agree that Miss Pomeroy's standards are very high, yes?"

At last, a question I feel I can safely answer. "Yes," I say. There is no denying that Miss Pomeroy's standards are very high.

"Good." He holds the stack out, as though to hand it to me. When I reach for it, he pulls his hand back. "No, you don't. I'll look after Eaton's from here. Back to steno with you. Understood?"

He doesn't wait for my answer. In the silence he leaves behind, I hear the clock ticking again. It's half past six and I am late for my meeting with Mr. Hearn.

———— ⊱❦⊰ ————

I will never mention to anyone what happened that night. Who would want to hear about the shame of a girl like me? A girl who goes to the lobby bar at the Mount Royal Hotel—by herself!—arriving almost an hour late. A girl who hides among the potted palms under the rotunda, hoping to spot someone that looks like a Mr. Hearn from Philadelphia, a colleague of her brother-in-law, in town on business. A pity date, no doubt, set up by her much prettier sister.

"Can I help you, Miss?" A waiter in uniform spots me between the palm fronds.

"I was supposed to meet someone. A man. Mr. Hearn? From Philadelphia?"

"With the General Motors group? They left for El Morocco a while ago, Miss. Will you join them there? Shall I call you a taxi?"

"El Morocco?" I shake my head, my cheeks burning. What kind of girl would take a taxi, alone, to a club?

"Are you sure I can't call you a taxi?"

My mouth is so dry I cannot speak. Instead, I rush out, sliding through the slush on Peel Street to the streetcar stop at the corner of Saint Catherine.

I am home now, huddled over my typewriter in my room, with a cup of weak tea to keep warm. Mother has turned off the heat completely, since it is raining now and it seems spring has arrived. She's settled the little boys on makeshift beds in the kitchen to keep them warm. I promised I would change my clothes and come down and tell her about my date, but surely I can go to sleep now? This day has been long enough, and I need to get under the covers. The air in my room is even colder than the outdoors.

# Chapter Twenty-Two

Mr. Sands said I was to go back to steno, but Mr. Lewin asked for me all week, and there's still one day left in this week, so I walk straight to the desk outside Mr. McAulay's office, where I plan to stay until I'm told otherwise.

Mr. McAulay is already there, along with Mr. Lewin.

"There you are, Miss Grant. Where is the Eaton's campaign?" Mr. McAulay's normally calm eyes are looking panicked. He's not been to the barber in a few days; stray whiskers escape his nose and ears, giving him a wild look.

Whatever it was that called Mr. Lewin away yesterday evening seems also to have kept him up all night. "I told him you must have put it away for safekeeping. Isn't that right, Miss Grant?"

"I—I gave it to Mr. Sands. He insisted." I stumble out the words.

"Ah. Sands," McAulay says. "Where is Sands? That fellow is never around when you need him."

"He called in with the flu," Lewin says. "Should I go see him at home?"

"Yes. And hurry. How am I supposed to deliver a presentation on Monday on a campaign I haven't even seen? What if I want changes?"

Lewin won't be flustered. "I can deliver it. For all that, so can Miss Grant. It's ready, Sir. You won't be disappointed."

The phone rings, drowning out Mr. McAulay's reply. "Mr. McAulay's office," I answer.

"June? Is that you? It's me, Ted Hearn. I understand you arrived after I left? I wanted to wait, but the others—well, we're a whole crew here."

I look up to the other two, quiet now, listening. "It's all right, I understand."

"Will you give me another chance?"

"Yes. I'd like that very much," I say. I look up to see whether Mr. McAulay and Mr. Lewin are still watching me.

"Let's try again, shall we? Tonight, five thirty? Same place?"

"Five thirty at the Mount Royal," I repeat. "See you there."

I hang up, and Mr. McAulay coughs. "Arranging your social calendar, Miss Grant?"

"Yes, Sir. Sorry, Sir," I stammer. The familiar heat spreads over my chest and neck and cheeks, and I start to sweat. Paired with the ever-present anxiety in the pit of my stomach, I wonder if I am going to have to rush away to the ladies' room, but then Mr. Lewin steps in.

"Surely you don't begrudge Miss Grant a little Friday evening fun? She's been such a help this week on the Eaton's account."

Mr. McAulay makes a grumbling sound that Lewin takes for assent.

"Good. I'll go track down that presentation," Mr. Lewin says, looking at his watch. "I'll be back before you're done with your morning commitments."

I smile down at my typewriter at this. I know what Mr. Lewin is really saying—that Mr. McAulay has time to go to the barber now.

———— ⁊⁊ ————

When Mr. McAulay comes back from the barber, and Mr. Lewin comes back empty-handed an hour later, it's Miss Pomeroy who steps in. She sends Lewin to find some early sketches and paste them onto new boards. She sends me to retype the copy as best I can, from an earlier version. She sits with Mr. McAulay and speaks to him calmly, and, when the props are ready, has Mr. Lewin and me walk him through the presentation.

We spend the afternoon in the boardroom, as McAulay runs through the campaign, line by line, stopping every minute to ask Lewin's opinion, to change a word, or to ask me to try calling Mr. Sands again. Miss Pomeroy stays the entire time and does nothing more than nod, calmly, when he looks her way.

For the last hour of the day, Miss Pomeroy calls the steno girls and the secretaries in and has them sit around the table. Marie-Céleste slides into the empty seat next to me and whispers, "See? I told you he needs to be surrounded by pretty girls." And in a way she is right. The presence of the secretaries and stenographers seems to ease the tension that Mr. McAulay has held tight all day.

Each time he finishes part of the presentation I clap and smile along with the other girls. And at the end of the day, I file out right on time, just another girl from the steno pool.

―――― ⁓⁓ ――――

When I dressed this morning, I did not know I'd be going on a date. I smooth my rough wool skirt as best I can as I follow the maître d' through to the center of the cocktail lounge.

"Would you like a drink while you wait, Miss?"

I remember Missie's story of the train to New York where she met her husband. He invited her to the bar car, and she asked for the same drink that the lady at the next table was having—a pink lady.

I order one of those.

There's a jazz trio playing, but I can't really hear the music over the laughter and chatter at the tables all around me. I look up at the white marble columns to the second-floor mezzanine. With all the greenery it feels like being inside a colonial courtyard in India or Kenya. I imagine girls in white dresses, daughters of colonels and ambassadors, twirling parasols to keep their skin from browning.

"Here you are, Miss."

I am surprised to see the waiter back so soon, so engaged was I in my daydream. He places a champagne coupe in front of me, a maraschino cherry floating at its pink and frothy center. He bows before he leaves. I am eager to return to my daydream, but when I look around the image is spoiled by the drudgery of winter coats, piled on the backs of chairs and filling the room with a damp smell.

I touch the drink to my lips and taste foam and red fruit and a bright sharp taste that must be the gin. I take a tiny sip and try not to make a face.

A man at the next table stands up and flings his arms out wide. The rest of his party erupts in applause and he holds his loosened necktie to his chest as he takes a deep bow. On his way back up he looks over to me, as though he can sense me watching, and winks. I put my drink back down and stare hard at the inlaid woodwork of the circular table.

"Miss Grant, is it?" I look up, expecting to see Mr. Hearn at last, but instead it is a clerk in front desk uniform, holding a slip of paper. "A telephone message for you." He hands me the white paper rectangle and then ducks away.

*Can't get away. Sorry. Leaving tomorrow. Maybe next time? Ted Hearn.*

I look down at my drink. A pink lady? What was I thinking? I should have ordered water while I waited. How much does a pink lady cost? Do I have enough money in my purse? Will I have to beg off and promise to come back tomorrow with the money?

The man at the next table is still standing, still watching me. He steps over. "Did you get stood up?" His words are slurred. He sways as he points to the message slip in my hand. "Come on, sit with us! Bring your drink!"

I am about to say yes—what choice do I have?—when a voice over my shoulder, strong and clear, says, "None of that now. Off you go." A voice I easily recognize.

"Mr. Lewin! What are you doing here?"

He drops his coat on the back of the chair and sits across from me, points to the message. "He called the office first."

The waiter appears out of nowhere. "What can I get you, Sir?"

"A glass of beer, please."

"Yes, Sir. Mr. Hearn, is it? And will you still be moving over to the restaurant for supper? Shall I push your reservation back a bit?"

"Sure, why not? Let's have dinner, shall we?"

I sip my drink and grimace again at the taste.

"How is your drink, Miss?"

I stare at the table. "It doesn't taste how I thought it would."

"Take it away, will you?" Lewin asks. "What would you like instead?"

I look up at him. His voice and eyes are kind. "A sherry?"

"Sherry it is," he says as the waiter whisks away the champagne coupe.

"Now, Miss Grant, what shall we discuss?" Lewin asks once the waiter is gone. "It's been a long time since I was on a date, even a pretend one. I will take your lead."

It was not a real date, I remind myself when I get home and snuggle under my quilt in the dormer window. My fingers are frozen, because, although the temperatures have plummeted yet again, Mother is holding out for an early spring and refuses to use up the last bit of heating oil by turning up the heat.

The sherry must have loosened my tongue. That, combined with Mr. Lewin's kind and calm demeanor. "Order anything you like," he said. "I can expense it. Surely it's only fair that McAulay buys us dinner after what he put us through today?"

Oh, I cringe when I think of it now. One glass of sherry and by the time the lobster bisque arrived (Lewin ordered for both of us) the words tumbled out of me. Father's stroke and Mother letting our maid, Christine, go, the move to Abbott Street and Missie getting married and moving away. And Daisy. Daisy and her boys. Daisy and Geoff. Daisy and modeling.

When I finished telling him about the modeling agency, Lewin takes the last bite of his chicken Kiev and tucks his cutlery in the four o'clock position. I look down at my own plate, my chicken untouched. I look around at the grand dining room, the enormous tapestries on the walls, velvet curtains, darkly veined marble, as though seeing it all for the first time.

Seeing my discomfort, Mr. Lewin, kind Mr. Lewin, starts to talk. As I eat my meal, he tells me the story of his morning. The wasted effort of the matzo ball soup to ease Mr. Sands's flu symptoms, which he went all the way to Saint Laurent Boulevard to pick up in a taxi, only to find the man not home.

And I stay silent. That was the moment I should have spoken up, about Mr. Sands at Geoff and Daisy's party. I should have said something then, but I didn't.

It was not a real date, I remind myself. But this feeling I have, this effervescent sparkle? A lifting through my diaphragm, where I normally slouch down to hide my height. This feeling of hopefulness?

Is this how normal girls feel after a nice date?

I know it was not a real date. Mr. Lewin is married, after all. But the feeling is nice. Nicer than I normally feel. Like I have a secret, a happy secret. I savor it as I fall asleep.

# Chapter Twenty-Three

My mind is a jumble of questions and worries as I slip out for my Saturday walk, soon after breakfast. Almost without thinking, I retrace my steps of a few weeks ago—along Saint Catherine to Greene Avenue—and this time, when I reach the railway bridge, I don't stop. Instead, I take a deep breath, as though diving underwater, and walk under the bridge.

It's clear I'm not in Westmount anymore, but at first I'm not sure why. The slopes are the same, as are the brick houses, but after half a block the subtle changes show themselves. The houses cower together, closer to the road. Plain lintels hang above unadorned doors. Each step takes me farther into this unknown land. Now there are no spaces between the houses, where curved metal banisters lead to second- and third-story dwellings. Here there are no landings, just plain front doors that open directly onto the sidewalk.

Three boys bounce a ball against the gray brick wall of a three-story walk-up. I want to warn them to stop before they break the front window, but their easy banter sounds nothing like the convent school French I learned. They fall silent as I pass.

Saint Jacques is busy with cars and Saturday morning shoppers. Women in small clusters, their hair tied with headscarves. A group of men outside a diner, smoking. I drop my gaze down to the sidewalk and keep walking. At the sound of steps behind me, I tense my shoulders and plow ahead, sure that someone will stop me. It is a relief to reach the store beneath Abbie's studio, where signs plaster the window—Bière, Cigarettes, Lait, Pepsi.

Halfway up the stairs I wonder what I will do if Abbie is not there, but I can hear her humming as I knock on the door. She lets me in, dressed in trousers and a plain sweater, her hair tied back in a bright-green scarf.

"June! What a surprise." She gives me a quick hug. "You are just in time for coffee. Sit, sit."

She gestures to the divan and returns to a table in one corner where she fusses with a metal espresso maker on a hot plate. I lay my coat over the divan but, rather than sit down, I circle the studio to take in all the changes. The rack of dress-up clothing has expanded to take up a full corner of the room.

"Edward has hired me the most brilliant instructor. Of course he's as old as my grandfather—*can't have you falling in love with your photography instructor,* is what Edward said. And see?" She is pointing to a console table next to the door to the windowless room. "Yesterday we set up a darkroom in there. It's all fascinating. We developed those prints together, and today I'm going to try to do most of it myself. Mr. Wilson will stand by and watch."

I pick up the first envelope and flip through the two-inch-square photographs inside without touching them. "Why, Abbie," I say. "These are wonderful." The pictures are mostly of children—I recognize several of the boys that followed us to the jazz club—was that only a week ago? White children and Black, individually and in small groups.

"Did you dress them like this?" I ask.

"Oh no, they chose their own costumes. I asked them what they wanted to be, and one of them said, 'Pirates,' and then they were off. The girls dressed the boys and then themselves. Then they each decided on their character and became the role, and I took their pictures."

I've stopped at one group photo. The girls are sitting on the divan, white blouses and pinafores and scarves and belts creatively tied around their waists and holding up their hair. They stare at the camera, fierce maidens, except for one who stares out the window as though lost in a daydream. The boys crowd around them in torn pants, white blousons, smudged railway coal on their cheeks, headscarves as belts and broomsticks as swords, their gazes frank and clear.

"My first series," Abbie says, at my elbow now.

"Abbie, it's really something."

She hands me a tiny espresso mug. "Here," she says. "Only one option for coffee with a bohemian—black and strong."

I laugh and take the cup from her; watch as she gulps hers back.

"Abbie," I say. "Really, these are striking. What are you going to do with them?"

She shrugs. "Give them away? Nothing? I don't know. Here." She tugs one of the pictures from another envelope and hands it to me. "This one is for you."

It's the picture she took of me on my last visit. The bright orange of the turned-up blouse collar comes across as serious gray in the black-and-white photograph. I'm wearing a men's hat at an angle. You can't see my hair at all, and I'm staring directly at the camera.

"I look like a man," I say.

Abbie nods. "A very handsome man." We're quiet for a moment, then she laughs. "You should have seen Mr. Wilson when this one was developing. He told me it wasn't proper to entertain men here by myself and the next time I want to take photos of a man I must have a chaperone."

I have a hard time tearing my eyes away. In most pictures, I look like a person who will do anything to escape my own skin, but here I look like a real somebody. A person of substance, not bothered by having my photo taken or by anything else besides. I hand it back to Abbie.

"No, no. Keep it," she says. "Now tell me about everything that happened at McAulay's this week. Everything."

She nestles into the divan and, while she's not looking, I slip the picture back in its envelope on the table. I don't want to keep it, though if she asked me why, I would not know what to say. I take up my mug of coffee, and joining her on the divan, tell her everything I can think of—working late on the Eaton's campaign, Miss Pomeroy's face when Mr. Lewin said he needed me all week, Mr. Sands—first at Daisy and Geoff's party, and then disappearing with the boards.

"Oh, June. That doesn't sound good."

"I know. But if I say anything, it could be worse for me. I'm the one related to Geoff, though Mr. McAulay seems to have forgotten, if he ever knew. And I was at the party too."

"Maybe Mr. McAulay will finally realize about Mr. Sands," Abbie says. "He's always sneaking around, disappearing places, not being in his office when he's supposed to be."

"Is that true? I never noticed before this week."

"That's because you're good, June. You don't see the bad in people."

I shake my head. I don't think what she's said is true at all—I see plenty of bad in Daisy. "But why? What would he be doing?"

Abbie drops her head back dramatically on the back of the divan. "Oh, June. He's trying to get information and use it—trade it or share it or gather it to use later—so he can get what he wants. Sometimes, I think it's all a big game of war or spies, or, or . . ."—she waves a hand in the air toward the console table—"or pirates for them. They can't help themselves."

I'm surprised at the anger in her voice. "It's not a game for me," I say.

She reaches out and takes my hand. "I know, June. I know it's not."

"The thing is, I do think Geoff might be up to something." I tell her about the list of McAulay clients on his blotter.

"Do you think he's trying to poach clients?"

"I really don't know."

She squeezes my hand and looks serious. "You'll simply need to stand up for yourself, or you'll get bruised up on the sidelines of some silly men's game," she says.

"But how do I do that? And not lose my job? I'm not you, Abbie."

"You don't need to be like me. Just say something. Say anything. Don't let them elbow you out of the way in their attempts to one-up each other," she says. The windows shudder in their frames and the street door slams. "Oh, here's Mr. Wilson."

I jump up and grab my coat.

"I would invite you to stay, but I'm sure it will be awfully boring for you." She hugs me again.

"No, it's fine, I should get back and help Mother. Thank you for the coffee."

Mr. Wilson, a tidy man in tweed and heavy glasses, nods and wishes me good morning and then presses up against the wall so I can pass him on the stairs.

Saint Jacques is busier now, and I duck my head and try to blend into the crowd. Walking briskly, it only takes fifteen minutes to reach Greene Avenue and cross under the bridge, back to my own world.

# Chapter Twenty-Four

"Looks delicious, Mother." Geoff is using his adman voice, like he's trying to sell us all on the Sunday luncheon we are going to eat anyway. He takes up the silver carving fork and stabs twice before piercing the breast of the shriveled roast chicken.

I'm to serve the cold potatoes and waxy carrots. Thankfully there's plenty of gravy.

"Monsignor McDonagh asked about you at Mass, Daisy," says Mother.

"Of course he did." Daisy has dark circles under her eyes, and her makeup looks like Steve drew it on. Or, more likely, that she drew it on last night and then patched it up this morning when she woke up just in time for lunch. Her voice is guttural and indistinct as Father's when he tries to speak.

"Well, I don't see why he wouldn't. It's his duty, after all, the care of our eternal souls."

"I told you, I've been going to Saint Malachy's. It's closer." She looks to Geoff, who nods.

"Right by the shops," he says. "Daisy can go to confession and be home in time to make supper."

I tilt my head up, scoop of potatoes midair, and look at Geoff, whose face is as placid and smiling as ever. And yet surely he's lying? Or does he simply believe that he's telling the truth? Mother has fed the little boys supper every night this week while Daisy has gone off in taxis. Off to meet Geoff, to help him with a big account. Or so she says. She hasn't cooked supper for her family once, or gone to the shops on Queen Mary Road, let alone to Saint Malachy's for confession.

It's as though Geoff knows how each person wants to appear, and then he treats them as though they already are that way. That's his gift. He treats Mother like she's still a great lady overseeing a fine house. Daisy, like a spirited flower who's thriving in the role of housewife. Father, the old patriarch fallen on hard times. And me—he has a way of including me, even though most of the time I'm convinced I'm an outsider in my own family.

"So, June, I hear you're working on the Eaton's spring insert for the *Gazette*. How's that coming along?" Geoff asks.

My thoughts race—How does Geoff know about the insert? From Sands? Could it be from Daisy?—as I reach for the plate that Mother hands me but don't grasp onto it, looking at Geoff instead.

"June, serve the vegetables, dear," Mother says.

I take the plate and lump the potatoes and carrots onto it and hand it over to Chris, still not sure how to answer Geoff. It's a relief when he keeps talking.

"I'm surprised McAulay opted for sketches. He should get with the times. We're moving all our fashion clients to photography. Why do you think that is, June?"

I want to ask if he's seen the sketches, but instead I hand Mother her plate; she insists on being served last, and even then will feed Father his meal before she touches her own. I can feel Geoff's eyes on me, waiting for my answer.

"Something to do with the research," I say. "I was mostly retyping the copy, over and over, for Mr. Sands." I try to look at him but I can feel the blush starting to rise at my own lie, along with that familiar sensation: anger. I want to yell at him to stop asking me questions. To stop his games. Doesn't he know I could lose my job? And what then?

"Daisy says you have a big new account, Geoff," Mother says.

"Yes, did she tell you? A cosmetic company called Derny." He pauses from cutting Steve's meat to smile over at Daisy. "Think of all the money we'll save on cosmetics, right, Daisy?"

Daisy's chuckle is so deep it sounds more like a cough. "What you need is a department store."

"Working on that." He winks at me as he says it. "But my plans will take time. We need to be patient, don't we, my dear?" He points his fork at Daisy as he says this. "Daisy misses all the free clothes from her modeling days. She thinks that if Collier and Moore had a department store client she'd have all the latest styles."

"Eaton's," Daisy says. "I want Eaton's." She's pushed her plate away and plays with a cigarette. "You promised me."

"Yes, well." Geoff shifts in his seat. "We both know that McAulay has Eaton's, for now at least. Like I said, it's going to take some time."

Daisy pulls a face as though she's a child. "What if I'm tired of waiting?"

Mother is focused on feeding Father his lunch and does not pick up on the tightening in the air around us. Chris has his head down, trying to cut the tough meat on his own, but Stephen, like me, has his eyes fixed on Daisy.

She wrinkles her nose, and again I'm amazed at how unpleasant she can make her otherwise attractive face. "What if I already took matters into my own hands? What if I went back to modeling? Why don't you tell him, June? Tell him! You've been dying to!"

Geoff won't be ruffled. "Did you think I didn't find out about that? We said, no more modeling. A man has his pride. Doesn't want his wife's face in every mailbox in town, even if it is just a sketch. What would people think?"

Daisy's chair back cracks against the gold-painted portrait frame as she stands up. She's pinned in place and can't get out unless Mother rolls Father's chair out of the way.

"Sit down, Daisy," Geoff says, his voice so placid it's almost eerie. "It's all over. When June gets to the office tomorrow morning, she'll find that I've looked after it."

Mother pauses with a forkful of chicken midair and, barely turning to Daisy, raises one eyebrow. "Lunch is not finished, Daisy."

But Daisy won't be stopped. She drops to the ground, crawls under the table, and squeezes out between my chair and Mother's. She stands and tugs her skirt back down, then turns to Geoff, her eyes murderous. "I wouldn't have to model if you'd kept your promise." She rushes outside without a coat, slamming the door behind her.

For a moment, everything is still.

Then Mother jumps up to roll Father's chair out of the way. "Daisy's not feeling herself today," she says.

"I'd best get her home. You're right, she's not herself," Geoff says, inching his way across Daisy's chair while gesturing to the boys to follow suit. "Thanks for lunch, Blanche. Delicious as always." He kisses Mother on the cheek as the boys grab their coats from their hooks and scamper out the door, all before I have a chance to get up from my seat.

---

Mother tips her head back in her armchair in the sitting room. Eyes closed, there's a pained expression on her face. She's rolled Father next to her as though he's in his own armchair. He stares straight ahead, and I wonder if the unpleasantness of lunch registered with him at all. Daisy seems to be getting worse, but I know Mother will refuse to talk about it. I clear the dishes as silently as I can, trying to make sense of Geoff and Daisy's exchange.

Before they were married, Geoff used to promise Daisy that she would never have to model again; he'd buy her all the new clothes she wanted. We heard him say it so many times, he sold the whole family on the idea. No one expected his parents, who'd never approved of

Daisy, to follow through on their threat to cut Geoff off from the family fortune if he married her. The truth only sank in when the ceremony started and the groom's side of the church remained empty. I am sure Daisy thought she could win them over eventually with her charm, or maybe with her children, but that hasn't happened.

There were whispers then, about Daisy. And the constant worry since: What if Geoff gets fed up? With Daisy. With working so hard. With being an outcast from his own family, and their fortune?

# Chapter Twenty-Five

Miss Pomeroy blocks my entrance to the conference room. She's wearing her brown suit and her "don't try that with me" face.

"You're needed back in steno, Miss Grant."

"But Mr. Lewin—" I look over her shoulder to where Mr. Lewin is waiting for Marie-Céleste to serve him coffee. Mr. Sands and Mr. McAulay are next to the panels at the front of the room.

"Mr. Lewin is not in charge of the steno pool, Miss Grant. I am." She crosses her arms and blocks the door, but I can still see over her shoulder, to the panels. They are the original sketches that were missing on Friday, except Sissy now has blonde ringlets and a heart-shaped mouth. Daisy's face has been erased completely from the sketch.

I look again to Mr. Lewin—the new sketch is in his unmistakable style—but when I catch his eye, he looks away.

"But do you know about Mr. Sands? He's trying to steal clients away." I hear the desperation in my own voice. Mr. Lewin has turned his back to me. Miss Pomeroy tilts her head and gives me a pitying look.

"I warned you, Miss Grant. Didn't I?" Her voice is low, coaxing. She puts her hands on my shoulders and turns me away from the conference room. "Back to steno, before you make a spectacle of yourself."

She closes the door and steers me in the direction of the steno office, staying right behind me the whole way to make sure I get there.

--- ୧୬୬୦ ---

I spend the day typing up letters in triplicate, and I don't make one mistake. After a while, if I don't look up or talk to them, the girls lose their curiosity and stop asking what happened and why Marie-Céleste is with Mr. McAulay now. Instead, they wonder whether Grace, one of the new girls, is trying to hide her crooked teeth by not smiling fully.

There's another new girl too—Dot—who has a date with one of the lawyers from the firm on the twentieth floor. She spends every spare moment looking through catalogs for the perfect going-away outfits for after her wedding.

The steno girls are all saying that Marie-Céleste went on a date last night, and I wonder if it was with Mr. Sands. I suppose she too will get married in time, but surely not to him? Helen, gray-faced and silent, will no doubt give her notice soon. Even the new girl, Grace of the possibly crooked teeth, is bound to get married eventually. They will all go and be replaced by ever-younger versions of themselves, and I will be left here with Miss Pomeroy and the men.

"Miss Grant?"

Miss Pomeroy's sharp tone brings me back to attention. "I'm sorry," I say. "I was lost in my thoughts."

She coughs. "There's nothing you need to think about, Miss Grant. Just type. Thinking will only get you into trouble, won't it?"

"Yes, Miss Pomeroy." I look down to the contract before me. The summer ads for Elizabeth Arden in the *Gazette*. I slow down and pay closer attention, so I don't transpose the numbers. If any thoughts come up I will send them away with one push of the carriage release lever and start again, mind blank, on the next row of letters and words.

# Chapter Twenty-Six

I spend the whole week typing contracts, without looking up, without speaking to any of the girls. I have been thoroughly punished, and the end of Friday comes as a relief.

I take the Saint Catherine streetcar straight home. I don't take the prettier route home along Sherbrooke. I don't get off a few stops early to whisper encouragement to the daffodils in Westmount Park. I know they are there, under the snow, waiting. The promise of early spring is gone now, swept away by cold wind and replaced with a frigid, unmoving mass of air.

"You're home early." Mother greets me at the door. I do not tell her the details, but she's pleased I'm back in steno, safe under Miss Pomeroy's watchful eye. I don't tell her I'd be home at this time every day if I didn't daydream on the way home.

"Would you like me to go to the store?"

"No, I went already." She takes my coat and hangs it up for me.

"Are the boys here?"

"No, Daisy has them. And she's cooking dinner. She even called for the brown sauce recipe."

She leads me into the sitting room, to the armchair that is squashed up against the wall. It is like sitting on a block of ice.

"How is she? Is she feeling better?"

"Daisy? Oh, she's fine. It was just one of her spells. You know how she is." I want to say her spells are coming more often, but I know that Mother will only change the subject.

"And Father?"

She shakes her head. "He's having a lie-down, but don't you worry about him. Can I make you a cup of tea? Or even, would you like a sherry?"

It's rare that she has no one to fuss over, and I let her fuss over me. I take the tiny cut-crystal glass of sherry and sort the mail.

"Do you think we might call for more heating oil?" I ask. "It looks like spring won't be here for a while yet."

"Let's try to manage, shall we? Stay warm as best we can? You need a new coat and hat. Let's wait." Mother sits across from me on the smaller armchair, just like she used to when Father came home from work. She has her own glass of sherry and a cigarette that she hasn't lit. The spaniels have followed her into the room and flopped at her feet.

"Do you want to do some writing before supper? Or shall we eat now?"

*Writing before supper.* Was it only a few weeks ago that I rushed home to turn my thoughts into poems before they escaped? It seems like worlds away.

"I'm very tired today, Mother. Let's eat early if you don't mind, then I might go to my room and read." Even as I say it I know that I will sleep, not read. I'd sleep all the way until Monday morning if I could. Sleep and forget. Wake up and then type in triplicate again. Pay the rent. Stay within the tracks laid out for me.

"I'll go wash my hands, then I'll come help feed Father his dinner."

Mother nods and leaves me in the room, lit only by a small lamp in the corner. Outside, a train passes on the tracks. I listen to the comforting rattle of the windows and wait for the toot of the horn as it crosses over Glen Road toward Westmount Station, same as it does every single night at this very time.

—— ⁓⁓⁓ ——

Saturday stretches before me with no plans. Abbie's parents have kindly sent Christine to help Mother today. I can hear them chatting in the kitchen like two old friends, happy to be together. When we lived on Côte Saint Antoine, Mother never had any reason to go into the kitchen, let alone sit in there. The kitchen was Christine's domain. The two would have tea together, midmorning in the sunroom, and plan the evening meal, but it was a much more formal encounter, nothing like what I see before me now.

Mother drinks her coffee at the table while Christine is at the sink, washing the delicates. Together they have strung up the clothesline that crisscrosses the kitchen. Both have their winter coats on against the cold.

I hesitate in the doorway—it feels as though I would be intruding to cross the threshold. Mother's fine silk underthings hang like flags on a sideways mast between us. Father is with them, his wheelchair in the circle of warmth from the simmering soup on the stove and the steam from a massive pot of boiling laundry. Already in my coat, I slip out the door without saying goodbye.

I set out toward Abbie's studio without consciously thinking about it. I walk right past Epicerie Lublin and along Saint Catherine, and when I get to Greene Avenue I don't even pause. Instead I turn and head south, downhill, and under the train bridge. By now I know the invisible barrier, the one that I imagined held me in place, exists only in my mind. There is no force that keeps me, an English-speaking girl from Westmount, from crossing into Saint Henri.

I pick up my pace, hoping that will warm my frozen feet.

Saint Jacques bustles with people despite the cold. There's none of the magical light of the golden hour that I saw in the taxi ride when I visited Abbie after work. Only ordinary people, bundled against the cold. Gray stone, brown brick, painted wood buildings dusted with coal, create a backdrop for a neighborhood teeming with life. Even the greened copper cupolas of Saint Cunigunde are dulled by the winter sky.

It doesn't take long to reach Abbie's studio. I side-slide around the cardboard boxes and up the steps.

"Abbie?" I call. The door falls open. Costume clothing covers the divan, and every available surface, and even some of the floor, is littered with lipstick-stained glasses, beer bottles, and overly full ashtrays. It smells like a billiard hall. I step inside and close the door behind me.

The console table is scattered with photos of young children, not in costume this time, just as themselves, their clear gazes startling. There's also a picture of François sitting on the divan with his bandmates behind him holding their instruments.

There's a quality to the pictures, something I can't quite name. *Frankness* is the word that comes to mind. Like Abbie has seen behind what the person looks like to who that person is, and by showing that, the person viewing the picture feels like they are seen too. The envelope with the photo of me in it is still there.

I normally hate to see photos of myself; really there have been so few. The pictures of Daisy's wedding, for example, make me cringe. Only fourteen, I towered over the rest of the wedding party. Daisy would have much preferred to have her bridesmaids all the same height; Mother was the one who insisted I not be left out. In every picture I'm looking in the wrong direction—at the other girls, at Missie, at Daisy—wishing I could be pretty like them.

In this picture, I'm not pretty. I'm strong and mysterious. And capable.

"Hello? Miss Abbie?" A key jingles in the door and it falls open, unlocked as it is. A woman stands there, her head wrapped in a brightly colored scarf; she's stooped forward from the weight of carrying a mop and broom and bucket and other cleaning supplies up the stairs. She steps back when she sees me.

"Miss Abbie not here?" she asks.

I shake my head. "I just dropped by, but she's not here."

"Wednesdays and Saturdays I come and clean," she says, stepping around me and putting the bucket down.

"I'll get out of your way," I say.

I navigate the stairs back down to the street and head farther east to the old mansion that houses Le Salon du Jazz. The front doors stand open and the sound of piano music draws me inside. The club is deserted except for François on stage at the piano. His fingers caress the keys as he plays Beethoven's *Moonlight Sonata*—music I recognize. There's a sadness in his rendition, almost dirgelike, that is familiar to me too.

He sees me but doesn't stop playing. He appears taller here, not the hesitant clerk from Epicerie Lublin or the young boy helping his father in our garden at the Côte Saint Antoine house.

"Miss Grant, you made it finally," he says when the echo of notes has stopped and he drops his hands into his lap.

"Yes, I got the note with this address on it. That was you, wasn't it?"

"Yes," he replies.

"Why just the address? I wasn't sure—"

"Mr. Lublin doesn't want me to bother the customers, and your mother—I'll always see her as Mrs. Grant, as she was when my father worked for her. But I had to find a way to tell someone."

"About Daisy?"

The self-effacing manner creeps over his face again. "Yes, I thought your family—your mother—would not want any . . ." His voice fades.

"Yes?" I ask.

He shrugs. "Any more upsets. With your father being so ill and all."

"Any more upsets?"

"I was worried. That it might be like last time."

"I'm sorry, I don't know what you mean."

He hesitates then, and I see the uncertainty come back.

"Please, François. I need to know, so I can help Daisy."

"It was a long time ago, when your family was still in the old house. I was eleven, twelve maybe? There'd been a big snowfall overnight. First snow of the winter. My father had so many driveways to clear that he got me to help. We started before dawn."

"I remember the snow that year—1937. The year of Daisy's debutante ball. I was twelve, too," I say, wondering that François and I are the same age. I'd always thought he was older than me.

"The Grant house—your house—was at the top of the street, so was first on our list."

"I didn't know you did the shoveling in the winter."

He runs his fingers along a few keys, a light melody I don't recognize. "We were usually done before anyone woke up. But that day, even though it was still full dark, all the lights were on at your house. And the sound, we could hear it from the street."

"What sound?" I ask.

He glances at me quickly, then back at the keys. Runs his fingers down to a lower octave and starts to crash out a minor chord. He lifts his hands and, as the notes echo away into the silence, he looks right into my eyes. "I've never heard anything like it. Not before, or since."

"Daisy," I say.

He nods. "We didn't have time to gawk. We needed to clear the snow for the ambulance that was coming up the hill. But I did see her when they took her out—just a glimpse. Arms strapped behind her back."

He pauses, shakes his head. "Her eyes—she looked right at me—like she was pleading for me to help her." He plays the opening chords of the *Moonlight Sonata* again.

I drop my hand from where it's been covering my mouth. "Mother always told me she went to the country, for a rest."

"Well, Miss, I don't know where the ambulance went. It might have been to the country."

I take a deep breath and let it out in a shaky sigh. "That's why you wrote the note?"

"Yes, Miss." He lifts his fingers so they are paused over the piano keys. I recognize the impatience in the movement; it's the same position I take when Marie-Céleste interrupts me when I'm typing. "I keep seeing her here, with that same wild look in her eye. I thought maybe I could help her now." He plays a chord. "Sorry, Miss. It's just that I only have a short time to practice."

"I'm sorry," I say. "I won't keep you. Thank you. For telling me. I'll look after it from here."

"Are you okay to walk, Miss? Would you like me to call you a taxi?"

"I can walk. It's not far at all," I say. My surprise at the short distance is obvious in my voice.

"It's true, Miss Grant. It's really not far at all," François says, and returns to his practice.

# Chapter Twenty-Seven

Mother saves a whole row at Mass for Daisy, Geoff, and the boys. She looks back, waiting for them to appear, and I want to ask, Why? Why, Mother? Why always Daisy?

But I know why. In the early years of their marriage, Daisy and Geoff made a point of attending Mass on Mothering Sunday. They'd buy a simnel cake from the National Food Shop. Somewhere between the war and the end of the war, between Geoff leaving McAulay's and starting out on his own, and between Daisy's ever-changing moods, the tradition got dropped, but Mother is ever hopeful.

Mother finally relents and allows another family to join us, and I can feel her disappointment and worry like a vibration between us.

Monsignor McDonagh reviews the seven deadly sins in his sermon. When he says that envy is the most joyless of states, a rejection of God's gifts, I feel a hot stab of shame and rage in my belly. I feel it again now, back in my room, where I am writing this by hand since there is no typing on the Lord's day. And I'd best follow all the rest of the rules, since I am sorely failing at my promise to give up envy for Lent.

Even after my confession yesterday—I stopped at Saint Cunigunde on my way home from Abbie's studio and confessed my rage at Daisy in halting French—I am swimming in a soup of shame. Daisy is my sister, and she has not been here in a whole week. She's been at home, not asking Mother, or me, to feed and care for her children and buy her cigarettes. Isn't that what we wanted, after all?

There is rage inside me, still. Yes, rage. Rage born of envy and fear and spite. Surely that must add up to a deadly sin all its own? With my rage, I nurture my envy. I collect bitter crumbs and rusted bits of metal and feed them to the monster inside me, which is always hungry for more.

I don't breathe air, but fire. I could set the whole block on fire with my rage. I want to explode with it. Instead, I fall to my knees and pray to God to take it away.

What else can I do? What else is there but to pray? Otherwise, my rage will surely consume me.

---

Back in steno on Monday morning, the week stretches endlessly before me. Most of us are here today, Dot, Marie-Céleste, Helen, and me. It is like old times, and somehow there is comfort in the familiar.

Dot has decorated for Saint Patrick's Day. There will be cupcakes during the afternoon, and I'm more excited than I'd care to admit for this break in the monotony, even though, with my Scottish and French ancestry, this day has little to do with me.

Is this my life now? A series of half-hearted celebrations? I think back to the real excitement I felt—Was it just two weeks ago?—when I stayed late to work on the Eaton's campaign. Excitement tinged with doubt at the time, but now, it seems bright and hopeful. I should have enjoyed it more when I had the chance.

Across from me, Helen coughs and then swallows. Over the weekend, her complexion has gone from dull gray to sallow yellow. Marie-Céleste sighs deeply and rolls her eyes dramatically when I look up at her. I keep my eye on my page and not the clock. Last time I checked, there was still over an hour until the morning break. I keep typing.

I must seem suitably humbled because none of the other girls make comments. They've all heard about my "case of nerves," as Miss Pomeroy has called it—when I accused Mr. Sands of trying to steal Eaton's away—but they are careful not to speak of it in front of me. I have not seen Mr. Sands or Mr. McAulay or even Mr. Lewin since that morning a week ago. Miss Pomeroy rarely lets me out of her sight.

"Miss Grant." Miss Pomeroy calls me to her desk midmorning. She holds up a message slip. "You picked up bad habits while you were gone from steno. We do not take personal phone calls at work."

Abbie has phoned me three times. I am desperate to call her back, but I don't dare. Midmorning, Marie-Céleste steps out to make a phone call, I'm sure of it, though Miss Pomeroy says nothing. I feel the familiar rage, dormant since my prayers yesterday, bubble under the surface.

Miss Pomeroy raps on her desk, and when I look at her she points to my typewriter. I turn back to the task at hand, a letter from Mr. McAulay to his fellow board members of the Montreal Association of Advertisers. A missive on the morals of ad men. Mr. McAulay is calling for a motion to appoint an ethics subcommittee. Member agencies that poach ideas and clients from other member agencies will have their membership revoked, and I wonder what prompted this action. Was there something more to my "case of nerves" after all? I wish I could ask Mr. Lewin.

Miss Pomeroy coughs and gives me her sternest look. I must stay focused. There are ten members of the board. Ten letters. I set to work.

Miss Pomeroy comes to stand next to me and holds her hand out for the final letter as I pull it out of the typewriter. I stare straight ahead as she reviews it, close my eyes and flinch as she tears it in two.

She picks up the other nine letters and reviews them. "Addressed to Mr. McMillan, but opens with 'Dear Mr. Crosbie.' Mr. Crosbie's letter is addressed to Mr. Sontag. And so on . . ."

"I'm sorry."

"Sorry? Is that what you are? You've wasted a whole morning, Miss Grant."

I hug my arms to my belly and hunch over the typewriter. I will not cry.

"You will stay until they are done. No breaks. No phone calls. Understood?"

"Yes, Miss Pomeroy."

"And I'll place a demerit on your file."

"Yes, Miss Pomeroy."

Around me the girls are typing with their heads down, refusing to look at me. When lunchtime comes, they file out, one by one without a word. In the afternoon, they eat cupcakes in a circle, surrounded by Dot's green streamers, and I keep my eyes on the page, matching the greeting to the address line, tapping my fingers to the long slow beat of my shame.

Abbie finally reaches me once I'm home. There is the sound of voices in the background.

"Where have you been, Junie? I've been trying to reach you."

"Yes, I was moved back to—"

"What? Oh, sorry. Just a minute." Her voice turns sharp. "Well, I won't be back here long."

"Abbie, who are you talking to?"

"I'm in the dépanneur downstairs. I have an update."

"Yes? What is it?" I feel a stab of hurt that she doesn't want to hear about steno.

"I saw J-P. At the club. He says someone named Margaret is going to call me. About the special jobs? She's the one that manages all the girls."

With all the noise in the background I can barely make out what she's saying. "Manages the girls . . . for special jobs?" I whisper, looking over my shoulder to see where Mother is. "What do you think that means?"

"Whatever it is I'm sure your nuns would not approve, but don't worry about me, I won't do anything too improper." She laughs then. "Only a little improper . . ." She pauses. "No, I don't work here." Then she hollers, "You have a customer! Sorry, June. I'll tell you more about it when Margaret calls."

"Who is this Margaret?"

"I just told you! The girl J-P talked about. The one that looks after things for him. Oh! I have to go. The gang is here. We're going to El Morocco. Do you want to join us?"

I say no, of course. The question I didn't think to ask until afterward is, What does all this have to do with Daisy? She would never do what Abbie is talking about. Would she?

But then, what was François so worried about?

Suddenly all the behind-the-scenes sleuthing seems ridiculous. An address written on an orange wrapper. Getting dressed in costumes and sneaking around Daisy's back. Abbie meeting with a lady manager. All to find out what Daisy is up to. Surely there's a simple explanation for everything?

It has now been a full day since my confession and prayer, and I still feel calm when I think of Daisy. Could it be that my envy and fury have consumed themselves for good? Maybe I have been overreacting about everything. I am an adult, and so is she.

If I want her to stop treating me like her baby sister, I must stop acting like one. An adult would simply make an appointment with her and discuss it. That is what I will do.

Another day passes in steno, same as all those that came before. I make an error—on an address again—one that would shock my teachers at the Mother House. Miss Pomeroy arches her brow and says, "This is your second demerit this week, Miss Grant."

Once home, I go into the living room and dial Daisy's exchange.

"Collier residence, Daisy speaking." Her voice is subdued, as though she's been tamed.

My own voice comes out high-pitched, and I can't stop the words from coming out all at once. "It's June. There are some things I want to talk to you about."

"June? Why are you calling me? Is it Father? Is he all right?"

"Father? Yes, he's fine." Of course she would think that. I never call Daisy, or anyone, if I can help it.

I hear the indistinct rumble of Father's cough coming from down the hall. It has gotten worse, and Mother's asked for a home medical visit. I can't imagine that the cold temperature is helping, as we've now used the last of the heating oil.

"I mean, he's fine except his cold is getting worse and it's awfully cold here."

"You should get some more heating oil."

"I know. Mother wants to hold out until spring, that it can't be much longer."

"Remember last year when we were trapped in the church after Easter Mass because of an ice storm?"

"Yes," I say, shivering.

"Easter is still three weeks away. It's just Mother being tight again."

"No, it's not. It's just, she wants me to buy a new hat. I've been saving for one." I take a deep breath and try again. "Listen, Daisy—"

"If Father is all right, then why are you calling me?"

"It's just—I am calling to invite you to lunch. There are some things we should discuss."

"Very well," she says, like she's trying to find out where the trick is.

"Thursday?" I ask. "I have my lunch break at noon."

"How about tomorrow? Wednesday is my Eaton's day."

"Your Eaton's day?"

"Yes. Wednesday I go to Eaton's for at least a few hours to do my shopping. But I have no lunch plans tomorrow."

"So, lunch at Eaton's then? Noon, tomorrow?" I was going to suggest Woolworth's. I will have to dip into my meager hat savings again.

"Fine," Daisy says and hangs up.

# Chapter Twenty-Eight

Daisy is late. I feel conspicuous, sitting in the center of the art deco splendor of the restaurant. I want to swivel my head and take in the colors—the orange walls, the green frieze above the entrance door, the bright, curved window almost at ceiling height—but I can't. I am surrounded on all sides by well-dressed ladies out for lunch, and it would be rude to stare over their shoulders.

I sip my coffee and peruse the menu, adding up the cost in my head as I go. I decide on the daily special; it's the cheapest option, even though beef seems like it would be heavy in the middle of the day and I'd prefer something simpler.

Just as I start to worry that I'll have to go back to work without eating anything at all, Daisy arrives. Cool and distant, accepting the glances that come her way as the Eaton's matron leads her across the restaurant. Her coat is off but she's kept her gloves on, and she's wearing the suit I recognize from the Eaton's fashion show.

She doesn't smile, just leans her cheek toward mine and kisses the air, first on one side, then the other.

"June, this is lovely." She waves away the offered menu and lights a cigarette. "Consommé and gin. On the rocks."

"And for you, Madame?"

I hesitate. It would be cheaper to not order a meal at all, but it would show fear too, and that won't do. "The beef, please," I say. I won't make it through an afternoon in steno on consommé alone.

Daisy watches me through the film of smoke, her innocent eyes at odds with her voice, throaty from smoke and late nights. "So, June. What do you want to speak with me about?"

In that moment I wish I smoked. Instead, I narrow my eyes and sit back in my seat, pretending to be every bit as cool as she is, as I work up the nerve to say what I came here to say. Before I have the chance to speak, two waitresses descend on the table, one with Daisy's gin and the other to refill my coffee.

I twirl my coffee cup in its saucer. I'd like to add milk, or better yet, cream. Anticipating Daisy's disapproval, I settle for drinking it black.

"What are you up to? There's something. At the modeling agency. Does Geoff know about it? You're lying to him. I'm sick of keeping your secrets, and we simply can't afford any trouble." I blurt it all out at once, my words tinged with anger.

Daisy sits back as though to dodge an object I've thrown at her. Disdain wafts off her in waves. "You are forgetting your little scene at lunch."

"*My* scene?" I think back to the last time Daisy and her family came for Sunday lunch, the week before last.

"Yes, *your* scene. You were going to tell him, I could see it." Daisy sips her gin and glances at me over the edge of the glass. "I just stepped in." She puts her gin down and shrugs. "They let me keep the money, and the suit." She looks down at the mid-weight wool she's wearing. "They're still using my body, even if Geoff made them change the face."

I nod. I know this part already, saw it play out before my eyes.

"What about the rest of it?"

Daisy takes a drag on her cigarette and holds the smoke in for a long time. She stares off over my shoulder as a cold smile settles over her features.

"Daisy. I asked you a question." My stomach growls, betraying my weakness. My hunger. Daisy is never hungry. At least not for food.

She exhales, and the smoke hangs over the table between us. "I don't see how it is any concern of yours."

The waitress swoops in again, this time with consommé for us both, and I realize the problem with ordering the three-course special: Daisy will nip at her soup like a bird and watch me eat. She won't say a word about my waistline but I'll feel her criticism with every bite.

Daisy ignores her soup, sipping instead at her glass of gin. "You were saying?"

I take a spoonful of soup to quiet my belly and let the words come out. "It's my concern because it's not respectable. I'm lying for you all over the place. Lying to Mother, lying to Geoff. Worst of all, I made a fool of myself in front of Mr. McAulay and the others at work. I spend half my time saying Hail Marys in penance for your sins."

She smirks at that.

"It's not funny, Daisy. Do you know what would happen to Mother and Father if I lost this job? Or to all of us if Geoff got fed up with, with . . ." I pause. "Well, with you."

"Is this why you needed to see me so urgently? To nag me? I get enough of that from Geoffrey and Mother; I don't need it from my baby sister."

"If you haven't noticed, it's your baby sister that is keeping a roof over our parents' heads. You'd just let them go out on the street, wouldn't you? Don't you care about our family's reputation?"

"Don't be ridiculous. They won't end up on the street; that's why they had three daughters. I'm sorry that you're the ugly duckling, June, but I know you won't let that happen. I got married and had children. I have my own family to look after now." She lifts her head and drops her shoulders in the same way Mother does when she does not want to notice something that is beneath her. "And, I am looking after my own family's respectability, as you call it. Do you have any idea how much it costs to start an ad agency? To keep a good house? To keep up with the fashions? To keep those boys in proper shoes and clothes? All with no help at all from Geoff's family, I might add."

And there it is, the truth of the matter. Daisy needs to make up the shortfall for Geoff's family fortune. I sink back in the upholstered dining chair.

"Geoff never had to economize a day in his life, until our wedding day," Daisy says. She swills the last of the gin. I take another sip of my soup, but it's cold.

"What would you like me to do?" Daisy asks. "To preserve this respectability you're so worried about?"

The waitress hovers but I wave her away. I lean forward. When I speak, my voice is as cold and calm as hers. It's like we've traded places. "Look after those boys. And Geoff. Stop modeling . . ." I hesitate. Should I mention the photo I saw on the wall of the agency? The one where it looked like the man was about to take a bite out of Daisy's neck, as though it were the forbidden fruit? The special dates that Abbie mentioned? "And the other business. Stop that too," I say finally.

Daisy raises her eyebrows, and a slow smile spreads across her lips. "You can't even say it, can you?"

I take a deep breath and try to meet her gaze steadily, but I can't, because I know she's right. Even if I knew what she was up to, I don't know that I could say it out loud.

She's won and she knows it. I drop the pretense, the coolness, the one-upmanship, and look straight into her eyes, pleading. "Go home to your family, Daisy. Please. Look after Geoff."

"In case you haven't noticed, I haven't been to Abbott Street in over a week. And as for Geoff, I've got him very well looked after, thank you."

Daisy grounds out her cigarette and pushes out her chair just as one waitress arrives to take away the soup bowls and another comes with my beef Wellington.

"Is everything to your satisfaction?" The matron rushes to the table to help Daisy with her coat.

"Yes, it was delicious. I'm sorry to leave you by yourself, June, but I have an appointment. Thank you for lunch." And then to the matron, "Will you be a dear and fetch my parcels and summon me a taxi?"

I dig in to my beef. No sense letting it get cold. Besides, now that Daisy is gone, I can eat without her silent judgment. I mop the gravy off the plate with the soft white bread—two slices!—just as Father used to do back when he could feed himself. I dab the gravy from the corner of my mouth with the linen napkin and sit back with a sigh, sated after my feast. No sharing a dry cut of meat, no rationing, and I ate the whole basket of bread. My stomach is pressed to the edges, but I feel satisfied in a way I haven't for a long time.

When the bill comes, I count out the coins and add a tip. It's enough for four lunches at the Woolworth counter, completely draining my hat savings.

I stand and wait several minutes for someone to get my coat, and finally get it myself before the matron appears.

"Would you like me to call someone to carry your package to the taxi, Miss?"

"My package?"

She holds up a golden-brown hatbox from Eaton's, tied with a wide blue ribbon.

"That's not mine."

She holds the box out toward me. "I believe it is a gift. Mrs. Collier asked that I give it to you, as she was in such a hurry for her next appointment."

I take the box from her, resisting the urge to rip it open then and there. She places my old hat on top. It looks unbearably shabby.

"Taxi?" she asks again.

"Thank you. I'll walk."

# Chapter Twenty-Nine

It's the kind of hatbox you'd take on a trans-Atlantic voyage. Cardboard the color of burnished leather. The lettering embossed in sky-blue—*T. Eaton & Co.: Canada's Greatest Store*—and the whole held together by a tantalizing blue ribbon, tied in a bow. It's too tall to fit on the hat shelf above the coat stand, and I have to carry it to my desk.

That's when the whispers start.

I place the box behind my tray, which is filled with the contracts I am to type in triplicate this afternoon. Marie-Céleste always keeps her hat on her desk, says looking at it cheers her up, and it's true. Her hats are always chic and well tended to.

It's Dot that finally asks: "Will you let us see your new hat, Miss Grant?"

I look to Miss Pomeroy, my fingers in formation over the keys.

The two clear lines between Miss Pomeroy's brows deepen and she claps her hands. "Back to work, everyone. Miss Grant will show you her hat during the break."

I will? My cheeks burn. I haven't even seen my new hat yet. I want to keep it away from them all. I know that in the unwritten code of the steno pool, gifts are for sharing.

I look down at the keys, determined to keep my focus for the next one hour and fifty minutes. I will not let this distraction earn me another demerit. It's automatic firing at three, and I've already got two.

At break time, Marie-Céleste sits on one corner of my desk, though she usually smokes on the balcony outside the mail room, gathering the gossip from the delivery boys to bring back to us. Dot is there too, in her yellow dress, her hands clasped at her waist as though she might fly apart from excitement otherwise. Helen, still sad and pale as she has been for weeks, red veins in her eyes from the strain of holding in her secret, stands behind.

"Let us see," Dot whispers, her hands flapping the air.

Marie-Céleste lays her hands on the lid as though she's going to open it, but Miss Pomeroy—even she has joined in—stops her.

"Tell us about your new hat, Miss Grant."

I tuck my too-large feet under my chair and crowd my shoulders down. Even sitting, I hulk over them. "It's a gift. I haven't seen it yet." I can't keep the sulk out of my voice.

"A gift from an admirer?"

"Miss Grant has an admirer?"

"It's from my sister, Daisy." It's only then I see the gift card, tucked in tight under the bow.

"Go on, Miss Grant, open it," Miss Pomeroy says. "Share the pleasure with your colleagues."

I want to hug the pleasure to myself, and the pain of it too. Because with any gift from Daisy, no matter how lovely, there will be pain. When will it come? Later tonight? Next week? I place the box at the center of my desk and slide the card out. Will they want me to pass it around, like the gift cards at the lunchtime bridal showers?

*Thank you for taking care of the boys during our dinner party. They love when their Auntie June looks after them! xo Daisy*

I drop my shoulders in relief and pass the card to Miss Pomeroy on my right. Of course Daisy would know about this part, the young-girl-birthday-party atmosphere, even if she'd never worked in an office in her life.

"How charming," Miss Pomeroy says, passing the card to Marie-Céleste.

With one tug, the blue ribbon cascades down. I lift the butterscotch lid, and Helen takes it from my hand.

"Oooh! I can't stand it!" Dot says at the sight of the pleated white tissue paper, sealed with a gold *T. Eaton* sticker.

There's a hush as I peel off the sticker. Miss Pomeroy takes it expertly—she's been to more bridal showers than any of us—and we all watch as she places it on the back of the card. "A memento," she says. "For your scrapbook."

The moment is as silent and graceful as communion. I pull apart the delicate folds, careful not to tear the tissue, to see the treasure nestled inside. We gasp as one.

"It's lovely."

"So stylish!"

"I was just at the hat counter this week, I don't think it's even out yet."

"It's exactly what I wanted," I whisper, and I know it is true, though I have never seen a hat like this before. How could Daisy have known? I hold it up like a baby for christening. Stiff wool felt in a bright shade of navy, a deep pleat in the crown, a flat brim. The wide grosgrain ribbon is the color of a wheat field in fall, and the brim edge is curled and bound with a thin silk ribbon in the same golden hue.

"Look at this." Dot's voice is tinged with awe as she turns the brim so I can see the yellow-tipped feather, bright-cobalt blue at its base. In a moment of generosity, I turn to Helen and see a flash of her old smile as I pass the coveted item to her first. As it makes the rounds, I allow the unspoken rituals of women and girls to hold me. I watch as it passes hand to hand, the feather, the edge of the brim, the cheerful blue wool.

"Come, let's see it on you." Miss Pomeroy does the honors.

From my seated position, I look to each of them, their expressions my only mirror.

Helen cocks her head. Marie-Céleste purses her lips in a way that's unattractive. Finally, Dot says, "Maybe if we fix her hair?"

They don't ask permission, we are beyond that now. Miss Pomeroy produces a comb and Dot some lipstick and powder and they land on me, poufing and lining and untangling. I stare straight ahead, swaying between shame and hope. I am still me, after all. But perhaps they can do something, these bright, magical girls?

"Try it on an angle this time." Marie-Céleste has taken over the stage direction.

I look to my mirror of girls and they sigh as one. "Oh yes."

"Just right."

Someone holds up a compact and I see what they are talking about. It is just right. It's me, but better. I can't wait to show Mother.

Then Miss Pomeroy claps her hands. "Girls, girls. Back to work."

I take the hat off and place it on top of the box, the feather facing me so I can see it. I settle back into the Red Lantern Taxi media contract. Just one more hour and then I will walk the long way home along Sherbrooke in my new hat. Maybe the sun will come out.

Mother will wonder why I am late, but no matter. Surely I am allowed an hour to enjoy my hat, before Daisy extracts her price.

———— ⤙❧⤚ ————

There is no walking home. The air that warmed briefly at lunchtime has plummeted again and the rain has turned to ice. I don't want the ice to ruin my new spring hat, and so I put it away in the precious box and wear my old one out into the sleet.

At home, Mother greets me at the door in her fur coat, carrying a lit candle on one of the silver candlesticks that was a wedding gift over forty years before.

"What's happening, Mother?" The house is completely dark. Are the boys playing some game? I feel a stab of anger that threatens to ignite in rage that Daisy has broken her promise so soon.

"June, oh dear June." Mother's face is drawn and she looks serious, no sign of her usual pleasure when she is playing with her grandsons.

"Are the boys here?"

"No, thank goodness."

"You're not playing a game? Then why are we in the dark?"

I start to take off my coat but Mother says, "No, keep it on." I find a clear spot on the shelf to place the Eaton's hatbox.

"It was a present, from Daisy," I say as Mother looks at it.

"Oh dear," she says. "Very kind of her, I'm sure. But still."

I follow her down the hall to the kitchen. She waits for me in the doorway and then closes the door behind me to keep the heat in. The silver candelabra—another wedding gift—is alight with white candles.

"It is not warming up, Mother. Are you sure we shouldn't get another quarter tank of heating oil?"

She sits down before the large silver teapot, which she has wrapped in an old shawl.

"Mother, what is happening? Why are the lights out?" I circle the kitchen table to give Father his kiss. He's got a fur car rug over his lap and three sweaters on.

"He's frozen! Father, are you all right?"

She sits me down and pours a cup of tea from the pot. She adds milk and sugar and hands it to me. The mug is cold in my hands. "He's as warm as I can make him for now." She fills her own cup and wraps her tiny fingers around it.

Mother. So small and so very strong. This was not what she was raised to expect, sitting in a frozen kitchen with no lights.

"Mother, why are there no lights?"

"It was my mistake."

"What was?"

"Remember, I said to give the electricity money to Daisy to pay our bill. She said Geoff was going to pay theirs, and she'd give it to him." She shivers again. "She must have forgotten."

I take Mother's hands and squeeze her fingers in my own. "She bought me a hat instead. And her things. She had scads of packages from Eaton's today." More than the electricity bill cost, but I don't say that to Mother.

"I'm sorry, June."

"It's all right, Mother."

"I wanted more for you."

"It's all right, Mother," I say again. And it is all right. "I'll look after this, but not until tomorrow."

"You'll have to ask Geoff to go," she says. "It's his name on the account. To reconnect. There'll be a fee."

"I'll look after it." We sit in silence for a while, holding hands across the table. Neither of us says what we are both thinking: Without Geoff, we'd have no electricity at all. And we can't tell him what Daisy did. If he gets angry with us for accusing her—or worse, if he finally gets so frustrated with her—well, we can't risk that. What would become of all of us if Daisy and the boys moved back in here for good? If mine were the only salary?

There's no choice. I will have to lie.

Finally, I say, "We'd best get Father to bed, so he'll be warm."

As if to concur, he coughs, a wet rumble deep in his throat. I stand and wrap my arms around him. "Did the nurse come?"

"Not yet."

Reconnecting the electricity will look after the lights, but not the cold. "Are you sure we shouldn't get some heating oil? Just a bit?"

"We still owe them from the last half tank. It'll only be a few more days."

I rub Father's shoulders and then steer his chair into the den.

"Let's move him, and then I'll bring you dinner in your room. You can write by candlelight. Won't that be romantic?"

But it's not romantic. It's too cold to think. There's no toast, of course, so I have a slice of bread with cheese and cold tea, and I have to type with gloves on. I feel I'm in a frozen cave, pushing to get out, the pinpoint light of one candle my only guide. Like the tulips frozen under the ice, waiting.

# Chapter Thirty

The woman at the Eaton's counter counts out the crisp bills until she gets to ten dollars and ninety-five cents. She marks the amount on a return slip that she hands to me, along with the money. The blue hat sits on the counter between us, its gold ribbon and bright-blue feather full of promises for some other girl.

"Is that how much it cost?" It's not enough to cover the electricity bill and the reconnection fee.

"Yes." She's wearing a dress from a few seasons ago; I can see a tiny fray at her sleeve hem and that her blazer has been brushed out plenty of times. "Sorry," she says. Her expression might be even sadder than my own.

I place the bills inside an envelope in my pocketbook and touch the rim of the hat one last time, brushing my fingers along the feather, wishing it a silent goodbye.

"A shame," she says. "It's such a nice hat. Did it not suit you?"

"It's not that." I squirm against the shame that rises in me, feel myself blushing, and then a spurt of anger. "It was my sister," I say in a vicious whisper. "She bought it without thinking."

She's holding it now in both hands, inspecting it for damage, though it was not out of the box long enough for there to be any. Her head is tipped, her eyebrows raised. I see that she is inviting confidences, in that secret coded language that I recognize from the girls at the office.

I shake my head. Gossip is surely a sin. And gossip about a family member? Mother would not have it.

"You've been most helpful," I say. "Thank you." I snap my pocketbook closed and shove my old trilby on my head.

"One minute," the girl says, holding her hand out for my trilby. "Can you wait here?" She smiles prettily to the woman in line behind me, and I think that I must learn to smile like that, if I am to get by in this world. No one can get angry at a smile like that.

She comes back a moment later with what looks to be my old hat, but she's brushed it and shaped it and tied a canary-yellow ribbon around the rim and fastened it with a dark-brown feather. "These were going to go to waste. Here, lean in?" She places the hat on my head and then adjusts it.

"There, see?" She points to the mirror on the counter. "Just a bit of an angle makes all the difference."

I bend my knees to take in my own reflection. "It looks like a whole new hat." I try one of her smiles, but on my face it looks like I'm making a cruel joke.

"I'm sorry, about your sister." She shoots a nervous glance back now, at the woman in line. Sweet smiles are all gone. "I hope when it's time for a new hat again, you'll come back to Eaton's."

Head held high, I walk toward the elevator. "Main floor," I tell the attendant when I get in. From the lobby I head down the street to where my next humiliation awaits.

———— ❧～❧ ————

Across Saint Catherine Street, Geoff swivels in his stool at the Woolworth's counter, waiting for me.

"Coffee? Bun?" he asks.

"I have to get to work. I'm already late." There will be no coffees and buns for me for a while.

"Come then, at least have a coffee." He raises a finger to the girl behind the counter, who slops coffee from her pot into my mug before I can say no again. My stomach is much too nervous for coffee.

Geoff is all cheerful bluster, even today, but then why wouldn't he be? He spent the night in a warm house, surrounded by his loving family. He could switch on lights and make all the toast he wanted. His hat hangs on the hook under the counter. His black coat is still on, but unbuttoned, showing his navy suit and pressed white shirt. His tie is wide and navy as well, polka-dotted with sailboats.

I hand him the overdue notice and pull the envelope of cash out of my pocketbook.

"There now, you spent the electricity money on a new hat, did you?"

"Is that what Mother told you?"

"Nothing to be ashamed of, June. Part of growing up. We all do it once before we learn." Then he laughs. "Well, twice, at most."

I want to smash the table. I am a horse, quivering, ready to gallop. Ready for the truth to burst out of me. I want to ask how many times Daisy has overspent on a hat. When will *she* learn? With effort, I restrain myself. Daisy is a problem that's been handed on to him. And he's been so patient with all of us. He could shrug us all off and go back to his own family and have a much easier life.

I talk myself down like this, rung by rung, until I think my voice is steady enough to speak. I hand him the envelope. "I'm still a dollar and forty cents short. I can pay you back on Friday."

He waves this away. "That's all right, June. Save it. Put it away for your new hat." He winks. "One you save up for this time." He clatters his coffee cup into the saucer. His smile is so earnest I can't look back at him. I add some cream to my coffee, hands shaking. The cup rattles as I lift it out of the saucer to take a sip. The coffee lands like hot acid in my belly, already full of anger and shame.

"It will be back on before you get home from work. I'll make sure of it." He's searching for my eyes, but I can't meet his gaze. The tears are hot and tight and threatening to fall. "June, tell me, what is it?"

The anger fills me and threatens to burst through once and for all. I clench my fists and hold it in, but I know it will be so much worse in the long run if I tell him that Daisy spent the money. He will not believe me; will think I'm envious of my prettier, more stylish sister. I stare straight at him, speechless, tears threatening to breach the dam, until I have contained myself.

"The heating oil," I say, breathless from the effort of holding it all in. "Mother says they will only come if they can fill it halfway. It's a waste since it's almost spring."

"Halfway? At this time of year? Those crooks. Why . . ." He pauses to light a cigarette. "They filled our tank to barely a quarter just last week. I'll call them."

"Mother says we still owe them from last time. She's trying to stay warm in the kitchen, but poor Father is freezing."

"Poor June. And all you wanted was a new hat." He pats my hand, and I have to force myself not to snatch my hand away. "She's in the kitchen in her fur coat, I bet. A spaniel on each frozen foot."

"Yes, that's exactly right." I sigh, feeling the emotions retreat inside me. Subdued at last. "What would we do without you, Geoff?" I say, my voice flat and quiet.

He narrows his eyes and exhales. "We'd all be lost without each other, June." Through the smoke his gaze turns serious. "Speaking of which, your changes, to my Derny campaign?" He taps out the ash and points his cigarette at me. "Brilliant. Simple, elegant. I've a mind to offer you a job. Wasting your talents as a stenographer, I say. I'd hire you as a writer myself."

I feel the thrill in my belly, of happiness and relief at the admiration, but it's snuffed out just as quickly by fear. I shake my head. I remember Mr. McAulay's unkind words about new, upstart agencies.

*Don't know the value of relationships.* I remember the posturing around the Eaton's insert. The letters I typed to the Montreal Association of Advertisers. "That's kind of you to say, but I'm happy where I am."

"You sure?" He stubs out his cigarette. "You let me know if you change your mind."

"I will." I want to ask him—Does he know? Does he know about the modeling office on Saint Jacques Street, the taxis?—I stop. What do I even know really? A photograph of Daisy. A warning from François. A mention that some of the models go on special jobs. Geoff will dismiss all of this with an affable smile if I bring any of it up.

"That all?" The girl behind the counter scribbles the total and tears the slip from her pad, handing it to Geoff. He chugs the last of his coffee and winks at her.

"All right then," he says to me. "Reconnect the electricity, order some heating oil, and pocket this," he says, taking up the envelope. He reaches into his coat pocket and clatters two dimes onto the counter. "I've got my marching orders," he says with a wink to the waitress as he stands. "Yes, by all means, fill Miss Grant's cup.

"Take a few quiet minutes, June, before you head to work. Stenographers rush about. But writers, well, writers need time to mull things over, creative geniuses that we are."

---

"Good morning, Miss Grant." Constant, the elevator attendant, steps aside to reveal Mr. Lewin, already in the elevator.

"Miss Grant."

"Mr. Lewin." I nod to him. I have not spoken to him since our "date" at the Mount Royal Hotel. Our pretend date, I remind myself. My cheeks burn as the doors close. I pull up my coat sleeve and check my watch and cry out when I see the time.

"Everything all right, Miss Grant?"

"I'm terribly late."

"Is that a problem?"

"I don't know. I've never been late before."

"Ah," he says. "Constant, shall I take mercy on this poor girl? Show her how it's done?"

I watch the line of Constant's dark neck duck down, exposing a line of tight frizz of black hair. His shoulders shake up and down with silent laughter. "I think so, Sir. Miss Grant is always on time." We wait in silence a moment, until Constant says, "Here we are, eleventh floor."

"Head up! Shoulders back. Good. Now, follow my lead."

I step to the door, ready to rush out as soon as they open. Mr. Lewin places his long fingers on my shoulder, as though pausing an overeager dog. "Wait. Take one step back."

I step back. The doors open and I have to hold myself back from running into the reception area.

Lewin stands next to me, bows his head, and tips his hat. "After you, Miss Grant," he says, full voice, then mutters, "Slowly now. With all the confidence of a Bethany or a Rosemarie."

This makes me smile, remembering Bethany in her summer seersucker stripe suit, the skirt so straight she had to sashay, rather than walk down the runway. I do the same, one foot out, both feet together as I step out of the elevator.

"Don't overdo it," says Mr. Lewin.

Marie-Céleste is on reception this morning. I try to catch her eye, to find some remnant of that camaraderie from yesterday, but she's not looking at my face. She's staring at my hat.

"Marie-Céleste, is it? I need you to send a message to Miss Pomeroy. I need Miss Grant this morning. No, scratch that, for the whole day. McAulay's orders."

"There's a requisition—"

He waves a hand and takes my elbow. "Look after it, will you? Charge it to the taxi account."

He steers me right past Mr. McAulay's desk and down the hall. The air is thick with cigarillo smoke as we near the art department. He pauses in front of the door next to the supply room and pulls out a key.

"You lock your door?"

"Art department thing. Bunch of robbers they all are." He yells this into the hall of closed doors, then hustles me in and slams the door behind me. He collapses on the couch, his coat across his legs like a blanket, and puts his hat over his eyes, stretches out his long legs, and settles in as though for a nap.

"Mr. Lewin?"

He raises a finger to his lips. "Just twenty minutes. All I need." Then he waves a hand toward the desk. "Get started if you like."

# Chapter Thirty-One

I perch on the one stool at Lewin's drafting table, my coat and hat still on. Is this even proper? In Mr. Lewin's office with the door closed while he naps on the couch?

He gives an audible sigh, almost a moan. He's absorbing sleep like a man in the desert, thirsty for water. His hat has slid down the long angles of his face and I can see his features now. Bags under his eyes like soft bruises; an uneven shave. The shirt cuff peeking out of his jacket sleeve is pocked around the buttons, as though it's been ironed by an impatient wife. Or by a man.

The table is littered with illustrations for the Red Lantern Taxi account. The top drawing is almost all black, except for the rosy glow of a Red Lantern rooftop sign and the outline of a taxi. The next sketch has the Red Lantern light at the bottom of the page, and, at the top, the yellow rectangle of a lighted window. With the next one, the view is through the back window of the taxi, a man in the back seat, tweed coat and hat, so clearly delineated I might look over his shoulder to read the newspaper he's holding up. I can see the back of the driver's head as well, all illuminated by the Red Lantern sign on the roof. And then in the distance, the outline of a handsome house, the solid wood door lit by lantern-shaped light fixtures on either side.

*Because the most handsome houses aren't next to the train station.*

The words pop into my head, and I reach for a pad of newsprint and scribble them down. And then the next, *Leave a light on, I'm working late tonight.* And then, simply, *We light your way home.*

I wrestle off my coat and hat and find a spot for them among the charcoal-smudged smocks and discarded ties that hang on the coat stand behind the door. The thoughts are coming fast now, remembering back to that first Red Lantern meeting. *Ask for us by name.* That's what the owner, Bruno, said at the original Red Lantern meeting.

I write: *We light your way home. Red Lantern Taxi. Ask for us by name.*

And then I write the phone number.

There's a sharp knock at the door. "Mr. Lewin?" It's Miss Pomeroy. She knocks again. "Mr. Lewin? Open up, please."

Her voice is like syrup running over a cleaver. Standing behind the door, I adjust my dress. I give Mr. Lewin's foot a shove. He shakes himself awake and sits up. "Is the baby crying?" Then he looks at me. "Miss Grant?"

It's my turn to hold my finger to my lips.

"Mr. Lewin, this will not do. Open the door, please."

Awareness fills his expression and he shakes himself awake, sits up, and looks around. He points to the stool, and I go back to my perch. He pulls his coat closed and stands for a second, uncoiling until he's quite imposing-looking. He runs his fingers through his hair. Finally, he opens the door and Miss Pomeroy falls into the room.

"Oh! Well! I was about to call the custodian." She bustles in, a sheaf of paper in her hands. "There you are, Miss Grant. I'm quite shocked at your behavior. You know perfectly well the process for requisitioning a stenographer, even if Mr. Lewin seems to have forgotten."

She's wearing her navy boiled-wool suit today. "It's not possible to requisition a particular girl, Mr. Lewin. You know that."

"Do I?" He gestures his hand to the couch. "Do sit down, Miss Pomeroy. I was just going to call for coffee." He whisks his coat off the couch and flings it over the coat stand. At her pinched expression he continues. "Now, don't be like that. Do sit."

"Miss Grant, will you call for coffee, please? Perhaps Miss Pomeroy can help us with our dilemma."

I pick up the phone and quietly give the instruction to Marie-Céleste. "Coffee for three in Mr. Lewin's office."

"What? You're too good to get coffee now?" Marie-Céleste asks.

"Miss Pomeroy takes milk, not cream, so send both," I say.

"What happened to your hat?" I lay the cradle back in the receiver without answering that question.

Miss Pomeroy and Lewin have joined me at the drafting table. "Mr. McAulay said specifically to have this campaign ready for next week's meeting. You know how he likes to prepare well in advance, and with Sands being, well, frankly unreliable, and Mr. Shoesmith on the Gillette account and Leblond just better left to the French accounts . . . well."

"Well?" asks Miss Pomeroy.

"Mr. McAulay says he's going to hire a new writer, but in the mean-time, well, you see my problem."

"No, Mr. Lewin, I simply do not. Miss Grant is a stenographer. I don't see how this has anything to do with her."

They stand on either side of me like siblings bickering over a par-ent's affection. I slide the newsprint pad with my rough copy over into Lewin's line of vision. I sit as straight as I can on the stool, cross my feet at the ankle, place them on the metal bar designed for this purpose, and stare straight ahead.

"She's nothing but a stenographer. She has no business having such aspirations."

"She's a better writer than any of the men on staff. She wrote that whole Eaton's campaign."

"Mr. Lewin, you shock me. I know perfectly well that Mr. Sands wrote that campaign."

"Look, let's not stand here and argue over her like she's a pad of paper. Requisitioning stenographers? What kind of idea is that? Do you see your girls as interchangeable cogs with no individual characteristics?"

Miss Pomeroy sucks in her breath. I too hold my breath and stare harder at the poster on the back of the door, an illustration of a cheerful circus scene. I wonder if it is Lewin's work, but this is not the time to ask.

"My girls are all equally trained. And they all get married eventually. There's no sense getting attached to any one in particular. Best leave it to me to assign them."

There's a knock and the door swings open. We all watch as Marie-Céleste rolls the coffee tray in with a practiced look of boredom. "Would you like me to serve, Miss Pomeroy?"

"Miss Grant can serve, thank you."

I know Miss Pomeroy takes milk; Lewin, black. I hand them each their cup and pour a generous serving of cream into my own. Since there is no room left on the couch, I head back to my stool. A new illustration is at the top of the pile now. A man in a suit carrying a briefcase, walking behind a man wearing a traditional red Turkish fez and holding a lantern lit by a flame. *Escort you home like a visiting dignitary.* I reach for the pad, but it's not there. I look over to the couch, where Mr. Lewin is holding the pad up for Miss Pomeroy to see.

"*Ask for us by name.* I love it. So simple. So perfect. Exactly what the client wants. I could have run this by five writers and not one of them would have come up with it."

Miss Pomeroy looks up at me, eyes narrowed. "How did you come up with it, Miss Grant?"

"It just came into my head."

"See?" Lewin asks.

Miss Pomeroy ignores him and levels her gaze on me. "Is this what you want? To be a copywriter?"

Am I allowed to say yes? It's not what I was trained for. Not what my family needs from me, and certainly nothing a young lady should want, if Miss Pomeroy's expression is any indication.

I meet her gaze. "More than anything."

Lewin sits back, slaps his thigh, and sighs. "There now, see?"

Miss Pomeroy takes up the requisition form again and hands it to him. "Sign this. I will look after it from here. You can have her for today. After that it's back to steno. Agreed?"

Lewin shrugs. "Agreed for now. Though I still say what a damn waste." He scrawls his signature all along the bottom of the page.

"Miss Grant? Remember your place."

"Yes, Miss Pomeroy."

She looks down at her paper, shakes her head, and walks out, leaving the coffee tray behind for me to clean up.

———— ⚜ ————

Writing headlines all afternoon is like being at the Mount Royal Park lookout on a sunny day in winter, when the air is so crisp and fresh and you can see the whole city and the river and beyond, like your life has finally started.

Is this how Dot feels when she's looking at going-away dresses? Marie-Céleste when she's gossiping with the boys in the mail room? Abbie when she's taking photographs? Daisy when she's shopping at Eaton's?

When I get home, it's warm and bright. The electricity is on, and the oil tank full enough to see us through, even if we have another late spring. François sent some Danish blue cheese for Mother. We have toast with blue cheese for dinner and warmed green beans from a can. My humiliation over the hat, over lying to Geoff to cover for Daisy, is all but forgotten with a full belly.

Mother is calling from the kitchen, where she and Father are sitting, warm, with the dogs at their feet. I will visit with them and then go and write a poem, maybe even two.

# Chapter Thirty-Two

I have a hat with a yellow ribbon, even if it isn't new. It is Friday, and after today I will have a weekend and a reprieve from the endless monotony of steno. I count my blessings one by one as I settle in to my desk.

"You're late, again, Miss Grant. That's twice this week."

I look up at the clock and indeed it is several minutes past the hour.

"I'm sorry, Miss Pomeroy."

"I told you not to start picking up habits from the art department. Putting on airs." Her voice fades as Helen scuttles in, even later than I.

"I won't let it happen again, Miss Pomeroy," I say. Anything to distract her from Helen with her sunken cheekbones and dark-circled eyes. Miss Pomeroy grunts and walks away without another word, and I'm glad that I've absorbed a little of Helen's trouble. I start in on my pile of contracts.

"I say, don't go," Marie-Céleste whispers, leaning her head back in Grace's direction. "Don't you agree, Dot?"

I try to drown out their whispers and concentrate on the contract before me.

"I don't see why not," Dot whispers back. "A date is a date."

"But last minute like that? For a show with tickets? You have to know you were not his first choice." Even in a whisper Marie-Céleste can convey that she would never settle for sloppy seconds.

Grace shuttles the carriage on her typewriter louder than is really necessary, making Helen jump.

"Maybe not all of us can afford to be as fussy as you," Grace mutters. "What about you, June? Do you have a date tonight? Or do you need to work late? In the art department?"

Marie-Céleste and Dot giggle. For a moment everything is silent.

I agree with Grace, but still don't say anything. I look down to the contract, the words swimming before my eyes, and gasp. I've done it again, flubbed the address.

"Miss Grant?"

How is it that Miss Pomeroy hears everything I say and sees everything I do, but is deaf and blind to all the others? I hear her chair slide back, but then Helen slides hers back too and rushes from the room without a word.

When Miss Pomeroy follows her, I roll out the three layers of carbon and start afresh. There will be no mistakes this time.

———— ◦⬭~◦ ————

"Miss Grant? Please wait and speak to me before you go."

The other girls file out, giddy with their evening plans, released at last. My stomach flips and I feel as green as Helen this morning. I tuck my hands into my lap, angle my ankles, and wait, without fiddling, until Miss Pomeroy approaches my desk.

All I want is home. To get away from the whispers and the clanging of typewriters. To replace it all with the sound of just one typewriter— my own—and the whistle of my thoughts through the air as I set them free after having locked them up all day.

Miss Pomeroy's face is drawn in heavy vertical lines. She stands before me, her hands clasped behind her back.

"I tried to warn you, Miss Grant. Girls dally in the creative department and come back with their heads so full of nonsense, they're no good to me at all." She pulls a contract from behind her back and places it on my desk. The spring media contract for Gillette. One of the ones I typed today—just before lunch or just after? I can't remember.

She takes a red wax pencil from the cup on my desk and slashes it across the top page. I press my nails into the flesh of my palm.

"This is your third demerit in one week, Miss Grant. What happened to all of your impeccable learning at the Mother House? Your almost-perfect record. Yes, I went back and checked your file this afternoon, to be sure. I could not believe you could have slid so far in such a short time, but here we are."

In the silence I can hear only my own short bursts of breath as I try to hold back my tears.

"I'm sorry, Miss Pomeroy. I won't let it happen again."

"You are right. You won't. Because you won't have the opportunity." She presses the red-slashed pages onto the desk under the flat of her palm. "Three demerits in one week, Miss Grant. I would never let a new girl on probation—Grace, for example—stay on after that."

I try to speak, but it's like I'm being strangled. I can't get any air. "I'm sorry," I whisper.

"I'm sorry too," Miss Pomeroy says. "I did try to warn you, but you would not listen."

"Am I fired?" I can barely whisper the words.

"Yes. Yes, I'm afraid you are. Please collect your things."

I look down at my desk. I have no things, beyond my purse, coat, and hat. I stand and head to the door to collect them.

"Goodbye, Miss Grant."

I don't answer—my breath is so shallow I have none to spare. The hall and reception area are deserted. Everyone has left for their Friday night drinks and dates.

Constant nods as I board the elevator. "It's cold out there," he says. When I don't answer, he hums a tune quietly to himself to fill the silence. "See you Monday, Miss Grant," he says when the doors open.

I don't correct him, just step out into the marble-columned lobby of the Sun Life Building for the last time.

# Chapter Thirty-Three

Outside the sky is brilliant blue and the air is pure cold. The sun has started its descent and the angles of light tinge the buildings with streaks of gold.

I can't go home, not right away. Instead, I cross into Dominion Square. I let my tears fall, and they immediately freeze to my cheeks. The benches are crusted with ice and, besides, I can't sit and sob in a public square. Mother would be more upset about that than me being fired. Instead, I cut across the diagonal path, past the statue of Robert Burns, and pause to let the words of the epitaph soothe me. *It's comin' yet for a' that.*

Father explained the significance to me once, when we were walking in the square on a sunny afternoon—after our reversal of fortune, but before his stroke. His voice was deep and sure. He knew our current state was not our fate. He would work his way out of it. It was only a matter of time.

"An independently minded man is better off than a prince," he told me.

I never thought to question him, but now when I read the words, *That man to man, the world o'er, shall brithers be for a' that,* I know they do not apply to me. The world has no place for an independently minded woman.

I turn away from Burns and start walking. Across from me, the entrance to the Windsor Hotel, where I know I won't be welcome without the generosity of Abbie's father. I let the stream of office girls leaving the Gazette Building carry me along Peel Street to the streetcar stop, but once I reach Saint Catherine, I keep walking.

Past the Mount Royal Hotel, golden and full of promise. A sign tells me there's dancing and cocktails and a twenty-five-piece swing band with three shows tonight. I reach Sherbrooke Street and my feet trudge forward of their own accord. My lungs open and press against the frozen air. My breath comes faster as the street climbs up the side of the mountain.

I'm surrounded by students now, young men, heads down against the cold. All of them wearing the same wool coat, the same tweed hat, the same galoshes over polished loafers. Men learning to be independently minded so they can make their way in the world. Up ahead, there's a young lady in a tightly cinched coat, stockings, and shoes, her face tipped toward the streaming sun. Imagine that, to be a girl studying at McGill. It's not such a rare thing anymore, I know, and yet it is so far out of my reach.

In front of me, a young man slows his steps and I have to step aside so as not to tread on his heels. The girl smiles and raises her own hand and I see she has nothing but a pocketbook. No satchel, no briefcase. He spreads his arms wide, blocking the sidewalk, a limp bouquet of three carnations in one hand. I have no choice but to stop and witness the moment. She's not a student at all. She is a girl waiting for her date. This is not an accomplishment, I want to tell her.

Rather, I step into the street with an "Excuse me" so I can keep on walking. At Doctor Penfield Avenue I press on. I pass the law faculty and keep my eyes firmly on the sidewalk, convinced that somehow Mr. Jack Ritchie from Toronto will look out the window at just this moment and see me. Feel sorry for me. I force myself to walk faster, sweating now under my coat, my breath chuffing.

If Daisy saw me, she'd tell me to collect myself, but I will not.

Perched close to the top of the mountain is Crow's Watch, a historic home that is now the Montreal Hospital for the Insane. Abbie says this is fitting given its gothic tower, which juts up into the sky. The very top is an observatory from which the original owner, Sir Hugh Armstrong, could keep watch over the city he'd helped build.

I must hurry; the afternoon light will not last much longer. I start up the steps to the mountain, going against the current. Other afternoon walkers are headed down the stairs, not up. A girl like me should not be alone on the mountain after dark.

I push past the ice-cold burning in my chest, past the frozen stumps of my feet and the dampness under my coat that will settle into cold as soon as the sun dips below the horizon. Up and up, I press, and when I reach the overlook, it is deserted. I circle the parapet until I'm at the center of the semicircular balustrade, the whole city spread out beneath me. The university, the shops and lights along Saint Catherine, the Sun Life Building, Saint James Cathedral, Dominion Square. Below all that, the ramparts of the old city, the spire of Notre Dame Basilica, the river and beyond, the mountains of Vermont. Below me lays the city my ancestors once claimed as their own as boldly as Sir Hugh Armstrong.

I kneel against the base of a column as though it were a pew. My elbows on the balustrade, my hands together, I drop my head. I pray to God to help me in my predicament. And as I look out at the sun casting angles across the city, my prayer changes. I pray to the city itself. I pray that it will open up just enough to find a space on the side of this mountain for me and my family to cling to.

Surely, this is a sin. Monsignor McDonagh would be shocked, praying to the very city. And yet, God looks over the city from the cross at the summit to the river that is our lifeblood. As the last ray of sun extinguishes itself, the city falls into shadow, and I pray for forgiveness.

I let my pride get in the way of the income my family needs me to earn so that we can all survive. Pride before the fall, indeed. I made this predicament myself. Why ask God for help now after I've messed everything up? Why didn't I listen before when Mother spoke to me, and Miss Pomeroy? Why didn't I heed their warnings? My pride got in the way.

*She's a natural copywriter.*

In my mind, the voice of God sounds just like Mr. Lewin. No wonder I'm in trouble.

The clammy cold inside my coat spreads across my shoulders and back and down my hips. I creak back into motion, crossing the crest of the mountain, following the trail that skirts along Beaver Lake; the cold has chased even the bravest skaters away. Down to Côte des Neiges Boulevard with the last of the light and into Westmount.

It is full dark now. The grand houses are lit at the doors and in the dining rooms. I imagine the maids setting the table, the drivers shuttling the master of the house home for the evening. I imagined such a scene so recently I half expect a Red Lantern taxi to drive past, and I wish one would. I could flag it down and be escorted home like a visiting dignitary.

I steer myself in the direction of Abbie's house, knowing I will be welcomed and warmed and fussed over. Christine will make me a toddy and John will drive me home. But when I get there, the very warmth of the light, the golden rectangle of the windows, the paths so recently cleared of ice, fill me with shame.

I've gotten myself into this mess and I must get myself out of it. I turn away from the cleared path toward the slick sidewalk that will lead me to the lower reaches of Westmount that we still call home, at least for now.

# Part 3

"Most of the girls I grew up with married the first man who proposed to them. I didn't. I've lived my entire life outside the 'magic ring.' Partly because 'till death do us part' seemed too much to promise.

"I kept thinking about how quickly I kept outgrowing books, for example. What would happen if I came to the last page of a husband?"

—June Grant on CBC's *The Sunday Edition*,
October 2001

"What happened to Daisy's debutante dress? Please tell me."

Flash of sunshine through leaded glass, the dining room suffused in light. Daisy in her slip, pouting, the seamstress with her stretched smile, the burnt velvet, tulle, and silk. Had I imagined it all?

Nothing like the plain, ill-fitting dress Daisy is wearing in her debutante photo. I take up the frame from the sideboard and crouch next to Mother in her armchair. "There was another dress, wasn't there?"

She keeps her eyes fixed on the far wall for so long I don't think she's going to answer me at all, and when she does speak, it's in a whisper, as though she doesn't want Father to hear.

"It was the winter of 1937, when it all happened. A long time later I found it had all been falling apart for years, but your father kept going just the same. Borrowing against the business to pay for our household expenses. He thought he could at least keep everything the same for Daisy, until she got married. Then we'd start to economize. Daisy was his princess, the apple of his eye. It was always like that. He could never say no to her.

"Daisy's dress for the Saint Andrew's Ball—you can't imagine the expense of that dress. It would be enough to keep us in heating oil for five years, the way we live now. The silk velvet was woven in Florence and then sent to a craftsman in Paris to have the pattern that Daisy had drawn herself burned into it. The white silk, the tulle. Oh, June, when I think of it now."

*She shakes her head and covers her mouth with her hand, and I think she might not be able to go on.*

*"What happened next, Mother?"*

*"What happened was Nathan came—your father's business manager. They locked themselves up in the study for hours. Nathan had been trying to keep it afloat, but there was no way to save the fur business. It was the Depression, people were desperate to sell their heirloom fur coats for pennies on the dollar, not buying new ones. Everything was due at once, all the expenses, all the bills, all the loans. No more extensions. And nothing we owned had the value it once had.*

*"Except the dress, you see. Not all families were struggling like we were, some businesses did just fine through those years, thrived even. And Daisy's dress, well, we sold it to the McGowans so we could make a payment and keep the Côte Saint Antoine house at least until Daisy was engaged. The McGowan girl wore it to the ball, and Daisy wore Aunt Lucie's old debutante dress. I tried to take it in as best I could, but I'd never really learned how to sew."*

*She looks at me then, her eyes lost. I reach for her hand but she pulls away, stroking the edge of the wooden frame instead. "She still looks lovely, of course, and she tried to make the best of it, she really did. But then, when she saw Cecily McGowan at the ball, in her dress. Well, she made a terrible scene. Tried to tear the dress right off the girl."*

*"You sent me to Grannie's. When I came back it was after the ball, and Daisy was away in the country." That's all I can remember.*

*"Yes, she went away to the country. To a friend's chalet in the Laurentians. By the time she got back, we were moving to Abbott Street and, well, she could not tolerate it here. She was determined to make a good match, a match where she'd never have to think about economizing or wearing a hand-me-down dress or worry about any of it.*

*"And we thought, after that frightful scene—and the gossip!—that there was no hope for a match for any of you. But then she met Geoff, and whether he hadn't heard, or didn't believe a word of it, we're still not sure.*

*His parents tried to forbid him from seeing her. And when they didn't turn up to the wedding—" Mother waves her hand as though to say that I know the rest of the story.*

*Then she continues: "It's no small thing for her, you know. The clothes, the dresses, the nights out, the beautiful house. And Geoff is doing well, isn't he? Even without his father's money to help him. He'll be able to look after her the way she needs to be looked after. With all her nice things."*

*She shakes her head as she takes up her newspaper again. "We just have to make sure that Daisy's temper doesn't chase him away. It would be terrible for her, without Geoff. Terrible for all of us."*

# Chapter Thirty-Four

During Mass, I think about all my lies. Upon review I find that every time I've lied, it's been to help me get by in the world.

I lied when I told Mr. McAulay that I did not write the Eaton's copy, but then I was lying to cover up for Mr. Sands, which is what I thought I needed to do to save my job. And where would we all be if I lost my job? (I gasp out loud, right in the middle of Mass. I have lost my job. I was fired. I had forgotten, just for a moment.)

But back to lying. I lied to Geoff. Or rather, I did not correct Geoff when he repeated Mother's lie that I had spent the money for the electricity bill on a new hat. Daisy spent that money, not me. But if I told him that, it would have upset him, and who knows what he would have done? Who knows what a man will do, when faced with the truth?

The truth is that we are completely dependent on Geoff to have electricity at all. Mother knows this, as do I. It was more important to have lights and heat than to tell the truth, and if this counts as lying, so be it, but I will not confess such lies anymore.

Envy is another thing altogether. As far as I can tell, I've made no progress at all on that front. I would still change places with Daisy in a minute, given the chance.

Pride and envy got me into this mess. I open my mouth and allow Monsignor McDonagh to place the wafer on my tongue. I will humble myself tomorrow when I go out in search of a new job. Any job. I will do this to pay the rent and the heat. I will do this so that Father is warm and the dogs have their ground beef and Mother her cheese.

——— ⁓ ———

"What do you think of this one, Father?" I ask him. "Secretary in a law office. And it's in Westmount. I would not need to take the streetcar. That would be another savings."

But would I miss going downtown? The feeling each morning of being shuttled to something new and ever different?

Mother has taken the dogs for a walk in the sun. Father and I are at the kitchen table. He's the perfect audience for my musings. We're never sure how much he understands, but no matter. Even if he understood it all, he could not repeat a word. I haven't told Mother yet, about my predicament. I hope to have another job before I tell her anything at all, though the weight of my silence makes my breath feel as heavy as Father's.

"I think this one will be popular, though, suitable for a proper Westmount girl. Someone whose parents would not approve of her going downtown every day."

Father makes a noise deep in his chest.

"You think that's funny, do you? Here, how about this one? A receptionist/model. Do you think I could be a model, like Daisy? Oh, but it's on Bernard. That's three streetcars at least. 'Must be a size six.' Really. Well. Never mind that."

I let one side of the paper fall on the table so I can lay my hand over Father's on the arm of his wheelchair.

"I've made a terrible mess of things, Father. I'm very worried. There's not much in here today at all."

"Huuuuuun . . . ," he gurgles.

"I know." I look into his eyes, murky with liquid and veined with red from coughing. Is he sympathetic? Angry? About to cough? Really, there's no way to tell.

I pull my hand away and get back to the paper. "Look at this one," I say to him. "'McAulay Advertising. A national firm, seeks copywriters. English. Excellent writer. Smart and efficient. Will train. Apply to Mr. McAulay, eleventh Floor, Sun Life Building.'"

Father coughs, like he's trying to dislodge something vital, deep in his chest. I let the paper drop and stand, hands on his shoulders, waiting for it to pass. There is nothing more to do.

I take the classifieds up to my room when I go, and even though it's Sunday and I'm not supposed to use a typewriter, I type an application letter to Mr. McAulay. The advertisement does not say that copywriters need to be men.

# Chapter Thirty-Five

"Fine morning, isn't it, Miss Grant?"

"Yes, Constant. It is." I have arrived at my usual time, dressed in my usual clothes, a letter addressed to Mr. McAulay in my hand. There is no reason for Constant to think anything has changed.

I will drop the letter off at reception and hope that Marie-Céleste isn't assigned to the front desk this morning, but when I step out of the elevator Mr. Lewin and Miss Pomeroy are standing at the reception desk, which is even worse. There's no stepping around them; I am a visitor like any other. When Marie-Céleste sees me (of course it has to be her) her eyebrows shoot up and her soft-pink painted lips form a perfect O.

"What do you mean, I can't have her? I filled out your infernal form." Mr. Lewin shoves a paper at her, then catches sight of me. "There you are, Miss Grant. We are fighting over you like a prize pig. Do you have any say in the matter at all?"

Miss Pomeroy turns and scans me top to toe. Then she nods. "Right on time, I see, Miss Grant. Good. Get to work."

Mr. Lewin sighs. "I need her on the Red Lantern account. The presentation is this afternoon."

"No, Mr. Lewin, you do not. You need a copywriter. Miss Grant is nothing more than a stenographer, one on very thin ice at the moment."

She turns to me. "Off you go, Miss Grant. I will be right there with your morning assignment."

I know better than to question. I can feel all of their gazes follow me as I head down the hall to steno. A job—any job—my old job! It will do. I tuck the letter up my sleeve as I go, but I don't throw it away. Not yet.

———— ❧~❧ ————

It is coming up to the lunch break at my not-so-new job, and it is clear: Miss Pomeroy has allowed me back, but I am to be treated as the newest girl. My desk is in the corner, looking out at the other girls' backs. I must not speak, or get distracted, or make a mistake, or I'll risk getting fired again. The others barely look at me in case my bad luck rubs off on them. But I am here. I am working. Miss Pomeroy doesn't take her eyes off me, but won't look me in the eye all at the same time, and I am too relieved and grateful to ask questions.

Still, I am determined to get my application letter to Mr. McAulay.

I look furtively to Miss Pomeroy and for once she is not looking at me. I unfold my letter and smooth it, then place it between two letters for Mr. McAulay to sign. I place a thick contract on top, to help keep it flat. Then I roll a fresh sheet of paper and start on the next letter.

Partway through the morning, Marie-Céleste slips in from her assignment at reception and drops a note on my desk. I jump in surprise. "She keeps calling," Marie-Céleste says. "It sounds important."

*Abbie Howard,* the note reads. *Come to the Windsor Hotel at lunch.*

I look around, frantic Miss Pomeroy will scold me, but she's not there.

"She's out checking on the girls," Marie-Céleste whispers on her way out. "Grace spilled the coffee cart."

It's just green-faced Helen and me left in steno, and Helen has not stopped typing. I do the same and for several long minutes there is nothing but the sound of the two of us. Miss Pomeroy, if she could see us, would be very pleased.

Suddenly, Helen stops typing and falls to the floor, retching into the garbage pail. I scuttle to the floor beside her and rub her back, the same as I did for Missie after her Saint Andrew's Ball—"Too much excitement," Mother said. "Too much champagne, more like," Daisy muttered, too quietly for Mother to hear.

"Oh, June. It's no use," Helen whispers.

"It will be all right, Helen. It will," I say, though what business I have saying this, I don't know. "I'll clean this up. Try to pull yourself together for these last few minutes before lunch."

I take the soiled trash bin to the ladies' room and rinse it out, then leave it in a corner for the custodian to find. I freshen my lipstick and, when I hear voices in the hall, I join a rush of girls heading to lunch. I crowd into the elevator with them before Miss Pomeroy sees me.

———— ◦✑〜✎◦ ————

The concierge at the Windsor bows and opens the door for me, and I feel every bit as rich and important as the other guests. Concierges make me want to spend all my time wandering the lobbies of the best hotels.

"There you are, June." Abbie runs up and takes my arm and rubs it. "Didn't you wear a coat?"

"No time, I didn't want Miss Pomeroy to see me." She's wearing a tea dress in a bright raspberry red with a dramatic cinch at the waist. "Abbie, you must be the prettiest girl here."

"Oh, shush. Come, we don't have a lot of time."

"But what is happening?"

"I'm going to meet the lady. She said we'd have a nice private chat, but I wonder . . ."

"Which lady?"

"The one from the agency. That J-P talked about. About the special modeling jobs?"

With all of my own problems, I had put it out of my mind for the weekend, but now it all comes rushing back. "I remember," I say.

"Margaret, her name is. I'm sure she's perfectly nice, but will you keep an eye on me?" she asks, pulling me toward the restaurant.

The maître d' does not flinch at Abbie's convoluted story, conveyed in hushed, almost desperate tones. I'm her sister, chaperoning her lunch from a distance, and Abbie will pay my bill. He only betrays his skepticism when he says, "Your aunt can come this way. Wait here please, Mademoiselle." Then to me, "Follow me, Madame."

He leads me to a table and is soon replaced by the waiter, who asks, "High tea for one?"

I nod and spread my napkin on my lap. I have a clear view of Abbie at her own table. In the time that the waiter takes to pour my tea, her guest has arrived, and though I can only see the back of her head, it is a head I would recognize anywhere.

I shift my gaze to take in Abbie, who refuses to look my way. If she does, she will surely give away the game that Daisy, my older sister, is sitting across from her. *A woman named Margaret.*

Marguerite, French for "daisy," is Daisy's full name.

The waiter deposits a tray of crumpets, cucumber sandwiches, and tiny tarts. Food for four people. My stomach is so unsettled, I don't know if I'll be able to eat a bite. Will they let me take it home? I wonder. What a treat for Mother and Father. For the boys, too, if they are there.

It's no good, I can't eat a thing, and surely I should be getting back? I look to the table, Daisy leaning forward over a tray twice the size of mine, whispering to a wide-eyed Abbie.

The shock of it settles deep inside me, and I tamp down the inevitable nausea. I will not be sick; there's no time for that now. Instead, I follow my anger, which has me standing. I take my purse, and at the querying look from the waiter, I make a sweeping motion over the tea tray, which he rushes to collect. I move and see myself move at the same time. I am propelled.

They both look up when I reach their table, Abbie's expression stricken; Daisy's shows only mild surprise.

"What are you doing here, June?"

"What am *I* doing? What are *you* doing?" My voice is too loud, too forceful, too full of emotion, which flares further at Daisy's shrug. "Managing girls for special dates? Is that what you've been doing all these nights when you go out?" I want to pull the plain, ugly words back, but what is the point of pretending?

Daisy swivels her head to Abbie like I'm not there at all. "Is this some kind of trick?"

Abbie shakes her head over and over, her voice appeasing. "No, I didn't—I didn't know it was you. I was a bit worried—didn't know what to expect, so I asked June to chaperone from afar."

"I see," Daisy says. Then she looks up at me. "Thank you, June, but we won't be needing your supervision. As you can see, your friend is quite safe."

She raises a hand, and before she lowers it the maître d' is at my side. "Madame, if you will follow me."

The waiter appears with a bakery box full of my tea things. He takes my elbow and guides me through the lobby, under the magical golden light of the chandelier. I stood here once, in line with 183 other girls, waiting to curtsy before Princess Alice at my Saint Andrew's Ball. Was that only two years ago? And a few weeks ago, I passed through on my way to dinner. I thought I might enter this lobby again one day, to watch someone lovelier than me, perhaps Abbie, dance on her wedding day.

But I'm alone now, on the sidewalk outside with a box full of crumpets. The doorman watches me from the warmth of the lobby, and I can read his expression clearly: he won't open the door for me if I try to come back. And Daisy, treacherous, lying, dangerous Daisy, is still welcome inside.

# Chapter Thirty-Six

I am so angry at Daisy I'd like to drag her out of the Windsor and home and make her answer to Mother. But I can't lose my job all over again by being late. Not when I've so recently gotten it back.

Dot is at reception, a far-off look in her eyes. She's smoothing the part of her hair with her left fingers, ever so slowly. I'm almost at the steno office before I register the ring.

"Did Dot get engaged?" I ask as I enter the office.

Miss Pomeroy shudders. "Yes, and the others are all in a flurry. I am counting on you to stay focused this afternoon, Miss Grant."

I must push what I just saw out of my mind. I must not make mistakes. I stare straight ahead as I take my seat. I can feel Marie-Céleste's eyes on me as I sit at my typewriter. No errors means no daydreaming. No thinking about Daisy, or how I'm going to get in touch with Abbie. It takes effort to focus on the dry language of the sales contract between McAulay and Associates and the Celanese Carpet Company.

I don't know how much time has passed when Miss Pomeroy calls to me, "Miss Grant." I look up, fully absorbed in the details of the proposed media buy for nylon carpets. French and English. Newspapers, magazines, radio. It's a big account. It will need one full-time writer, possibly two.

"Yes?" I look up. The desks around me are empty. "Is it break time already?"

Miss Pomeroy shakes her head. "Everyone is out on assignment. I need you to deliver coffee. The trolley is ready for you in the kitchen."

I nod and lift my fingers from the typewriter. Standing, I smooth my skirt and shake down the sleeves of my blouse under my jacket.

"Lipstick," Miss Pomeroy says.

I reach for my purse and refresh my lipstick. Then I look at her again.

"That will do," she says.

In the kitchen I find the waiting trolley. "Coffee and biscuits for seven," the chit reads. "Conference Room A. Account: Red Lantern Taxi."

One wheel on the coffee cart is off-balance and squeaks. I have to fight to keep it rolling in a straight line, but when I get to the conference room it won't turn; the cart just presses harder into the door hinges with each push.

Mr. Roscoe from the accounts department is standing at the front with Mr. Lewin's poster-size mock-ups on the three easels. He's holding a pointer, but he's dropped it to his side in order to glare at me. They are all looking at me. Mr. McAulay, Mr. Lewin, the whole accounts department seems to be here. And then, on the other side of the table, the clients, Bruno and J-P, both stare right at me.

The heat rises from my chest to my throat and up to my cheeks, which burn bright as a Red Lantern roof light. I try lifting the trolley on one side to unstick it from the doorjamb, but I only manage to rattle the coffee cups.

"Uh—as I was saying—lighting your way home. You, the conquering hero, uh . . ." Mr. Roscoe tries to start up again.

I crouch down and lift the stuck wheel away from the corner of carpet that has it trapped. Half standing, I lift one side of the trolley and move it several inches, then clank it down. Coffee sloshes from the carafe onto the cinnamon swirl buns. With a final clank and squeak, I get the trolley in place. I stand behind it, hands behind my back, ready for service, and turn to watch Mr. Roscoe blunder through the end of my presentation.

"In this situation, it's you, reading the newspaper, who is the conquering hero." He hasn't even bothered to memorize it. He's reading from the notes I typed up. "Home for a reprieve, to be feted and adored, before heading out again." He ends the sentence on a high note, as though asking a question.

Mr. Lewin jumps up. "Thank you, Mr. Roscoe. Now, gentlemen, I would invite you to have a closer look at the artwork while we all enjoy a cup of the coffee that Miss Grant has so spectacularly delivered for us." There's a chuckle around the room as the men stand and begin to drift toward me.

I pour the first coffee for Bruno. "Cream and sugar?"

"No, black."

"Quite an entrance," says Mr. Lewin.

"I'm terribly sorry. One of the wheels is completely stuck. Here, will you take this bun, please?"

"But it's wet!"

"Please? Will you just take it?"

He shrugs and takes a large bite. "Practically don't need the coffee." He winks at me, pointing the bun in my direction. "It should have been you up there."

J-P keeps trailing to the back of the line. He comes to get his coffee once all the others are looking at the artwork. "I've seen you before, haven't I? Where was it? At the club?"

I smile, aiming for mysterious. Nonchalant. "Coffee?"

He leans closer. "Never mind the coffee. Where was it? Were you at the club?"

His face is less handsome up close. His breath smells like mints, not coffee and cigarettes like the others. He steps back and his face relaxes back into his regular, charming assemblage of features. His smile is gracious on the surface, but the suspicion is still there underneath. "No coffee for me, thank you. Just a bun."

Using the tongs, I place the bun on a plate and hand it to him. He looks down at the plate, smiles, but does not take it. He waits, staring at my shaking hand. I want to shove it at him and yell, "What are you turning my sister into?" He looks at my face and it's like a light has turned on, and his expression turns hard and angry. He's about to say something when Mr. Lewin sidles up and draws J-P away, saying: "Come tell me which of the drawings you prefer."

I manage to serve the others without spilling or stammering. As soon as I can, I run out of the room and to the ladies' room. I splash cold water on my face and stare at myself in the mirror, taking deep breaths to calm down.

What happened, really? What did he say that upset me so much? It wasn't his words so much as the kaleidoscope of his expression. The cold and hard expression just under the surface of his smile. A feeling, more than something I could point to.

I pull a fresh swath of towel through the dispenser and dry my face on the rough, striped cloth. My hands are steady as I refresh my lipstick and stare back at my reflection. Resolute.

I go in search of Dot to help me retrieve the trolley. I dig the wheels out of the carpet while she flashes her engagement ring around as she steers. The meeting is back in full swing, with J-P and Bruno asking questions. No one notices us leave.

I wish I could stay to hear which campaign they choose, but I can't think of an excuse. I just manage to steal a call in to Abbie—she's not home—before getting back to the carpet contract. There's still time to finish it before the end of the day, if I don't let my inner state of turmoil distract me.

At home everything is quiet, except for Father's coughing. Daisy and the boys are not there, and Mother says she has not heard from her all day. I tell her Abbie treated me to high tea, and we eat the cucumber sandwiches with our can of chicken soup.

I call Abbie so many times I worry Mother will start to ask questions, and it's only when I am heading for bed that the phone finally rings.

"Abbie? I've been calling and calling."

"I know, June. I got your messages here, and at the dépanneur."

"But what happened at lunch? What did Daisy say? Have you seen her? She hasn't been here tonight at all." While her presence makes me angry, her absence tonight has made me frantic. "I don't know what to do. Do I tell Mother? Geoff?"

Abbie sighs. "She stopped talking when you came up to us."

"But—"

"Listen, June. Everything will be all right. I'm trying to find out. Just leave it with me."

"Will you tell her to stop?"

The line goes quiet for a moment. "I'll try, June. I promise. Now I have to go, or Mother will start about being on the phone so late."

I hang up the receiver and head up the stairs to my own bed. The clarity of purpose that overtook me at the Windsor has deserted me now. Who was that young woman, so clear and forceful, who marched right up to Daisy and confronted her? She's a stranger to me as I climb under the covers and listen to the sounds of Father's coughing through the floorboards until I fall asleep. I want her back.

# Chapter Thirty-Seven

There's a buzz in the air as I arrive in the morning with just a minute to spare.

"Mr. Lewin and Mr. Roscoe landed the Red Lantern Taxi account," Marie-Céleste whispers. "And there's going to be a party!"

"Which pitch did they choose?" I ask her.

"Oh, I don't know. Does it matter? Quick. Start typing."

"It matters to me."

The rest of the details come to me in whispered snippets over the morning. The party is to be a dinner in the Sun Life executive dining room.

"It's a small gathering; only those who worked directly on the campaign will be invited," Miss Pomeroy eventually tells us.

Marie-Céleste pouts artfully. "I wonder who Mr. Sands will invite. All the others are married. There's no talking them into letting you be their date."

Of course this sets off Dot, who lifts her antique diamond-studded band into the air. "You make it sound like a curse, being married. I'm sure their wives will enjoy an evening out, after all those late nights working on that campaign."

Dot has more to say—about what she would wear if she were married and her husband had worked on the Red Lantern campaign—but the rush of hot anger to my ears drowns out the sound of her voice. I worked on that campaign too, at least at the beginning. Just me and Mr. Lewin in his office all that day, until Miss Pomeroy pulled me away.

"Did you hear me, Miss Grant?" The rushing sound subsides. I can barely hear Marie-Céleste's low voice from the desk in front of mine, speaking with her lips closed so that Miss Pomeroy does not catch her.

"What?" I say.

"Something about a conquering hero."

"'Escort you home like a conquering hero, or a visiting dignitary,'" I whisper back, not bothering to keep my lips shut.

"Something like that."

Miss Pomeroy coughs and we all start typing again. No more whispers, only the clack of keys.

———— ⚮ ————

"Would anyone like a scone?" Mother has arranged the leftover scones, tarts, and crustless sandwiches on the cake plate from her wedding china. "June was invited to tea at the Windsor yesterday, and we still have leftovers."

"Were you, June?" Daisy sits back in her chair as though the scones are on fire. She sucks on her cigarette, the ash dangerously long. "No, thank you, Mother. I'm watching my figure." She looks at me as she says this.

I look down at the lovely strawberry tart on my plate, just a little dry at the edges, and the baking soda biscuit I was about to slather with butter. I put the butter knife down, my mouth suddenly dry.

Mother holds the plate out to the boys, who each make a selection. Then she goes back to feeding Father a bite of scone. "Did you see anyone interesting?" Mother asks.

"Chris, close your mouth when you chew! Heavens!" Daisy cries out.

It's my turn to narrow my eyes. "No one interesting at all." I look right at Daisy as I say it.

For once, Daisy lets things drop, with a glare in my direction. A relief for now, but no doubt she'll be back later to tug my hair and make me promise things.

When the phone rings, Daisy jumps up. "Let me get it, Mother."

Of course it's for her. "Hello, darling," we hear, and then she's listening. She's back a moment later, breathless.

"Geoff wants me at his client meeting. Says it's terribly important for business." Hand on Mother's shoulder, she kisses the top of her head. She's already got her coat on. "Do you mind, Mother?"

"But it's Missie's day to call! You'll miss her."

"Chris will talk to her, won't you, dear?" Daisy kisses the tops of the boys' heads and mutters motherly things about good behavior. I wonder what it must be like to have this convenient cloak of motherhood to put on and take off at will. "Goodbye!" she calls from the door.

I scrape my chair back and stand as though I too have somewhere to go, but the phone rings again.

"That must be Missie. Quick, June. Answer, will you?"

There's more than the usual confusion, since Missie has called early and Mother and Father are not in their places yet. And of course, the boys are here too. Chris tells Missie about the letter to the editor he's going to write about the wartime airports being turned into weather stations. (He's in favor.) This leads to the inevitable discussion of what a brilliant young man he is, and then there's a long silence in the room as Missie tells us all about the baby's nursery and how she's as big as a house and she might need to make more maternity dresses, but wouldn't that be a waste as there's so little time left? (Mother assures her she'll wear them again next time.) Father's deep cough interrupts this flow and then there's the worry about him and why hasn't Mother called the doctor and should he go to the hospital and more reassurances from Mother and the script races to the end—these calls cost a fortune and Missie must go—before anyone even remembers that I'm in the room, let alone remembers to ask about my date with Mr. Hearn.

I stand in the doorway, barely listening. I slide my fingers into the pocket of my skirt and feel the perforated edge of the taxi chits that I always keep with me now. The call takes forever, and then Mother needs my help. Only once Father is settled and the boys are tucked on either side of the sofa, Steve asleep, Chris watching me in the dark, do I call a taxi of my own. I ask them to send Tomasso.

———— ⚬⁓⁓⚬ ————

"Waiting for someone?" the bartender asks me.

"Sherry, please," I say, nodding. When he slides the tiny glass across the bar, I ask, "Can I pay now?"

"A quarter."

I count out two dimes and a nickel and snap my pocketbook closed. I'm the only woman alone at the bar or in the whole place, and I wonder what people must think.

"I *am* waiting for someone," I say aloud, though I'm not sure who I'm saying it to.

I take a sip of the sweet drink for courage and look around for Daisy. There's a lull between the eight o'clock show and the ten o'clock show and the stage is deserted. No François in sight, but the tables are crowded with people, couples and groups and parties of just men in suits. No Daisy.

The cigarette girl comes up to me with her tray, but I shake my head. She leans against the bar and nods to the bartender, and I swing back around to face my drink. I take another sip and look up to see them both staring at me.

"Who'd you say you were waiting for?"

I take a tiny swallow of my sherry. "Marguerite," I say.

The bartender cocks his head and the cigarette girl narrows her eyes, and that's when we recognize each other at the same moment.

"Say, weren't you here a while back, in the kitchen?"

I nod. It's the girl in the blue dress from my first visit here, the one who led the man up the kitchen steps to the Superior Models office and closed the door.

"Were you looking for Marguerite then too?"

I nod.

"What do you want with her?" the bartender asks.

I want her to go home to her children. I want to know what she's up to. I want her to stop. I don't say any of this, I just say, "I heard about the dates. I need to make some extra money."

The cigarette girl's eyes rake over my unfashionable coat, which I've kept on, my woolen stockings, and my clunky boots. "You're hardly her type," she says.

She juts her chin to the bartender. "I need another pack of Export A's." She opens the pack and arranges the cigarettes one by one on her tray.

"What is her type?"

She darts her smoky eyes at me. "Pretty, friendly. You have to make your patron feel good, you know? That's what Marguerite always says."

"And you don't think I can do that?" I know I can't do that, but how does she?

She looks at me more closely, assessing. "You look like you worry about things too much. Our patrons? They have enough to worry about; they just want to feel good," she says again.

"And is that what was happening last time I was here, when you went upstairs?"

Her face closes like a clamp. I reach for her arm, but she's turned away from me. "Export A's, Chesterfields?" she calls as she walks away.

I don't finish my drink, but jostle my way to the door, where Tomasso is waiting outside to drive me home.

"You okay, Miss?"

I nod and watch Saint Jacques pass by outside the window. "I was looking for someone, but she wasn't there."

Abbie's studio is dark as we drive past. I don't talk the rest of the way.

"Ask for me anytime," Tomasso says as he turns into Abbott Street. "Anytime at all."

# Chapter Thirty-Eight

The chatter in steno this morning is all about the Red Lantern dinner. No one from the steno pool is invited. Not even Miss Pomeroy.

By afternoon, the topic has turned to our own Friday night plans. Dot and Marie-Céleste have plans—Dot with her fiancé, of course, Marie-Céleste with someone new. She won't say who, but she has not mentioned Mr. Sands all week. Helen, back from a sick day but looking none the healthier, is mute on the subject. Grace is spending time with a friend.

"That means she hasn't been asked on a date," Dot says, but only once Grace is back at reception, where she's been stationed for today. "What about you, June?"

I'll be sitting with Father so that Mother can have a rest, I want to tell them. I'm just happy that Daisy has been back at home with her own boys. Abbie has been too busy with wedding plans to return my calls. I want to say that I wish everyone would just stay home and have a quiet night. But there's no time to say any of it because Miss Pomeroy interrupts.

"Miss Grant. Mr. Lewin would like to speak with you."

*With me?* The girls follow my steps to Miss Pomeroy's desk from the corners of their eyes. "Hello, Miss Grant speaking."

"June? I told her that you have notes you didn't return. So, look ashamed and apologize now."

It takes a beat for his words to sink in, but then I drop my gaze to my feet. "I apologize, Mr. Lewin."

"Now tell me you'll return them right away."

"I'll return them right away, Mr. Lewin."

"Good. Come to the twentieth floor."

"The—"

"No, don't say that part out loud. Just get some papers and come to the twentieth floor."

"Yes, Sir."

Miss Pomeroy shakes her head when I tell her. "And you were doing so well this week, Miss Grant."

"He'd like me to bring them now," I say.

"Yes, of course. Don't dawdle."

I nod, then scurry back to my desk. In my drawer there's a legal pad with some ideas I scribbled about the Eaton's account. It feels like a lifetime ago. I grab it and head for the elevator.

When I tell Constant that I'm going to the twentieth floor, he just nods. When the doors open, I step out, unsure what I will find. An office of some sort? But it's just a hallway.

"Over here." Mr. Lewin is farther down the hall, looking out the window over Dorchester. "Come see."

The windows this far up do not open. On the parapet outside, nesting in a depression in the gravel, is a falcon.

"Her name is Scarlet," Mr. Lewin says.

The angular end-of-day sun illuminates the brilliant yellow of her claws. The falcon named Scarlet shudders, her gray and white feathers articulating outward.

"What is she doing, when she does that?" I'm not sure why I'm whispering. There's no one else around, and Scarlet seems unperturbed at having an audience, but a hushed voice seems respectful.

"I'm not sure what it's called exactly. But at some point an egg will come out." Lewin is whispering too.

I touch my fingers to the window, wishing I could reach through to feel how soft her feathers are. The swaying dance requires all her focus, with the end-of-day bustle of the city below, and Lewin and me watching her through the window. She ignores it all.

"I put in a good word for you, with Mr. McAulay." I can feel the weight of his presence close to mine, but I can't take my eyes off Scarlet. "That was clever of you, to put your letter in amongst the letters for him to sign."

"He got it then." I smile, but the relief at knowing my ploy worked is soon replaced by uncertainty. "Was he angry?"

"Angry? No. I told him he was crazy if he didn't hire you. You've already proven yourself by landing us Red Lantern."

I nod at his words, drawing them inside me. I feel them soothe the gnawing in my stomach that has been growing all week.

"Like a conquering hero . . . ," I say.

"Or a visiting dignitary," he finishes.

I don't dare look at him, but I can feel every inch of the space between us. We are not touching, but there's part of me that is reaching toward him, and him toward me. We meet, invisibly, in the air between us, igniting and circling upward. This is it, I think. This is why girls feel excited after a date. But then I think, This isn't it at all. Other girls are excited at the prospect of marrying the man, not writing ad campaigns with him, and I know suddenly that this is what excites me about Mr. Lewin. I stare straight ahead at Scarlet, who lifts her head and looks straight at me with her yellow eyes and yellow beak. "Have you ever seen her lay an egg?"

I feel, rather than see, him shake his head. "One minute there's no egg, and then there's an egg. Just like that." He snaps his fingers and I feel the invisible web between us dissolve. I step back, hugging my arms.

"Look, Miss Grant, about the party. It's mean of McAulay not to invite you."

I shrug, aiming for Daisy nonchalance, but I'm not sure I can carry it off. "I'm not bothered. Besides, I've got other plans."

"I'm glad. It'll be a bore anyway, these things always are. But I say you should have a chance to find that out for yourself."

Maybe it's the golden hue of the afternoon sun, but his skin looks less sallow than the last time we worked across from each other. He's in his shirtsleeves, his blazer left behind on some chairback at some point in the day. The slanting light illuminates every thread on his shirt. The cuff and collar are all smoothly pressed, no frays, no missing buttons.

He looks back at me, his eyes kind. "I hope you'll celebrate in your own way. You've done a very good job."

Down the hall a crowd of rowdies tumble out of one of the elevators. "This way, boys."

They follow their leader, heading our way.

"Her name's Scarlet," one of them says, which makes them all laugh.

"I bet it is."

"Shall we go?" Lewin asks. I nod, and take one last look at Scarlet. I feel oddly protective of her, but she has her head down again, feathers puffed out, focused. No band of Friday afternoon jokesters will distract her from her task.

"Hold the elevator," Lewin calls. He holds one arm out like a protective shield, to keep me from being jostled as we pass the revelers in the hall.

Once in the elevator, I realize I've been holding the legal pad in one hand all this time.

"You'd best take this," I say. "The notes I forgot to give you."

"Ah, yes, of course. Don't let that happen again, Miss Grant." His voice is stern but he's grinning when I look up at him.

I smile back, feeling settled—certain of my place—for the first time in days. I know where I belong; a writer, working alongside Mr. Lewin. And it means so much more to me than a date, or an engagement ring, or even marriage. I hug that feeling to myself as the elevator whisks us back down to the eleventh floor, wishing I could knit it closer and make it last.

——— ⌾⌾⌾ ———

I can tell something is wrong as soon as I get home.

Mother is not pacing by the door, as she normally does when I'm late. There's no offer of Friday night sherry, no jostling from George and Elizabeth for floor space as I take off my coat.

"Mother?"

"June?" Mother's voice is a high wail that has me running back to the kitchen, coat half on.

"What is it?"

Father is at the kitchen table in his wheelchair, his face gray and drooping, his brow glistening with sweat. Mother's arm is draped over him, holding a blanket in place. "The blanket keeps falling off. He's sweating and shivering all at the same time."

I come closer, try to tuck the blanket around his shoulders, but he's shaking so much it won't stay. I touch the back of my hand to his burning forehead and look to Mother.

"Did the nurse come?"

She shakes her head.

"He needs a doctor," I say.

"I called Daisy and Geoff, but there's no answer."

Father tries to cough, but only manages to sputter like a weak engine. His eyes are closed, his breath a heavy wheeze. I pull up a chair on the other side of him and lay an arm across his shoulder. Mother, her head laying on his chest, her arm across his waist, looks up at me. The dogs, asleep at her feet, are quiet for once.

"What should we do?"

Mother shakes her head. "Geoff will know. Surely, they'll be home soon? I'll try them again in a minute."

"I haven't seen Daisy in a few days, have you?"

"No," Mother says. "I haven't. Not since she picked up the boys on Wednesday morning."

"We can't wait for them. We need to get him to the hospital."

"But the cost, June. An ambulance is terribly expensive."

I look across at Mother and see something new in her. Something I've never seen in all these years. For the first time I can remember, Mother is afraid.

I go to the front room and call Red Lantern Taxi. I ask them to send Tomasso.

# Chapter Thirty-Nine

We spend the weekend at the hospital, Mother and Father and I. Other than taking a brisk walk home each day, to wash and change clothes and walk the dogs (and this morning, when Geoff finally came and brought her to Mass), Mother will not hear of leaving Father's bedside. When she comes back after Mass, she ties the palm cross to Father's bedpost and prays on her knees for what seems like hours.

Daisy graced us with her presence on Saturday. She came alone, no Geoff, no boys. She wore her black boiled-wool suit and a tiny square black hat with a little black veil angled prettily over her fine features. She kissed Mother on each cheek and made a great show of her tears.

I stood to wait out in the hall so I didn't have to watch her theater, which lasted only five minutes before she came out again.

"It's a little early to start mourning, don't you think?" I whispered, so Mother would not hear, and out of respect for the others on the floor.

"Don't be hateful, June."

"Me, hateful? Where have you been? I called and called."

She looked up at me, the contempt in her eyes clear. "Why? Why did you keep calling? Why does everyone keep calling and expecting me to fix everything? Can't you do anything on your own?"

My mouth dropped open as I searched for some sort of reply. "Daisy, it's Father. He's—he's dying."

Daisy straightened her fur stole and shook her head. Her eyes were bright, too bright. "There's just too much to do. I can't possibly fit this in. Father will understand."

I grabbed hold of her arm, trying to hold her there. "Too much to do? Like what? Like modeling? Going out on the town? Sending your girls on dates?" The words tumbled out of me all at once and I clapped my hand over my mouth, remembering Mother, just inside the door to Father's room. Mother, who taught us to never speak of unpleasant things.

Daisy shook her arm free and stepped away from me. "You won't understand, June, since you're not married, but I have my own family to look after now. Just like Missie. You don't see her here, do you?" She waved one arm behind her like she was erasing me as she clipped back down the corridor and out of sight, leaving me alone with our mother, and our dying father.

—— ෴ ——

I have to go to work tomorrow, so I have come home to get some proper rest. Mother has asked me to write to Missie, but I am to tell her not to worry, and most of all not to come; that Father is getting better and that he will be home soon.

I think this is a lie that helps Mother cope. Lies to make life just a little better. That give a person hope. It seems Mother tells those too.

But poor Father. Oh, Father.

Mother says he will be on the mend and back home with us in no time, but I'm afraid that's not what I saw in the doctor's eyes, when he came in to examine Father this afternoon.

In which case, poor Mother.

# Chapter Forty

I wake with a spaniel clamped to each leg and only feel the frigid air when they scamper down, barking with excitement at the prospect of breakfast. Once dressed, I barely have time to take them for a quick walk, just to the train tracks and back, but when I open the door the dogs shrink back inside.

Abbott Street is an enchantment of icicles. Ice encases the scraggly branches of the tiny trees along the sidewalk, which itself is a sheet of ice. I merely manage to coax them as far as the patch of grass next to the street, which is as slick as a skating rink. Once they are settled back inside, I take Father's old walking stick in one hand and his long black umbrella in the other. Using these props for support, I set out, skate-walking down the sidewalk.

On Saint Catherine, the tinkle and groan of ice in the wind echoes between the buildings. The street is a frozen canyon. A dozen huddled figures waiting at the bus stop tell me all I need to know about the status of the streetcar. I turn away from them and head east. I must get to work. Miss Pomeroy will not accept an ice storm as an excuse. At least not from me.

I cross the arctic landscape, one treacherous penguin step at a time. At the corner of Atwater, with five or six blocks behind me and many more ahead, I almost turn back.

A car has crashed into a light standard. The hood dented, the pole bent over, and no one in sight. I want to climb inside the empty back seat, wrap myself up in Father's coat, breathing in the smell of him until the ice has melted and the streetcars are running again.

Instead I sit on an ice-crusted bench and face the white tundra of Cabot Square, where Mother and Father used to walk during their courtship and the early days of their marriage. Tree branches clink against each other like champagne glasses at a wedding. There is not another soul in sight.

The streetcar stop at the corner is deserted. Even the most persistent would-be passengers have given up the wait. The cold seeps into me as the ice melts under my seat. My stomach churns with hunger, and I imagine the hot cup of coffee and warm bun waiting for me at the office if I can get there. My knees and hips ache with the effort of bracing against the ice. My fingers are cramped from grasping the walking stick and the umbrella. I might freeze to death just sitting here alone in the no-man's-land of Cabot Square. I could turn into an ice sculpture, the cold seeping inward until I'm stuck in place. Tomorrow, or the next day, the storm will be over and the ice will melt again. Droplets will fall from the trees and soak into the scraggly garden beds at the edges of the square. The running liquid will carry a message to the daffodil bulbs that it's time to wake up, but by then it will be too late for me.

The thought that I could freeze to death without last rites propels me to my feet like a rusted machine. I inch around the bench and face the street, each step a potential chute that would bring me tumbling down. I pause at the sidewalk, facing across Saint Catherine, waiting, as though something, or someone, will come along to rescue me.

Should I go back home? But what about Miss Pomeroy? She's sure to be shorthanded today, and I don't have the grace of taking a day off. I am not sick myself, and Father being in the hospital will not count. Not to Miss Pomeroy, anyway.

I am turning in the direction of the Sun Life Building, still eight endless blocks away, when I see a vehicle inching along Saint Catherine toward me, a red light on its roof. The taxi approaches slowly, as though in a dream, and just as slowly I raise one arm and wave the umbrella in the air. A Red Lantern taxi, ready to whisk me where I need to go. *Like a visiting dignitary, or a conquering hero,* I think, as I step gingerly down from the sidewalk and step-slide my way to the rear passenger door.

I almost slide underneath the car completely when I swing the door open, all tangled up in the walking stick and the umbrella.

"It's a mess out there, Miss," says the driver. A new one I've never seen before. "Where to?"

"The Sun Life Building," I say, reaching into my coat pocket. "I have a chit."

---

I needn't have worried about arriving late. The steno office is as deserted as the street; even Miss Pomeroy has not made it in. There are no letters or contracts to type. No clacking keys or whispering girls. As I head to the coffee room, it feels as though I am in a dream.

"Miss Grant, you are the answer to my prayers." Mr. McAulay stands at the coffee maker, holding the filter basket in the air like it's an alien object. "Do you know how this works?"

"Yes, Sir." I take it from him and start to scoop the coffee. "Cream and three sugars?" I ask, and when he nods, I say, "I'll bring it to you, Sir."

"Bring one for yourself, too. I've got something to discuss with you."

He's gone before I can ask what it is. As I wait for the coffee to percolate, I imagine possible scenarios, each one darker than the last. Surely, if he were firing me, we wouldn't sit down for coffee first? And he'd wait for Miss Pomeroy?

"There's no milk," I say, when I carry a tray with our cups and the sugar bowl into his office a few minutes later. "But I did find some cookies."

"Never mind that," he says. "Here, sit." He gestures to the couch, not the hard steno chair where I normally sit to take dictation.

"Do I need a steno pad?"

"No, Miss Grant. Just sit and enjoy your coffee. I can't imagine how you managed to get in."

I place the tray on the coffee table and take my seat. "Would you believe me if I told you a Red Lantern taxi saved my life?" I add sugar, to make up for the lack of milk.

He chuckles and reaches for his own cup. "How's your father? He had a stroke quite a few years back, I remember."

I swallow a sip of my overly sweet coffee. "Yes, and now he has pneumonia."

"That's no good. How's your mother faring?"

I think of Mother sleeping in the chair at Father's bedside, in her fur coat, still wearing lipstick. Her stubborn insistence that Father will be fine despite what the doctor says.

"I've never seen her this scared before," I answer finally.

He puts his cup down and tents his fingers, tapping the pads of his fingertips together. "When my wife died last year, I was terrified. Nothing made any sense without her." The pain in his expression, when he looks up at me, gives his eyes an unfocused look. "It still doesn't," he says.

My stomach chooses that moment to growl with hunger. Mr. McAulay claps his hands together. "Better have one of those cookies, Miss Grant," he says, holding out the plate.

I take one. Outside, in the main office area, a telephone is ringing. It stops and then starts again. There is no one to answer.

Mr. McAulay holds up a letter. At first I think it's my letter, the one I wrote to him to ask for the copywriter job, but then he hands it to me. It's a letter of resignation from Mr. Sands.

"He's going to work at Collier and Moore," Mr. McAulay says. "It seems you were right all along, Miss Grant."

"I'm sorry, Sir," I say, handing the letter back to him. "I didn't want to be right about that."

"That's what I like about you, Grant. You don't mind being wrong. You don't insist on taking credit for your ideas. You know what to do without even being asked. Frankly, we need more of that around here.

"Lewin tells me I should bring you on. As a writer. Says I'd be crazy to interview a new young buck when you're better than three of them put together."

I nibble on the edge of a cookie, willing my stomach to stay quiet.

"What do you think of that?" he asks.

I take a deep breath to find my courage and look up at him. I nod decisively. "I want that more than anything." I want to say more—that I don't care about taking credit, he can have all that, if only I can spend my days writing, preferably with Mr. Lewin—but I stop myself.

He laughs, like he's pleased with me. "Well, then. Let's give you a shot. Why not."

I smile and look down at my coffee. I don't dare raise it to my lips, knowing my hand will shake.

"Are you all right, Miss Grant?"

"Oh, yes," I say, remembering to give him the expected smile. "I'm very happy."

"Good, good. We'll start you today. Thirty-five dollars a week. Good?"

"Yes." I swallow. That's twice what I'm earning now. More money than I ever hoped to earn.

"You'll be in the supply room for now. There's a desk at the back. You can clear it off."

He stands and turns to his own desk, where he picks up a stack of reports that he holds out to me. "Your first client, Celanese Carpet Company. You'll work with Lewin. Study up on nylon. I want a list of all the advantages of nylon carpets and three campaign ideas, with illustrations, on my desk a week from today. Any questions?"

I swallow the last of my cookie and stand, taking the stack from him. "What about Miss Pomeroy?" I ask.

"What about her?"

"Isn't she going to be angry?" I already know the answer. She'll be furious.

Mr. McAulay shakes his head, and then he smiles. "Miss Grant, you're one of the writers now."

"Yes, Sir."

"Most of my writers don't even know who Miss Pomeroy is, and they certainly don't care if she gets angry."

———— ⁂ ————

Over the course of the morning, more people start to arrive. I can hear voices passing in the hall, and the phones are answered after a few rings.

I pull the desk in the supply room away from the window. I find an oak chair on wheels that lists to the left but is otherwise in good shape, and two plain wooden chairs that will do nicely for guests. I slide the chair behind the desk and sit with my back to the window, facing the door. I sharpen a dozen pencils and place them in a cup. I start to take down a steno pad from the supply shelf, but think better of it and reach for a legal pad instead. Then I settle in to read the stack of industry reports about making carpets out of nylon.

Nylon is more interesting than you might think. It's certainly more interesting than typing contracts. I immerse myself in the topic and forget altogether that I am in the supply closet. Nylon is very versatile and can be used for anything from stockings to blouses and nightgowns, drapery sheers, and now carpets. Because it's a man-made fiber, it keeps its shape. In a carpet, this means less vacuuming, which is a big benefit for housewives. I'm so busy thinking about all the things housewives can do with the free time that nylon carpets give them that I don't hear Miss Pomeroy come in.

"What is going on here?" She's wearing her brown suit today, and the cleft down the center of her face is especially severe.

I remember what Mr. McAulay said and steady my voice before answering. "This is my new desk. I'm a copywriter now."

"According to whom?"

"Mr. McAulay."

"Since when?"

"Since this morning."

This interrogation might've gone on longer except that a man from maintenance peeks his head around the door.

"Excuse me, ladies?" He steps into the room, holding a telephone. "I was told to install a phone in here?"

Miss Pomeroy's eyebrows shoot up. I manage to keep my calm on the outside, but inside I'm shouting. My own phone!

"Yes, right here at this desk," I say.

"This is your office? In the supply room?" asks the maintenance man. He walks between the shelves of office supplies, and Miss Pomeroy has to step aside to make space for him.

"That's right," I say. "This is my office."

"Right. Well, this will take about ten minutes."

He waits, phone in one hand, a length of wire in the other, a belt full of tools hanging from his waist. I realize he's waiting for us to leave.

"Fine. I'll come back then. Thank you."

Miss Pomeroy and I walk out into the hall together. Once there, she turns to me, her expression thunderous. "Mark my words, Miss Grant. When you are finished playing writer, when they are done with you, there's no coming back to my steno pool. Understood?"

She doesn't wait for me to answer, but turns on her heel and heads back to the steno office without another word.

——— ❧～❧ ———

It's hard to concentrate on the properties of nylon with a telephone sitting right there on my desk. There are so many calls I need to make. To the hospital, for one. And then Daisy, and Abbie. If Father is ready to come home today, I will need to arrange for help. From Geoff, or Mr. Lublin? Possibly even from Tomasso, whom I have not had a moment to think about, or thank, since he left us at the hospital doors on Friday. I negotiate with myself: one hour of reading about nylon per phone call, plus an extra phone call at each break and at lunch.

I have not made it through my first hour before Marie-Céleste comes in. She doesn't pretend to look for supplies, but beelines straight for my phone. She doesn't ask permission, just makes her call and leans against my desk, her back to me. I drop my eyes back to my paper and try not to let her distract me, but the words before me suddenly have no meaning. When she's done, she shifts to face me, half sitting on my desk.

"So, you have Mr. Sands's job now, is that right?"

I lay the pencil flat under the line I've just read five times, to keep my place. "That's right," I say.

She swings the heel of her shoe on and off, on and off, and picks up a pencil from my cup, testing the sharpness against the tip of her index finger.

"What we can't figure out, then, is how come they didn't give you Mr. Sands's office?" The arch of her brows conveys innocent curiosity, but I'm not fooled. The veneer of friendship, always thin with the girls in steno, has scraped off completely now.

"I don't know," I say.

She shrugs, as though just as mystified as I am. "The girls are wondering if you're making the same salary as Mr. Sands. He made fifty dollars a week. But I told them it would be rude to ask."

"Thoughtful of you," I say.

She nods and stands, places the pencil back in the cup with the others. "Well, see you later," she says, but I call her back.

"Marie-Céleste? When you go back to steno, will you tell the other girls that I made a fuss and wouldn't let you use my phone?" Those eyebrows again. How does she get them to arch like that? I continue: "Make sure Miss Pomeroy hears you."

She nods, slowly, as if taking in all the layers of what I am saying. "All right," she says finally, "but if I need to make a call?"

I hold my open palm out toward the telephone. "By all means," I say.

She smiles at this and starts to walk away, but I call her back again.

"One thing, though. It's making calls only, all right? Don't give this extension out, or I'll tell any suitors that you already have plans."

Arms crossed, she rolls her eyes elaborately before she waltzes out. Pleased with our understanding, I look up at the clock. An hour has passed. I can make my first phone call now.

---

I cannot reach Daisy, or Geoff, or Tomasso, or even Abbie. In the end I use my desk phone to call Christine, who speaks with Mrs. Howard, who speaks with Mr. Howard, who sends their chauffeur to the hospital to bring Mother and Father home.

By the time I get home, my head filled with the seemingly infinite uses of nylon, Father is back in his den. Mother is sitting in her usual chair, a bowl of soup in front of her, the dogs in a heap at her feet, the smell of fresh-baked bread in the air.

Christine stands over a pot at the stove, speaking quietly to Mother, but she stops when I come in. It is such a relief to see her there in the kitchen, as she had been every day of my early childhood. She takes my coat and sends me to wash my hands for supper. Then she serves supper before she lets me go in to see Father.

"He's sleeping. Leave him be," she says.

It's the kind of hearty supper I remember from childhood—beef and barley soup, the broth thick with chunks of meat and vegetables, served with a slice of Christine's fresh-baked soda bread.

When I do go in to see Father, my full belly dulls the shock of how shrunken he looks. It's as though the trip to the hospital and home again has taken everything out of him. His breath is wet and loud, his eyes closed, his hands folded over his chest, on top of the blankets, as though he's already been prepared for his funeral.

"He's so still," I whisper. I know it's a silly thing to say. He's paralyzed. But even paralyzed, there's been a force running through him this whole time.

Where is Daisy? She has not called or stopped by or offered to help. I have not seen her since her short visit to the hospital, when she was no use at all. In her funeral clothes, like Father had died already.

It is hard to fathom a world without him in it. Poor Mother. Should I go to her?

She's in her room down the hall, smoking cigarette after cigarette. Much more than her usual one or two per evening. But how can I talk with her and not tell her about my new job? It will only worry her. Best to stay in my room and try to sleep as best I can. I don't want to burden her, but it's more than that. I want to hold on to my good feeling. I don't want anyone, not even Mother, to take it away.

It's finally happened. I'm a writer now.

# Chapter Forty-One

"We need just a word or two. Not even a real headline. Something that captures the very essence of spring," Mr. Lewin says.

He's sitting across from me in my supply room office, as he did all day yesterday. It's almost lunchtime on Wednesday, and I am beginning to think the entirety of my new job will be to sit across from Mr. Lewin, matching my words to his images.

Between us, my desk is covered in drawings of the Eaton's girls for the spring insert in the *Gazette*, which is to run in two weeks' time. Sissy, featuring Daisy's body and another model's face, stares up at me.

"Is something wrong, Miss Grant?"

It's like my eyes are stuck on the drawing and I can't tear them away from Sissy.

I sigh. "What do you think it would be like to be that pretty?"

Mr. Lewin lifts up the cover page and holds a loupe over the drawing. Then he puts the loupe down and crosses his hands on his lap. He drops his gaze and I wish I hadn't asked the question. I've embarrassed him.

"Never mind," I say. "I'm being peevish."

"But Miss Grant, don't you see?" he says finally. "Imagine if your only job was to be pretty? All your life, to be an ornament."

Sissy's face on the desk starts to swim as my eyes fill with tears.

"Miss Grant," he continues. "What happens when an ornament loses its shine? You have something so much more than that."

I feel something in me shift. Ideas that had been there all my life sift and re-sort themselves. My mouth drops open, but before I can speak, the phone rings.

I shake my head to clear the emotion, and pick up the receiver. "Miss Grant speaking."

"June? It's Grace. There are some people here at reception to see you."

"To see me?" I jump up from my seat. Is it about Father? Has the worst happened? "I'll be right there."

Mr. Lewin has stood too and is looking at me with concern. "Miss Grant?"

"There is someone to see me at reception," I say. "I think it might be—my father is ill, you see—" I stop explaining and rush out the door, Mr. Lewin right behind me.

At the reception desk, Geoff is waiting for me, Stephen in his arms and Christopher at his side. "I don't know what to do. I have to work," Geoff says.

Chris looks up at me, his eyes blinking. "Grannie can't have us because Granddad is dying," he says.

"I know, Chris. But I can't look after you, I have to work too," I say.

"We won't be any trouble at all," he assures me. "That's why I stayed home from school. I'll watch over Steve. We won't bother you."

I look to Geoff. "But where's Daisy?"

Geoff's eyes are hard, and when he speaks, his voice is all repressed rage. "I have no idea where she is. She didn't come home last night. Or this morning. You need to babysit. I have to work, and then I'll try to find her somehow."

My mouth is half open, ready to tell him where to start looking. To spill Daisy's secrets at long last.

"If I may—" Lewin starts, but Geoff interrupts him.

"No, you may not. I don't even know who the hell you are. I need their aunt to help, since it turns out my wife is completely unreliable."

"This is my colleague, Mr. Lewin," I say. "And I cannot babysit, because we—"

Lewin holds a hand up. "If I may," he says. He nods to Geoff. "If you'll allow it—if you'll accept it—I think I can help."

———— ⚮ ————

Mrs. Lewin waits for us at the top of the sweeping staircase that is carpeted with a once-red runner, faded to pale pink. She's not elegant, or even particularly pretty. She can't be more than a few years older than I am, but her face is lined with fatigue and what looks like sadness. Her plain features brighten as she greets the little boys. She has a plump, bald-headed baby in her arms—I cannot tell if it's a boy or a girl.

She spares a smile for me too, but with the boys she seems transformed. She drops down to their level to greet them and a curtain of unfashionably straight, and not terribly clean, hair falls over her face. The baby grabs a handful of it and starts sucking.

"Chris, and Steve." She repeats their names. "This is Arthur Junior, but we call him Drumstick." She wiggles his plump thigh as she says this. The boys stare at the baby, until Drumstick breaks out in a gummy grin, making all of us laugh.

"Can I help put the baby down?" Chris asks. "I'm good at putting babies to sleep."

"Oh, are you? Well, thank goodness, because we do have some trouble with that around here." She looks up at Lewin as she says this, her expression suddenly blank and sad. I shift on my feet, and it's like she notices me for the first time. "You must be Miss Grant," she says. I expect her to say something more—that she's heard about me or is pleased to meet me—but instead she stands up from her crouch and leads us inside.

"My little Drumstick does not think he needs any sleep at all. It's the one point we disagree on."

The Lewins live in an apartment on the second floor of a converted mansion. By the light streaming in the broad windows I can see how pale Mrs. Lewin is, the dark circles under her eyes, the deep fatigue beneath her smile as she chatters with the little boys. But I'm soon distracted by the paintings that cover the walls of what was once the great room but that now makes up the sum total of the Lewins' home.

Landscapes, cityscapes, portraits, all done in oil.

"The paintings," I whisper.

"Oh yes, that's my talented husband." Her voice sounds hard, almost resentful. "Some of the ones in the back are mine. I used to paint too, before—"

Lewin bats a hand and goes to the kitchen, carved into a window-less corner. "Boys like cookies, don't they? Have we got any?" He roots around on the counter with his hands, touching everything like a blind man.

"In the cupboard, Arthur."

Have I heard his first name spoken before now? I don't think I have. To hear it from his wife's lips, in such an ordinary, domestic tone, makes me blush.

"No, the next one. There you are."

He comes back with a tin of shortbread and offers them around. The boys look to me before taking one, and I nod. Chris says "thank you" without prompting.

"You'll be all right then?" Lewin asks her. "We'll come back for them later."

"Or leave them. We'll be just fine, won't we, boys? We have a cot just your size, Stephen. And Christopher can fit on the sofa. We'll be happy for the company, won't we, Drumstick?"

Christopher nods and follows her to a large sofa, draped with col-orful cloths and piled with laundry. She settles with the baby on her lap and looks up to me. "Keep them here as long as you like. I am sorry about your father, Miss Grant."

"Thank you," I say.

She nods, then looks back to the boys. "Now, tell me all of your stories while we eat the rest of the cookies."

None of them look up at us as we leave. I follow Lewin slowly, taking in every detail as I go: the art, the piles of books, the colors everywhere, the creative mess layered over faded Victorian grandeur.

"Back to work for us, then," Lewin says as he leads the way down the curved staircase.

"Are you sure Mrs. Lewin does not mind?"

He shakes his head. "Quite the opposite. It will do her a world of good." He pauses on the steps as he says this, and I stop before I bump into him. I wait for him to say more, to say something about why Mrs. Lewin seems so sad, and for a minute it looks like he will speak, but then he seems to think better of it. He adjusts his hat back on his head and starts walking down the stairs again. When he reaches the front door, he holds it open for me. I nod and step through the doorway, my mind full of stored details of his domestic life to take out and think about later.

———— ❧❧ ————

"Any news?" At the end of the day, Lewin appears between the shelves of the office supplies. "From your sister, that is?"

I shake my head.

"And your father?"

"Still the same as this morning."

"That's good then, that means we have some time."

"Time?"

"Yes. Shall we go look for her? We can commandeer a taxi and check out every jazz bar and dinner club in town until we find her." He gestures to the piles of reports about nylon on my desk. "Nylon can wait," he says.

"But what about the boys?"

"I'll go check on Mrs. Lewin and make sure, but I'm sure she's fine." He looks pensive for a moment. "She's probably happier than she's been since—well. Why not let them stay overnight?"

I reach for my coat. "If you're sure."

"Where would you like to start?"

Tugging my coat on, I say, "I should go to Abbie's studio first. I can do that while you check on Mrs. Lewin. Then we can meet at Le Salon du Jazz?"

He looks at his watch. "See you there in an hour?"

I almost rush out after him before the tug of obligation brings me back to myself. Returning to my own desk, I call Mother and tell her not to worry and that I'll be spending the night at Daisy's. Then I head out to find a taxi to take me even farther into the city.

———— ⁓⧢⧢⁓ ————

Along Saint Jacques, the sun is setting, but the streets look crowded together and plain. Up ahead, Saint Cunigunde church is dull against the piled-up clouds.

"I'll wait here," Tomasso says as he pulls up outside the dépanneur. I pick my way past today's collection of beer cases and cartons of cigarettes and push open the unlocked door at the top.

The mess from my last visit has crossed from untidy into squalor. Even the cleaner seems to have given up. Almost every item of clothing from the clothing rack is draped or spread or piled, on chairbacks, across the divan, on the floor.

On closer inspection, the clothing rack is not quite empty. There is one black suit hanging there. Daisy's mourning outfit—the one she wore to the hospital on Saturday.

Candles in wine bottle holders have dripped down to form wax sculptures. The wax is hardened and cold. My hand brushes the table as I step closer, and I look to the mess there: another bottle of Chianti, its heavy base woven with straw, a white candle half burned down, an ashtray shaped like a swan overloaded with lipstick-stained cigarette butts. Daisy's black box hat with its lace veil has been discarded among piles of costume beads and bangles.

Today the photographs on display are mostly of young women, dressed for a night on the town. I recognize the cigarette girl from the jazz club. Her blonde hair is in ringlets and her dress cuts a deep V across her chest. There's a girl with dark hair slicked back and tiny cowlick rings around her forehead. Her head is dropped back, her eyes closed as though she's given way to pleasure. A more proper-looking young woman with dark hair framing her long, but pretty, face, her eyes innocent, leaning forward, as though listening attentively.

There are photos of them individually, in pairs, in small groups. And there is one of the girls all together, crowded around the divan, laughing and talking with one another, champagne coupes in hand, as though ready for a great party.

The picture is like nothing I have seen before. Abbie seems to have captured the essence of each of them. Their beauty, yes, but their individual personalities shine through as well. The cigarette girl is leaning forward and talking to another one of the girls, as though sharing a secret. The girl with the long plain hair is slightly separate from the rest of them, staring off into space, a little bit dreamy. At their center is Daisy, small and lovely and yet regal, staring straight into the camera lens, her expression a mix of satisfaction and daring. Just try and stop me, it looks like she's saying. A dozen girls, and Daisy at their center. Daisy and her girls.

It's the only photograph with Daisy in it. I pull it down from the line and slip it into my coat pocket. At the end of the row I find my own photo—the one from the time I pretended to be Abbie's manager.

It stops me again to see myself like this. I look brave and ready for anything, which is exactly how I need to feel on this evening of searching the nightclubs for my missing sister.

I rummage through the discarded piles of clothing until I find the blouse, the men's trousers, the overcoat, and the fedora from that photo of me. Then, standing at the back of the room so I can't be seen from the curtainless window, I dress as I did that day. I stand the collar of the blouse up under the coat and, using the tiny wall mirror, angle the hat the same way the steno girls did that day in the office, until I am quite satisfied. My reflection shows a brave and capable young woman. One who feels perfectly comfortable going in and out of nightclubs in trousers. One who looks more courageous than I feel.

I fold my skirt and blouse, roll them up, and carry the bundle of clothing down to the street, where Tomasso is waiting to take me to meet Mr. Lewin.

# Chapter Forty-Two

The crowd is already forming for the early set when we arrive at Le Salon du Jazz, but the musicians are not yet on stage. Lewin nods slowly as he takes in my changed appearance, but he does not comment.

I hand him the photo. "Daisy is the one in the middle," I say.

He nods. "Yes, of course. Our Eaton's girl. I'll go ask the bartender if he's seen her."

I go straight for the kitchen, which again is crowded with instruments and music stands. A few musicians are there, warming up, the sound even more discordant than usual. François is there, and he stops talking when he sees me.

"Miss Grant," he says.

"Have you seen Daisy?" I ask him.

He cocks his head, his eyes sad. "She was here last night until late with your friend, the blonde one." He twirls his finger next to his head to indicate curly hair.

"Abbie," I say.

"A couple of gentlemen bought them champagne, and they all left together after the second set. Around one thirty?"

"Thank you, François. If you see her, will you tell her . . ." I pause.

"Tell her what?"

"Tell her to come home."

"Is your father okay, Miss?"

I shake my head. The grief I've been holding at bay threatens to crash across me like a wave. "No, he's not."

François nods his head back toward the servants' staircase. "Have you checked upstairs?"

———— ❧～❧ ————

The cigarette girl answers my knock. She's wearing a red dress today, and her face is carefully made up, her freshly rolled hair shiny and smooth. Her bright smile drops right off when she sees me.

"Oh," she says. "It's you."

"Who is it?" a voice calls from inside. A man's voice.

I step past her into the room.

J-P stands at the edge of the room divider, smoking a thin cigar. The air is sharp and heavy with the smell of it.

"You," he says. "Where is she?"

His so-called handsome features are twisted in anger as he steps toward me. He grabs my arm and hisses the words again. "Where is she?"

I shrug his hand away, but he holds on tighter. "I came to ask you the same thing."

"She was supposed to be here hours ago," he says. "All the girls are ready for her."

"She's a married woman with children. You have no business asking her to model, or do whatever it is you have her doing."

His eyes squint in confusion. He loosens his grip on my arm enough for me to twist it free. "Modeling? Abbie doesn't model. She takes pictures. And no way has she had babies. You can always tell."

I remember now. He knows me from my visit with Abbie. He does not know I'm related to Daisy. "I'm not talking about Abbie. I'm talking about Daisy."

"Daisy? Who the hell is Daisy?"

There's a slam behind me and I jump. Lewin has pushed the door open and he steps into the room. "Everything all right?" he asks me. "J-P," he says, nodding at the man. "Have you seen Daisy? It's important we find her."

J-P steps back, his hands out in front of him. "I don't know any Daisy. No girls called Daisy."

I remember the pictures of the models and turn to the wall, jabbing my finger at it. "This. This is Daisy." Daisy smiles up at me, her eyes filled with knowing. "Marguerite."

"Oh, Margaret," he says, nodding at the photo. "She's like my den mother. She looks after all my girls. Takes them shopping, does their bookings. Makes a pretty penny while she's at it."

I too nod at the picture. "That is Daisy. She's my sister. A wife and mother to two young boys. Our father is dying, and her family needs her to come home."

J-P shrugs and drops his hands down as though shaking off any responsibility. "She came to me. Said she needed to make more money. Like real money, that's what she said. More than modeling. She's too old to model anyway. Too old for all of it really. But she's good with the girls, so I put her to work. What could I do?"

"You could just stop. Be satisfied with a modeling business and a taxi business, surely that's enough?" Lewin says. "Does Bruno know what you're doing?"

That shrug again, as though it could not be helped. "Bruno's old-fashioned. He goes home at five o'clock. Spends the money I'm making for us both on his nice house in the suburbs and doesn't ask questions."

"But it isn't right," I say.

He lifts his hands up and lets them drop. "Businessmen from out of town. Widowers. Cheered up by a beautiful girl on their arm. The girl gets a little money out of it, enough for a new dress and a hat. Keeps her in new shoes. There's no harm to it."

"The harm is to their reputations. Their future lives. Their morals," I say.

He shakes his head at my words. "Look, I'm just a businessman. There's a need, I fill it. I'm in the business of pretty girls and taxis. Some old widower wants a girl on his arm, I send one to him in a taxi. Young bucks from out of town take a taxi to a club and want company? Driver picks up some girls on the way. Simple as that."

"But aren't you worried about the police?" Lewin asks.

J-P shrugs and takes a drag of his cigarette. "Police like pretty girls, too."

I open my mouth to say more, but let it close again. "I need to find Daisy," I plead.

"Have you seen her?" Lewin asks.

He shakes his head. "Not since sometime last night."

The girl by the door has been watching this exchange, but has not said a word. As we step out into the hall, she follows us and grabs my arm. "Try Rockhead's Paradise," she whispers. "I saw her there last night. Her and the other one, with the curls."

I nod, and Lewin lets me step around him so that I lead the way down the stairs. We take the main staircase this time. Downstairs, the first set is in full swing, François and his band up on the tiny stage. I raise a hand to him as we step out.

—— ❧◦❧ ——

At Rockhead's Paradise, Mr. Rockhead himself gives me a red carnation for my lapel. He fusses over me as though I'm as special as the other girls and somehow finds a seat for us in the crowded club.

"Best I can do, I'm afraid. The first show is about to start."

Lewin nods, and once he's gone says to me: "We can see the crowd from here."

We are visited in turn by the cocktail waitress and the cigarette girl. Lewin orders me a sherry and buys a cigarette for himself, though he does not light it.

It's like entering another world. Like another city has lived inside the city I've known all my life. The room is electric with anticipation. Everyone yelling to be heard and yet conversation is impossible.

I sip my sherry and scan the tables. There are many men—American, I'd say, with that same clean and confident look and straight white teeth as Missie's husband. But there are women too, and plenty of them. Girls from offices looking dazzled and hopeful, older couples finishing a meal, enjoying a show in the days leading up to Easter.

"What would Monsignor McDonagh think?" I mutter.

"What did you say?"

"I wonder what our priest would think," I shout.

Lewin shrugs and then joins the clapping as the lights dim. He leans toward me and whisper-shouts in my ear, "He'd no doubt love it like everyone else."

The crowd is suddenly hushed. There's a long moment of anticipation, and then the spotlight follows a line of chorus dancers onto the small stage. They are wearing tulle headdresses and strapless satin bodices with tutus that barely cover their derrieres. It's my last thought for ten full minutes as they sweep me, and every single person in the room, into an enticing world that only has room for beauty and light and sequins. A world where legs are long and shapely, where skin is only smooth, golden perfection.

Next comes a magician, and then a comedian, and then a jazz band from Harlem, playing their first night in Montreal. During their set, I come back down to earth. I spend those minutes scanning the other tables, looking for Daisy, the jazz notes intruding on my thoughts. Will I ever let this music carry me away? I think it's better not to, on the whole.

I'm still buzzing from the show when we land back in the taxi.

"Where to next?" Tomasso asks.

"Take us uptown," Lewin replies. "We'll start at El Morocco."

I'm inside the famed El Morocco at last, so packed with patrons that there is not one seat available. Young people, Americans, a table with three young married couples on a triple date.

"Is it always like this?"

Lewin nods. "Every single night."

"Even Sunday?"

"Not until after midnight, but yes."

And then the show starts. There's a cheer for the burlesque dancer who's come from New York and will be here every night this week. Three shows a night.

The music starts, just one trumpet player off to the side of the stage, playing a sultry melody, and Miss Edna begins to sway, arms outstretched, rattling the bangles at her wrists like a tambourine. She takes these bracelets off, one at a time, and tosses them into the crowd. I see an older man catch one and present it, like a gift, to a smiling woman who surely must be his wife.

Miss Edna begins to unbutton her blouse, her hips still moving to the slow music, until it is open to the architecturally constructed bodice beneath. The crowd is silent, as though in a communal daze. It's like this almost plain-faced woman, with spectacular curves and a very small waist, has secretly let us into her boudoir; except those in the crowd must not have had older sisters. It reminds me of sitting on Missie's bed as a young girl, watching her and Daisy get ready for dates. Only the opposite, of course—they were putting clothes on, not taking them off.

I allow my gaze to drift, more interested in watching the spectators than the show itself. The young wives on the triple dates glance back and forth between the stage and their husbands' faces. The older women are more contained, as though allowing themselves the pleasure of absorbing youth itself on full display. The American men can't restrain themselves from calling out, trying to claim Miss Edna's attention.

By the time Miss Edna is wearing nothing more than two sheer triangles over her breasts, attached by almost invisible string (yet another use for nylon, I think), I am quite sure that Daisy is not here. The lights fall dark and Lewin and I head toward the door.

"I did not know," I say quietly, as we make our way through the crowd. "It's like I haven't known anything at all."

Lewin doesn't hear me, of course. He leads me back to the taxi, and we hit four clubs along Saint Catherine in quick succession. It's all a blur of music and lights and smiling faces, and at the Normandie Roof at the Mount Royal Hotel, I almost forget to look for Daisy completely.

"Hungry?" Lewin asks, when we are back out on the street.

"Famished," I say.

Bens Delicatessen is our next stop. Even Tomasso joins us. Lewin orders for us all—smoked-meat sandwiches, French fries, enormous pickles, and glasses of cherry Coke and ice. More food than we'll have on Easter Sunday at home. The spiced meat, the rye bread, the hot salty potato fries, the sour pickle washed away by the childlike sweetness of the cherry Coke—it's like I'm eating more than food.

I'm eating the laughter and the life and the very teeming essence of this city that I did not know before now. My city. Even here it is too loud to talk. Smiling faces everywhere. Young, old, Black and white, French and English. I look at every face, looking for Daisy and for Abbie, but also looking for laughter, taking it all in.

Suddenly, I'm filled with longing. To be alive and free, fully immersed in taking a bite from my smoked-meat sandwich. I want to be here, really here, not worried about Daisy, looking for Daisy, trying to stop her. I want for just one moment to be part of it all.

"I don't see them. Do you?"

Tomasso shakes his head.

On our way out, Lewin shows Daisy's picture to Ben himself. He shakes his head.

"Her? I'd remember her. I wish she'd come in. It looks like she could use a good meal." He laughs at his own joke, and we fall out into the night, which is as bright with lights as the indoors.

I look at my watch. "It's almost three o'clock!"

"Good time to go to Saint Laurent. It'll be warming up by now."

Café de L'Est, Faisan Doré, Saint Germain des Pres. More jazz, two more chorus lines, a trapeze, and a seal wearing a bow tie. Fatigue overtakes me, and I register only blurs where I should see faces. Now the patrons speak French, the air more subdued, thicker with smoke and secrets. There's no sign of her. The city is enormous and alive. She could be anywhere.

The sky is lightening with dawn when we slide into the back seat of Tomasso's taxi and head back to the office.

"Catch a few hours. You can use my couch. I'll go into Mr. McAulay's office."

"Sleep here?"

"That's how it's done. You'll be surprised how rejuvenating it can be. Lock the door behind me," he says. "That way you'll have notice if someone is coming."

I slide off my shoes and curl up, using my coat as a blanket. It's surprisingly comfortable. With the buzz of the city in my feet, the pulsing jazz in my veins, and the laughter of revelers echoing in my eardrums, I sink into a tunnel of sleep.

# Chapter Forty-Three

I feel surprisingly chipper the next morning, after a few hours' sleep on the couch in Lewin's office, as though the music and lights and conversations from the night before are still spurring me on. I know I need to call Mother right away, to see how Father managed overnight. But I also know she will ask when Daisy will come to see him, and I don't want to lie. I can't tell her the truth, that I was out all night looking for Daisy and that the boys slept at a stranger's house. And Geoff. I suppose I should call him too.

I decide to head to the ladies' room to tidy up as best I can before I call anyone, and before the office starts to buzz. I'm not the first one there. Helen is seated on the wide windowsill, the sash opened to the cold morning air.

"Helen, you startled me. You're here early."

She doesn't answer. I'm not even sure she sees me. I can understand not wanting to talk, so I leave her alone. I use the stall to change back into my skirt and blouse from the day before. I wash my hands at the sink and pat my hair with my wet fingers to smooth my curls as best I can. Some lipstick and a breath mint will have to do. I'm turning to leave, when I see Helen has fallen asleep, her body curled toward the open window. She looks dangerously close to pitching out the opening altogether. I reach over her to pull the sash down and that's when I see the blood staining the front of her dress.

"Oh! Helen!"

She slowly blinks her eyes open and I see she is not sleeping at all. Her gaze is empty.

"June," she says. "I lost the baby."

The door opens. There's the sound of voices and laughter and the others are upon us.

"Hélène?" Marie-Céleste takes charge with a clucking, motherly tone I haven't heard from her before.

"What can I do?" I ask, but it's like a curtain has closed all around them. With Marie-Céleste's coat covering the stain and Dot's arms around her and Grace holding the door, they lead Helen out. I follow them helplessly to the elevator.

"Come to my apartment and rest," says Marie-Céleste.

"It'll be all right, Helen," says Dot.

"Oh, Helen, are you very sad?" From Grace.

"Grace, you stay here. Tell Miss Pomeroy that Helen has taken ill and that Dot and I will be back soon."

Grace jostles past me. The doors open and the other girls step inside. I make to step into the elevator car too, but Marie-Céleste shakes her head at me just once.

"Lobby, Constant. Please hurry."

I step back and think what a silly thing that is to say; the elevator only goes as fast as it goes, after all. I watch the doors close on the tableau of three girls, sisters of sorts, looking out for one another. Who would look out for me if I were the wounded bird? I go back to the ladies' room, but I'm not needed there either—Grace has already finished cleaning up the mess. I head back alone to my new office in the back of the supply room.

The night on the town has opened up a new catalog of images in my mind. Even a parade of chorus girls and jazz musicians, a big band, a magician, and a circus act could not crush the nylon carpet fibers at

285

the nightclub. I make note of this thought and get back to the reports, and my allotted hourly phone calls.

I speak with Christine, since Mother is at Mass for Maundy Thursday. No change in Father.

"How is Daisy?" Christine asks. "Your mother keeps asking when she will come."

I almost blurt out that we never found her, but then I remember I told Mother I was going to sleep at Daisy's house. "She's fine," I lie.

"Your mother misses those boys, but best not bring them here just yet. She doesn't have the energy to look after them right now."

I get back to work on the nylon carpets. An hour later when I call Mrs. Lewin, she assures me that the boys are just fine.

"It's nice for the little Drumstick to have something to look at other than boring old me," she says. "Why, I even folded all the laundry and picked up the house. We'll go to the park later—just for a bit, though; it's cold. They're fine." She seems unperturbed by the fact that Mr. Lewin did not come home.

"Did you find their mother? It's just that little Chris keeps asking."

"Not yet," I say.

"Well, not to worry. I'm sure she'll turn up." Her voice turns cheerful, and I wonder if it's because Chris is listening.

By noon, the beat of the city that made me feel so alert in the morning has started to wane. My stomach feels unsettled, and I'm wondering if I might find a way to nap under my desk, when my phone rings.

"Miss Grant speaking," I answer.

"Oh, June. Thank goodness you're there. You need to come."

It's Abbie.

I rush to the Mount Royal Hotel, and Abbie lets me into the second-floor suite.

"I don't know what to do. She wasn't like this last night."

The suite opens into an entry area, a crystal chandelier hangs over a Napoleon-style round wooden table with an inlaid mosaic top. I can't see the pattern; it's hidden by a hillock of tangled clothing: stockings shaken loose from their packaging, slips and bras and other underthings, blouses and skirts, all of them in black.

I hear Daisy's voice from the adjacent room. "What do you mean you don't have it in black?"

"Daisy?"

I push open the door to the dimly lit bedroom. Daisy is on the still-made bed, leaning against the headboard, her legs stretched out in front of her. She's wearing a tightly cinched black silk robe that barely covers the tops of her thighs, and a pair of silk slippers complete with short, pointed heels and pom-poms over the toes. She has a cigarette in an ebony holder in one hand, the telephone receiver in the other. Her nails are painted the same deep red as her lips.

"No, no. Gray won't do at all. Has to be black." She listens. "Fine. Send that one."

I step closer. Lined up along the base of the bed are bags and boxes, Ogilvy's, Morgan's, Eaton's, stacked one on top of each other and side by side, arranged by size, tidy as Christopher's toy soldiers.

"Yes, and the hat. Suite 274 at the Mount Royal Hotel. As soon as possible. Yes, charge it to the room."

I gasp. Who will pay the bill?

"My name? Why, I'm Miss Howard," she says, then smiles. "That's right. Howard Ship Lines. That's my father's company."

She hangs up at last.

"Daisy, what are you doing?"

She looks in my direction, but not at me. It's like she can't see me, or anything else. "The deliveryman from Simpson's will be here soon. Send him in when he comes." She lifts her chin in dismissal, a gesture she learned as a child, when she'd order the servants about at the Côte Saint Antoine house.

"Daisy?" I say again, but it's no use. She drops her head back and takes a deep draw on her cigarette, and I'm left looking at her swanlike neck.

I take a step closer. "Daisy."

Her head snaps up. I've never seen her eyes so dark blue and feral. "I said, listen for the door. That is all."

"Come, June." Abbie pulls my elbow. I follow her back through the entry to the living room area, which has two clusters of seating in the same Empire style as the entry table, and tall, sheer-draped French doors overlooking Peel Street.

"Mind the glass," Abbie says, steering past a shattered bottle to the second cluster of sofa and chairs. Every surface of the coffee tables and side tables is covered in wine and beer bottles, dirty glasses, full ashtrays. The table in front of me, when I sit on a blue velvet armchair, has a half-empty bottle of gin and three glasses, along with a cluster of hairpins, Daisy's wedding ring set, and a pair of clip-on earrings that used to belong to Mother.

"There's coffee. Would you like some?"

I nod. The leftover thrum of energy from the night before is completely gone.

"And eggs? She keeps ordering food, though I don't think she's eaten a thing this whole time."

I shake my head. Abbie hands me a cup and sits across from me with a coffee of her own in her hands. She's wearing one of the flapper dresses from the rack at the studio; this one the color of candied ginger. Her curls spring wildly from her scalp; her eyes are smoky with last night's makeup.

"Abbie, what's happened?"

She shakes her head. "It all started out as a bit of fun. What day was that? Tuesday, I think. We dressed like flappers, and I was taking photographs of some of Daisy's girls at my studio. Then Daisy gathered

288

us all together. There was a party of businessmen in town, and they needed company for their night on the town. I went along, just for fun. But that was two days ago."

She reaches among the detritus on the side table and pulls a cigarette out of a gold case and lights it. I watch her lips, pale without lipstick, as she sucks the smoke into her lungs.

"Oh, Junie, I'm sorry." She unfolds herself from the chair and goes to the doors and tugs them open. They lead to a semicircular balcony. The sounds of the street seep into the room, and Abbie comes back to sit down. "It's so stale smelling in here."

"Mr. Lewin and I were out all night looking for you and Daisy," I say.

"Oh, were you? Of course you were. I'm sorry."

"We went to the Normandie Roof, but we didn't see you there."

"Oh, we never made it there. Last night, was it? Last night we only made it as far as the Palm Room, and then the party moved here." She waves a hand. "It's all a blur."

"But Abbie—"

"Oh, June, I know. It's all gone wrong, but it started out in good fun. Daisy said wouldn't it be a ball to get a hotel room, and I laughed and said I'd just gotten my trust and why not? So we rented the grandest suite we could, and said we'd live exclusively at the Mount Royal for a few days, for a laugh." Her voice fades. "But Daisy—does she ever stop?"

I shake my head. "Something has to happen, to make her stop."

"What did I say?" The shriek comes from the entry hall. A door slams. Abbie and I jump to our feet as Daisy careens into the room, a Simpson's bag in one hand, the ever-present cigarette holder in the other.

"I said, listen for the door. I said, the man from Simpson's was coming. Didn't I say that? Can't you even get that right?" She raises the Simpson's bag in the air and throws it, hard.

We watch its trajectory as if frozen in place. It narrowly misses Abbie's head and explodes like a grenade on the table between us, shattering the gin bottle and glasses. I jump back, but too late. Shards of glass, like so much shrapnel, fly in all directions, and one lands on my cheek, just below my eye.

"Stop it, Daisy!" Abbie's voice is strong and sure, but it's no use. Daisy climbs atop the coffee table, her slippers skittering on the crowded surface until she finds purchase.

"You can't get anything right! Nothing!" She screeches the words at me.

I hold my palm up to my stinging cheek, try to catch and hold her gaze. "Daisy," I say, my voice calm. "You need to come see Father."

"Father? What use is he to me?" She looks around, blindly. "This is all his fault. All of it."

"He's dying, Daisy." For a moment I catch her gaze and hold it. "He needs you. To come and say goodbye."

There's the honk of a horn from the street, and her eyes shift in the direction of the sound. She holds out her hand with such authority that I drop my own hand from my cheek and hold it out to her. She takes it for balance as she steps down from the table, striding through the broken glass as though it can't touch her. She picks up the Simpson's bag and heads to the open windows. She pushes aside the sheer curtains and steps out onto the tiny balcony.

"All I need is one good dress to wear to a funeral." She yells the words out, over the street, across the city. "My father is dying, and I cannot find one dress."

I look to Abbie.

"She's been like this for hours," she whispers. Exhaustion lines her face, and she seems shrunken in her flapper dress, like she's tired of playing dress-up.

"This one won't do at all," Daisy calls out into the street. Through the sheers, I see her holding up a dress that she's pulled from the bag. "This would suit an old lady, or a girl in an old lady's body, like my sister June . . ." She yells my name out over the city street like a slur.

There's another honk from below. Daisy holds up the dress like a flag. She waits for the wind to catch it and then she lets it sail out into the air.

"Hey, lady," a voice calls. More honking.

I look to Abbie and nod. She slips out of the room and into the bedroom. I step out onto the balcony. Daisy has a pair of shoes out of the bag now, one in each hand. She's waving them back and forth. More cars honk.

"Daisy, come inside," I say. I move closer to her. There's a crowd that's gathering below on the sidewalk across Peel Street. Cars stop, their drivers roll down their windows and look up at Daisy. At me.

She throws one shoe. It plummets like a pheasant that's been shot midflight and lands with a thunk on the roof of a car. The driver waves a fist, and a chorus of honking starts up. I try to grab the other shoe from her hand, but she's too quick. It sails through the air, and there's a shatter of glass from below.

I wrap my arms around her and grapple her to the ground. "Daisy, stop," I say, breathless, trying to hold her down.

But Daisy is an expert at wriggling away from anything that tries to hamper her freedom. She pulls my hair and spits in my face, kicks her legs. When I relent even the slightest bit, she crawls over me like a crab, then rights herself, and runs into the suite.

She's barefoot now—did she throw her slippers too?—and she runs right through the broken glass into the entry hall. She returns seconds later, her arms full of the pile of clothing that was on the table. Her feet leave bloodied footprints in the carpet. Her black robe falls open in front.

"Just one dress!" she calls again. She throws a pair of stockings out onto the street, and then an opera-length black glove.

"Any more stockings?" someone calls from the street.

"Send down the other glove!"

Daisy turns and leans her elbows on the iron rail of the balcony. She digs into the pocket of her robe and pulls out a cigarette and lights it. She narrows her eyes at me as though daring me to try to stop her.

"Oh, Daisy. Think of the waste," I say. Me, who hasn't had a new pair of gloves since before the war.

Daisy throws her head back, her arms out, until her hair hangs down over the edge of the balcony, and laughs. Below, people on the street are pointing up, and some of them start to laugh along with her.

"Any more shoes, lady?" a man calls out.

Daisy spins around and yanks a black skirt from the pile at her feet. She throws this over, followed by a pair of stockings and a brassiere, which raises a whoop from the crowd.

"Allez, Madame!"

"Just stop," I plead, to no avail.

"June, come inside," Abbie says from the doorway. "The doctor's here." I squeeze past her into the suite, where three men wait. One in a suit, two ambulance attendants with a stretcher.

The suited man nods at me and steps outside. I can hear him talking quietly to Daisy, but she ignores his calm assurance.

Two policemen enter the suite, along with one of the front desk clerks and a housekeeper.

"Get away from me!" Daisy yells at the doctor, and then she turns back to the street. "Get him away from me." She turns to her audience now, and then clambers onto the railing. The sash on her robe gives up completely and the robe flutters open.

Everything happens at once. The crowd goes from cheering to jeering. The policemen move surprisingly quickly. Daisy is inside, and the ambulance attendants have her in hand. The doctor administers the dose in the syringe hidden in his palm, and soon Daisy is nothing more than a trapped bird, cinched in to the stretcher, panting.

"Best take her up the hill," the doctor says.

"Can I stay with her?" I ask.

One of the ambulance attendants nods. I look to Abbie. She lifts her hands, then looks to the hotel manager and the housekeeper. "I'll stay and look after things here," she says. "Don't worry, June."

# Chapter Forty-Four

"Medical history?" The clerk in the lobby of the Montreal Hospital for the Insane has a nasal voice that is at odds with his broad shoulders and well-padded body.

I stand across from his desk—he has not invited me to sit down, and he seems to be in a terrible hurry.

"I—I don't know. I mean she is healthy enough."

He grunts. "Any children?"

"Yes, two."

"Has she done anything like this before?"

For a moment the ornately wallpapered room seems to expand and begin to spin. I press my feet firmly into the polished wood floor and put a hand onto a white plastered column to hold myself steady. I look at the clerk, who is tapping his pencil, waiting for me to answer. I do not have the luxury of falling apart.

"Miss? Has your sister done this kind of thing before?" He looks down at the page in front of him. "Climb naked on a second-floor balcony and threaten to throw herself off?"

"That's not what happened," I start.

He clucks and shakes his head. "That's what the police report says right here. Now just tell me. Has she ever tried anything like this before?"

"She's always had moods," I say. "But no, nothing like this. At least not as far as I know. But she hasn't been herself lately."

"Any particular reason?" He's got his pencil poised over a box in the form, waiting to fill it in. It's not a big box. Not big enough for the whole story—our family's loss of fortune during the Depression, Father's stroke, Geoff's family cutting him off.

"Our father is dying," I say simply.

He grunts and writes something in his little box.

"Anything else?"

"Not that I know of. As I say, her husband—"

"Yes, her husband." He looks at his watch. "The thing is, he's not here, is he? I'm off in an hour, and tomorrow is Good Friday."

"He could come Saturday?"

He shakes his head. "No visitors over Easter."

"But—"

"No," he says. "Simply not possible. She'll be asleep anyway. After an episode like that, Dr. Thompson will keep her sedated." He tears the bottom portion from his sheet. "Give this to the husband, and tell him to come on Monday. You may go upstairs and see your sister to say goodbye. But be quick about it; visiting hours end in thirty minutes."

On another day, walking up the curved staircase, running my hand along the richly carved wood, would have awakened a grand story in me, but there is no time for my imagination today. Instead, I trudge up the stairs in my heavy shoes. The carpet runner on the stair treads, once grand, is now old and faded. The landing leads to a long, high-ceilinged corridor of bedrooms. And though I would expect grunts and cries of despair coming from the patients of a hospital such as this one, it is completely silent.

Daisy, when I find her room, is thankfully sound asleep, felled by whatever it was the doctor gave her. She's wearing a flowered hospital smock I'm sure she'd have refused if she knew about it. Why can't she stay like this? Subdued and compliant. Why does she always have to stir up so much fuss? Why can't she just be good?

I look at my watch. I'm surprised it's only midafternoon. The girls in steno will be taking their afternoon break, and I have almost a full day of work to make up. Was it just this morning I woke on the couch in Mr. Lewin's office?

I must go home to where Mother sits vigil. I must call Geoff and tell him what has happened. Tell him to pick up the boys from Mrs. Lewin on his way home from work.

I start to tuck the blankets around Daisy's feet, and I see that in their rush to quiet her mind, they have ignored her body completely. Her feet are covered in splotches of dried blood from the broken glass, and dirt from the balcony.

At the sink, I fill a basin with cool water and take three flannel cloths from a pile. I place the basin on a chair at the foot of the bed. Gingerly, I rinse Daisy's feet. Once I am sure I've removed all the shards of glass, I start to wipe at the dirt and blood. I refill the basin three times until her feet are clean as a baby's. I tuck the blankets around her again.

"Rest well, Daisy," I whisper.

I drop the dirty cloths into the hamper and rinse the basin. Standing at the sink to wash my hands, I catch a reflection of myself in the mirror. A rivulet of blood has dried on my own cheek from the shard of glass that landed just under my eye. I wet another cloth and wash it off, then press the cloth hard into the little dent on my cheekbone. I hope it won't leave a scar.

Once it stops bleeding, I toss the final cloth into the hamper with the others. I rush down the grand staircase again—there is simply no time for poems or stories—to find a phone and call a taxi.

I have never seen Mother break. Never. Not when Father had his stroke. Not when she had to let Christine go. Not when we left the Côte Saint

Antoine house. Not when Daisy threw tantrums and stole the rent money to buy new shoes for a dance. Not when, at the age of fifty, she opened her scrapbook to the recipes she'd written as a young bride-to-be, never expecting to have to set foot in the kitchen, and taught herself to cook.

Not even earlier this week, with the slow dawning that Father was leaving her. I could see she was afraid, but she did not break.

But now, as I tell her that her Daisy is lying, sedated, in a hospital for the insane, it is too much. I tell her everything. My long night of searching through bars and clubs and cabarets. Daisy, in a black silk robe, perched like a crow on a balcony rail at the Mount Royal Hotel. Daisy, shrunken and sedated, strapped to a bed in the asylum.

Mother does not slump. She does not cry out. Her spine, a straight rod, begins to shake, and she squeezes her eyes shut with the effort of holding it up. Like an earthquake under a great column, the edges crumble off, but the structure stays standing, despite itself; a witness to a changed world.

When I finish telling her, we sit at Father's bedside together for a very long time, not speaking. I can hear Christine in the kitchen, humming as she makes a tray for our early supper. I can hear Father's strained breathing, can smell the decay on his breath. I want to take Mother's hand in my own and tell her everything will be all right, but Mother never has been one for affection. Besides, how can I tell her that, when I don't know that it is true?

Mother turns toward Father and takes one of his hands in hers. Tears streak down her cheeks and she says, "James, Daisy has gone to visit friends. Remember the ones with the chalet in the Laurentians? She won't be back for a while. You know how Daisy is, always wanting to spend time with her friends. She sends her love."

I hear Mother's words and I know they are a lie, but I also know they are a kindness. What good would it do to burden Father with worry in his final hours?

And so, I reach out and cover her small, dry hand with my own. "Everything will be all right," I tell her. She tilts her head and smiles as she draws her hand away, and I know she's seen right through my lie to the kindness behind it.

Then she says: "Please ask Monsignor McDonagh to come."

When he arrives, Monsignor McDonagh delivers last rites to Father and offers absolution to Mother and me. I pray for Father, for Mother, for Daisy. I feel the great grief of Jesus's betrayal more keenly than I ever have before, and yet, I feel no peace. I am praying still, falling asleep in my chair, when Christine sends me to bed.

"I will sit with your parents," she said. "You need to sleep."

# Chapter Forty-Five

I do sleep. Most of the night and through the next morning. When I finally wake it is to the full light of morning and a heavy, heavy heart. I feel none of the absolution and the full depth of grief of Good Friday. I dress and go downstairs. Mother nods to me, and asks me to sit with Father while she and Christine go to the service.

While they are gone, Missie calls. Too pregnant to travel to see us, she cries on the phone. I stretch the cord as far as it will go and she says her goodbyes to Father. "If it's a boy, I will name him after you," she says at last. "You were a good father."

I weep as I put down the phone. I pull my chair closer to Father's wheelchair, which is now permanently in the bed position. I hold his hand and lay my head on his chest, listening to his breathing.

"You are a good father," I whisper to him. "Kind and good."

Tears slide from my eyes. There is no one to hear me weep, except Father, and he can't tell me to stop. And so I weep. I weep for my parents, and for Missie, who can't be here, and for Daisy, who could have been here but caused so much trouble instead. I weep for Geoff, who wants a proper wife, and the boys, who ache for the kind of mother they will never have.

And I weep for me. For the life I am supposed to want, but will never have.

"I'm sorry, Father," I say. "Forgive me."

I stay there with my head on his chest, listening to the whisper of his breath, until there's a gasp and a sigh and Father is gone and I am all alone.

—— ⟍⟍⟍ ——

The service at the cemetery chapel is a simple one. The altar is stripped; there is no music. It is Holy Saturday, after all, and this is the best we can all manage on short notice.

Afterward, we stand in a semicircle around the family crypt, where Father will join his ancestors. We've picnicked on this very spot more summers than I can count, Daisy and Missie and I climbing over the crypt while Mother handed out sandwiches and kept the ants off our blanket. Now, in this cemetery at the very top of the city, the brown grass is frozen and there are still patches of snow. The trees are bare with their winter branches, but I am sure I can feel the pulse of spring under my cold feet.

Geoff and the boys are here, of course. The boys are clean and tidy and dressed in their very best, without the assistance of Daisy, or Mother, or even me.

The Howards are all there, Mrs. Howard pale and serious, Mr. Howard gruff and awkward, his hands on Abbie's shoulders as though keeping her in place. Christine stands with them, as though she has been reclaimed.

Mr. Lewin is there, along with Mrs. Lewin and little baby Arthur, a kindness that brings tears to my eyes.

Even Mr. McAulay is there. After it's all over, he presses my hand in both of his and nods and nods. I think he's not going to say anything at all, but he does find some words at last: "Your father was a good man. They don't make them like him anymore." As though the factory that produced good men closed down after the first war.

It's my turn to nod. "Thank you, Sir," I say.

One by one they all come by, to shake our hands, to kiss our cheeks. Mrs. Lewin hugs me close. Mr. Lewin himself shakes my hand and leans in to my ear. "I'll be at the office tomorrow afternoon. We need to get those nylon ideas together. Work is the best medicine." I shake his hand and nod, but in that moment his words are as meaningless as the rest.

At last, only the Howards remain, and while Mr. and Mrs. Howard console Mother, Abbie pulls me along to an oak tree next to Thomas D'Arcy McGee's grave and hugs me close.

"I'm sorry, June. I'm sorry for all of it."

"Oh, Abbie, it's not your fault." I know she's not just talking about Father, but about Daisy too.

"I was trying to help, to keep her from getting in trouble."

"I know you were."

She looks back to her father. "He doesn't. He blames Daisy, and, well, you in part."

"Me?"

She frowns and drops her head down. "Well, maybe I had to exaggerate a few things, to stay out of trouble myself. I'm sorry." She looks up at me. An errant curl has escaped her black cloche hat and she tucks it away. "He'll get over it eventually. Forgive me?"

"Of course," I say.

"Father says I've spent a whole year of my income, in less than a month. With the studio lease and the hotel, and the damages." She pauses and laughs. "And all my new black clothes."

"Oh, Abbie. I'm sorry."

She waves this away. "No. Don't you see? That was my fun. I can't regret it now, can I?" She reaches into her pocket and pulls out a skeleton key on a blue ribbon. I recognize it as the key to her studio.

"I'm not to go back to the studio, even though I paid for a full year. I told him . . ." She looks over her shoulder, drops her voice. "I told him I would give it to the poor. For someone in need." She hands me the key. "Will you go there? Pack away my things? Find someone to take it?"

I nod. "Of course. Of course I will."

She hugs me again. "Thank you, June. You are a true friend. And now you won't hear from me for a while. I'm to be very quiet, until I'm properly married."

I smile at her. "How will you be quiet, Abbie?"

She shrugs and shakes her head, her eyes bright. "I am told I can be irrepressible again, but only once I'm safely married off."

She takes my hand in hers. "Goodbye, June." She lets go, and then walks away to join her parents.

I watch them go, and then join Mother and the boys and Geoff, waiting to drive us home.

# Chapter Forty-Six

The Ladies' Committee at the church have done their best to prepare a nice Easter feast for us, but the mood around the table is anything but festive.

Geoff puts in an effort to be a good host—we are at his and Daisy's house, after all—but we are all more than a little fragile. He gets the boys to set the table with Geoff and Daisy's wedding china while I put the lukewarm meal onto serving platters, but it's no use. The boys miss Daisy, and Mother is bereft without Father. Geoff tries to be jovial, but I am too lost in my own thoughts to pick up the conversational gambit. After I put away all the leftovers and wash the dishes, I call a taxi. I ask Red Lantern to send Tomasso.

"Are you sure you won't stay, June?"

"No, Mother. I have to work tomorrow, and it will be easier to come and go from home."

Mother has brought her suitcase and the dogs and will stay with Geoff and the boys until Daisy comes home, maybe longer.

"I know, June." She pats my hand. "I will miss you."

"Daisy will be home soon, and so will you," I say. Consoling, meaningless words.

―――― ⚬⌒ ⌒⚬ ――――

Tomasso opens the door for me as I slide into the taxi.

"Where would you like to go, Miss Grant?"

Something sparks in me when I realize that no one will know if I don't go home straightaway. There is no one waiting for me. No dogs to walk or feed. No boys to look after. No Mother to worry over me. "Please take me to the Hospital for the Insane on Pine Avenue."

Tomasso looks at me in the rearview mirror. "Are you sure, Miss Grant?"

I shake my head. "It's not like that. I just want to drive by and stop for a minute."

"No problem, Miss."

At the hospital, I stand on the melting snow just inside the rusted iron gates. I look up to the four-story tower crawling with naked ivy branches and shiver with more than the cold. It's a blue-sky day and the breeze has an uplifting undertone to it. Undeniable spring, at long last. I stand alone as the snow melts under my feet, exposing brown grass and mud, and stare up at the imposing building, its many windows staring back. I count the windows until I find the one I think is Daisy's.

I think back to the start of Lent, when I begged God to release me from the grip of envy. I have to admit that my prayers have been answered. I don't envy Daisy now.

I close my eyes and breathe in the cold spring air and whisper the words that Monsignor McDonagh said this morning at Easter Mass. *Don't be afraid. I am with you still.* "Don't be afraid, Daisy." I whisper the words into the air that holds just a hint of promise of spring, and climb back into the taxi.

At Abbie's studio, Tomasso comes inside and together we clean up, using some empty boxes from the pile on the steps. I pile all of the photographs into a small box, which I will keep for Abbie. Tomasso makes several trips down the stairs with boxes of photography equipment and costumes, which he loads in the trunk of the taxi. With both of us working, it does not take long. I brush off the divan and place it square under the window. Then I take one photograph—the one of the street urchins dressed as pirates and laughing on the divan—and, using a nail pounded in the wall by some previous tenant, I hang it on the wall. Off-center, but still, it is something. A mark, of sorts. Something of Abbie.

"Bonjour? Hello? Mademoiselle Howard? Are you moving out?" Heavy steps on the stairs and the owner of the dépanneur appears, out of breath in the doorway. "Oh, hello."

"Hello," I say. "Miss Howard has been called away."

"Yes? And you are?"

"I am her manager." I straighten my spine and look straight at him. "I am making arrangements for her. A new tenant will be moving in."

"What tenant?"

"A couple. Husband and wife. They will come and introduce themselves."

"Mais, c'est—" He starts to complain in French, but I hold a hand up.

"It's paid in advance, yes? For one year?" I repeat the words in my own rusty French.

"Oui, mais—"

"Yes. Paid in advance. There will be no problem with the new tenants." My voice is so certain that he can't help but repeat my words.

"No problem."

"Exactly," I say. "I expect they will arrive tomorrow."

Tomasso drives along Saint Jacques, where families in their Easter best are out strolling in the sun, heavy coats over spring dresses. At 1919 Saint Jacques, the Red Lantern taxis are lined in front of the building, lights extinguished, drivers with the day off.

"Even taxis take a day of rest," I say.

Tomasso shrugs. "Some, not all. And only because it's Easter. They'll start up again at midnight."

And I know they will. The taxis, the lonely visitors from New York and Pittsburgh, the girls to keep them company, the music and dancing, the nights out in the clubs—the city keeps spinning, as it always has, and perhaps as it should. It will simply do so now without catching my family in its wake.

Even Saint Ambroise Street is kissed with spring sunlight as Tomasso pulls up outside Helen's duplex. A few families have opened their doors to the warmer air, children spill out to play on the stoops after Easter lunch. I ring the bell to the second-floor apartment. The young man that appears in the doorway is a cleaner, handsomer version of the man I saw lurch at Helen the last time I was here.

"Is Helen home?"

He looks at me quizzically. "Hélène?"

"Yes. I'm a friend from work. I'd like to speak with her, please."

He calls up the stairs, and a moment later Helen appears. She's pale, but her eyes are clear and her hair is brushed and shining. She's wearing a spring dress in coral pink, with a warm cardigan over the top. She looks up at the man and squeezes his hand, smiling shyly. "It's June, from work. It's okay. You go up. I'll be back in a minute."

We step away from the door and find a sunny spot on the sidewalk. "Are you feeling better, Helen?" I ask.

She nods. "I'm sorry if I scared you."

"Did you get the help you needed?"

She nods, but then shakes her head. "For now. But we need to get away from here. From his brother." These last words come out as a whisper.

"I understand." I pull out the key, and the slip of paper I have wrapped it in, which has the Saint Jacques Street address of Abbie's studio. I explain to her why I've come. I press the key into her hand and fold her fingers over it.

"June, are you sure?" she asks.

I nod. "I am sure."

"Paid until next March?"

"Yes," I say. "There is a couch there and not much else. It's very basic, I'm afraid. The bedroom doesn't have a window, and the bathroom is on the landing, but it will be all yours."

For the first time in weeks, her smile actually reaches her eyes. "Thank you, June," she says. "Thank you."

——— ☙❧ ———

Finally, I ask Tomasso to take me to the Sun Life Building, which is gleaming white in the spring sun.

Mr. Lewin is in his office, as promised. He smiles at me when I come in and gestures to the stool at the drafting table, where I take my seat. "Sunday is the best day to get things done, I find," he says.

I open the research file in front of me and start reading. Mr. Lewin sits on the couch, sketchbook on his lap, moving his pencil along the page in swirls and circles. I know enough now to know this is his way of thinking, the same way I might think and write, or think and read.

We stay like this for a long time. I feel the connection between us grow in the silence. And yet, I don't blush. There's no stuttering or awkwardness, just this silence. It is something different from the stories that Daisy and Missie tell me, the fairy tales about marriage. Different from that hope and expectation. Different still from the raw calculation in the exchange between Daisy's girls and the men visiting from out of town. It is the simple silence of colleagues, at work on an idea.

"Let's get started," he says. "Tell me everything you know about nylon carpets."

After two hours, we've outlined the three ideas we think Mr. McAulay will happily take credit for, including my inspiration after our night out—*Even a parade won't crush it*—and Lewin sits up.

"That's a wrap for today, don't you think? Mrs. Lewin's parents are expecting us for Easter dinner. Would you like to join us?"

I shake my head and get my coat. "I've got plans," I say. Which is true in its own way. I have poems to write. "See you in the morning."

Outside, Tomasso is waiting at the taxi stand, leaning against the hood of the taxi. He crushes his cigarette underfoot when he sees me. "Ready to go home, Miss Grant?"

"I think I'm going to walk. Will you drop the boxes on the stoop? I'll bring them inside when I get home." Already I know I will save them for Abbie, for someday. For when she needs them or wants them again.

"Would you like me to wait there and help you?"

I shake my head. "No, thank you," I say.

He limps around to stand next to me on the sidewalk. "Miss Grant," he says, "I wonder if you would go to a movie with me sometime?"

I hear the words and I don't feel anything. No surge of hope, or despair. I just know that it is not possible. Not anymore. There is no sense wasting his time, or mine.

"I'm afraid I can't, Tomasso. I'm sorry. I hope you'll understand." I smile, to soften the blow of my words.

His dark eyes look dejected as I say this, and I want to take my words back but I don't. He frowns and his eyebrows pucker together and I think he might stomp his foot, but still I don't change my mind. When he looks at me again, his eyes are hard.

"I think I should drive you."

"I'm going to walk," I say.

"It's a long way."

I wave away his objections. "It's really not that far. Besides, it's a beautiful afternoon."

And it is. I walk the long way home, along Sherbrooke Street, whispering words of encouragement to the tulips and crocuses all the while, and it is glorious.

# Author's Note

June Grant was a distinctive person. She was quiet and rather shy, extremely intelligent, and most of all, funny. More than a decade before the start of second-wave feminism, she began her career as an advertising writer in a well-known Montreal agency. She worked there for over forty years.

In her free time, June wrote: poems, short stories, and later, novels. While some of her early work appeared in *Chatelaine* magazine, her novels were never published. It was after her retirement in the 1990s that she began to write humor pieces and was "discovered" by the producers of the CBC radio show *This Morning*, which later became *The Sunday Edition*. Some readers may remember her radio essays on poetry, mysticism, and life, which turned into the popular segment "Ageing Dangerously," airing every month or so, as part of CBC's Sunday morning show from 1997 to 2004.

June never married, and when she died in 2014, her books, papers, and personal archives, including her advertising portfolio and the scripts of her CBC essays, were passed on to me. These formed the basis of my research for this novel.

While the events depicted in these pages are fictional, many details and significant dates are drawn from June's life and work. I invented this story of gentle suspense and adventure, but I did strive to convey June's character—her voice—as I knew her, and as so many Canadians experienced her and loved her through the radio: distinctive, intelligent, and most of all, funny.

The depiction of the rest of my ancestors in this story, particularly my grandmother, Daisy, is fictional. I like to think that if Daisy knew I had turned her into such a beautiful and troubled villain, she'd have a good laugh.

The Montreal depicted here, while grounded in research, is very much a city of my imagination. I consulted many books, archives, and several experts, and then deviated from the facts as it suited me, or to satisfy the needs of the story.

Any visitor to, or resident of, Montreal will know that street, business, and place-names in the city now are almost exclusively French. This novel is set in 1947, thirty years before the Charter of the French Language, or Bill 101, was passed. I deliberately chose to use English street and place-names throughout the novel as a way to capture June's experience of the city, during a time when an anglophone could go about their day without reading or speaking a word of French, unaware of the important changes to come.

Originally, Montreal was the home of neither the English nor the French. The unceded Island of Montreal has served as a place of meeting and exchange for many Indigenous peoples, including the Anishinabeg and the Kanien'kehá:ka Nation of the Haudenosaunee Confederacy, and is the home of many diverse Indigenous people today. I humbly acknowledge that I have maintained the privilege to tell the story of my ancestors on this land, and in my own language, while colonial policies of assimilation deliberately tore this same privilege away from many Indigenous people and communities. In a gesture toward reconciliation, I am donating a portion of my royalties from this book toward cultural development and language revitalization projects initiated and led by the Kanien'kehá:ka in the community of Kahnawà:ke.

# Acknowledgments

When I started on this journey of telling my great-aunt June's story in novel form, I certainly did not expect so many people and organizations to jump in with support. It amazes me still, and I am more grateful than I can express. This book exists because you said yes.

Generous funding from the Columbia Basin Trust through the Columbia Kootenay Cultural Alliance allowed me to travel to Montreal for research. Funding from the Canada Council for the Arts provided editorial and research support and precious time to write.

Thank you to the Thompson Nicola Regional Library for their support through the Writer in Residence program. In Kamloops, thank you to Judy Moore, Catherine Schmidt, all of the TNRL staff, the many writers I worked with, and Shelley Joyce and family.

At Lake Union, thank you to editor Erin Adair-Hodges for "getting" June right from the start, and for treating her, and me, and this work with such thoughtful attention. Thanks to Devon Frederiksen and Tanya Fox and everyone at Amazon Publishing who contributed their careful attention to the editorial and production process. Thank you to Gabriella Dumpit and the marketing team.

A big thank-you to my agent Wayne Arthurson and everyone at The Rights Factory for holding such a big vision for what I thought was my little Canadian book.

In Montreal, thank you to the librarians and archivists at the McCord Museum and Archives, the Westmount Library, and McGill and Concordia University libraries. An especially "gros merci" to the Bibliothèque et Archives nationales du Québec, whose online resources make it possible to write a book set in Quebec while living in rural British Columbia during a pandemic.

Thank you to Professor Magda Fahrni of the Université du Québec à Montréal, who was so generous with her time and knowledge, and who connected me with grad student Annick Desmarais, the most delightful research assistant I could have hoped for.

Thank you to CBC producer Karen Levine, who went above and beyond. Thank you to David Gutnick, Lesley Forrester, Carolyn Burgess Le Dain, Gertrud Le Dain, Molly Christie, James Allen, and the late James Routh, who all contributed to my research. Thanks to the Colliers—Geoff, Stephanie, Steve, and Barb.

Sioux Browning, story structure rock star, thank you for being my mentor and friend. Thank you to Janice Weaver for early editorial support. Thanks to beta readers Sue Adam, Alison Clarke, and Jocelyne Stephenson and to my mom, Carol Collier, for reading so many times.

Thank you to fellow writers Rachel Greenaway, Jane Byers, Sandra Wong, Angie Abdou, Linda L. Richards, and Lisa Johnson. Thank you to my ride-or-dies Jillian Harvey and Sarah Beth Hughes, to Cate Baio, Serene Stewart, Michelle Mayer Hunt, Julia Gillmor and the Mountain Women hiking group / text chat, and Terry Toews. Thank you to Jen Groundwater and Ruth Linka for helping when asked.

To my husband, Ron Sherman, thank you for carrying my books, and so much else, for all these years. To Graeme and Eric, our sweet boys who are now somehow grown men, it's such an honor to be your mom.

Finally, to my readers, for your fierce belief in this project, for following along, month after month with *The Aunt June Files*, and for your conviction that you would hold this book in your hands one day. What is a writer without readers, after all?

# About the Author

*Photo © 2021 Julia Gillmor*

Deryn Collier has dreamed of writing mystery novels since reading her first Nancy Drew in the second grade. She has written two previous novels: *Confined Space*, which was nominated for a Best First Novel Award by the Crime Writers of Canada, and *Open Secret*.

After moving to Montreal as a teenager, Collier instantly fell in love with the city, later graduating from McGill University. These days she lives in a small town in the mountains of British Columbia with her family, and though she has lived there for many years, she still considers Montreal to be home.

Collier enjoys gardening, sewing, and swimming year round in a glacier-fed lake and regularly overshares about these hobbies on Instagram. She writes a newsletter to her readers called *The Aunt June Files*, where she shares a behind-the-scenes look at her work and research in progress. Visit her website at www.deryncollier.com to subscribe.